HALF HITCH

HALF HITCH

Donald Junkins

iUniverse, Inc.
New York   Bloomington

for Tommy:

another corner

of the story—

from your old team-mate,

Don

April 2010

Deerfield

Half Hitch

iUniverse books may be ordered through booksellers or by contacting:

iUniverse
1663 Liberty Drive
Bloomington, IN 47403
www.iuniverse.com
1-800-Authors (1-800-288-4677)

ISBN: 978-1-4502-0279-4 (sc)
ISBN: 978-1-4502-0281-7 (dj)
ISBN: 978-1-4502-0280-0 (ebk)

Printed in the United States of America

iUniverse rev. date: 3/30/2010

for Travis Barnes and Joe Crocker

Half Hitch

"TRUMAN ORDERS U.S. AIR, NAVY UNITS TO FIGHT IN AID OF KOREA," *New York Times*, June 27, 1950

Chapter 1

▼

Shouts of men off to the north came clear in the morning air, and Cal left the pasture road and ducked under low pine branches, then knelt in front of a stone wall and looked down through an oak grove. He was worried about being shot by another hunter and was glad to be off the pasture road, but he didn't know where Joe was. Tipping his hunting hat back and scanning the woods, he could feel the sweat drying on his forehead.

He took off his right glove and gripped his father's Winchester carbine, the butt end resting in the pine needles, and studied the openings between the oaks. He was relieved not to be walking toward the deer drive where men would be posted somewhere further up the road. The sun slanted between openings in the oak grove below, and his little cavern under the low branches by the stone wall was soft and dark, the woods hushed. Shoutings from the deer drive were moving off to the north, and the only sounds in the silent grove were the soft tickings of the brownish yellow oak leaves drifting to the ground.

Cal loved the leaves in the woods in the fall. Maybe a deer would be circling back, away from the drive. Cal had never killed a deer, except in dreams, and they were always bad dreams.

A week before, coming out of *Old Testament* class, Cal spotted Joe Sterns in front of the elevator.

"Going up or down?" Cal asked.

"I'm going down to check the mail, then I'm going to play ping-pong with Prestwood if I can get past Paul Bennington's office. I've already gotten three tickets for parking too near the trash out back and he's probably looking for me. You?"

"I'm going up and read some Steinbeck, then I'm taking the MTA down town. I see Miss Green today after work. Hey, you want to go deer hunting at the lake next week? It's Armistice Day."

"Sounds good, I'll have to work it out with my church."

Jim Toffert was holding the elevator door open with his hand. "Heretics are descending next door. You Unitarians can go up with us into the light or you can stay lost. What'll it be?" Toffert's eyes glistened, and his neck bulged over his turned around collar. "Come come boys, let's be precise."

Cal stepped into the elevator, calling to Joe, "Where do you want to eat tonight?"

Joe called back as the door closed, "Chinatown. I'll come up to your room at six." The elevator rose.

"Hey Jim, I hear your bishop has been fondling one of his secretary's breasts, maybe both of them. Can it be true?"

"Listen, my son, Steinbeck is putrifying your imagination. You're a wayward boy from *The Wayward Bus*. An apt title, very apt. My dear bishop denies that trashy story, and you would be well advised to elevate your thoughts. The library, my son, or the Devil's dorm on the top floor where you and your deer killers congregate?"

"I'm elevating to the higher regions. Give my regards to Barth and Brunner and the boys, Jimbo."

Looking out the window of his room, Cal watched the shells on the Charles River moving like pencils with bug arms. He opened the window latch and lifted in his apple bag. The apple was cold and the first bite made one of his back molars ache. As he stared at the autumn river, he pictured himself back at his former university, *walking across the campus under the maple trees, sitting in Mr. Robert's American Westward Expansion class in Massachusetts Hall, putting on his shoulder pads in the locker room beside the cage.*

A silver jetliner was rising from Logan over Cambridge, glistening in the early November sun. Where the wind whipped the river surface, dark shadows merged and disappeared.

"My fraternity brothers are in Korea," he thought, *"and I'm in a Methodist seminary reading about Gnosticism."* He picked up Steinbeck's

Cannery Row and lay down on his bed to read. There was a knock on the door.

Before he got across the room, it opened and Clare Prenay was sliding in sideways and closing the door behind her.

"How did you get up here? Geez, did anyone see you? What are you doing?"

"Hi."

"What did you do, just come up the stairs? This is a frigging men's dormitory. What if Travis comes back?"

"I said 'Hi.' Be nice. The stairs from the library are wide open."

"So you just came up?"

"I'd love to see Trav."

"Terrific, he'd love to see you."

"Did you tell him?"

"For Christ's sake, Clare."

"You're not supposed to swear. I thought all you boys told each other your conquests."

Cal pushed the lock button on the door. "If he comes back, you've got about seven seconds to get in the closet while he's getting his key into the door."

Clare walked to the windows. "It's cold in here. Is this monk temperature? The view's peachy. I knew a boy once who drove one of those boats. He was a Harvard boy. He had wonderful latissimus dorsals."

"Clare, what's with the bimbo talk? You've got to get out of here."

"How can I learn if you don't teach me?"

The door lock clicked back and forth and Clare moved fast and closed the closet door behind her as the room door opened.

Travis Gaines came in holding his glasses and earmuffs in one hand and an armful of packages in the other. He went directly to the sink and looked in the mirror.

"Hi Trav. You look cold."

"Hey man, it's cold out there, my sinuses are killing me. You know what they told me at the speech clinic? I speak a 'deep South dialect of the American Negro.' At least they understood me at Filene's Basement today. You going to chapel? Howard Thurman's going to talk on the first chapter of *Mark*."

"No, I'm hitting *Cannery Row* again."

At the sink, Travis poured salt from a Morton's box into half a sinkful of water, and scooping the water with one hand, snuffed it up his nose. "At least you don't have sinuses like mine."

"It's your Deep South American Negro nose."

"Shit."

"I'll bet you can't wait to tell your father."

"He'd tell me it's what I get for going to a damnyankee doctor."

Travis tied his necktie and put on a suitcoat. He opened the door to leave. "Where're we eating tonight?"

"Chinatown."

"Where?"

"Where do you want?"

"The Imperial."

"OK. I'll be at Tremont at six-thirty unless you want to meet at Park Street and we can change to the red line. Joe's coming here at six."

"Tremont. We can walk over faster."

Travis left and closed the door. Cal pushed the lock button again.

"You can come out now."

Several seconds passed. "Trav has *gone*, Clare."

Cal opened the closet door. Clare was looking straight at him, not moving her eyes. She was naked except for the black garter belt holding up her silk stockings. "How are you feeling, Cal?"

CHAPTER TWO

▼

Cal heard a stick break, and peered down over the stone wall, scanning the silent oak grove. The hootings of the deer drivers had stopped. Another twig snapped, down and off to the right, and he thumb-pressed the cock on his gun, holding it as he squeezed the trigger and released the cock, carefully taking it off safety. He realized that he was holding his breath and breathed out. As he listened, he held his breath again.

The first movement Cal saw was the rack of antlers moving slowly from behind a large oak, then the head appeared, then the neck and shoulders. Cal sighted just below the shoulders and squeezed the trigger so slowly it became like the dream in which the trigger won't fire the gun. Aiming just below the shoulder, he was concentrating on holding the gun steady when he remembered that it was down hill, and while still applying pressure to the trigger, minutely lowered the target spot.

Later, he paced off the distance at ninety yards. When the gun fired he saw the deer leap forward and disappear, then bound and disappear again. Cal stared, holding the gun at his shoulder. The woods were silent.

He vaulted the stone wall and ran down through the oaks toward the spot where he last saw the running buck, and scanned the ground for blood. His father had told him to find the blood first, and the blood would lead to the deer. Cal's heart pounded

He studied the leaves, walking back and forth along the line where he thought the deer had run. For ten minutes he paced, looking for drops of blood.

"Did you fire?"

Joe was standing in his red hunting clothes twenty yards away, holding his double barrel shotgun in one hand, his red hunting cap pushed back on his head.

"Yeah I fired. I'm sure I hit him but I can't find any blood."

"Which way did he go? Was it a buck?"

"A *big* buck. He ran along here. He was coming along this line, right along here, toward that grass. I'm going back to where I think I hit him."

Cal walked back, bending over, studying the fallen leaves. When he spotted a glistening drop of fresh blood on a yellow leaf on the ground, he called, "I found the blood, Joe! Over here! I hit him!"

Joe called, "The deer's right here."

CHAPTER THREE

▼

Cal left the MTA at the Arlington Street station and walked past the Ritz Carlton Hotel. Across the street, the maple trees along the Public Garden were bare against the November sky. He had taken this walk to Miss Green's apartment over a hundred times, and he always had the same feeling of anticipation and hope, three times a week, week in and week out, except last summer when Miss Green went on vacation. The only thing now different from the beginning was that he knew he would talk. For months he had brought dreams written down on paper to read to her, now all he had to do was close his eyes and say the first thought that came into his head. She handed him a Kleenex when he needed it. Occasionally at the end of the fifty minutes she said, "You worked hard today. Good job."

Sometimes in a silence Miss Green would repeat a word he had used a few minutes before so that he could pursue it. Sometimes she would repeat something he said toward the end of the hour and connect it to something he had said near the beginning so he could hear the two words or phrases together. In an early session, he talked about his revulsion toward his mother's body—she once told Cal that when he was a baby she didn't take him off the breast early enough and had lost the shape of her breasts. Cal realized immediately why he had hated the taste of milk as a child, especially warm milk, and had refused to drink it unless it was almost ice cold, even then holding his breath as he guzzled the whole glass without stopping.

At the beginning of a much later hour he recounted a recurring dream of his mother putting him to bed. As soon as she kissed him goodnight and closed the bedroom door, the window over the porch roof opened and a figure dressed in black would enter and approach his bed. Terrified, he shrank into the covers, but at the moment the shrouded figure bent over Cal, it merely threw warm milk in Cal's face and the dream ended.

At the time of this later session with Miss Green, Cal was reading Milton's "L'Allegro" in Konigsbauer's Art of the Religious Tradition class, and he used the word "Miltonic" to describe his mother's joy whenever he was nice to her. At the end of the hour, Miss Green pointed out that it sounded as if he had said "milk tonic." After that session, Cal thought often about milk tonic, how something that made him gag could be related to someone he loved.

Little pieces of things were coming together, yet even when he didn't understand the meanings of his dreams or the reason why he "imaged" the things that came to him during the sessions with Miss Green, he *felt* better about himself. He believed that he was holding on to a rope, and that if he held on long enough, he would find himself at the end of it. After his previous session, he realized he had to talk with Miss Green about Clare, and he was apprehensive.

Across from the Public Garden where the pond was now empty of swan boats, Cal crossed Commonwealth Avenue. As he walked, he looked across to the statue of George Washington on his horse, holding his upturned sword that attracted vandals. He thought of the broken sword of Washington he had seen outside the state house in Charleston, South Carolina, smashed on the night the South Carolina regulars fired on Fort Sumter.

As Cal crossed Berkeley Street, he thought how stable the brownstone houses of Old Boston seemed. Over in the Public Garden loomed the statue of the doctor who first administered ether as an anesthetic. He entered the next brownstone building and climbed the stairs. The hour with Miss Green would be without anesthesia. She would be standing across the room when he entered, holding one wrist in the other hand, smiling at him. He would smell the cigarette smoke.

Once, he passed an older man coming down the stairs from her apartment. He must have been in deep trouble and stayed too long. Miss Green always broke off the hour at fifty minutes so her patients would not run into each other, but also so she could use the time to make notes and look over her previous notes on the next patient. Cal could always smell her cigarette, but he never saw it, and there were no visible ashtrays in her apartment. Miss Green knew that women smokers intimated Cal. At the top of the third flight of stairs he knocked gently, and after a few seconds, he heard her say, "Come in."

Miss Green stood across the room, holding one wrist and smiling. She said, "Hello."

Cal said "Hello," crossed the room and preceded her into her small office where he sat down in the familiar chair. She sat across from him next to her desk and smiled at him and waited. Behind Cal, a couch covered by a hand-made spread had been pushed against the wall. Cal wondered if some of her patients got to lie down on that couch. Cal looked at Miss Green and closed his eyes and began to talk.

CHAPTER FOUR

▼

"LYNN SUFFERS MILLION DOLLAR LOSS FROM HURRICANE: Streets Blocked by Fallen Trees," *Daily Evening Item* [Lynn, Mass.] Sept. 22, 1938

In the fall of the year when Cal was six, Beech Brook Reservoir seemed as calm as the lake on the cover of his father's *Liberty Magazine*. Nearby on the shore, the water reflections of beeches and maples seemed as real upside down in their perfect colors as those pointing into the sky. Looking from Fairchild's Point, Cal could also see the pines on the water side of Beechnut Street, dark and heavy green, and Cal would always remember the dead wood duck he held in his hands on that day.

It was a Saturday morning and he and Joe Sterns were looking for crawfish. Joe was his best friend. A year earlier, when Cal's mother assured Cal that he would like first grade, she offered Joe Sterns as the reason.

"Joe Sterns will be there, Cal, and you will like him."

"Why will I like him?"

"Because he's a nice little boy, Cal."

"How do you know, mama?"

"Because I know his mother from the Ladies' Aid. They live down at the end of Grant Avenue, right across from the reservoir."

Cal's mother always knew what she was talking about. Cal and Joe became friends in first grade. They played together on the schoolyard swings at recess, and they shared their colored pegs. Right after recess, the first graders had to put their heads on their wooden desks to rest, and after Miss Wells read to them from *Raggedy Ann*, they could play with their pegs while Miss Wells taught the second graders. Joe sat behind Cal, and during rest time Joe kept his eyes open and sometimes would poke Cal in the back with one of the colored pegs and whisper, "Time's almost up."

Joe could run faster than any first or second grader on the playground, and he could move his hands fast. He caught flies on his desk and collected them in the inkwell until it was so full of soggy, ink-soaked, dead flies that he couldn't jam in any more without squishing ink onto his desk. Then Joe lost interest in fly catching and concentrated on his idea for *Ferdinand the Bull*. Miss Wells had been reading *Ferdinand* to the class for several days, and Joe kept whispering to Cal that it sounded just like the Schick test. During the first week of school, the class had lined up in the back corridor where Miss Dobson, the school nurse, sat in a chair in front of the janitor's sink and gave each pupil a needle in the arm to protect against diphtheria. Each afternoon when Miss Wells picked up *Ferdinand* to read, Joe would say in Cal's ear, "Here comes the Schick test again."

The day after she finished reading *Ferdinand*, the class marched up to Miss Shoreham's room to listen to the radio broadcast of the coronation of King George VI from Westminster Abbey in London. It was the first time the class had been in Miss Shoreham's room, and they knew that she was very strict. The first and second graders had to stand along the back aisle next to the ferns on the windowsill and the plants with long stems trailing to the floor. Miss Shoreham told them not to touch any of the plants. Nobody dared make a sound and the class had to pay attention to the radio full of static and crackling sounds and no one could hear much.

Everyone could tell that it was quiet where the man was talking because he sounded like he wasn't supposed to be making any noise. Joe was pretending he was not interested, but Cal knew he was because Joe stopped elbowing Bruce Thomason right after "My Country Tears" was over and the radio man started talking in a loud whisper. When the class went back down to Miss Wells's room, Joe immediately raised his hand and asked Miss Wells if the class could play *Ferdinand the Bull*, acting out the parts. She told Joe it was an extremely clever idea and he could be in charge of the play if he thought about it at home and told the class the next day how to go about it.

Joe never worried about what was coming next, and he came to school the next day with his plan. Miss Wells said that Joe was the "The Director" and he could pick the actors, and every day for a week the class acted *Ferdinand the Bull* after they recited the Pledge of Allegiance and Miss Wells read the 100th Psalm about the long lasting gates. Cal was bothered that Joe never picked him to be Ferdinand, and he always had to be the picador. Joe changed the actors for the part of Ferdinand, and Jane Hood and Wilfred North got to be the sad bull, but Joe always took the role of matador for himself. Joe said that Cal was the Shick man, and shouldn't complain.

After a week, *Ferdinand the Bull* was forgotten because the class began reading the big Dick and Jane and Spot book on the front wall over the blackboard. The class had little books just like the big one, and they were supposed to keep them inside their desks except during reading time when they took turns standing and reading a few sentences from the big book as Miss Wells pointed with the long wooden marker. When she turned the page of the big book, that was enough for the day and the class could read in their own small-sized versions, except that no one was supposed to go past where Miss Wells left off in the big book on the wall.

When the class came to the chapter when Dick and Jane went to visit Grandfather and Grandmother, Cal got sick with scarletina, and when he returned to school three weeks later, Miss Wells had collected the little books. Cal had to ask Joe how the story ended, but Joe could hardly believe that Cal hadn't peeked ahead to read the ending. Joe said that he had read the whole book through to the end in the first week of school because it was easy to pull it out a little way from inside the desk and keep the edge of it in his lap so Miss Wells couldn't see him reading it. But Cal told himself that knowing the ending wouldn't be as much fun if he secretly turned the pages by himself.

In the fall of the year when they were in the second grade, Cal made his visit one Saturday morning. The sun was bright and warm, and Joe's mother walked them across Beechnut Street to the reservoir and said she would come back and call for them in an hour. Joe said they were going to hunt for crawfish under rocks in the shallow water where red and yellow leaves floated near the shore. He said the crawfish were good bait for bass fishing.

Joe and Cal walked by the water's edge to a point where it was shallow a long way out. Nearby was the cove with pine trees growing at the edge of deeper water. As soon as they reached the end of the point and could see into the cove, several ducks jump-flew from the surface and leveled off across the reservoir toward an island and a small cove where the big boys swam in the summer.

"They're probably mallards," Joe said.

"What's mallards?" Cal asked.

"Ducks with green heads, except for the females, but they could be wood ducks, except I didn't hear any noises. Wood ducks go "oo-eek" when they fly.

"Ducks fly really fast."

"My father says they fly faster than any bird except a woodcock after it whistles."

"What's a woodcock?"

"They have long beaks and look like professors of history. That's what my father says. He says all they need is glasses."

"*My* father went hunting once and came home with ducks that were all black. He said for my mother to put them in salt water for a week, and they rotted."

"Those were ocean ducks. They aren't much good. You should see a wood duck. They're all rainbow colored, and my father says they melt in your mouth."

"I wish we could catch one."

"You have to be lucky to shoot a duck. You have to aim way in front of them, and you have to have a dog that'll swim out and bring them back in his mouth."

"My dog Pickles would eat them. He kills chickens."

"A bird dog drops them right on your feet."

Joe took off his shoes and rolled up his pants to his knees and stepped into the water. Cal followed him and watched him carefully pick up rocks the size of his hands and move them. Then Joe said under his breath, "OK, right there." He put his hand very slowly into the water in front of him and held it still, then moved it very quickly to the bottom.

"Missed him," Joe said.

"What was it?"

"A crawfish, a little one. You can tell them because they look like tiny lobsters, but they're brownish like the rocks. You can look right at one and not know it."

Joe caught five crawfish that morning before they heard his mother call from the shore. Cal missed several because each one moved faster than he could make his hand move. Joe said that the trick was to grab them from the back because they moved backwards by flapping their tails back up underneath them. They moved so fast when they flapped that Cal couldn't see where they went. Each time that he missed, he lifted another rock. Joe let him hold one of his and it pinched Cal's hand and he dropped it and Joe laughed.

"They can't hurt you," he said. "A lobster can take your finger right off."

CHAPTER FIVE

▼

"GERMANS ENTER SUDETANLAND: Czechoslovakia Area Will Soon Be Divided,"
Daily Evening Item [Lynn, Mass.], Sept. 30, 1938.

After lunch, Joe and Cal were playing glassies at the edge of the dirt
road in front of Joe's house, waiting for Cal's mother to come down from
Pine Ridge Avenue, and they saw Buddy Thomason and Eddie Churchill
and Frank Kendall coming from the reservoir. They were fifth graders
from Miss Shoreham's room. Buddy and Eddie were laughing and Frank
was dangling something from his hand. Cal and Joe could see that it was
a dead duck.

"Can we see the duck?" Joe called to them.

The older boys crossed over to Joe's front yard and Frank held out the
dead duck by the neck.

"Can I hold it?" Cal asked.

Frank handed it to him by the neck. Cal took the body in two hands
and held it with the neck dangling over his right hand.

Joe reached over and ruffled the feathers with one finger.

"How did you catch it?" Joe asked.

"Luck," Eddie Churchill said. "Pure luck."

"It was a fluke," Buddy said.

"I got it though," Frank said. "I got the son of a bitch."

"We scared a bunch of ducks up, Joe said. "They flew across the
rezzy."

"We saw 'em," Buddy said. "We were in that cove behind the island. We saw them land in the water."

"I just smacked him," Frank said. "He flew up right next to me and I batted 'em. He went down and I grabbed 'em. I got the son of a bitch and I'm going to eat him."

"Pure luck," said Eddie. "You'll never do it again the rest of your life. You're bitchin' lucky, Kendall, it's a fuckin' fluke. If we hadn't stopped walking when the mallards came into the cove, he wouldn't have spooked. You're a real bird dog, Kendall."

"I got 'em didn't I? You guys didn't get him. I got the son of a bitch right out of the air. Wham. I clipped him and he went down and fluttered around and you guys just stood there."

"You drop-kicked him about eight yards, you screw," Buddy said. "He's probably all broken."

"He'll eat just the same, won't he? You guys are just jealous."

"You're a great man, Frank," Eddie said.

"Fuck you, Churchill, I got the duck. I'm going home and cook 'im."

After they left, Cal remembered the yellow and red and blue feathers of the wood duck. There were white stripes on his green head, and blue feathers on his back near the tail. "It was so soft," he said.

"Frank must have walked right on to a pair nesting in the woods. That's why they call them wood ducks. My father says when you kill one the other one keeps going back to the same place for days, looking for the mate."

"It was so soft and pretty."

"Mallards are pretty, too," Joe said. "And they're bigger. When they're dead, they make wood ducks look puny."

CHAPTER SIX

▼

"CHAMBERLAIN CALLS UNITED STATES THE MOST POWERFUL NATION IN THE WORLD: Announces $350,000,000 Loan for Czechoslovakia," *Daily Evening Item*, Oct. 5, 1938

Joe and Cal were best friends until the Sterns moved to Mapleton Center when Joe and Cal were in the fifth grade. They had always been on the same side when they played football at recess and when they played "Buck Buck, How Many Fingers Up" against the telephone pole at the edge of the playground along Grant Avenue. They said that they would go out for the high school team together when they got bigger.

After the Sterns moved, Joe and Cal talked once on the telephone, but then they forgot about each other until seventh grade when both were in Miss January's class in junior high school. Joe was playing halfback on the Mapleton Center sandlot team, and Cal played for the Mapleville team. Joe could still run faster than Cal and he was now a little bigger and much stronger than Cal, but they made a plan that Joe would wait for Cal to catch up before they tried out for the high school team. Once in the seventh grade and once in the eighth grade they played against each other and both times Joe's team won by a lot of points.

One fall afternoon, when Cal didn't have to go to band practice, they agreed to meet at Bly Field and watch the high school team practice. They each rode their bikes to the practice field.

"Eddie Sikorski is the best football player in America," Cal said as they sat on the top row of the visiting stands looking over the practice field. It was a cool fall day and the first shadows from the maple trees were just beginning along the west side of the field. Off to their right beyond the field house, Hyacinth Pond was almost brown with summer weeds. The home stands across the game field were empty and gray and shiny in the last rays of the sun. Cal felt warm and good inside. The stadium was a special place for him, and he dreamed of the day he would play on the high school team. Cal and Joe agreed that they would try out for the team when they weighed 140 pounds. Joe had weighed 130 for two years but Cal was gaining. Maybe when they were in the ninth grade they would be big enough.

"How come they call him 'Shipwreck'? Cal asked.

"It's a joke," Joe said. "He's dangerous when he runs. Nobody wants to tackle him. He goes every which way. Coach Whately calls him a dumb Polock, but he likes him. He only calls him that when he makes little mistakes. Eddie laughs. Maybe he'll do it today. If Eddie really screws up, coach calls him Edward."

"He's the nuts," Cal said.

"So's Farrington."

"Last Sunday the *Boston Post* said, 'Farrington 14--Marblehead 0.' Jesus, it was great."

"Wasn't it great when Eddie took the kickoff and ladreld to Mike so he could block for him?"

"There's Bonny White, the one on the bike."

"Who's she?"

"She's over here all the time."

"I never saw her in school."

"She's been in reform school. She does it."

"She's coming over. What'll we do?"

"Don't do anything. Just shoot the breeze. She's OK."

Bonny White was fourteen, small boned with softly chiseled features and nut-brown hair. She pushed down her kickstand with her foot, looked up at Cal and Joe and smiled.

"Whatcha doin'?"

Joe said, "Just catching practice. How's it going?"

"OK. Just riding my bike. I have to be home before dark." She took her hands off the handlebars to see if the bike would steady against the wooden bleachers, and ducked into the open back of the stands under the boys dangling feet.

On the practice field, Coach Whately yelled, "Cut inside when it spreads like that, Sikorski. Don't think, will you? If you cut back, everything goes the other way. If you think, you'll screw it up. Run it again."

Sikorski got to his feet and jogged back to the huddle, a little grin on his face. Coach Whately said, "K 9 Red Outside."

Joe said, "Watch Eddie run it this time. They won't touch him." Cal was watching Bonny pull herself up through the wooden planking of the stands. She was wearing a white T-shirt and her breasts softened against the edges of the last plank as she pulled herself through.

"Made it," she said as her bike fell over on the grass. "The hell with it. It's an old bike anyway. Who're you?" She was looking directly at Cal.

"I'm Cal."

"Is that your first name or your last name?"

"It's short for something else."

"Am I supposed to keep asking you questions?"

Joe said, "He's Calvin Calculus, named after a Greek poet who was lousy in math."

"You're always a wise ass, Joe. Tell your mystery buddy he doesn't have to be nice to me."

"You can tell him. He's going to be the next great football player for Mapleton High School."

"O la."

"I'm Caleb Newsome. I live in Mapleville. Joe and I have been friends since first grade."

"I live in Maple Hills. I'm Bonny. Thanks for the introduction, Joe."

"No sweat. I couldn't get a word in between you two."

"I bet. Did you tell him all about me?"

"I didn't tell him anything. I told him you've been in reform school."

"Yeah, that's where I've been. Do you think I'm bad, Calvin Calculus?"

"I don't even know you. I don't think anybody's bad."

"Boy, that's something. That's not the way I heard it."

"You heard about me?"

"No, but I heard about bad. This is a great conversation. I got to be going before my bike stands back up by itself. See you around."

After Bonny left, Cal said, "She's pretty."

"Yup, she's pretty. You want to get fixed up?"

"Did you ever fuck her?"

"No, but I know guys who did?"

"She just does it if you ask her?"

"Yes or no?"

"I never fucked anybody. Where would we do it?"

In the twilight, the players on the practice field crashed against each other, and the scrimmage lasted a long time. The soft autumn air was punctuated by Coach Whately's voice rising and falling in the late afternoon. Riding his bike homeward, Cal pumped up Oak Street hill. The streetlights came on, and he passed the path in the woods he would have taken if he had been walking. As he stood up on his pedals and pumped hard to see if he could make it to the top of the hill without getting off his bike, he thought of Bonny White's breasts against the wooden planks of the visitors football stands.

CHAPTER SEVEN

▼

Cal closed the door to Miss Green's apartment and hurried down the stairs. *I did it*, he said to himself, *I talked about her.* Outside the brownstone building, the early Boston darkness was soft and receptive. Cars crowded all three lanes of Arlington Street, their early headlights beaming toward Tremont and Copley Square. Leaves from the overhead trees fell softly around him as he passed Ursaline Academy. He was euphoric with relief, but puzzled by the dream he had related to Miss Green near the end of the session.

Crossing Commonwealth Avenue, Cal knew that he had three hours before meeting Travis and Joe, and as he walked, his thoughts went back to the university, *walking from football practice to the sloping east side of the college pond where he would meet Joannie, and they would join hands and sit by the water watching the two swans as the reflection of the chapel gradually disappeared from the water. Then they would walk to Johnson Hall where Cal would eat with the football team at training table and she would eat with friends from her dorm. They would meet again at the library and in the furthest reaches of the stacks on the second floor Cal would ease his finger inside her panties, then they would walk to the main reading room and open their books.*

Before today's session with Miss Green, Cal had determined to talk about his relationship with Clare. Earlier in his room, after he had hurried her down the stairwell to the library, his erect penis pulsated for a long time as he thought of her standing before him in her garter belt and silk stockings, and he wished he had screwed her. Yet, sitting across from

Miss Green, as soon as he closed his eyes, it was Joannie who was lying beneath him.

After graduation, he had read her Dear Cal letter near the end of the summer when he was working in Montana, chain-sawing switch-track ties for the Great Northern Railroad at a small sawmill in Martin City. Later that week he bummed a ride from a woman whose husband had run off with another lumberjack's wife, driving with her young daughter to Fargo, North Dakota. Cal then bought a Greyhound bus ticket for Boston with the nineteen silver dollars in change he had received when he broke a twenty dollar bill to buy a pack of gum earlier in the summer in Kalispell. Four days later in Boston he got another bus to the Cape where Joannie was summering as a waitress in Dennis.

Sitting across from her in the front seat of her mother's green Chrysler sedan on an isolated sandy road, with the late summer smell of scrub pine and bayberry bushes coming through the open windows, Cal cried and pleaded with Joannie to come back to him. In the bushes outside, the cicadas vibrated in the August Cape Cod heat. She listened patiently to Cal and shook her head and waited for him to stop crying. Then she drove him to a friend's apartment near the beach.

That night, Cal took his first alcoholic drink and got drunk on rye whiskey. One of Joannie's girl friends sat with him on the lower steps of the Narragansett Inn, their bare feet touching the cool sand as Cal poured out his self-pity until four o'clock in the morning. The next day when he saw her, Cal pretended he didn't know her.

Today he had told Miss Green the Joannie story for almost the whole fifty minutes, then opened his eyes and remembered his dream from the night before. Every detail of the dream was clear in his mind, the long wharf in the mist leading to the other shore, the Indian professor, Chakravarty, sitting in the wooden gazebo reading a stone tablet with Bengali writing on it, then doing chin-ups on a suspended bar, smiling at Cal as his mustache disappeared, then the broken silver clarinet on the linoleum floor with tiny boxes of mouthpiece reeds strewn around it, then the amphitheater in the Far West and the long trail up the mountain where he seemed to have been a long time ago, then passing by caverns as crowds descended the mountain, then entering the high pass with the great boulders in the dark, looking across to a far valley.

Now as he walked along the late afternoon Boston sidewalk, a voice inside his head said, *"Being in seminary is like staying in childhood."*

Cal had almost reached the Arlington Street subway station when he saw her, and the heavy stone was in his stomach again. Her head was tilted forward, and she had that same funny little sexy hitch in her walk. She didn't see him as they passed on the sidewalk. Cal could have touched her, but he kept walking, then turned and stared after her. Then he began to follow her. The coincidence of her physical presence on this day at this moment seemed preposterous.

Yet there she was, walking directly in front of him. Inside his head he could hear Joe: *"There's no such thing as fate."* Joe's favorite comment was that life mirrors the after supper neighborhood game they both played as kids, Red Light, finding the runners one by one and racing them back to the lamppost goal. The point was to capture all the players and then run free. He could hear Joe saying, *"If you can't get her out of your mind, get another girlfriend."*

Cal called to her.

She turned and looked at him. "Oh hi," she said, "long time no see."

"What are you doing in Boston?"

"I work here. Wednesdays I meet my mother for dinner. You?"

"Gee, that's great. I'm still at Z.U. May I see you sometime?"

"I'm getting married in March. He's an intern at Mass. General. I'm in kind of a hurry. Bye."

She was walking toward Beacon Street to meet her mother who never approved of him because he was going to become a minister. He watched her disappear across Berkeley Street.

Cal turned and walked back toward the subway station where she had emerged three minutes before. Passing it, he looked down the half-lighted steps of the stairwell past the intent faces coming up from underground. He turned the corner at the Arlington Street Congregational Church and walked toward Copley Square. *She's been right here.* He stopped in front of the Copley Bookstore and looked in the window, but the dust jackets of the featured books were merely colored objects. *I could have called her, all that time.* He crossed against a red light, stepping between cars, turning the corner at the public library. A taxi driver blew his horn and yelled, "You color blind, asshole?"

Half way across Exeter Street he was almost hit by a black sedan driven by an old lady wearing a polka dot kerchief around her head. All the windows of her car were open. She slammed her brakes and Cal jumped back and stared at her. Her windshield wipers were clicking back and forth. The woman started to back up so she could give him more space but the car behind her honked and she slammed the brakes again. Cal then realized how far he had walked and started to cross back toward the movie theater, turning to see the old woman inching her car ahead, moving her hand back and forth near the side of her face as if she were brushing away flies.

Cal stood reading the theater marquis describing *Raintree County* with Elizabeth Taylor and Montgomery Clift. Cal tried to remember the name of the author of the book. Lock something. He taught at Simmons College here in Boston while writing it, then committed suicide. Ross Lockridge. *How could anyone commit suicide?* The poster said that a northerner torn between two women married one of them who later fled south with their little boy during the Civil War.

Inside the theater, a wounded Yankee soldier, Montgomery Clift, was carrying a little boy on his back in the dark, trying to escape north through Confederate lines. At the edge of a gorge that blocked their way, the only escape was straight down. He rolled off the edge, dropping into the darkness of the gorge. Cal was sure that the boy would be killed.

Although Cal had planned to watch the movie up to the point when he had entered the theater, he stayed through to the end again.

Walking to Chinatown, Cal couldn't erase from his mind the scene in which Elizabeth Taylor found the doll after the fire, half of its face burned off. Cal knew that he was the doll, and that one half of him had been lost somewhere.

CHAPTER EIGHT

▼

Inside the entrance to the Imperial restaurant in Chinatown, Cal climbed the steps to the second floor dining room and saw Joe and Travis at a corner table, eating with their fingers from baskets. The smell of deep fried egg rolls and seafood hung heavily in the room.

"Well, I'm late but I'm here."

"Did you hear somebody say something, Trav?"

"I didn't hear anything, man, 'cept some Yankee street noises."

"My apologies, guys, I need some slack. Big day at Miss Green's, then two cars barely missed me and I ended up in the Exeter Theater watching *Raintree County*."

"The Yankees still win the Civil War?" Travis asked.

The waiter came over and Cal ordered noodles and shrimp. Joe and Travis stopped eating and waited for Cal to resume talking.

"You won't believe what happened before the movie," Cal said.

"Clare told you she's pregnant," Joe said.

"Not about Clare, though she actually walked up to the room by the back stairs from the library and undressed in the closet and I kicked her out. Later I saw Miss Green and talked about Joannie for the first time and afterwards bumped into her on Arlington Street."

"Go back to the Clare part," Travis said.

"She was bareass in the closet when you came into the room."

"Whoa," Travis said.

"I like Clare," Joe said.

"You never heard the bimbo routine. Today she was rhapsodizing over the latissimus dorsi of a former boyfriend who rowed for Harvard."

"She was just trying to get your attention," Joe said.

"It feels like I just fantasized a whole afternoon. Listen, you guys, I actually talked about Joannie with Miss Green for the first time and then right afterward I ran into her on Arlington Street after I left Miss Green's. You know what kind of a coincidence that is?"

"What took you so long?" Joe asked.

"Come on Joe, everything isn't fate. I walked to Copley and almost got hit by a taxi and then by an old lady in a car on Exeter Street by the movie theater, then went in for the last third of *Raintree County* and stayed over and saw the whole thing again.

"Not to get philosophical, old buddy, but maybe some of your answers are somewhere in the right questions," Joe said. "You told me yourself that in the *Gospel of Philip* when Peter asks Jesus why he loved Mary Magdalen more than the Disciples, Jesus said, "Why do I not love you like her?"

"Wait a second. Slow down here," Travis said, "I think I missed something. Catch me up, OK?"

"*Gnostic Gospels*," Cal said. "New stuff they found in old jars about five years ago."

"I don't know any *Gospel of Philip*."

"There's a team translating a whole bunch of Gospels that were kicking around in the second century and were supposedly lost. Some of it's mind-blowing."

"If my bishop knew I was listening to these ideas he'd have my Augusta ass back in Georgia so fast my daddy would think his rebel son saw the light in Yankeeland and turned tail for the red hills and the grits and pone. What's it supposed to mean," Travis said.

"Maybe Cal is just trying to figure out why he's in seminary." Joe said.

The waiter put the noodles and shrimp in front of Cal."

Travis said, "I'll have a ginger ale."

The waiter looked at Joe. "One more beer?"

"Ginger ale for me too," Joe said.

"Cal said. "Do you really think, Joe, I'm here just to figure out why I'm here?"

"You know that song we all sang at parties at college, "We're here because we're here because we're here?" Joe said. "Why do you think that Jesus answered Peter with the same question?"

"Do *you* think Jesus was screwing Mary Magdalene?" Cal asked.

"You're the one who told me that the Gnostics thought so," Joe said.

"I hope no one is recording this," Travis said.

"Peter was just a literary straight man in that exchange with Jesus," Joe said. "How many questions have real answers? He was either kissing Mary M or he wasn't. If he was, the reason was obvious. No?"

"And the reason why I'm in seminary is obvious?" Cal said.

"What does your Miss Green say?"

"She doesn't say, she listens."

"Same thing."

"Can we back up a little?" Travis said, eyeing the entrance on the other side of the dining room. "They're still pushing Bethlehem and the Crucifixion back where I come from. I'm only here in Boston at the indulgence of one Bishop Moore in Georgia, who merely allowed me to come up here to the double talk capitol of Yankee propaganda. Even Professor Roth says that the account of Holy Week in *John's Gospel* is more historical than the accounts in *Mathew, Mark,* and *Luke.* What do you say to that? Don't look now but Cripswell and Lovell just came in. There are more behind them. They've got Burwell and Mary Lou Manning with them. We better get rid of the beer bottles."

Joe held his empty bottle on the table. "Let the fledgling preachers gasp. They get a thrill out of watching sin take place before their eyes."

"Lovell's really OK," Travis said, waving his fork in recognition when he saw Mary Lou pointing toward them. "Don't let his big wet lips scare you, he's only an actor. It's not catching."

"I heard he just got the assistant job at First Unitarian over on Beacon Street. The head guy over there is slick."

"Stacy Cockburn," Cal said.

"He's from Harvard. All those Yankee Harvard types get the Unitarian jobs. Prestwood told me he's a good preacher, though. They're coming over."

Travis stood up and said, "Nice to see y'all. Grab a table right here."

"Hel-*lo* Travis Blain," Mary Lou said. "It's so nice to see you again. How're you making it in this awful Yankee weather? Y'all know each other, I'm sure." She pointed: "Joe, Cal, Ray, Cripsey, y'all sitting up back together in Dr. Roth's history class. Susan and I have to sit down front because we're new and we don't want to miss anything. Dr. Roth's so wonderful, don't you think he is? I could just sit in that class every afternoon forever. I just don't want him ever to stop talking."

Joe and Cal stood up to shake hands all around, and Mary Lou patted the air with her hand: "Now you boys just sit yourselves down and eat your dinners. We just came over to greet you and now we're going to find ourselves a table and just stuff ourselves."

Cripswell stood there smiling, reaching out his little ungloved hand toward Cal, who took it as he was sitting back down. "Oh goodness," Cripswell laughed, "I forgot how defiantly you shake hands." He lightly slapped with his gloved hand at the hand that failed him, saying, "You be ready the next time." He laughed again and cocked his head to one side. "See you."

Susan Burwell looked directly at Joe and said, "Bye men, eat well."

"Don't forget your doggy bags," Ray Lovell said, grinning, as the four turned and walked across the room to a wall booth.

"Both of their fathers are preachers," Joe said.

"Who?" Travis asked.

"Susan and Mary Lou."

"They're all ministers' daughters. That's what D-R-E's always are, ministers' daughters," Cal said.

"They are if they're from the South," Travis said.

"All Directors of Religious Education come from the South, don't they?" Cal said.

"No, there's a bunch from the mid-west and some from the far west," Joe said.

"Just a joke," Cal said.

"They're actually very civil," Joe said.

"Most of them are prudes," Cal said.

"What's a prude?" Joe said, sipping his ginger ale as Cal worked on his noodles.

"Who, Burwell and Manning?" Travis said.

"Some of them are probably prudes, who knows," Joe said, "It depends on what a prude is to you."

"Who'd want to screw a D-R-E?" Cal said, cornering the last noodle in his bowl with his finger. "They all think God's a preacher just like their father."

"If you believe in God," Travis said."

"It's a good question," Joe said. "I'll bet a D-R-E in bed is as good as any other woman. Nice is not always goody-goody. The first Saturday night after we got here in September, I saw Susan at the Old Howard for the midnight Rose La Rose strip show. She was with those three D-R-E's who hang around together at lunch at the corner table in the cafeteria. One of them is that really tall one with the long blonde hair, the terrific ping-pong player. They were sitting right in front of me and I didn't know it until Susan turned around and looked me in the eye at intermission, smiling, and said, "Hi Joe!" She never flinched, and she didn't say anything like, "What are you doing here?"

"I'm starting to get it," Travis said. "It would have been like Jesus saying to Peter, "You ask me why I kiss Mary Magdalene on the mouth?"

"Maybe that's not a joke. Susan looked right at me one minute after Rose left the stage at the end of the first act, bareass. She started the second act bareass and ended the show in an evening gown."

"What's so great about that?" Cal asked, picking up Joe's leftover rib.

"The show? It was a great show. Rose la Rose is very classy."

"I mean about Burwell recognizing you."

"I didn't say it was great, I said that she's not necessarily a goody-goody because she's a D-R-E. She didn't spook, that's all. And I'm telling you, she isn't."

"You know her, I can tell," Cal said. "How come you're holding out on us?"

"Who's holding out? If you weren't bubbling over with the Clare and Joannie show, some unrehearsed D-R-E might just slip behind the curtain. D-R-E's may not know all the ways of the world, but they know that preachers sleep with their wives. It's comfortable to go to bed with men who talk to God every Sunday. Why shouldn't they want to marry preachers? They bring that to seminary, but no more than we would-be preachers all bring the guilt of our mothers with us."

"Did I do that?" Travis asked. "I may need a beer. I've already gotten too much information from this meal. I'll bet a Richmond dollar that Lovell and Cripswell aren't talking about their mothers right now."

"Did you see Cripswell look at the empty beer bottle?" Cal said.

"He's harmless. He's one of those guys in your Konigsbauer Art class. He'll end up editing *intent* magazine and directing pageants at Presbyterian Student Movement conferences. When he's forty he'll marry one of those Southern widows a foot taller than he is, and when he's in his fifties a church janitor will open the assistant minister's office door one Monday morning and find them intertwined in a strange and awkward position. I'll wager you a whole trunk full of Richmond dollars that he keeps a bottle of Harvey's Bristol Creme hidden in his room." Joe finished the last of his ginger ale.

"Not Pabst Blue Ribbon?" Travis asked as they put on their coats near the cash register.

As the door of the Imperial Restaurant closed behind them, Joe said, "That's what Susan drinks."

As they walked toward the subway station, Joe said to Cal, "We weren't very good listeners for you tonight."

"It's better if I save it for Miss Green, anyway. I'll see her day after tomorrow."

CHAPTER NINE

▼

Cal broke the huddle and crouched behind the center. His arm was loose, and Joe was catching everything close to him. It was only a game of touch football, but Cal's whole body and mind were into it. He felt warm all over, working up a sweat. "Don't let that guy come up the middle," he said to his center, Bill Truckee, who nodded. "Joe! Red light!" Cal yelled at Joe, his right end.

Joe said, "Yup," looking straight ahead.

Cal took the snap, spun and faked a shovel lateral to Evers Candy flaring around right end, stepped back with the ball poised behind his right ear. He looked to the sidelines as if he were going to throw the ball to Candy, and saw Clare standing next to Travis, but it barely registered. Nothing mattered when he had a football in his hand.

Behind Cal, the Zion University Bridge was just beginning to silhouette against the double towers of the School of Sacred Thought across the river. Some of the cars crossing the bridge had turned on their lights. On the Charles to his left, coxswains were counting beats for the rowers. The long shells were strands of beads moving up and down the river.

Cal knew exactly what Joe was planning to do, and Joe knew where Cal would put the ball. Cal heard Bill Truckee grunt as the incoming lineman tried to arm lift him out of the way, and he heard him grunt again, but Bill was keeping his man in front of him. Joe took two steps and started to buttonhook, then made a complete turn and accelerated. The linebacker had over-committed himself and Joe was already behind him a step as the safety moved to cover Joe. Ten yards deep, Joe performed the same maneuver, drawing the safety by angling directly at him before straightening his course and Joe was in the clear. The ball hit his fingers seven steps further. Joe crossed the goal line thirty yards away from the nearest defender, his third touchdown, and they were leading by twenty with five minutes left.

Rawley Bengal, the playing-coach, ran onto the field with another player: "We'll finish it up. Nice going, Cal. Beautiful, Joe."

"Cake," Joe said, jogging off beside Cal. "Nice chuck, Q-B. You're on today."

"Yo." Cal looked up and this time it registered that Clare was standing on the sideline. "What the hell is Clare doing here?"

"Be nice to her for a change, will you? She came to see you play."

They jogged over and Clare said, "Good job."

"Thanks," Cal said. "Thanks for coming, Trav."

"Hi Clare," Joe said.

"You're glue fingers, Joe," Clare said. "You don't drop anything."

"Story of his life," Cal said.

"I've dropped a few," Joe said. "Cal was on today. It was too nice a day to drop them. I'm out of here, guys, heavy date with my church history paper."

"I'm gone too," Travis said. "I told Bertha I'd work the Smorgasbord tonight."

"So long everybody," Clare said, walking toward her car. "Bye Cal."

"OK, see you Clare, thanks for coming," Cal called.

"Have you totally lost it, Cal?" Joe said.

"Come on, man," Travis said.

"What do you mean, you guys? What did I do? I didn't invite her. I didn't ask her for a date. Am I supposed to go home with her? I've got things to do too. I've got a paper to write."

"Heck, I'll take her to dinner if you won't. Hey Clare! Hold it a second will you?"

Joe started to run toward Clare. She was unlocking her car at the edge of the field, just off the Cambridge Parkway, but Cal grabbed Joe from behind. "OK, OK, I'll go with her."

"Don't do yourself any favors, Cal," Joe said. "Sometimes you're as classy as a turd."

Cal left Travis and Joe, who were watching him, and ran toward Clare.

"I was thinking, Clare," Cal said, "Why don't we . . . let's have a bite somewhere. Let's go to the Wursthaus, you want to?"

"You don't have to do this, Cal," Clare said, "I know you have studies to do. I told my girlfriend I'd meet her. But thanks anyway. I'll be seeing you."

"No, gee Clare, it would be great. Come on, do it for me. We'll celebrate the game."

"I know you're upset with me, Cal. I shouldn't have come to your room the other day. I made a fool of myself. It was really dumb. I'm ashamed. I shouldn't have come today either."

"No, I was dumb. I was a jerk about the other day. Joe said. . . ."

"You told Joe? My god, Cal, do you tell Joe everything? What'll he think I am, a putt-putt girl? Do you swap notes? You're such a shit, Cal. Do you think I go around dorm-crashing in my garters? Maybe you think I just play the preacher circuit with my pussy. I happen to like you, damn you. Get out of my way." Clare pushed him and started to open her car door.

"Wait, Clare. I didn't really tell Joe anything. I apologize. Don't go. I've had some things on my mind."

"Yes, you've got things on your mind. You've got John Steinbeck on your mind, and you've got football on your mind, even your church fucking history paper on your mind. You've got everything on your mind except me, and you've made me feel like I don't have any shame, and I'm a lousy person and a sex hungry vamp, and I don't know what else. And you're a liar. You told Joe, all right, and Travis, and for all I know maybe even some of those creeps over there in your monk warren. Get away from me. You've had your last shot, Mr. Goodbar."

"Come on, Clare, I know I've got problems. I . . . "

Clare shouted through the closed car window: "You got problems. Right! You got problems. Try joining the world!"

Clare edged her car forward, waited for the traffic to clear, and pulled out onto Massachusetts Drive toward Cambridge.

Cal knew that she was right to leave him standing there alone, and because she was hurt and angry, he felt protective toward her. He wanted to comfort her now that he had wounded her. When she cried he wanted to soothe her, but the other voice said, *"She deserves it. She's not like Joannie; if you give up Joannie, you lose everything."*

Cal walked along the Charles River in the November twilight. Joe began to talk inside Cal's head, answering the other voice. When Cal heard these two voices arguing, it was always Joe's voice trying to clarify, trying to persuade. It wasn't a preaching voice, it didn't reprimand Cal, but it needled him, tried to put him off balance. Joe's voice said, *"Joannie left you when you hitchhiked west, she didn't want to marry you. She wants something you don't have right now. Let her be."*

"You need Joannie," the other voice said. *"She came back twice before. If she comes back, everything will be all right."*

"Nothing will be all right. Nothing will be changed. You're trying to prove something to yourself that has nothing to do with Joannie and Clare."

"Don't listen to him. Call her sister and find out where she's staying."

"Do you really want her to reject you again?"

"Joannie pulled you down into the sand and said, 'How can I love you standing up?'"

"Who were you thinking of when you were with Joannie?"

Cal walked along the edge of the river toward M.I.T. *Ma told me that if I went to medical school, she would help me, she had money tucked away. She said, "Don't tell your father."*

As he looked across the water, Cal remembered the afternoon of his first day in seminary when he walked along the other side of the river, all the way to the Boston Pops concert shell where people were lying on the grass and reading newspapers. Small rented sailboats eased across the water—a scene from a Seurat painting: warm colors, blankets on the grass and wine bottles in minute specks of color. Stopped time in early September.

On that afternoon, he met Cripswell for the first time. Cal had left the river and cut across the intersection of Beacon and Arlington at the corner of the Public Garden He was sitting on a bench near the statue commemorating the use of ether as an anaesthetic when Cripswell sat down beside him and began a conversation that revealed they were both seminarians at Zion University. They decided to eat dinner together, and walked to a Swedish Smorgasbord restaurant on a little side street across from Boston City Hall that Cripswell had read about in a guide to Boston restaurants.

When they began their walk back to Memorial Avenue along the Charles, it was still light outside, and the evening was pleasant and warm. They passed under the MIT Bridge, passed Kenmore Square, and passed The Ramparts where the president of Zion University lived. As they reached the Fielding Drive walkway overpass, Cripswell suggested that they sit by the river for a while before going in.

It was nine o'clock and it had been dark for an hour. The river moved slowly before them as they talked about their former colleges. Cal suddenly sensed that Cripswell was stalling, that he didn't want to return to the dormitory. "I'm going to cross back now," Cal said. He put one hand on the grass to push himself upright and Cripswell covered his hand with his own.

"Wait," Cripswell said. "Can't we stay a little while longer?" He pressed Cal's hand.

Later, Joe told Cal that he hadn't anything to worry about, that it wasn't catching, and he could have been kinder. But Cal had quickly gotten up and pulled away his hand: "I pass, Crips, I'll see you around."

Cripswell started to say something, but Cal interrupted him: "Don't say it, it's OK, I'll see you around."

"Good night, Cal," Cripswell said sadly, and Cal crossed Fielding Drive in back of Monroe Chapel, and inside his dorm took the elevator to the sixth floor.

That evening now seemed a long time ago. Cal thought, "Joe's right about Cripswell, Joe's right about all of us." Cal stopped at the edge of the river and looked toward Back Bay. The twin Renaissance towers of the seminary etched their yellow lights above Monroe Chapel. Cal could see the row of dormitory windows on the sixth floor. His room was in darkness. He looked down at the river and studied the water. A condom was lodged between two rocks at the edge, and part of it floated in the current. Cal took a stick and flipped it out where it disappeared into the slow moving water.

CHAPTER TEN

▼

"ALLIES STORM INLAND: Normandy Coast Invaded Early Today," *Daily Evening Item*, June 6, 1944

After school, Cal rode his bike to Bly Field and met Joe. "Is she here?" Cal asked.

"Relax, she'll get here," Joe said. "Let's watch practice."

They climbed the small wooden visitor stands and sat on the top row looking out over the football practice field. The high school team was practicing punt coverage. They stood in two lines on either side of the center and the punter. When Babcock kicked the ball downfield, two players ran down to tackle Farington or Sikorski who were taking turns.

"I couldn't tackle them," Cal said.

"Yes, you could. You'd have to," Joe said.

"Sikorski would run over me."

"He runs over everybody. So what? It doesn't hurt."

"Did you ever tackle anybody as big as him?"

"No, but I could. You just tackle him, that's all."

"He'd just take one step and I'd bounce off and look like a fairy."

"You wouldn't look like any fairy. You're always worrying about how you look."

"No I don't. I just don't want to look like a fairy."

"If you're playing football, you don't look like a fairy."

"Fats does."

"Fats is practically blind for crying out loud. You can't play football if you wear glasses."

"Kendall does."

"Frank isn't a fairy. He's just scared to hit. But he isn't scared when he's mad. You ought to know."

"He's never caught me yet."

"He will, if you keep pushing it. Why don't you throw him the ball once in a while?"

"He's way bigger than us. He should play with Maes and those guys."

"There's Bonny. You don't need me. Go talk to her."

"What'll I say?"

"Do you want to screw her or don't you?"

"I don't know, I told you."

"Well, let's get out of here, then. C'mon."

"No, stay here. I'll go talk to her."

"I'm not going to wait for you. I'll see you in school tomorrow."

Cal jumped down from the wooden stands and got on his bike.

"Hi," Bonny said. "What's up?"

"Hi. What do you say?"

"I say anything. What do you say?"

"Where do you live, anyway?"

"In Oz."

"Did you see the movie?"

"My aunt took me."

"Did you like it?"

"I hated all those dirty little men marching around. Are we going to stand here doing this?"

"Where can we go?"

"We can ride someplace."

Cal followed Bonny along the road by Hyacinth Pond, toward Maple Hills. After a mile they came to a field and a little hill. She got off and pushed her bicycle across the field and up a wooded rise covered with large boulders. She pushed the bike between the boulders to the top of the hill and set it on the ground. She pointed to a group of houses on the other side of the ridge. "I live three streets over there," she said. "I can't stay here long." She sat down with her back against one of the boulders. She was wearing dungarees and a light green sweater over her white t-shirt. Her sweater was open and Cal could see one of her breasts outlined under her t-shirt.

"So you didn't like the little men," he said. He sat down beside her.

"Did you?"

"I liked the tin man."

"He had lipstick on, for Christ's sake.".

Cal had never heard a girl say "for Christ's sake" before.

"What other movies have you seen? Did you see 'Thirty Seconds over Tokyo'?"

"What are you going to do, anyway?"

"Just feel you up a little."

"When? I haven't got all night. My mother told me to be home before dark. She'll kill me if I'm late."

"When did you have to go to that other school?"

"Who are you anyway, the Question Man? You did this the other time. I have to go home." Connie started to get up.

"No, not yet." He reached for one of her breasts. He tried to slip his hand inside her sweater, but she arm-lifted his hand away from her. Cal was surprised at her strength.

"You're strong," he said.

"I'm strong enough for you," she said, picking up her bicycle. Cal grabbed her from behind, groping for her breasts.

"You little shit," she said. "You'll get my t-shirt all dirty. That's all my mother will need." She swung an elbow at him as she righted her bicycle.

"Wait," Cal called.

"Sayonara, beetle," she said as she coasted between the boulders down the other side of the ridge.

The next day at school, Joe sat down next to Cal on the low concrete wall of the school grounds. Cal was eating his lunch.

"What have you got?" Joe asked.

"Peanut butter and raisins."

Joe opened his first sandwich. "Fried egg," he said.

"I never get tuna fish anymore."

"I never get caviar."

"We ought to trade with Serino. He always gets peppers and eggs. It's the nuts. He hates it."

"How'd you make out yesterday?"

"Nothing. She's a tough broad."

"You're a jerk. What did you think she was going to do, beg for it?"

"She wouldn't let me touch her."

"So that's the whole story?"

"I don't know. She was just sitting there."

"Where?"

"In the boulders near her house."

"She was just sitting there?"

"Yeah, she was just sitting there, and we were talking about the movies."

"I'll bet she loved that. Who were you, Charles Boyer?"

"Who's Charles Boyer?"

"Never mind. So then she left?"

"Yeah, she just left. I wanted to feel her up, but she got mad and left."

"And that surprises you."

"Yeah. I don't know. I felt funny. She was wearing dungarees. I didn't know what to do. I never touched a girl's cunt before. I thought you had to get them hot and stuff."

"Right. So you grabbed one of her tits."

"Geez, she arm-lifted me. She got a knuckle right into my wrist."

"On the whole, it didn't go too well, I guess."

"Tough girls scare me, Joe. I don't know what to do."

"They're just girls, Cal. Don't let it bother you."

"She thinks I'm a jerk."

"No she doesn't Cal, she doesn't think about you at all. You'll probably never occur to her again."

"What if I look for her?"

"You won't. I guarantee it. I'll swap you an apple for that tangerine."

Cal handed Joe his tangerine. A few minutes later, the lunch bell rang and Joe and Cal walked into the junior high school.

CHAPTER ELEVEN

▼

The late afternoon shadows darkened the silent classroom as church history Professor Edwin Roth paced with the fingertips of both hands poised under his chin, seeming to push the words higher as he looked beyond the unreflecting windows toward the misty darkness of the First Century Church. His words were soft and eloquent as they spoke of Jesus and his followers and the beginnings of the fall of the Roman Empire.

Dr. Roth was famous for his lectures, and no one missed his late afternoon classes, scheduled to begin as day waned and the setting was right for journeys into the past. Dr. Roth was an actor, and his eccentricities were human, his weaknesses attractive to the young seminarians. He allowed no one to enter his classroom after the bell sounded, and would only smile as the locked classroom door rattled after the beginning of class, his lecture uninterrupted by the folly of student lateness. The dean of the seminary referred offhandedly to Professor Roth's classes as "inspirational church history," as if to both denigrate Roth's verbal forays into speculation and reconstruction, and to laud his rhetorical skills in the service of more scholarly motivation. The dean was suspicious of all romantics, and Professor Roth's romanticism sometimes collided with the dean's intellectualism.

The dean's own classes were discussion seminars where students presented and defended. The dean taught the history of philosophy and a course in the history of social thought and action. Cal read Marx and Lenin for the first time in his course. Professor Roth lectured on Abelard and Heloise, Augustine, St. Francis, always dramatizing emotion, always humanizing the battles of the spirit and the flesh.

The dean was a fact man. Know the text and decide what it means. The dean was famous for quoting Bishop McConnell's challenge to the Council of Bishops during the McCarthy hearings: "Anyone who does not know the difference between Communism and Socialism is not qualified to take part in this discussion." Roth was famous for quoting St. Augustine who was supposed to have cried out, "Lord, make me pure, but not now." The dean was tall and angular and balding and cerebral. Professor Roth was short and barrel chested and silver-haired with ruddy cheeks. The rumor was that he had a drinking problem. Up at the front of the classroom, the words were softly streaming from his lips:

Think back with me now. Let your thoughts drift into the late afternoon darkness, back to the Galilean twilight of the beginnings of the first century. These are the fortunate days for you, your student days still before you, days of reflection and study before the duties of the world devour you, a time to turn the pages of time itself, a time to let the past instruct you, a time to think back on the gentle Jesus of the Gospels, not the Jesus of the charlatans of history, the beady-eyed Jesus of the Fourth Gospel casting sinners into the fire, but the Jesus of history who said "Do not call me God. Call no one God but God," who said "The Kingdom is not of this world, it is within you," who said "Give to Caesar what belongs to Caesar," who held the cool mud from the Jordan River against diseased eyes closed by crawling flies so that the poor cried out, "I was blind and now I can see." It is right that we are here, in the late afternoon, thinking our ways back into the mists of history, quietly reflecting on those early Christians who gathered together in hidden rooms, who made their peace with a higher and more noble power, who gave up the world to claim their own kingdoms, who were hunted down and stoned, who felt the yokes on their shoulders of a foreign and less noble power, and who finally with their faith, their sacrifices, their battle cries of forgiveness and absolution, sent the Roman eagle screaming back to Rome.

In the back row, Cal whispered to Joe, "He's got it going now."

Joe nodded: "Perkins just slipped me a note. There's a *Kairos* meeting in his room after class."

Up at the front of the room, Dr. Roth paced, his hands propping his arched neck like stone, and the words flowed over the students' heads like olive oil.

"Schweitzer in his village in Lambarene knew. Schweitzer the musician, the doctor, the theologian—there in dark Africa, playing Bach on the organ, reading the texts of Renan and Strauss and Reimarus, cutting and sewing and healing the broken black bodies from the forgotten forests of time itself, Schweitzer knowing the gentle Jesus of history. 'He comes to us as One Unknown,' he said, 'as of old, by the lake-side. He came to those who knew Him not, and he speaks to us the same word'. . . ."

Cal looked away from Dr. Roth, fighting the tears that had formed in his eyes, and waited for the mist to dry, his head turned to the window and the shadows of the backs of the brick buildings beyond the parking lot. The black fire escapes wavered as Cal struggled in his own mind against the warm and soothing rhetoric of his silver-tongued teacher and his own unhappiness. One tear rolled down his cheek and Cal let it reach his chin before rubbing it off with his wrist. He was moved and he hated it. *"Don't think about what he is saying,"* he said to himself. *"Think about the lake. Think about the lake at dusk with the white perch rising. Think about the whipporwhill, and Uncle Orion and dad sitting by the fish table, smoking their pipes."*

He could still hear Professor Roth: *"He speaks to us the same word: 'Follow thou me!' and sets us to the tasks that He has to fulfill for our time. He commands. And to those who obey Him, whether they be wise or simple, He will reveal Himself in the toils, the sufferings. . . ."*

Cal tried to block out the words coming from the front of the classroom. He didn't want to hear the words. He hated how he listened until something in his head clicked and the tears formed, and he had to fight against the emotion. He was always moved by words of softness and understanding, and he had no defense against them. He hated it. He hated this seminary, this building, this life that was not his, this pretension of do-goodism, this ministry. He hated the word "minister." He hated the word "preacher." He hated these people. *No, not these people. He loved Joe, he loved Trav. He liked Don Grapple and Jack Ward and Ben Perkins, the* Kairos *editors. He loved old Dr. Loyalton, the* Old Testament *professor. He liked Holmer, the homiletics teacher, even though he was an actor and a beefy, jowly fake. He even liked Brewer, the beagle-eyed* New Testament *professor who played touch football with the boys at the annual September picnic during the first week of school, and who was going through a divorce. And Dr. Roth. Cal loved this class with Dr. Roth. When the class ended late each afternoon, and Cal was left alone with the early evening darkness, history ended for him and he was back in the present that he hated, with no future, no life, nothing to look forward to. Cal knew he had lost Joannie, he knew that his former university was gone forever for him, his fraternity brothers gone, the afternoons on the practice field and the walks across campus every evening under the maples in the fall gone, walking past the chapel, past the campus pond to Johnson Hall and training table all gone, and Moose Greenville and Fuzzy Grillo and Gigi Romer. But Joe was here. Joe was always here. Without Joe, Cal wouldn't be here. But where would he be? Joe probably knew. Joe had the answers, why he was here, where he was going.*

Cal heard the words coming from the front of the classroom. He had blocked the tears, and his mind was clear again. Cal knew the lecture was almost over. Dr. Roth was quoting Schweitzer again, and Cal was wide-awake, waiting for the time lapse between Roth's final word and the ringing of the bell. Roth was famous for ending his classes a second or two before the bell rang. Everyone in the class was watching Roth and listening, caught between the power of Roth's rhetoric and their anticipation of his uncanny sense of timing. An actor always knows, and Roth was both actor and teacher. His eyes were on the windows and the darkness outside. His chin was lifted high on the tips of his fingers. His voice was clear and unwavering. He said the last words of the class:

". . .*the sufferings which they shall pass through in His fellowship, and as an ineffable mystery they shall learn in their own experience Who He is."*

One second passed. Another. The bell rang, ending the class. Roth smiled at the class in triumph, and the class broke out in laughter and applause.

Joe turned to Cal: "He's good."

"Too bad there wasn't a historical Jesus."

Susan Burwell edged past several students waiting to file out of the rear door and brightened in front of Joe and Cal:

"Wasn't that the best lecture you every heard?"

"He makes it real, all right," Joe said.

"And his timing. He's just wonderful. 'Who He is,' one second, two seconds, and the bell rings. He's magic." Susan stepped through the door, holding it for Joe, who waved at her that he was going to linger with Cal, and she left, saying "See you men."

"She's got the hots for you," Cal said.

"Where's *that* coming from? She wasn't exactly washing my feet with her hair just then."

"I'm serious. Have you got something going with her?"

"Would I hold out on you, old teammate? You set such a celibate example for the rest of us disseminators of the *Gospel*, we put our disseminations on hold, in order to revere you."

"Did I hear someone say 'inseminate'?" Cripswell appeared from the group at the blackboard discussing Roth's lecture.

"Only as in 'artificial,' my boy," Cal said.

"Come come, fellow seminarians," Cripswell said, "We are all lost sheep together. Do not growl in such friendly pastures. You will be mistaken for the big bad you know what."

"Right." Cal nodded impatiently and turned to Joe: "Where's the *Kairos* meeting? Jack's room? Let's go."

"*Kairos*, the *critical* moment," Cripswell said. "Actually, you boys do good work. It's quite an excellent endeavor. You have my congratulations on the last issue. A literary magazine with art work, and in a Protestant seminary. It's quite extraordinary. How did you get the dean to approve?"

"*Creative* moment, Crips. You make it sound like an orgasm." Cal turned to go.

"The dean believes in free speech, and he doesn't have to put up any money," Joe said.

"Then do not tarry. Carry on with the work of the Lord. On to your meeting in the upper caverns of the *creative* ones."

In the elevator, Cal said to Joe, "Cripswell's such an asshole."

"That rhymes. Put it in a poem."

"Ward wouldn't like it."

"Perkins would. He's itching to get something scatological into the magazine."

"Doctor Jansan would really have something to carp about then."

"How'd you know about Evelyn? That's what the meeting is about."

"I don't know anything. She came sputtering to me as I was doing work study when the last issue came out, that's all. She found a comma fault and a misspelling and said that as the head librarian she was responsible for ungrammatical periodicals being housed in the stacks of the library."

"Well, she went to the dean with it."

"So? The dean's a social justice man, he'll never knuckle under to Jansan's sputtering. Do you think?"

At the sixth floor, the elevator door opened and they stepped out. Joe said, "We've actually got the ivory tower that Roth talks about. We're in a tower right now. This meeting is a tower meeting. I've thought a lot about it lately. We're students of privilege, not of the *Gospel.* This isn't Lambarene, Africa. This isn't even Mt. Vernon Street downtown where this seminary began before the Depression. Think about it. Did you ever see anyone in the chapel on the second floor during the day? Did you ever see anyone from this place preaching on Boston Common on a Sunday morning? Everybody goes to Harvard to hear George Buttrick preach, or to Trinity to hear Ferriss, or to the Universalist Church on Tremont Street to hear someone talk about some Bengali poet, while Father Feeney is spewing his garbage on Boston Common. And we're going to this meeting because an old maid librarian is upset about a comma fault."

"Maybe we ought to go down to the Common some Sunday ourselves. Should we cut the meeting?"

"No, Let's go to the meeting and get it over with," Joe said. They opened the door to Jack Ward's room and stepped inside.

CHAPTER TWELVE

▼

"What's the Dean want us to do?" asked Cal. The other five members
of the *Kairos* board looked at Don Grapple, the editor. They were sitting
on the two chairs and the two twin beds in the room that Ward shared
with Perkins. The magazine had been Grapple's idea. A year before, he
mentioned it at a late night bull session with Cal and Jack Ward, and
they talked about it again later with Joe and Ben Perkins and Jake Foster.
When they talked vaguely about the policy of an art magazine, written
and put together by themselves as seminary students, Grapple had said
that they certainly were not going to turn down a piece sent to them by
Robert Penn Warren, and that they could get most of the material from
other students and some faculty.

Cal had asked, "Who's Robert Penn Warren?"

"He's the greatest writer in America," Grapple said. "He wrote *All
the King's Men*."

"His newest one is *Band of Angels*," Perkins said. "I hardly think he's
going to submit to us."

"I'm just saying 'if.' I didn't say he would. We should be open to
everybody, that's all," Grapple said. "I know an artist who teaches at the
Museum School who works in ceramic mosaics. I bet I can get him to
design something for a cover."

"How are we going to get it printed and put together? Physically, I
mean," Jake asked.

"We can do it. That stuff is easy on a verityper. It's like a double typewriter and it justifies margins. Maybe the School of Communication will help us print it. We can collate it ourselves."

Three months after that meeting, the first issue came out, with Grapple as editor, Perkins as assistant editor, and the rest of them on the editorial board. Grapple's artist friend, David Holleman, designed a cover in black and red depicting Joshua and the battle of Jericho, and Cal learned how to justify margins on a verityper, typing into the early hours of the morning several nights in a row in a one light bulb room inside the School of Communication. The magazine was Grapple's baby, but each of them did what he asked, and they learned how to put a magazine together. They were very proud of the first issue and expected great praise from everyone.

What they actually got was a mixture of surprise, skepticism, questionings, hostile silence, neutral silence and friendly distance. The only verbal hostility came from the seminary librarian, who went on a polite but vigorous crusade to clean up the magazine's syntax and punctuation or put the "inexperienced artists," as she called them, out of business.

The battle was fought inside the dean's office, and the tremors from Miss Jansan's polite outrage were only detectable in the dean's squinty-eyed but gentlemanly questionings of what he called "the legitimate issues" in Miss Jansan's complaint.

"The dean called me in," Grapple now reported.

"I thought the dean was above this stuff," Cal said.

"Is this what he means by the Social Gospel?" asked Jake Foster.

"Hold it," Grapple said. "The dean's a good guy. He's trying to deal with Dr. Jansan more than he's trying to squelch us. I could tell that he doesn't want us to put down Dr. Jansan."

"Who'd want to put her down?" asked Perkins, grinning.

"Don't be a smart-ass, Perkins," Ward said. "Keep your smutty little brain out of this."

"It's just a joke. What's everybody so jumpy about?"

"If everybody's jumpy, it should be about something else, not this. This is so unimportant that it seems important. It isn't important. But it's part of what's important. At least that's what the dean said to me. He made sense. He says he knows we're doing things that might seem out of the ordinary to seminary faculty and students, but that we have to keep focussed on what we're actually doing."

"What are we actually doing?" asked Perkins.

"We're publishing a fucking magazine," Ward said.

"How interesting. Does Miss Jansan know that?"

"Goddam you, Perkins, are you aware how juvenile you are sometimes?" Ward said.

Jack Ward was diminutive, thin, and balding. He played the organ at a big church in Duxbury on Sundays. In college, he was a music major at Blair College in Oregon, and he was shrewdly intelligent and feisty. He argued constantly with Ben Perkins, his roommate, who was precocious with words, and who irritated Ward. They lived in the same room in a state of controlled armistice, for Ward had never forgiven Perkins his comment during Holy Week of their first year at the seminary when Perkins referred to the hymn "O Sacred Head Now Wounded" as a lament on the circumcision of Jesus. Ward said that Perkins had wrecked that hymn for him forever, and he'd never forgive him. He later told Perkins that he would forgive him but to cut out making jokes like that about things Ward cared about. Perkins agreed but couldn't resist occasionally forgetting his resolution.

"So what does the dean want us to do?" Joe asked. "Try harder on the comma faults?"

"That's about it," Grapple said.

"So you called us here for that?" Cal asked.

"What's the big deal?" Grapple said. "You want me not to tell you that the dean called me into his office? Anyway we have to set an evening when we can do the next cover."

"What about Holleman?"

"We can't keep asking him," Grapple said. "And we said we'd do the Mondrian. How about next Wednesday at my apartment? Miriam has an art lesson."

There was a knock on the door and a voice called out, "Cal! Are you there?"

It was Cripswell. "A girl named Clare has been calling you, or someone has been calling you about her. Dorothy Jones came out of the dean's office and asked if anyone knew where you were. I heard you say you were having a meeting, so I told her I'd come up and try to find you."

"What's wrong with her, calling me during school? See what I told you, Joe?"

Cripswell said, "I think it's more than that, Cal. I think this person's been hurt. You better go to the office and check with Dorothy."

CHAPTER THIRTEEN

▼

Joe stood over the dead deer, his red hunting cap tipped back on his head. The huge buck was prone in the dried grass at the outer edge of the oak grove, his white belly fur shining in the sun. "You hit him all right," Joe said, grinning.

"He's as big as a cow," Cal said.

"He's no cow. That's the biggest rack I've ever seen."

Cal grasped one antler and tugged. "I can hardly move his head. We'll never get him out of here. Look at these four points. This rack's big enough for eighteen or twenty points. The tips are filed sharp as a knife. He must have honed them on a rock or something."

"This thing will dress out way over two hundred pounds."

"Take a front leg. See if we can drag him."

Cal and Joe laid down their guns and tried to move the deer. "No soap," Joe said. "What do you want to do?"

"I've got to get a frigging license for one thing. We can't get him home without a tag on him."

"You got your knife?"

Cal touched his father's hunting knife on his hip.

Joe said, "I'll dress him out. You go get the tag. How close can you get the car?"

"I don't know. The pasture road is driveable, I think. You ever dressed out a deer before, Joe?"

"I never saw a dead deer this close. I guess I'll manage."

Cal handed him the knife and drew a line with his gloved finger on the buck's white stomach from the top of the rib cage to the anus. "The business is in here. Save the liver and the heart. Will you know them?"

"We'll see won't we? If the warden finds me, he can point them out."

"No warden will come in the woods, don't worry about that. We're a long way from nowhere, Joe. God, it's beautiful in here. I'll hurry back."

Cal left Joe standing and looking at the deer, holding the black and silver knife in his right hand. Cal headed back up through the oak grove toward the camp, and the car.

Three miles back to Acton Four Corners, and Cal parked his '50 Plymouth outside Emory's Variety store next to an old pickup with a small dead doe in the back. Emory's store was the closest tag station, and Cal knew that if he bought the license here he'd have to take it to a different tagging station later.

Two men and a young boy in red hunting clothes stood around Emory's stove. The men sipped coffee from paper cups, and the boy held a half full coke bottle. "Morning," Emory said as Cal waited for him to go behind the counter.

"Where'd they get the doe?" Cal asked.

"Hey Josh, where'd you shoot the doe?"

"Up in the orchard," the taller of the men said.

Cal turned and asked him, "Was she a single?"

"Four of 'em. Jumped 'em just at daylight. Might of hit one of the others but we couldn't find it."

The boy said to the tall man, loud enough for Cal to hear, "I did hit it, dad."

The tall man said, "We'll go back later and look around some."

The other man said, "That deer's in Hancock County by now. Be a smart waste of time to go back there today."

Cal spoke to Emory: "Well, I better get me a license. Out of state."

"Just fill this out," Emory said, handing Cal the white out of state license form. Filling in the description of his own weight, eyes, and hair, Cal thought of the dead deer lying in the woods, and Joe dressing him out, alone.

As Cal left the store, the tall man said, "Good luck to you now."

Cal drove back to the lake and followed Red Gate Lane, a dirt road that circled behind the lake and continued toward a high ridge above an old wood lot. Beyond the ridge, the road dipped for an eighth of a mile and entered a pasture bordered on three sides by alder trees. Grass grew in the middle of the road. Cal drove slowly through the pasture and up an incline that followed along a stone wall. After another fifty yards he stopped the car. He had been gone two hours. The woods were quiet. He took the car keys, closed the car door quietly, and stepped into the pines.

From the stone wall, Cal paced off ninety yards down through the oak grove where Joe and the deer should be. He had made a good shot and his father would be proud of him. *Cal could hear his father saying "Attaboy!" and patting him on the shoulder.* He smiled to himself and looked toward where Joe should be gutting the buck in the tall grass. "Joe," he called, and Joe's head lifted above the grass where he was kneeling, cleaning out the bloody cavity where he had pulled out the deer's entrails. The sun was shining on the yellow grass where the deer was lying with its legs propped apart. Joe's hands were crimson with blood.

Joe had placed a freshly cut alder bough between the buck's hind legs to keep the cavity seam open. "You're just in time. I'm finished. This is one big animal. Look at the size of the heart."

Cal wired the white deer tag onto the deer's antlers. "Now we're at least legal. I've got the car up in the road. We've got to get him up there somehow."

"How?"

"I don't know. What if we cut a couple alders and see if we can tie his hooves so we can carry him?"

"You mean on our shoulders?"

"Yeah. Like a palanquin, only upside down."

"We can try it. That's a heavy deer, though."

Cal and Joe cut two alder saplings for poles and used the leather lacings from their boots to attach the hooves of the deer. With the poles on their shoulders they tried several times to lift the deer off the ground. At first the thin ankles and the shiny hooves slipped through the lacings wrapped around the poles. Then Cal pushed his knife between the ankle bones and their cartilage, then looped the lacings through the slits, but when they lifted again there was still too much weight for the poles. "Talk about dead weight," Cal said.

"He must go two hundred and fifty pounds," Joe said.

"We should be able to lift that much," Cal said.

"Not this way we can't," Joe said. "It's not like carrying a piece of timber where you can get a solid grip on each end. Everything collapses into the middle."

"We're just going to have to drag him. How far is the car?"

"She's close. I've got her right up by the stone wall."

"What are we going to do when we get him to the car?"

"We'll figure that out when we get there."

Joe and Cal put the lacings back in their boots and each took a front leg and tried to pull the deer. At first it seemed impossible, but when they got good leverage with their feet and they pulled together, they managed to move the deer six inches or so, then another six inches, and another until the deer was out of the grass and into the leaves where it went easier. They managed to drag the deer up into the oak grove. They pulled and rested, pulled and rested. "Another hour," Joe said.

"Maybe a half. But we can't possibly be home before dark."

"I'm happy if we're out of the woods by dark."

"We've still got to take him to a tagging station. We can't take him where I got the license. We can go over to the Ross Corner Store in Shapleigh. We buy groceries there in the summer. Ross really likes my father. It'll only take us another twenty minutes. We can drive right to Sanford from Shapleigh."

A half hour later, up at the stone wall, they lifted the head of the deer onto the top boulders and slowly pulled the neck and chest up far enough that the head draped over the other side. By pulling and lifting, knocking down some of the fieldstones that had not been disturbed for decades, they managed to get the carcass over the wall. It was only twenty feet through the heavy pines to the car.

Cal opened the trunk. "The trunk isn't that big. I'd love to put him on the fender so we can show him off," Cal said, "but we don't have enough rope."

"Let's just put him into the trunk."

"I don't think he'll fit."

"Most of him will. Let's try it."

"I'm going back and get the guns," Cal said. "Take a breather."

When Cal got back to the car with Joe's shotgun and his father's carbine, Joe had the deer's head in the trunk, and part of the deer's shoulder braced on his knee against the rear bumper. "I don't think he'll go," Joe said.

"If we can lift his butt, he might." Cal laid the guns carefully on the back seat of the car with a sweater between them so they wouldn't knock against each other and scratch the blueing on the barrels.

Together, they lifted, braced, lifted, and managed to get the rump of the deer into one side of the trunk. The body was still soft and pliable and they were able to tuck the legs inside the trunk also. When they finished pulling and pushing, with the trunk cover lowered, only part of the neck and the grand antlered head with its white tag could be seen.

Cal drove carefully along the pasture road with the heavy carcass in the trunk. Underneath the car, the grass hump in the middle of the road occasionally rose up to rough against the under-frame. It made a soft squishing noise. Two hunters with their guns on their shoulders and their hats tipped back on their heads stepped aside to let the car pass. Looking in the rear view mirror, Cal saw one of the men point to the rear of the car as he drove slowly away.

CHAPTER FOURTEEN

▼

"1500 BIG BERTHAS SHELL ENGLAND AS NAZIS START BLITZKRIEG: All signs Pointed Today to a Zero Hour for a Nazi Offensive Against England," *Daily Evening Item,* Aug. 13, 1940

Cal opened the cellar door that led to the kitchen and waited, listening. He had walked home from school for his noon dinner and he saw that his father's car was already in the driveway. Cal listened for the tones of their voices to see if they were quarreling. The four stairs leading to the kitchen door were always Cal's No Man's Land. After several seconds he heard his father shout, "What of it?" and Cal's stomach turned over. He mounted the four stairs and turned the knob of the kitchen door that would open to the eternal battlefield of his parents' unhappiness, and the violence of their voices would again break over his head like shellfire.

He entered the kitchen and they both looked at him. It never occurred to Cal to run from the house, to flee the sounds of his mother's tearful self-pity and his father's self-righteous pathos. Cal's first instincts were to witness, believing that he could heal their wounds, but his presence only enforced his own sense of naivete and impotence. For years he had listened to the corrosive bickerings that always led to the plaintive agonies of his mother and the silent isolations of his father, and Cal yearned for the calm between the barrages. Every time he entered the house on 82 Pine Ridge Avenue, he was afraid that the battle might have resumed, that any tranquility was merely temporary armistice. Their fighting drew him like a magnet.

Eventually, Cal would cry out, "Make up, daddy." Cal would be crying himself. His father would look at him, look at his mother, and become silent. Cal's mother would whimper, inconsolably, unreachably. If it were noontime, Cal's father would rise from his half-eaten dinner and leave through the back door, get in his second hand 1938 Buick and back out of the driveway, scraping the fender of the car on the hedges as he negotiated the curved driveway into the macadamed street recently surfaced by Roosevelt's Works Projects Administration. He would return to the General Electric Company, River Works Division in Lynn, where as the General Foreman of Building 63 he had supervised the construction of the turbine for the aircraft carrier *Hornet*. He was now building the turbine for the aircraft carrier *Wasp*.

When Cal opened the door to the kitchen, his father sat at the kitchen table, watching him enter. Cal's mother was standing at the sink, looking out the window toward the Wardwell's house next door. She turned to look at Cal who had walked home from the yellow three-roomed, Mapleville School, a quarter mile down maple-lined Pine Ridge Avenue.

All the streets in the neighborhood were named for trees and famous men. Every day, Cal ate noon dinner with his father, until gasoline rationing began, and then his father carried a lunch that his mother made each morning. Cal's mother got up at 6:30 to make his father's lunch, and Cal and his father got up at 7:00. When gasoline rationing began, the noontime quarrels stopped, only to resume in the evening and on weekends, except when they went to the lake in Maine, four driving hours away.

Cal never told anyone that his parents quarreled, and he wondered if his friends' parents loved each other and enjoyed each other's company. When he visited their homes, he listened for the spoken tones that would betray signs of a quarrel, but he never heard them. When the Bonds, who lived across the street, disagreed, Mr. Bond told Mrs. Bond to shut up, and she did. Next door, when young Ev Wardwell came home drunk, and ground the gears of his Chevrolet car as he negotiated his driveway, Teresa Wardwell was silent as Ev passed by her in the kitchen. Cal's mother, watching out the window, could see into the Wardwell's kitchen, and said out loud, more to herself than to Cal, "She never said a word." Next door on the other side of the house, Mrs. Teddington lived alone with her sons

Avery and Bobby. Mr. Teddington had died four years before. Cal never heard any grown up neighbors quarreling.

Cal entered the kitchen and said "Hi." His father nodded to him and his mother said softly, "Hello Cal, sit down honey and eat your lunch." She pointed to his seat at the round kitchen table where he always sat, just beneath the red framed kitchen mirror on the wall, and at the edge of the window with its view of the back yard. Half of it was his father's Victory-Garden which he had planted the previous Saturday, and half of it was nicely groomed grass which Cal had cut with the push lawnmower while his father turned over the soil of the garden with a pitch fork. As his father later secured the cut poles for Kentucky Wonder beans into the freshly forked earth, then pushed the seed beans an inch into the soil in a circle around the poles, Cal played with his rabbit Bingo in the grass. Just underneath the window, against the house, a bed of Lilies of the Valley bloomed, a bouquet of which Cal would pick later in the month for his grandfather's grave, on Memorial Day.

Cal's mother had prepared Campbell's tomato soup and a cheese sandwich for Cal's father, and he sat at the table, watching Cal. His father hadn't touched the sandwich, and the spoon was submerged in the still full bowl of soup. He looked from Cal to his soup and stared at it. Cal's mother remained at the sink, staring out the window at the hedges separating their driveway from the Wardwell's lawn. Cal took a bite of his peanut butter sandwich and chewed, waiting for the argument between his parents to resume. His mouth was dry as he chewed the soft, white Wonder Bread and the thick peanut butter, and his stomach was upset.

He wished he had chocolate milk instead of white milk.

"Give me a couple dollars, then," his father said. "I've got to get gas and a haircut."

They were arguing about money again. It was usually about money, but sometimes they had argued about something Cal didn't understand that had to do with the visit of Cal's Aunt Phyllis two months earlier. Cal kept chewing but he had no appetite. He knew what was coming. He tried to swallow but the saliva-sogged bread and peanut butter wouldn't go down his throat. He took another bite of his sandwich and chewed with his mouth full.

"What happened to the five I gave you on Monday? That was for the week," Cal's mother said.

"Jesus Christ, Sal, do you want me to squeeze every nickel like you do until it screams?" Cal's father glared at the back of Cal's mother's head as she stared out the window.

Cal's mother was silent. Cal watched his father who looked sick to his stomach and as if he was going to cry, but Cal had never seen him cry and knew that he wouldn't. He got angrier until he exploded, and then the yelling increased until his mother began to cry and his father's face looked sadder and more pained as he yelled.

His father had not taken off his double-breasted brown suit coat and he looked dignified and lonely as he sat at the noon dinner table wearing his newly ironed white shirt and the tie Cal's mother had given him the previous Christmas. She had ironed his shirt the night before. His father's wavy hair was silvery gray, and his blue eyes intense as he stared at the back of his wife's head. His hair had turned gray in France during the battle of Chateau Thierry in World War I, and Cal had always known him with gray hair. The lines around his mouth were deeply grooved and when Cal watched him shaving he often wondered how the razor could go around the lines without cutting the skin.

"You needn't swear in front of the boy," Cal's mother said without turning her head.

"I needn't be parceled out nickels and dimes like a kid either," Cal's father shouted.

Cal watched his mother, who didn't move. He had seen her pummeled by angry words from Cal's father for as long as Cal could remember, and Cal knew her heart-hardened, despairing look better than any other picture in his mind of his mother. Later, Cal learned that she had been adopted out of a state foster home, and the kindness in her life had come from her foster father and her foster-brother Nate who was unambitious, generous-spirited, and funny. He made her laugh with his simple, wry observations, and his dependable good cheer took her mind off her essentially lonely childhood. Her foster father was good to her and soft spoken, and her foster mother was breezy and unsentimentally dependable, without affection.

One Sunday, Uncle Nate was riding in the back seat of the family car, next to Cal, returning from a weekend at the lake. Crossing the bridge between South Berwick, Maine and Somersworth, New Hampshire, hearing the uneasy rumble of the loose wooden timbers as the car tires jostled them, Cal's mother commented on her dislike of crossing that bridge. Nate said drily, as quick as a puppet answering a straight man, "I'd rather go over it than under it." The remark might not have seemed funny to those outside the family, but Cal and his mother and father broke into laughter, half from anticipation that Uncle Nate's comment *would* be funny, and half out of appreciation for his cheerful ability to prefer comfortable danger to uncomfortable safety.

Uncle Nate worked for Cal's father at the G.E., and later when Cal worked one summer during the Second World War as a sweeper in Building 67 where they made blades for jet engines, he visited his father one lunch time, and his father walked him through his building. Each worker stood up as Cal's father passed, introducing Cal to each one, except Uncle Nate, who good naturedly remained seated, talking to Cal and watching the copper coils wind and wrap into their proper configurations inside the inner coil of the turbine. When they passed on, Cal's father remarked, "Nate's the only one in the building who doesn't stand up when I walk by." He said it with a mixture of acceptance and ironic humor, for Cal's father had known Nate all his life, and had spent carefree childhood summers with him while Nate was growing up in High Pine, Maine. Cal's mother adored her foster brother Nate. The story of Cal's mother's marriage to his father was another story that Cal did not learn until later.

Cal's mother also adored Cal, whom she called "the sunshine of my life," and Cal spent hours during his seminary years talking to Miss Green, trying to unravel the mystery of why Cal's mother allowed Cal to listen to the endless arguments and why Cal hadn't fled the house until the arguments were over.

"Eat your lunch, Cal, you've got to eat," his mother said, turning to look at him from the kitchen sink.

"I'm not hungry," Cal said, chewing.

"Does that surprise you?" Cal's father thundered at Cal's mother. "Who the hell can eat with your sourpuss, hangdog expression in the same room?"

Later, in his second year at the seminary, Cal read Valery Searles' book on violence, which claimed that emotional violence could be more traumatic and destructive than physical violence, and Cal began gradually to understand his voluntary participation in the cruelty of those terrifying parental fights. His father never struck his mother, but they tortured one another, and their torturing prompted Cal to both blame and punish himself as a reprisal for his inability to save his mother and comfort his father. In his desire to assuage their pain, he blocked off something in himself, and the only path to its discovery lurked on the other side of this Protestant seminary he was drawn to, without knowing why, during his college years while deliberating his future.

He went to seminary partly because Joe did, but he was drawn there by the same magnet that drew him to the corners of rooms to listen to his parents punish each other, to search and confirm the catharsis of his own guilt for his failure to save his parents from their pain, to explore what he felt to be the inner cages of Hell itself. He knew by his nature, armed with the rhetoric of blood-washed Calvary lyrics, that the only exit from the violence and cruelty of his argument-stained childhood home was through the little white church of that same childhood vale.

During Sunday-evening church services, the sparse congregation would sing the lyrics to the "Little Brown Church in the Vale" as "the little *white* church." Three maple-lined streets over from Cal's Depression-built home on Pine Ridge Avenue stood the white clapboarded Mapleville Methodist Church where Cal brought his two pennies to May Rice's class in Sunday School as a first grader, then later his nickel to Mr. Chase's junior high class, then to Andy Frank's Sunday afternoon teenage group called "Sons of Christians." It was in that little white church of Strawberry Festivals and Saturday night bean suppers, Christmas parties with lantern-flashed messages of Santa's progress crossing the North Pole on his journey to the basement of the little church in the Mapleville vale, Halloween parties with five cent grab bags for the kids, church auctions, minstrel shows, May Day picnics, summer trips to Salem Willows and Asbury Grove, Sunday morning worship with communion once a month, and the Sunday Evening Services with hymn sings led by Mr. McAlister or Andy Frank, that Cal was unknowingly being guided to the seminary.

Cal spent a childhood of outdoor hours playing touch football in the neighborhood streets, and tackle football in the vacant fields between the sporadic houses. When the Second World War ended, the community expanded, as if a field-eating Cyclops had appeared during the home-building explosion that not only destroyed the playing fields of his childhood but the neighborhood itself, with its influx of strangers, its new fast moving cars, its sweeping destruction of space and quietude. The neighborhoods that were New England in the thirties and early forties disappeared, and the childhood church he was nurtured in disappeared with it, burned to the ground by vandals in the late fifties.

From the sink, Cal's mother walked to Cal's chair and put her hand on Cal's head, then patted his cheek. "Drink your milk, then," she said softly, "I bought you some coffee flavored syrup for it." She took a bottle of dark liquid from the cupboard and a tablespoon from the silverware drawer next to the sink.

Across the table, Cal's father sat solitary, drained, and furious. He stared at Cal's mother as she stirred two tablespoons of coffee syrup into Cal's glass of McAdams milk, delivered at the door that morning. Its cold white color changed to creamy knaki. Cal sipped the transformed liquid and said, "It tastes good."

"God damn it, Sal, give me the two ones. I've got a job. You want me to lose that too, along with the rest of my self-respect?"

"You never had any self-respect, Lem," Cal's mother said. She took Cal's uneaten soup to the sideboard next to the sink and wrapped the bowl in wax paper. Then she wrapped the uneaten half of his peanut butter sandwich in wax paper and put them in the Frigidaire in the pantry.

As she closed the Frigidaire door, Cal's father shouted, "Will you give a guy the god damn ones or will I smack some sense into you?"

Cal had crossed the room and was sitting in the corner next to his mother's ironing board. He watched his father clench his fists.

"You won't hit me, Lem. Don't talk like a fool."

"I can't eat my dinner because you turn my stomach. Can I get my haircut and gas for the car, or do I have to walk to work too?"

"Norm Harman walks to work. It wouldn't hurt you. It might improve your disposition."

"There's nothing wrong with my disposition that not having to look at your face wouldn't cure."

"There's nothing wrong with my looks that a little happiness wouldn't change."

"You've never been happy a day of your life. Don't blame me for your sour puss."

Cal's mother had gone into the dining room and returned, opening her pocketbook.

She handed a two dollar bill to Cal's father, who took it without a word and put it in his pants pocket. He went out the back door without saying goodbye. Cal heard the engine of the family car start. Then the engine died and Cal's father re-appeared through the back door.

"I'm going up to ma's after work. Then I'm going somewhere else. Don't wait supper for me, I don't know if I'm coming back or not." He went out the door again and this time slammed it.

"Maybe that wouldn't be a bad thing," Cal's mother said softly, but loud enough for Cal to hear.

Cal heard the car engine start again and then the whine of the reverse gear as Cal's father backed out the driveway, scraping the fender against the hedges as he negotiated the sloping curve where the driveway crossed the sidewalk, into the street.

"Is daddy coming back?" Cal asked, watching his mother from the corner.

"He's coming back. He wouldn't miss the chance to make me pay for this noontime."

"What if he doesn't come back, mama?"

"Cal, come back to the table and sit down. I'll warm up your soup. You've got to eat. You're a growing boy."

Cal walked over and sat down at his seat again as his mother got his soup from the Frigidaire and took it to the gas stove. Then she went into the change purse of her pocketbook and fished out a nickel.

"Today's Wednesday, Cal. Here's the nickel to put into your pocketbook for our day at Revere Beach when school gets out."

Above the sink, a red tray was nailed to the side of the dish cupboard, and Cal's little brown leather pocketbook rested there beside a metal fingernail file, a small jar of Vaseline, and the comb his mother used to comb his hair before he left the house each day. Cal could just reach it if he stood on his tiptoes. He took the nickel from his mother, snapped open the leather purse with his fingers, and dropped the nickel in with the rest of the nickels and pennies.

At the stove, his mother was staring at his warm soup.

CHAPTER FIFTEEN

▼

Ross Tompkins stepped carefully down the front steps of his country store, smiling at the sight of the antlers hanging over the rear bumper of Cal's car. "Well now, you done all right, sir. That's a right handsome beast. Let's have a better look here." Cal lifted the trunk door and exposed the full body of the buck. Ross said, "Say, that's a specimen. You tell your dad I said his boy trimmed him this year. I'll just write it up and you get him home to Massachusetts 'fore the snow starts."

"Here's the rest of the tag, Ross. Thanks a lot. I'll tell my dad you said 'Hi.' If we come back for some ice fishing, we'll come over. He's doing better, and he almost came with me this time. My mother's being a little careful with him for awhile." Cal waited for Ross to shuffle back up the steps and then headed toward Sanford.

"Ross looks the same as he did the first time I came to the lake with you ten years ago," Joe said.

"They all look the same," Cal said. "The faces never change. Their bodies move a little slower each year, but you have to look for it to see it. Then you come back some year and one of them is gone."

"There's something about Maine people that makes them special. All country people have it, I guess, but I really feel it in Maine. We picked Armistice Day to get out of the city, Cal, and we came to the right place," Joe said.

"It was no armistice for that buck in the trunk. What do you think about those antlers, Joe?"

"We should have asked Ross. He'd have an idea. It's some kind of a fighting deer, I'll bet you. Bucks don't have four prongs sharpened like that for nothing."

"He came through those oaks like a king," Cal said. "He was lifting his feet like a prancer in slow motion, barely moving. He must have been coming off that drive that was pushing toward the lake. When I hit him he must have gone four feet in the air."

"You know what Emily Dickinson said."

"What?"

"The wounded deer leaps highest."

"Where does she say that?"

"It's the first line of one of her poems. It's only four lines. It ends with 'And then the brake is still.' It's a terrific poem."

Cal was quiet for a long time, thinking about the deer and the poem. He drove through Sanford and took a left onto route 99 toward Kennebunk. They passed the farmhouse where Cal's grandparents lived when he was a little boy. Cal pointed out the place where he rocked the double-seat swing, standing and holding the hanging supports, playing train conductor. He pointed out the Baptist church where he was taken out of Sunday school the day his father was gored by Cal's grandfather's pet cow.

When they reached Wells, it was snowing, heavy at first, and then lightly. Cal turned off the windshield wipers. The snow turned to light rain and he turned the wipers on again.

"I don't know what I'm doing in seminary, Joe. I really feel out of it. Let's clear the hell out, Joe. Let's join the marines. Half of my fraternity brothers are in Korea."

"Mine too. It's a different life than college, that's for sure. And it sure isn't Korea, whatever *that's* like. I miss college life, too. You have to do what you feel. The Church isn't what anybody *else* thinks it is, it's only what *you* think it is. Something's clicking, at least for me, so far."

"When I was a little kid, I had this dream every once in a while. I talked about it with Miss Green. It was more of a feeling than a dream. I felt like I was falling off the edge of the world. I could hear my mother and father arguing outside my bedroom in the hall. My mother was wailing, and she said 'Jesus Christ.' I never heard my mother swear. It was a despairing, anguished cry of lostness and I was falling off the world into space. Sometimes, even in the daytime, I could feel myself slipping into that place where I was falling. I'd get like that at night and get out of bed and walk downstairs, wide awake, but in my mind I'd be in that falling place. They couldn't wake me up. My mother thought it was from reading comic books, so she threw them all away. She even threw away the first Superman comic book."

"I'll bet the dream stopped."

"Yeah, it did. How'd you know that? I know that the comic books weren't giving me that dream."

"It makes a kind of back-assed sense, that's all. Our minds use even the slightest change sometimes as a reason to make a major adjustment. It's the way our unconscious works to fool us into making rational connections. One of the men in my church had chronic diarrhea for six months, and went through several specialists. They did all the tests, one after drinking radioactive barium. Then one day his family doctor told him that most diarrhea problems could be traced to what he called the 'mother problem.' So the guy started thinking of his relationship with his mother and the diarrhea stopped within a week. A year later, the guy's wife left him, and later he found out that when his diarrhea problem started, his wife had just begun to have an affair. His unconscious was trying to tell him something. When he refused to listen to his unconscious, it finally decided to let him off the hook. It wasn't trying to kill him, just tell him something about himself."

"You mean about his wife."

"No, himself."

"How do you figure that?"

"I'm not sure, but I think it has something to do with the way everything works, life, God, Jesus, the Church. The guy's unconscious was not trying to rat on his wife. It was trying to tell the guy to wake up."

"You mean his wife was having an affair because the guy was a jerk."

"Not necessarily. His wife's problem was his wife's problem. The guy's problem was the guy's problem. His unconscious was trying to tell him that he had to start taking care of himself. Whatever change in his wife's behavior that was evident and not evident at the same time, because the guy chose not to allow himself to see the evidence, was indication enough that he had a problem and he should do something about it. We know things that we don't allow ourselves to know."

"You mean that I know something about myself that I don't allow myself to realize?"

"Maybe, Cal. I don't know. I know that you just told me that you're unhappy. I know that you're seeing Miss Green three times a week. You tell me you feel lost, but you must be doing something right. The deer came to you, today."

"What do you mean, 'came to me?' I was there when the deer came by. The drivers pushed the deer in my direction and I was lucky enough to be there when he came by."

"But you were waiting for him, and he came to you. He didn't come to me."

"But that was an accident. It was luck."

"Or fate."

"Come on, Joe."

"No, I'm serious. Something's afoot. I don't mean spooky. I mean, something is happening that we can all become part of if we're open to it. And the mysterious thing is that whatever it is, it's inside of us. Forgive the sermon, bubba, but this is what Jesus meant when He said that the Kingdom is within us. This is what Roth is getting at when he talks about the historical Jesus being the Son of Man. Roth always makes the point that Jesus said, 'Do not call me God.' The liberal humanist tradition in the Church is dying right now, and the Church itself may be dying with it, but it will be revived again sometime in the future. All the formalists in our seminary right now hate the liberal humanists because they think that the humanist denies the divinity of Jesus, but they make a huge mistake. The divinity in Jesus is exactly his humanity. That's the miracle, the meaning of the godhead in Jesus. The Gnostics knew a lot more than the orthodox Churchmen of the first and second centuries did, and that's why they were branded as heretics.

"When did you figure all this stuff out, Joe? All I know is that Jesus isn't God, and that Jesus probably didn't even exist. At least not the Jesus of the Gospels."

"You may be right. But it doesn't matter. The historical Jesus probably did exist, but we know nothing about his life. Someone existed whose life became a convenient starting point for a myth that caught fire when the world needed such a myth. The world needed a Jesus so it created one. And a Buddha, and a Confucius."

"And a Gandhi?"

"Sure. Within a year of Gandhi's death, stories of his miraculous healing power were already circulating along the banks of the Ganges."

"This stuff really interests me, Joe, but I am not cut out to be a minister. Seminary is just another graduate school for me. I don't know what to do. Everything is screwed up. I came to seminary and lost my girlfriend. I got involved with Clare sexually and then acted like I didn't know her. It's my fault that she's in the hospital with broken bones right now, and won't even see me. I'm eyeball deep in psychiatric mud. I'm cutting all my classes except church history, staying in my room days at a time. The only thing that I like is playing touch football and hanging out with you and Trav, and reading Steinbeck, and I'm going to run out of Steinbeck pretty soon."

"How is Clare?"

"You tell me. You've seen her. Her mother won't let me near her. She's got the hospital people so on guard that as soon as I get anywhere near Clare's room some nurse tells me politely that I can't see her."

"It's only been a week. Her mother was the one who called you. You'll be able to see her soon."

"I feel really shitty, Joe. Let's put the deer on the fender. We're in Danvers already. In twenty minutes we'll be in Mapleville. My dad'll see us coming in the yard."

"Let's do it."

Cal pulled the car to the side of route 1 and parked in front of a large merchandising store where he bought two coils of clothesline. Passing cars slowed down as Cal and Joe dragged the deer to the front end of the car and wrestled it somehow onto the rain-soaked hood, draping it head first over the right fender. They anchored the hind legs by criss-crossing ropes over the top of the car to the rear bumper, and tied the antlers to the front bumper. They tugged the ropes and made sure everything was taut, and Cal eased the car into the right lane of the highway.

Cal started honking the horn a block from his parent's home on Grant Avenue. As he swung into the driveway he could see faces peering between the parted curtains in the living room. A dark blue sedan was parked in front of the wooden garage beyond the house. As he rolled to a stop at the lighted back porch, his mother was standing there waiting for him.

CHAPTER SIXTEEN

▼

"Is it dad, mama?" Cal asked.

"Oh Cal, no, daddy's OK for now, it's your cousin Russie." Cal's mother reached for him and he held her. "Lillian's here," she said.

"Russ is dead."

"I'm afraid so. I'm so glad you're here, and with Joe. Lillian's in shock. She brought the telegram from the War Department. Hello Joe, come dear, get out of the car and come inside."

Joe had rolled down his window and waited. "Mrs. Newsome, I'd just as soon string up this deer in the garage. I can see you've got trouble enough. . . ."

"Joe, you come in the house with us. It's a blessing you're here. Cal's first cousin has been killed in Korea and my sister's here. Oh, and you boys got this nice deer. It'll get all soaking wet in this rain."

"It's already wet, mama. What happened?"

"We don't know a thing. We better go in. Lillian got the telegram and that friend of hers who owns the milk company in Middleton drove her down. Pauline's here, too."

"The telegram says he was killed, mama?"

Cal's mother nodded and waved Cal and Joe past her into the house. In the living room, several people were sitting in chairs around Cal's father's bed. Cal's father was sitting up, propped by pillows. His hair had been combed with water, and it looked more silver than white to Cal. He was also wearing his octagonal reading glasses without the metal rims, which made him look distinguished and businesslike.

"Hi, Aunt Lillian. Mama told me. I'm so sorry. Hi, dad. Pauline. Mr. Penthhurst. This is my friend, Joe Stearns."

"Hello, Caleb," his aunt said. "It's one more thing, isn't it?"

The stark quietness of the New England living room with its yellow curtains pulled down after dark, one yellow water stain on the white ceiling, a framed embroidered poem on the wall above the stand-up radio, the Maxfield Parrish painting of "Sunrise" above the piano, all seemed to drive each one in the room deep inside themselves, but deeper also, there was present that intimidating and undefined sense of failure that is always there when someone in the family dies. Cal felt it instantly and knew that it was driving each one in the room somehow out of the room, as far away as each could get. Only the formality of the talk reminded the listeners that they were physically here against their wills. The unspoken guilt of New England family grief pressed the four walls into each of them.

Later, Joe told Cal that he felt it also this night, that Cal wasn't imagining it. In the ritual silence, a thousand inadequacies dissolved in family blood-guilt, and each member took his place in the pecking order of tribal penance. In the silence, Cal flung himself on the barbed wire of domestic no man's land. Home is where they tell you your cousin has been killed in the war and you feel accused by kindness and love, and a dead deer stiffens on the car outside in the rain.

"Hi boy," Cal's father said, "You and Joe got a deer."

Cal asked softly, "How're you doing, dad?"

Cal's father held up the telegram in his hand and shook his head. "It only says the one thing, doesn't even tell what happened. I thought last week when the paper talked about a big tank counter-attack, Russ would be in the thick of it."

Cal looked at his aunt, her face frozen in a quizzical half-smile. Sometimes she looked like his mother, Cal thought, but not now. Cal's mother did not smile when something bothered her, but would hold her other arm at the elbow, or she would bite her lip and squint, but Aunt Lillian would look stunned and smile, as if she knew all along that the worst would happen. Then she would speak abruptly, from an inner room somewhere else that she had settled into. A door had opened and she had gone in and closed it behind her. Then she smiled as if rigor mortis had set into her facial muscles. Cal's mother had talked about it once when she told Cal about the state taking the three sisters from their mother and the girls went to the orphanage and then to different homes. She said Aunt Lillian had that smile when she left the orphanage. Cal saw that smile at Uncle Hal's funeral and at Russie's going-away party. Cal tried to think of something to say to her, and he began, "Aunt Lillian, . . ."

She looked at him and said, "It's all right, Cal. No one can do anything about it. It's done. Don't concern yourself with it. We'll all be fine."

Russ's sister Pauline sat like a stone.

Later they would learn that Russ had been chosen to lead the counter-attack against the Chinese, and that he had been awarded the Silver Star posthumously. He was the youngest major in Korea at the time.

Cal's mother said, "Cal, you and Joe should eat something. You must be starved. Have you eaten anything at all today? I can warm up some pot roast in a second. Joe, you could eat something, couldn't you?"

"Mrs. Newsome, I better go out and get that deer strung up in the garage."

"You go ahead, Joe. I'll call you when it's ready." She looked at Cal as she left for the kitchen. "Cal?"

"Yeah, OK, mama. I'll go with him. Gee Aunt Lillian, what a time to bring a deer home. I'm really sorry."

"Tush, don't be maudlin Cal. You wouldn't be here without it. It doesn't matter. It's the way things are, and the dead deer doesn't change things, does it? You go on out now, and hang up your deer."

Outside, Joe had switched on the porch light and untied the rope through the antlers. "I can't undo the knots holding the hind legs," he said.

It was raining harder and the deer fur was matted in dark splotches. The blood on the edges of the stomach cavity was clotted and shiny, as if it had been lifted out of a medieval Italian painting. "Cut them," Cal said. "I'll get the doors."

Inside the garage, Cal roped the rafter overhead and they strung up the deer by the antlers, Joe bear-hugging the deer and raising it, inch by inch as Cal helped while pulling the other end of the rope.

"What a time to show up with a dead deer." Cal said.

"The man said home is where when you have to go there they have to take you in. Once you decide to return, there's always some kind of death waiting whether it's yours or someone else's. If you don't bring it, it'll be there anyway."

"Nobody here ever read Frost, but I bet Russ did. He was a smart kid. He was cocky and smartass, but he knew what he was doing. We'd go up there to West Lawrence to visit when we were kids, and I always got pushed around. I was a little afraid of Russ but I liked him. I guess I didn't really like him but I admired him. He had this high-pitched voice and that easy god damned smile. After we both went off to college, I saw him only a couple of times, but all that young cockiness had turned into a kind of reserved confidence. My father really responded to him. Even when Russ first got accepted to West Point, my father said he'd become a general. He'd have loved it if I went to West Point. Maybe I should have."

"Maybe. Speculation is like playing dodge ball. We all end up in the middle sooner or later. The only question is what position we're in when the ball hits us."

"Even if we get hit in the back?"

"I'm not sure *what* I mean, Cal, but it's all kind of a game. In the games we played as kids, somebody was always "it," and it doesn't really change when we get older and the names of the games change."

Joe and Cal stood and talked on either side of the hanging deer. Joe took a cloth off the workbench and began to wipe the rainwater from the wet matted fur of the deer. "What are you going to do with this specimen, anyhow?"

"Hang him for a month, then cut him up. Do you mean that it doesn't matter that Russ went to West Point and I went to the state university? It sure matters to Russ. He's as dead as this deer, and I'm back where I started. I went off to college a hundred miles away to get away from everything that's in this house right now, and I end up ten miles away in a freaking seminary. Tell me how I got back here. How did you get back here, Joe? We both grew up in this neighborhood and we both end up in the church. Have we ever really gone away, Joe? That little church three streets over from here burned last year, but it's still in my head. Can we ever really burn it out?"

"Maybe it didn't work the best way for you that it might have, Cal, but something was at work for both of us. We just have to follow along and see where it takes us."

"You mean where she goes nobody knows and we just have to follow. It's a carnival, Joe. We grew up on the merry-go-round, shot baskets for the kewpie dolls, and ended up on the Ferris wheel. Did all this end up for you in the right place? I guess it must have, you seem so relaxed at the seminary. You don't seem to mind going off to that crumby little church in Braintree every weekend. You even seem at home here, right now in this garage."

"Don't make me into anything big, Cal. The Church is big, and we're all little. We're all trying to stay alive. You know so many things that I don't know about, like today and this whole adventure with the deer. I left all this when I left the neighborhood a long time ago when my father died."

"All what? You're the one who knows things, Joe. You know about people, you get along with women, you've read the Russians."

"The Russians. Come off it, Cal. You shot this beautiful deer, one shot, ninety yards."

"You gutted it."

"I cut its heart out."

"*We* dragged it out of the woods."

"Yeah, we did."

"Let's go in."

"OK, let's go in."

They closed the garage doors and went into the house to eat pot roast.

CHAPTER SEVENTEEN

▼

Cal sat in the dean's office, waiting for him to come in, trying to read a short story that Ron Grunfield had submitted to *Kairos*. He read the same paragraph several times, and the dean came in and sat down.

"So Caleb, how are you?" the dean asked as he sat down at his desk.

"I'm OK dean, sir, I'm fine. I'm just looking over a story that Ron Grun submitted to *Kairos*. I know Miss Jansan is unhappy with the magazine. We can do better, sir."

"Professor Jansan is a stickler about some things, but she's a serious person. Don't take unkindly her interest in your magazine."

"Yes sir, that's the best way to put it, I guess. She's a stickler, all right."

"But she's fussy, too, is that the right word? Maybe even a little zealous? What do you think?"

"Well sir, maybe she could help us proofread. Grapple and Perkins and I read that stuff about ten times, and we missed two misspellings and left out a comma. But it was a pretty good issue, I think, and it's not like we aren't trying to make it perfect. Do you think we should ask her or would that seem impertinent? What do you think, sir?"

"I can hold her off for now, Caleb. Why don't you and the other men make a few more go rounds with the final copy of the next issue, and we'll see how it comes out?"

"Thanks a lot, sir. We appreciate it. Did you tell Grapple or shall I tell him? We talked about all this at our meeting the other night, and we all want to do the right thing. Is that it, sir?"

"Fine. You tell Grapple what we decided."

"Sir, could I talk to you about something else? I've been meaning to come in and talk to you about something on my mind, and I've been sort of delaying it, I guess."

"Sure, why not? In fact, I want to talk to you about something else myself. You go first."

"Well sir, I don't exactly know how to say this, but I've been a little confused is I guess the best way to say it. I like it here a lot, and some of my courses are really terrific. This is a great school, sir, and I'm lucky to be here."

"But you're not sure you belong here, right?"

"You know that, sir? Yeah, that's it, I guess. I just sort of wanted to come clean about it. I wanted to tell you some things. To tell you the truth, sir, I've been seeing an analyst for some time now, and I feel like it's some kind of a rope sir, and if I hold on to it, maybe I'll get to the other end of it."

"And you're afraid that I won't approve?"

"I don't think I'm afraid, dean, it's just that, I feel, well, yeah, that's what I've been afraid of. Like I'm sneaking out of here three times a week to get an injection of something."

"Something like health, perhaps, Caleb?"

"I'd like that to be what it is, dean."

"Caleb, the Church needs health in its ministry more than it needs anything else. You hang on to your rope and you'll most likely find a surprise at the other end. The surprise will be none other than you, yourself. Are you able to pay for this analyst without hardships that will affect your work here?"

"Yes sir, she charges me only five dollars an hour. She charges that to ministerial students. Her regular fee is a lot larger than that. The going rate is fifty dollars an hour."

"Yes, I'm aware that the price for this sort of thing is in that vicinity. She must be a very good person to take this interest in the ministry."

"She is, dean, she's terrific. She's one of the top psychiatrists at Commonwealth Hospital."

"I gather that one of the things you talk about with her is the young lady who visited you last week in your room?"

"Sir?"

"Caleb?"

"I'm sorry, dean. I didn't know, well, I didn't think anybody had seen her. I apologize for that whole thing. I didn't plan it, she just came up, and, . . ."

"You mean, it was all the young lady's fault."

"No, I, it wasn't all her fault, of course, it was my, I take full responsibility for it. I just didn't plan it, and nothing happened, sir. She didn't stay long, and we talked, and that was it, I guess. I'm sorry for the whole thing. Am I in serious trouble, sir?"

"I don't know. Are you, Caleb?"

"That's certainly the question, sir. I know that much. I mean from your point of view, am I in big trouble?"

"Let's say for now that your point of view is probably the key to my point of view. So you better go first."

"She's in the hospital, dean. She totaled her car the other day and she won't let me come and see her. She's pretty upset with me."

"She must be, to total her car for you. She must be also pretty upset with herself. Exactly what are you doing to make the situation better for her, and for yourself? Are you in touch with her parents?"

"Well, I tried, that is, her mother told me that she didn't want to see me and that it would be better if I stayed away, at least for now."

"Her mother doesn't want to see you?"

"No, her daughter. The mother is a nice person. Both her mother and father are nice persons. They, it's kind of a mess, sir. I've got to go over to their house and talk to them. I've got to do that. I'm going to go over and talk with her mother and father, sir. Maybe they'll let me see Clare. I've got to talk to Clare. I've got myself into a mess, sir. I haven't done very well, sir. I've messed up my life. I don't know if I belong here or not. I don't know about the Church, sir. I really don't. I don't feel like it's me. I don't know what's going to happen. I didn't expect to be in here telling you all this stuff, sir. I'm really sorry. I don't really know what to do. I'm kind of lost, sir. I guess I'm that hundredth sheep in the old Bible story."

"We're all that hundredth sheep, Caleb."

"Yeah, well, I see what you mean, sir."

"Caleb, if you feel the need to come back and talk, do so."

"Thank you sir, Yes, I will, thank you. Goodbye, sir."

Outside the Dean's office, Cal ran into Perkins on the way to the elevator. "I see you've been in the Lion's Den," Perkins said.

"Yeah, we talked about Jansan. He'll hold her off if we can do better next time. Are you going up or down?"

"It all depends on how you look at it. I'm going vertically up but I'm going horizontally down. Get it?"

"What's 'it,' Perkins? Yeah, I'm going up."

"'It' is the sixty four thousand dollar destination. Be my guest." Perkins waited for Cal to enter the elevator first.

CHAPTER EIGHTEEN

▼

Cal edged in front of two first year students and sat down in the chapel pew as Rex Rehnquist was playing the prelude to the mid-morning service. Cal sat next to the wall, beneath the stained glass window of Hosea forgiving his adulterous wife. The music was modern, and the high expansive notes of the powerful organ ricocheted from all sides of the chapel. Sunlight streamed through the stained glass windows and Cal felt the cartoon simplicity of the colored pieces of glass fitted together to form the great myths of the Church: Jesus kneeling in Gethsemane, Peter standing on a great rock holding a huge key, Micah holding a pruning hook and a ploughshare.

Cal studied the life-size carved wooden apostles behind the solidly carved communion table in the place of an altar. This is the liberal church of the mid-twentieth century, Cal thought, the reform minded Presbyterian Church, the church of works, not faith. *No, it's the church of faith through works. What's the difference,* the voice said. *The difference is in emphasis,* the other voice said. *There is no faith without manifesting it in good works. Then what about those who only stand and wait?* A third voice interrupted: *"You're the lost sheep, you better find the shepherd."*

Cal concentrated on the carved wooden figures, chiseled and cold, the carved wooden pews, the carved podium holding the thirty-pound *Revised Standard Version of the Bible.* It was like the imitation wooden wallpaper he had chosen for his bedroom when his parents moved into the new house on Grant Avenue after he left for the university. It wasn't the unpainted secondhand tongue and grooved wood of the camp walls at the lake in Maine, these carved wood sculptures were shiny and slick. They weren't like the worm-eaten wooden sculpture of Donatello's screaming Mary Magdalene in the Uffizi museum in Florence.

Everyone in the chapel was standing up, reciting the Nicene Creed. The whole congregation of ministerial students recited it by heart. Cal read the words on the page but was thinking of something else.

That day in Rome, Cal had gone to the Protestant Cemetery to find Keats' grave. He had wandered through several sections of the graveyard, occasionally recognizing names, such as Goethe's son, and came upon the headstone over Shelley's grave, which struck Cal because he knew that only Shelley's heart was buried here. Cal pictured Shelley's drowned body washing up on shore, then on the funeral pyre and the blazing logs. An ex-pirate, Edward Trelawny, pulled Shelley's body from the burning pyre and cut out Shelley's heart. Cal wandered further through the maze of headstones, and actually came upon the headstone of Trelawney. Not finding Keat's grave, Cal re-traced his steps to the entrance gate and asked the old attendant, "Keats?" The old man pointed and drew a half-circle with his finger in the direction of the pyramid outside the cemetery, to the left, around the corner. Within a few minutes Cal found the famous headstone, and as he stood there, something happened that he never forgot.

Cal was looking at the inscription, "Here lies one whose name was writ in water," thinking of Keats and his friend Severn. The graveyard was quiet, and over the wall where the Egyptian pyramid rose near the north city gate, sounds of the Rome street-traffic were muffled, intensifying the quietude of the headstones and the brilliantly green grass of the cemetery. There was no one else in this section. Suddenly someone was walking toward Cal.

As the figure got closer, Cal could see that it was a beautiful young woman, elegantly dressed. She held a single red rose in her right hand. Cal was standing back from Keats' grave and he could see that the young woman was so singularly concentrated that she was unaware of him, though he stood only several feet away from where she stopped, her head bowed as she stood before the grave. She never looked at Cal nor gave any indication that he was there. Her hair was raven black and she was wearing high heels and a trimly cut blue suit with a high white collar. Her features were classical, and her face could have been one of the maidens on the frieze of the Parthenon. She was so fixed on Keats' grave that Cal did not feel as if he were intruding on her privacy by being there and watching her. Her intensity was overwhelming as she stood before the grave for several minutes, then slowly and deliberately bent over sideways with her knees still close together and placed the red rose on the grass directly in front of Keats' headstone. She lingered in that position only a moment, and then rose and left without any seeming awareness of Cal's presence.

Cal was very moved by her intensity and emotion, silent and undistracted. He felt that this woman was experiencing some great grief, and that Keats somehow, dead as he was, through his poems and the sufferings of his brief life, gave solace to her. Cal himself left the cemetery soon afterwards, and thought no more about the woman until he saw her again, weeks later at the Uffizi museum, as he was looking at Donatello's worm eaten wood sculpture of the screaming Magdalene. She was standing before the sculpture in rapt meditation as Cal entered the room, and he was drawn to her by the same concentrated intensity that he experienced in the cemetery. Cal stepped toward her and watched her from a short distance, feeling the same sense of overpowering but controlled distress that he had felt before. The young woman never changed her expression but seemed to radiate an inward dedication to some personal ideal. She knew exactly who she wanted to place herself in the presence of, and exactly what she would feel and retain from her interaction with the object of her attention. This time Cal noticed her black eyebrows and the way her hair was coifed at the sides of her face so that it barely covered her ears, but was still waved in a way to expose her sculpted facial features. The serene expression on her face was not neutral, but relaxed in a mysteriously powerful way, as if she were determined to see something through, singularly and without distraction. She had created a distance around herself and was unapproachable. She turned and left as suddenly as she had in the cemetery. Cal never saw her again, and he never forgot these two incidents, weeks apart, which had become one in his mind.

Suddenly, in the mid-morning chapel service, he was re-called to the present when the young student beside him nudged him with a hymnbook, as if to ask if he wanted to share it. Everyone was standing, and the student/faculty congregation was singing the first verse of "The Church's One Foundation." Cal stood, accepting the boy's invitation, and began singing, mouthing the words he knew by heart, but still thinking of the woman in Italy. He was so drawn to her sorrow that she became for him a sort of icon, and he fantasized that she had lost someone she loved very much, just as Donatello's sculpture of the young Mary had incarnated her inconsolable grief over Jesus' death.

As the hymn continued, Cal sang, but his thoughts continued to range over this mystery woman and the Magdalene and the unknown person of Jesus himself. Then an image of Joannie came to him. She was lying in a sand dune at the Dennis beach on Cape Cod. Back from the water where the heavy beach grass began, she was tanned and the faint remnant of lipstick had deepened her lips after swimming. Her bathing suit was still damp and a light film of sand was powdering from it as she reached up to him kneeling beside her.

It was three weeks into the summer and he had just told her that he couldn't see her any more. He had a job in Truro at the Lighthouse Restaurant as the dessert man, and he had not been over to see her at the Inn where she was waitressing. His high school girlfriend had written to him, and he couldn't get her out of his mind. Joannie's mother didn't approve of Cal because he had plans to enter the ministry, but she treated him well, and she had told him two hours earlier that Joannie had been in a numb trance the previous three weeks. She made it clear to Cal without telling him directly that she didn't want Cal toying with Joannie's emotions.

Joannie was silent when he told her, and it was clear to Cal that she was suffering. He told her he didn't think he loved her. She reached up to Cal and gently pulled at him and said, "How can I love you if you do not lie down?" It was not a seduction, but an assurance, a reaching up to Cal who was moved as he thought about it later, and the next fall at the University they got back together for several months. They broke up after Cal became indecisive again.

Now sitting in the morning chapel service, these memories and images alternated in his thoughts. The mystery woman, the Donatello wood sculpture, Joannie, and Clare. Oh god, Clare, Cal thought.

A student was standing before the lectern at the front of the chapel, reading from the *Gospel*, but Cal did not hear the words. Then Cal was standing, singing another hymn, holding his own hymnbook that he had unconsciously lifted from the pew rack in front of him. Then he was reading from the responsive reading at the back of the hymnbook. Then Dr. Becker was standing in the pulpit, his mouth moving. Cal didn't hear the service going on around him.

He was thinking of a typescript he had read just before he decided to read the rest of Steinbeck. A young British student from Oxford had lent him a paper that described new findings in a Qumran cave. Cal had seen the young man reading at lunch in the cafeteria one day, and he sat down next to him and after a while they were talking about the typescript he had set aside when Cal sat down.

Cal was fascinated when the British student told him about the Gnostic Gospels, *Philip, Thomas,* and *Mary Magdalene,* that scholars were at work translating. Professor Roth had lectured on the fistfights during the Council of Chalcedon in 325 A.D., and how the *Revelation of St. John* had won election into the Canon by one vote. The Gnostics were excluded as heretics because the Church Fathers wouldn't tolerate any theory of Jesus that underscored His humanity at the expense of what they considered to be the Godhead, but Roth had apparently no knowledge of the Gnostic Gospels.

Cal tried to imagine the uproar at the Council during the discussion of the passage in the *Gospel of Thomas* where the author warns that there will be no Kingdom until man becomes woman and woman becomes man, or the passage in the *Gospel of Philip* when the Disciples go to Jesus and ask him why he kisses Mary on the mouth so often, and He replies with the question, "You ask me why I kiss Mary on the mouth so much?" None of the *Kairos* staff had known of these things as Cal talked about them at a staff meeting when they were evaluating a poem about Mary Magdalene that had been submitted to the magazine.

Ward pugnaciously said, "Where the hell did you read that? Is that straight or are you making it up?"

"I'm not making it up. I read it. Why do you think that there are four Gospels and not eight?"

"I read the *Apocrypha*. There's no *Gospel of Philip* or *Mary Magdalene* in there," Foster said.

"It's not in the *Apocrypha*. The same gang that found the Dead Sea Scrolls held some stuff back. They made a private deal with two British scholars who are now on a team of translators who specialize in Aramaic. They haven't published anything, but they've talked around about it, and some of the stuff is in circulation."

Grapple said, "The Q Source thing is the exploder. They've been telling us since we got here that *Mark* is based on a group of sayings of

Jesus. If they could find that manuscript, they would get further back one more generation."

Perkins said, "They're already back to 40 A.D. Maybe Jesus kept a diary."

"Yeah, good Perkins," Ward said. "Keep the discussion right on target."

"Hey, what if he did keep a diary?" Perkins asked.

Cal said, "Look, there probably wasn't any Jesus. The only historical reference is in Josephus, and it's not a theological comment. He mentions 'the Christos.' That only means that someone had called the so-called Jesus 'the Christ.'"

"Josephus was a Jew," Perkins said.

"They were all Jews for Christ's sake," said Ward.

"Don't complain about me," Perkins said.

"You know what I mean," Ward said.

"Look," Cal said, "These same Brits are talking about Q. They say that it's right in front of our eyes, that if you compare the Gospels, you can tell by some new word analysis what the original manuscript said. They eliminate stuff and get back to the Q source. It turns out that Jesus was what they call a Philosophic Cynic."

"A cynic?" Perkins said. "I've always liked that about Jesus."

"Not in the negative sense," Cal said, "but in the largest philosophic sense, like the Greeks. Not a cynical philosopher but a Philosophic Cynic, one who questions, and who lives by a certain code of denial and good will."

"Really, where the hell did you get all this?" Grapple asked Cal.

"There's a guy right here at school who's been talking to me. I can't tell you who it is because it would get hot for him."

Grapple said, "We're studying in the most liberal theological seminary in America and you're worried about someone's theological beliefs? We've got atheists here, for crying out loud. Bricker and Hope on the fifth floor are Universalists, and they don't believe in anything. No one bothers anybody about that around here."

"Iliff in Colorado is the most liberal seminary," Perkins said. "We're the second most liberal."

"Perkins, why don't you just stay out of this?" Ward snapped.

"I'm just keeping the discussion accurate," Perkins said. "I'll bet I know who you're talking about."

"It really doesn't matter," Cal said. "The guy is open. It's got nothing to do with heresy or orthodoxy, and there's nothing theologically surreptitious about it, but there's no point in calling attention to him."

"All theology is speculation anyway," Foster said. "This is just the old debate about faith. They argued this question in the second century with the Gnostics. They didn't settle it and we're not going to settle it."

"The 'homousion' debate. Known now as the great homo debate." Perkins grinned. "We can put it in *Kairos* and call it 'The Great Homo Debate Number Two.'"

"If we all say 'please,' will you quit it?" Ward asked.

"The real reason why nothing would happen is that ordinary Christians don't really care," Cal said, "except for the Fundamentalists. They'd raise hell. Everyone who comes to a seminary or leaves the real world to serve God, or whatever, brings private motives usually so hidden that motivations are irrelevant."

Joe broke in for the first time, and said softly, "Yeah, it makes a difference, but you're right, Cal, it's personal."

Perkins interrupted Joe, "As Jay Gatsby said, 'It's just personal.'"

Ward shook his head in disgust, but Joe said, "And he was right. It was Gatsby's sadness that made the comment seem so right. That book made Gatsby's success seem crappy, but Gatsby was never crappy."

"I agree, Foster said. "It wasn't Gatsby's pathos that was so moving, it was his naivete and his simplicity. But Tom and Daisy were as pathetic as dinosaurs."

"There are a lot of single-minded good guys in this seminary that are like Gatsby," Joe said, "untouched by all the shit in the world. The only difference is, they're innocent and Gatsby wasn't."

"But Gatsby wasn't pathetic," Grapple said.

"The best guys in this seminary aren't pathetic either," Joe said, but the Protestant Church and the modern reform movements are still on the ropes. Our generation is the turning point. Once the real emphasis in the church shifts to social work, it attracts people without religious zeal."

"You think the late twentieth century social gospel zealots could have saved it?" Foster asked.

"Nothing could have saved it after World War II," Joe said, "the country's too affluent. Neo-orthodoxy is where the theological debate is going on right now, and 19th century liberalism is going to lose that battle. The liberal Protestant Church makes fun of the Four-square Gospel people right now, but once affluence arrives, the fundamentalists will take over. What comfortable middleclass American family is going to go to church on Sunday to listen to a sermon on the Social Gospel? People over forty maybe, but their kids will never buy it."

"So idealism and optimism are killing the Church," Grapple said.

"No, the lack of great church leaders and the wrong times are going to kill the liberal Protestant church," Joe said.

"Even in the Methodist Church, the bishops are so hung up on alcohol and tobacco, they can't smell the rot in the empty churches they visit once a year," Ward said.

"They can smell it," Joe said, "If we can smell it, they can smell it."

"The southern Methodist bishops smoke cigars," Perkins said, "to kill the smell."

"Alcohol *is* an enormous problem," Foster said. "And they may be proven right about tobacco. The new research is pointing in the direction of lung cancer and circulatory problems."

"Sin is bad," Perkins said.

Ward pushed Perkins on the shoulder: "Ben, if you can't shut your mouth, get out of here. You're such a piss ant when you get like this."

"Sin is sin no matter how the Church defines it," Foster said, "and the Church sticks its nose in, just as all reformist institutions have stuck their noses in from the beginning of time."

Joe broke in again, "But the Church is more than a reformist institution. It's a transformational institution. The Church doesn't reform, it redeems. The question is whether the theology surrounding the person of Jesus is crucial to its redemptive charter."

"If you really mean 'charter,' you're talking divine origins," Grapple said. "You're saying that God founded the Church, and all the old stories about Peter and 'Upon this rock I found this Church,' have historical substance."

"The myths have historical substance whether they originate in historical fact or not," Joe said. What interests me about what Cal is saying about Q and the British scholars is what it really means for the people in the churches we'll be ministers of. What we learn here in Boston is a social message that's been so distilled that the heroic element in religious zeal is missing. The sacrificial aspect of Christianity is what is transformational, without the self-pity, and it's where the fundamentalists have got us because the Cross is the centerpiece of their theology. It's fake because the sinner doesn't really pay, unless you call self-flagellation paying. But nobody pays in liberal Protestantism either. In reality, we all pay. Hemingway had it. Remember in *The Sun Also Rises* where Jake says the bill always comes. He makes a list of the ways we pay. It's an interesting list, and it includes money, but the other things are what tell us about what Hemingway knew. He says we pay by learning about things or by experience itself or by taking chances. Since when has the Church learned anything new or taken any chances?"

"But the transformational Church doesn't ask you to pay because it sets you free from all that. Freedom is free," Grapple said. "Ask and you will receive." It's the central invitation of Christian history. The substitution theory of the Atonement describes it perfectly. Jesus paid for our sins. It may be a bloodthirsty and seemingly nutty theory, but it's the theological theory that attracted the early slave Christians and it appeals to the down and outs today."

"And it apparently appeals to the upper middle class," Foster said, "Methodism under John Wesley in England was founded as a lower class breakaway from the higher class Anglicans. This is not the Church of the twenties or thirties in America. This is most of the Protestant churches of the upper middle class since the end of World War II. The Substitution theory of the Atonement is becoming easy to sell to people who have two cars in their double garage and own summer cottages in Maine. They think their parents paid when they were kids, and they want the luxury of leisure as their own payback now."

Cal said, "Exactly. So if history in America eliminates sin, and history then eliminates the historical Jesus who was the personal center of modern Protestantism, what you have left is a social institution, not a religious one."

"Why can't social be religious," Perkins asked. "Don't flip out, Jack, I'm just asking."

"It's a good question," Joe said. "It can be, but it has to be centered in something, it seems to me, that is truly transformational. The Catholic

Church still maintains the orthodox interpretation of the sacraments, and the Communion wafer is the Body of Christ, the literal flesh of God. Protestantism has always maintained the Real Presence idea, Jesus residing with the bread of the sacrament, but the bread is not the real body. 'Take this in remembrance of me,' means exactly that. 'Remember me as you partake of the symbols of my body and blood.' But take Jesus out of the memory and what do you have? If you have good works instead of faith, you have the same social institution, and all the old questions about the Social Gospel remain. How does the liberal Church re-create itself, generation to generation? Does the second generation liberal church retain the fervor of the first generation?"

"Does the minister's son go into the ministry?" Perkins said.

"Exactly," Cal said. "And if he does, or his sister does, what is his or her motivation?"

"If you don't have the tragic sense of loss that comes out of real experience, I don't think it will survive. I agree with Hemingway. We have to pay or we can't know. It's what knowledge is. It's what 'experience' means." Joe leaned forward, in concentration, and it was quiet in the room. They all respected Joe more than anyone. "Each one of us has to get what we need out of the Church, out of the life of the ministry. If we don't need to be ministers, we better not stay in the profession. It's what being 'called' means. We can talk about it as if the call comes from outside, from God, but the call is from within. Jesus said, or someone else said, if you prefer, and put it into Jesus' mouth, 'The Kingdom is within.'"

The room was quiet for a little while, and then Joe said, "Knowledge is transformational in Christianity. It's at the center of the myth of Paradise, which is paradoxical, because the payment is part of Paradise. We're all in the Church because of experiences in our lives that have delivered us here. Most of that is hidden beneath the reasons we come up with when asked, because reasons are never the reason. If we're lucky and things even out in our lives, we stay in the Church to find out how it all ends. If we're lucky in a different way and things even out, we leave the Church to find out how it all ends somewhere else. But we pay. The trick is to pay without self-pity."

For the next hour, the *Kairos* editorial board took turns arranging the black lines of straightened coat hangers into rectangles and squares of red, blue, and yellow paper on the floor of Grapple's apartment, and they finally agreed on an imitation Mondrian painting that would be the next cover of the magazine. After they left, Joe said to Cal, "Grapple's word for the lost Q source is a good one, an 'exploder.' It'll change the nature of the liberal Protestant Church. It means a lot to you, doesn't it?"

"Yeah, but it's just stuff. I don't belong in the Church anyway. It would be my excuse. I'll never take a church. If I didn't have this youth group job in Wellesley, I could never get credit for the Ministry and the Church requirement."

"And you'd never have met Clare."

"Yeah, and then there's Clare."

"Just for the record, I like Clare."

"You keep saying it, Joe. I think I *love* Clare. But there's something wrong with me. When I was in love with Joannie, I kept breaking it off because I couldn't get my high school girlfriend out of my mind. Now I make Clare's life miserable because I can't get Joannie out of my mind. If I fall in love with someone else, I won't be able to get Clare out of my mind, I can see it coming."

"Clare know about this?"

"Yes and no. I can't admit it to her because I'm afraid to let her go. She knows I feel an overwhelming darkness and guilt if we make love, and she thinks she can help me. She used to, anyway. I can't really talk to anyone but Miss Green. But I have to talk to Clare, I know it now. At the same time I haven't been able to give up Joannie."

"Hasn't she given you up?"

There was a long silence, and Joe's voice again: *Hasn't she given you up?*

It was not Joe talking, but Joe's voice in Cal's head as he sat in Marsh Chapel. Dr. Becker was in the pulpit, preaching. His jowls hung from his great jaw, and his beady eyes blazed as he talked. He was winding up to wind down. Cal had daydreamed through the whole service.

"It is more difficult to mediate a home dispute than it is to take an army to war," Dr. Becker thundered. Cal wondered if Dr. Becker was having trouble with his wife, and then he forgot Dr. Becker.

Cal didn't hear the end of Dr. Becker's sermon. He was thinking again of the mysterious woman at Keat's grave. The image changed to Donatello's wormwood sculpture of Mary Magdalene screaming.

Cal left the chapel while Rex Rehnquist played the postlude. The rest of the congregation sat and listened to the end. It was a seminary tradition.

CHAPTER NINETEEN

▼

"CHURCHILL OUSTED AS PRIME MINISTER: Election Returns Favor Attlee,"
Daily Evening Item, July 26, 1945

On a Friday afternoon in mid Indian summer, the woods in back of Grant Avenue were birch yellow except for the red sumac at the bottom of slide rock on the north side of Appletree's Pond. The long hay-like grass on both sides of the path to the valley was as soft as hair. Esther was lying on her back on the ground, and they were all waiting for someone to go first, and there were jokes, and everyone's eyes were alert and furtive. You could smell the heat of the woods in the late afternoon. Cal was glad Joe wasn't there.

Cal was watching Carrie Wormstead. She had black hair cut short around her ears and she was whispering to fat Norma Brophy who laughed out loud. Carrie and Norma had walked up from Sterling Street and Cal wondered who told them. If Carrie's brother Ron knew she was here he'd beat her up.

The day before, they had been playing football in Maes's field. Cal had tackled Tommy Remis up against the wire fence at the edge of Mr. Bartosh's garden, and it had been a lucky, perfect tackle because Remis had jumped up as Cal dove for him and Cal got him square in the stomach. Remis had the wind knocked out of him and praised Cal, who knew that Remis was exaggerating, but was flattered. As Remis was recovering his wind, they all sat around on the grass at the side of Pine Ridge Avenue, and someone had the idea to screw Esther Mackin. When the idea grew into a gang-bang, Frank Kendall asked if they thought she would agree to do it.

"She's dumb, she'll do it," Fred Bingham said.

"She's a hair lip for chrissake," Irving Wallace said.

"She's an epileptic, you assholes," Jamie Ahl said.

"Who said she's an epileptic?" Frank said, and asked again, "Will she do it?"

"If she does, will you fuck her in front of everyone?" Fred asked.

"I don't know. Maybe, maybe not."

"If you would, you'd fuck a rotten pear," Jamie said.

"We're not all Romeos like you, Bingham," Jamie said.

"Let's get Johnny Gray to ask her," Remis said.

"He's only in the seventh grade, how do you know he can get it up?" Fred said.

"How old do you think Esther is, jerk? They're same as us. They both stayed back," Irving said.

"Esther stayed back twice," Jamie said. "Old Lady Wodehouse wouldn't let her out of the fifth grade until Mrs. Mackin went to the superintendent of schools."

"She's been putting out for that Belgian kid from the flats for a year," Irving said.

Cal stayed out of the discussion. Johnny Gray lived down the street from him and was his best friend since Joe moved away. He wondered if Johnny would do it. They talked a little about sex, but Johnny never said that he screwed a girl. He was a funny kid. While he talked, he would always turn his head as if he were talking about something else. Johnny referred to his penis as his "dink." But he had guts. He crawled into that cave on Pirate's Glen with Cal, and he had to go in on his back, wriggling into the dark without a light.

Walking up Pine Ridge Avenue on his way home, Cal passed the Mackin house. It still had the Dewey stickers on the cellar windows that he had stuck there the previous Halloween. Ralph Mackin was the only Democrat on the hill. Cal wondered if Esther was inside the house. What would she be doing? She *was* a little slow, and she had a tooth that was almost black. Cal didn't know what epileptic meant but he didn't think she was one.

Esther was lying next to her underpants in the yellow grass with her dress pulled up. She was giggling. Cal had a boner on and he was nervous. All nine kids were crowding around, looking. Norma Brophy said, why don't you hop on, Cally Wally? Then she said "Ha!" and laughed.

"Your turn, Cal," Irving said.

"Come on, Newsome," Jamie said.

Everyone was looking at him. Fred Bingham was buttoning up his fly. He had just gotten off. Cal was tempted. He looked at Esther's knees. She was grinning and she looked pleased. Her dark eyes made her look as if she were seeing something no one else could see. Cal said, "OK," and moved toward her upturned legs in the grass. Then he suddenly changed his mind and backed off. "Not me," he said, and everyone was watching him. The woods were quiet. It seemed like high summer and there were beetle-like noises in the air. One of the girls said loud enough for everyone to hear, "Fairy." Cal rubbed his arm across his nose and was looking at Esther's knees again when all of a sudden Johnny Gray slid between Esther's legs with his pants down to his ankles, and he was pumping like a jackhammer.

CHAPTER TWENTY

▼

The Cambridge hospital looked like a pile of square cakes piled on top of each other with candles burning everywhere. It had been snowing for a half-hour when Cal got off the subway in Harvard Square and started walking. It had seemed too warm to snow, but it was coming down in half-dollars, and the sidewalk was white. As he stood on Massachusetts Avenue, looking up at the hospital, he wondered if Clare would really see him. Her mother had been distant and evasive on the phone, merely telling him that he might try to see her now, she wouldn't promise anything, it was all up to him, and Clare might change her mind, she was only delivering a message. Cal had asked her what the message was, and Clare's mother was vague. Something about Clare not being as angry as she had been before.

Cal had tried to talk to Travis about it, but Travis said, "It's your show, bubba." Joe was at his church in Braintree for some kind of church anniversary that Bishop Lord was going to attend. Joe had merely said on the phone, "Tell Clare that I'm cheering for her."

Cal said, "Hug the Lord for me."

"You can count on it. Hang in there, kid."

Cal thought, there is no rhapsody on this windy night.

Cut the literary crap, the voice said.

Cal thought, *Eliot is a high church jerk, but he understands malaise.*

He's a whiner, the voice said. You're a whiner. Reach down and grab your balls and pull up. There's a person inside of that building who cares about you.

Cal crossed the street and pushed through the doors.

She was lying in bed, propped up, reading. She seemed to know that he was there, but she didn't look up.

"Hi, Clare."

She looked straight at him with a seemingly neutral expression on her face, and said nothing.

"Can I come in?"

"Hello Cal. Yes, you may come in."

"I guess I never learned from the 'May I' game when I was a kid."

"Well, you may if you can, then."

Cal stared at the bandages on Clare's face, one on the left side of her forehead and one on her left cheekbone. Her left shoulder and upper arm were in a plaster cast. She looked very beautiful.

Cal and Joannie were running into the water at King's Beach at low tide, across the puddles, then in the ankle-deep cold water, lifting their feet higher as the water got deeper, then Cal was stumbling and spread-eagling into the knee-deep ocean. Joannie jogged into the water, slowed to a walk, then dove and swam for thirty yards before turning on her back and floating.

"It's freezing," Cal cried out.

"It's wonderful," Joannie called, backstroking straight toward Egg Rock.

After their final exams, they had gone to Joannie's home in Duxbury for two days, and now they were spending three days in Mapleville before Cal would hitchhike to Montana and Joannie would drive to the Cape to waitress in Dennis. It was late June, and the early summer sun warmed the sand of the beach so that Joannie had rolled off their blanket and lay in the hot sand for several minutes. Then she jumped up and ran into the ocean. Cal knew that she was thinking of the long summer alone. Cal waded toward Joannie as she floated and slowly backhanded. He studied the long arm of Winthrop Point curving toward Spain. Then the first sailboat of summer was rounding the furthest tip of land. A single helmsman slowly tacked toward them. Cal could barely make out a blue diagonal on the sail and he recognized the boat as a plastic-hulled sailfish. All of a sudden it capsized.

"There's a sailboat in trouble," Cal called to Joannie.

"There always is," she called back.

"I'm not kidding, it just capsized."

"Are you going to save the drowning sailor?"

"He's too far away."

Joannie continued to backhand slowly away from Cal.
"What shall I do?" he called. "Where are you going?"
"I don't know, Cal." She was floating away.

In the hospital room, Clare said, "Are you still here, or are you somewhere else?"

"Yes, I'm still here. I'm sorry."

"Don't worry," Clare said, "The scars will disappear. Sooner or later, it'll still be my face. And this thing will be gone in a month." She pointed to the cast on her shoulder. "I'll be out of here in a couple days."

"Why didn't you let me come to see you?"

"Because I knew you'd just talk until I started to cry, and I'm tired of the talk and I'm tired of crying."

"Are you angry with me?"

"Of course I'm angry with you. Is that the point? Is that why you wanted to see me, to ask if I'm angry with you? You and your precious little conscience!"

"Clare, can we talk?"

"No we can't talk. I know what that means. It means that you talk and I listen. It means that you start talking about your childhood and a zillion things that don't mean anything to me. I'm finished with that."

"We have to analyze the situation, Clare."

"We don't have to analyze a thing, Cal. You don't *analyze*. You just get squishy, and you smear the squish all over me, and I feel lousy, and I think everything's my fault, and I don't know what's happening, and I hate it. And I hate you most of the time."

"Come on, Clare, you don't hate me. Don't say that."

"Cal, I think I do. I spend most of the time worrying about you and your psycho-squishy feelings about everything. And even if I don't hate you I something you and I know that it's killing me and I have to get away from it or I'll die. Or part of me will die. Or something. I'm not a talker. When I try to talk to you I end up not knowing what I'm talking about, but I still feel what I feel and I feel that you're bad for me. I know that that hurts you but I can't afford to worry about your hurts any more. I didn't let you come here to see me because I wasn't strong enough to face it, but I think I'm strong enough now. I don't know for sure, but I'm hearing myself do it, and it feels good. I don't want to hear about your other girlfriends and all your honorable honesty. I don't know as much as you do about a lot of things but I know the difference between confession and forthrightness and you can sweat your little honesties that you have hurt people with all your life. I want someone who can just say what he thinks because he knows himself. If you don't know who you are, honesty is just a front for confusion. You can say what you think until you foam at the mouth, but if the thoughts are just bubbling up from a pot that's all crap, you just use people who take you seriously."

"Jesus, Clare."

"That's right. Jesus. You figure it out."

"I need some time, Clare. Maybe I *can* figure it out."

"Maybe. But not on my time, Cal. Whatever direction you're going in, I'm not going to be dragged along behind. I was willing to go along with the ministry and all that as long as you wanted to do it, but you don't want it, and you know it and you won't do anything about it, and it's a whole big dark thing out there, and if Joe weren't there for you to leech on, you wouldn't be anywhere near that seminary, and you know it."

"You think I'm a leech?"

"No, actually I'm the leech, and I'm un-leeching myself. Before you walked through that door I didn't know what was going to happen when you did, but it's happened, whatever it is, and you have to face it whether you think you're willing to or not. It's real. And you have to take it and I can't worry about you. I don't want you to call me any more, Cal. And I want you to respect me enough to go now. No more talk. Just face it, and go."

"Clare . . . ."

"I don't have the energy to scream, Cal, but I'll try if you don't leave. You've always talked yourself out of everything, and it doesn't take any courage for you. For once in your life, just bite your tongue, and do the courageous thing. Not for me, for yourself."

Cal started to say something, and Clare raised her right hand as if to say stop right there, and Cal got up and left.

CHAPTER TWENTY-ONE

▼

The lights inside the Boylston Street subway station loomed ahead as the MTA subway car rounded the underground curve, then stopped and waited in the Sunday morning darkness at the red traffic signal. Inside the car, the twelve seminarians stood by the middle doors, holding on to the overhead straps, waiting for the car to move into the station.

"How do you feel, Jack?" asked Cal.

"I just hope the chute opens when I jump," Ward said.

Jake Foster turned to Ward and said, "We'll stand in a curved line behind you. Just try to get eye contact with one or two people and talk to them."

Ward nodded as the underground signal turned green, and the car rolled into the deserted station. The twelve seminarians stepped from the car to the cold concrete platform and filed past the woman selling newspapers and candy. She was wearing earmuffs and smoking a cigarette. She watched the well-dressed young men in their dark winter overcoats push through the doors and mount the steps to the Boston Public Garden. They were all bare-headed except one who wore a tweed cap.

Walking up the stairs, Ward said to Perkins, "Are you going to wear that frigging hat, Perkins?"

"It's just a hat. It's cold out."

"It's tweed, Perkins."

"This is my tweed yarmulke to show respect for your preaching."

"Perkins, try to be inconspicuous, will you? You look like a gooney bird in that hat. All you need is a putter. Right now I can't even remember my text. If I look at you and forget what I'm saying, I'll start to laugh. Stand behind Foster, will you?"

"Your text is *Hebrews*. Why don't you have me read it at the beginning, then you won't forget it."

"Because you might screw it up."

"I won't screw it up."

"Promise me you won't read something else for one of your 'juxtapositions' or something."

"Actually, I have a better text from *Hebrews*, but I'll read yours. I'll be your faithful servant, your strong right arm, the mighty rock upon which you can build your . . ."

Cal walked next to Ward and listened to the conversation, smiling. He knew that Perkins was trying to keep Ward from thinking about what he was about to do. The twelve seminarians were approaching the south side of Boston Common, and a brisk wind was blowing from the north, sweeping down from the State House on top of Beacon Hill. They were headed for a spot on the Tremont side of the Common, directly opposite from where Father Feeney would be haranguing his weekly crowd on the Arlington Street side of the Public Garden.

"Don't finish it, Perkins. I prefer your hat to your cliches. What's your *Hebrews* text?"

"It refers to my hat. 'They shall all wax old as doth a garment.' It's the King James lisp version. Get it? 'Old as doth.'"

"No, I don't get it, but I pity the church that gets you."

"Who gets me gets poetry. Old as doth a garment. Old as doth. Doesn't that sound great? It doesn't matter what it means, it sounds wonderful."

"This is the place, Perkins, just read the right text."

The twelve seminarians stood at their pre-picked spot on the Common about a hundred yards equidistant from Tremont Street and the Park Street Station. Eleven of them formed a half circle behind Ward's back as he stood in the middle and began to sing "This Is My Father's World." Cal was standing on one end, and Jake Foster was on the other. They wanted to make sure that no one stepped in behind Jack's back and started trouble. They all joined in the hymn.

A week before, they planned this Sunday morning service on Boston Common during a late night bull session. Jim Toffert and his high church friends had scotch-taped a red and black sign on Cal's and Travis's door with the words, "PEST HOLE OF ATHEISM: Ex-communicant Method-baps, Universalists, and other Non-believers Reproduce Here." It was a form of retaliation for a series of *Boston Herald* articles about a prominent Anglican bishop and his claims of innocence to charges by a female parishioner that the bishop fondled her during a counseling session. The article had appeared mysteriously on a downstairs classroom bulletin board.

Underneath the humor, however, and the ongoing theological division between liberals and conservatives in the seminary, was a conscience-biting dispute between Cal and some of the young high church theologians who had accused the *Kairos* staff of exploiting the liberal seminary environment to cover their non-religious, literary ambitions. Further underneath the banter, a classic confrontation simmered between self-styled reactionaries and self-styled radicals. Cal, because he cut classes to read Steinbeck, became the target. Clare's visit to his dormitory room frosted, as it were, what the *Kairos* staff referred to as the "buns of the high church boys." Cal had told the staff about the Clare incident, and it amused them. Cal also knew, however, that probably everyone else now knew because the dean knew, but there was nothing he could do about it.

Cal had said to Joe, "I can't put up a signed notice on the bulletin board saying 'Attention! I didn't screw her!'"

"You're not really the target," Joe said. "They think we're all about literature, not the *Bible*. It doesn't matter that we have our own churches. It matters what they think we think. We're the do-nothing liberal Church that talks about social betterment but doesn't do anything about fundamental spiritual belief. The sacramental church has always despised the lecture circuit church. For them, our text is Shakespeare, not the *Bible*. And it's double trouble for them because we're supposed to be part of the same Mount Vernon Street seminary that sent its young men into the streets to preach the Gospel to the poor. Even Dr. Roth makes that distinction. Before the seminary moved here to Memorial Avenue, it seems to have had some aura of action, not talk. Some of it was Salvation Army stuff, but they did some good things. Not all of what they did copied Clyde Griffiths' family in Dreiser's *American Tragedy*. You *know* who's down there in the Public Garden every Sunday? Father Feeney, ranting against the Jews. Even the Catholic Church doesn't want him. And the liberal boys railing against tobacco and real wine in the Communion, go off to their Youth Groups on Sunday nights while their Methodist bishops in the Old South smoke Havana cigars and move in high circles. When we go after their own diocesan bishops they resent it. Can you blame them?"

Cal said, "Maybe we ought to be preaching on Boston Common too."

"Maybe," Joe said. "Is that what you want to do?"

"I don't know what I want to do," Cal said. "I want to finish this thing with Miss Green and see what happens. I lost Joannie and now I've lost Clare. All I've got is Miss Green. What the hell is a sermon more or less on Boston Common?"

While the twelve seminarians were singing the hymn, several people walking by slowed to listen. Some of them stopped. When they heard the "Amen" sung at the end of the hymn, some moved on, but a few stayed. Ward looked hard at Perkins, who had taken off his tweed cap and stuffed it in his overcoat pocket. Perkins' hair was awry on the top back of his head, and he fiddled with his glasses as he said in a loud, stentorian voice, "Hear the word of the Lord from the Book of Hebrews, Chapter 3, verse 6: 'Christ was faithful over God's house as a son, and we are his house if we hold fast our confidence and pride in our hope.' And also verse 13, 'Exhort one another every day, as long as it is called today.'" Then Perkins smiled, and when Ward almost smiled too, he began to talk. Perkins took out his tweed hat and put it back on, stepping back slightly as if to let Foster's arm and shoulder screen him from Ward's vision.

Ward was the smallest of the group, but he stood in front of his fellow theology students with the confidence of a conductor. He pointed with his left hand to the Public Garden behind him while keeping his eyes on an old couple standing a few feet in front of him, staring at him out of curiosity.

"Right now," Ward shouted into the wind, "Someone is spewing hate in the Public Garden of this historic city. This very minute, as we stand before you, one of the great haters of our time is rabble-rousing with his small band of followers to turn neighbor against neighbor and citizen against citizen. 'Great' is the wrong word, for no hater is great. Hate makes the hater small. Hate is the footman of despair and the handmaiden of grief, and hate separates us from ourselves as it pretends to separate us from our fellow neighbors and citizens.

"Just now you heard the words of the other story, not the hate story but the love story, when my fellow student of the Gospel read from the *New Testament.* We stand before you in the presence of those words, and ask you to join us in the only hope firm unto the end. The words are these: 'Christ was faithful over God's house as a son, and we are his house if we hold fast our confidence and pride in our hope.' I ask, whose house are we? Are we ourselves the houses of the Lord? Are we the Tabernacles of Christ? Are we the living Kingdoms of God if we hate one another?"

As Ward preached, other passers-by stopped to listen. Cal caught Jake Foster's eye, standing at the other end of the curved human backdrop, and they nodded to one another, signaling their pleasure at Ward's early success in addressing the small crowd. Not only from the sidewalk, but from the interior walkways of the Common, people began to migrate toward the little spectacle. As newcomers approached the backs of the semi-circle of seminarians, they fanned around to better see the small man with the high forehead and thinning blonde hair ruffling in the wind. Some edged closer to hear better, some listened for a minute or two and walked on. Cal kept his eye on one man, however, who had walked slowly from the direction of the Park Street Station and remained behind the semi-circle at a distance of perhaps twenty-five feet.

"*Isaiah* says, 'This is the day that the Lord hath made.' Did you ever think about today, right this minute, as being the first time in the history of the world that this moment is happening? That we are experiencing the newest moments not only of our own lives, but also of the planet earth? We, who are alive, breathing and thinking and dreaming and hurting and feeling during the very cutting edge of time itself. I'm not trying to be profound. I'm trying to accept the incredible responsibility to honor the privilege of being alive. Today will be today only until the bell tolls midnight. Today is wherein our hope lies. The writer of the book of *Hebrews* in the *New Testament* says, 'Exhort one another every day as long as it is called today.'" Ward's eyes were watering from the cold wind. He loosened the scarf tied around his neck. He swept his arm towards the semi-circle behind him.

"We are here to exhort you, and exhort ourselves,—today! We are here to ask you to join us in one of the many mansions of our Lord's house, to exhort one another and to join in confidence and hope, being firm in the firmness that will carry us to the end, in the love of our Lord."

"Hey kid. Pssst!" The man who had been standing behind the semi-circle of backs, watching for several minutes, had seen Cal looking at him, and had snapped his head upward and called in a loud whisper, trying to get Cal's attention. Cal looked at him and nodded his head sideways. The man wore a navy pea jacket with torn elbows, army fatigues, and sneakers. He stood with his arms crossed. He hadn't shaved for several days. Cal tried not to look at him, hoping that he wouldn't do anything disruptive, and glanced again at him. The man snapped his head upward as if to say "Hey, you!" but Cal turned away. The man came closer.

"Hey priest, are you bemused?"

Cal shook his head, nodding toward Ward, suggesting that the man be quiet. Then Cal looked at Foster, who was watching Cal's interaction with the man, and Jake nodded that he could see what was happening. Cal hunched his shoulders and furrowed his eyebrows as if to ask Jake what to do. Foster nodded his head sideways, as if to say, 'don't do anything.' When Cal glanced toward the man, he was standing several feet closer. Cal had stopped listening to Ward.

The man called in a raspy whisper, "Hey rabbi! Did you hear me? Do you think I'm a nut?" He took two more steps toward Cal. Cal pointed toward Ward and shook his head. The man nodded his own head and pointed to Cal, and he was now standing within several feet of Cal. The man had a large scab across his forehead and a bloody scrape on his cheekbone. Cal looked at Jake Foster, who was watching.

Travis and Prestwood and Bennet were also watching, and Ward kept preaching, unaware of the small drama going on behind his back.

"You see twelve theology students standing before you, but we're only students of the Lord, students of confidence and hope, students of today, students of the cutting edge of time. Our text today is, 'We are his house if we hold fast our confidence and pride in our hope.' Our text is the Lord's text. Our text overcomes hate and dissension and the doctrines of despair."

As he talked, Ward noticed that several people were looking at something going on behind his back, and he thought that he had lost his audience. He glanced at Perkins who was motioning to sing a hymn, pointing to his mouth and making a conducting motion with the first finger of his left hand. Ward thanked the crowd for listening and asked them to join with him in singing Beethoven's 'Hymn to Joy.' As Ward and the other seminarians sang, they moved together in a less formal grouping while most of the small crowd dispersed.

Cal stepped from the singing group to move away from the man in the navy pea jacket. The man was motioning to his lips that he wasn't finished with Cal.

CHAPTER TWENTY-TWO

▼

"NEW ATOM BOMB ROCKS JAPAN: Hits Harder Than 20,000 Tons of TNT," *Daily Evening Item,* August 6, 1945

"Hey fancypants!" The boy outside the ramshackle house had been chopping wood, and he called to Cal as he was turning the corner of the dirt road. He had almost made it to the path through the woods that would bring him to Appletree's Pond and Grant Avenue, then through North's Field to his own house on Pine Ridge Avenue. Cal's legs itched. He hated his scratchy wool suit. He shouldn't have taken this shortcut.

"Hey, I'm talking to you, slick hair!" The boy put down his ax and started walking toward Cal.

Cal was sweating. The wool suit was a bad idea. His mother had told him, but he had pleaded with her to wear it.

"You're only in the seventh grade, Cal," she had said, as if that had something to do with wearing the suit.

"But it's not really a date, ma. We're just going to take the bus to Swampscott Beach and come back."

His mother had questioned him, trying to find out more about the girl who had so attracted Cal: "Where are you going to get the bus from, Cal?"

"Bly Street. She lives in Mapleton Center. She's going to get on there."

"What's her name?"

"Marian Gray."

"Why is she special?"

"I don't know, ma. Geez, we're going to take a bus ride, that's all."

"Why your Sunday suit? You always wear long underwear under those pants, and it's going to be warm today."

"It's May Day, ma. It's a holiday. I don't want to wear long underwear. You can see it above my socks."

"And you don't want her to see your long underwear?"

"No, ma, come on."

The day was in the low eighties. Cal perspired on the bus and the perspiration made his legs itch more than usual. The scratchy wool was almost unbearable. Cal and Marian Gray got off the bus in Lynn on the beach road to Nahant, and walked along the sidewalk next to the deep sand. Cal almost forgot about the wool scratching his legs. He pointed out Egg Rock. Marian said she knew it. She had a little space between her front teeth and a slight lisp. She was wearing a red checkered skirt and a white blouse. She opened the collar of her blouse as they walked along the beach, and little beads of sweat formed above her upper lip. Cal carried his suit jacket on his arm and loosened his tie. On the way back from Nahant, the bus waited in Central Square Lynn, and it got hotter. Cal's thighs felt raw. As the bus idled, the smell of the exhaust came through the open windows. Marian said that sometimes she got carsick. Cal said that he hoped that she didn't this time. When the bus passed through City Hall Square and rolled along past the Lynn Common, Cal pointed out the YMCA.

"I go swimming there sometimes," he said.

"Is it nice," she asked.

"Yeah, I can play ping-pong, and sometimes pool. You have to take turns checking the stuff out."

When the bus arrived in Mapleton Center, Marian got up to get out and said, "I made it."

Cal said, "See you in school."

Two stops later, the bus was at the corner of Bly and Oak Street. Cal got out and walked down the winding hill past the storage warehouse, and crossed the small bridge over the Mapleton brook. Going by the field where the Mapleville neighborhood team played Mapleton Center in football, Cal remembered the dirt road that led through the poor community on the Mapleton Center side of the hills that led to Mapleville. He could cut out Oak Street and the long walk up Grant Avenue.

It was a big mistake.

Out of the corner of his eye, Cal saw the boy angling toward him, walking at the same pace as he. Up ahead, where the path into the woods began, two more boys were waiting. One was half-sitting on a bicycle. Cal could see that he was smoking a cigarette. The afternoon sun was hot, there was no wind, the woods were silent. The new leaves on the trees were bright green.

The boy holding the ax jerked his thumb toward Cal and said to the two boys blocking the path, "This is Fancypants Slickhair. He's one of the Mapleville Slickhairs."

"What are you doing down here, Slickhair? Or should I call you Fancypants?" The boy on the bicycle smiled at Cal.

Cal started to walk around them and the boy standing next to the bicycle stepped in his way. The boy on the bicycle moved it next to Cal, cornering him. Cal forgot about the cigarette in his hand. "I'm just going home."

"Where you been in all those pretty clothes, Fancypants, having a little date with your teacher?"

"Are you screwing your teacher, Fancypants?"

"No, I just went to the beach."

The boy blocking the path gave a yelp: "Hey Brownie, he's been to the beach. He's been swimming in his fucking wool suit!"

"You know what I heard, Fancypants?" asked the boy holding the ax, "I heard there's a kid named Fancypants who lives in Mapleville who said he could fight me."

"Is that true, Fancypants?" The boy on the bicycle tried to mess up Cal's slicked-down hair, but his hair stayed in place. Cal's mother always put a teaspoon of sugar in a quart of water and used the solution to comb his hair. When the water dried, the sugar held the hair in place, and it felt like cardboard to the touch. The boy looked at his hand and marveled: "Jesus, boy, you wearing a wig?"

Cal felt a sharp pain on his wrist and cried out. "Ow!" Then he saw the cigarette. "You burned me!"

"Why would I do that, Fancypants? Are you going to fight Brownie or not?"

"I don't want to fight. I didn't do anything to you. I'm on my way home."

"He's on his way home, Brownie."

"Yeah, he's on his way home."

"How come this is your way home, Fancypants? It don't look like the way home to me. How come you think it's the way home?"

"It's a shortcut, that's all. Can I go now?"

"He wants to know if he can go, Brownie."

"What about our fight, Fancypants?"

"I don't want to fight. There's nothing to fight about. I didn't hurt anybody."

"You didn't hurt anybody. Isn't that sweet? Let me tell you something, Fancypants. You give me a pain in the ass. And you make my eyes hurt. You come sashaying through here on your shortcuts, hustling from your nookie on the beach in your teacher suit, with your hair all pretty and nice, and your fucked up hairdo, and your pretty necktie, and you make me want to puke."

Brownie took Cal's loosened necktie in both hands and tightened it. "And you stand there and swallow shit as fast as it's spooned into you. How many cigarette burns would it take to make you fight for yourself? You and your fucking shortcut. Let me give you some advice, Fancypants. Don't take any more shortcuts. If we ever see you down here again, you'll get an ax handle right up your tight little ass. Now fuck off. Let him go, Wally, he's a goddam little shit can."

The boy next to the bicycle stepped aside to let Cal pass along the path. As Cal passed between them, the boy on the bicycle pushed his cigarette at Cal's face to scare him, and Cal flinched and started to run. The other boy tripped him and Cal fell down, soiling the knees of his Sunday suit, got up, and kept running.

CHAPTER TWENTY-THREE

▼

Cal couldn't decide whether to talk to the man in the army fatigues. Something in Cal wanted to get away, and something else made him hesitate. The man had used the word "bemuse," and his baiting intrigued Cal. He had switched from priest to rabbi to minister, and he hadn't been really disruptive.

Jake Foster called to Cal, "Are you coming?"

"No, I'm covered."

"Did I break up your ministerial party?" The unshaven man in the torn pea jacket hunched his shoulders in the cold wind. "I was just doing you a favor. You're not interested in all that crap."

"Why do you say that?"

"Let's just say I could spot you a hundred yards off. I'm in the know, brother. How about buying me a beer?"

"Why should I do that?"

"Ah, the question and answer game. Non-directive counseling. Carl Rogers. The Rogerian technique."

"You've read Rogers?"

"You're still doing it. How about the beer? It's cold out here."

"I don't know. Why did you ask if I'm bemused?"

"You're hooked, kid. Curiosity is the handmaiden of temptation. You better watch out."

It began to snow. Not heavy flakes, but light, swirling gusts of snow dust. The gray spring light made the buildings on Tremont Street appear opaque and impersonal. The eleven seminarians had walked off toward the Park Street subway station, and Cal didn't know why he hadn't gone with them. He knew that this man wanted something from him, and he was both afraid and drawn to him. Cal didn't want to walk away from him, but he didn't know how to talk to him. It wasn't physical fear. He was afraid of the man's confidence, his recklessness. Cal knew that Joe would have either talked with the man or walked away from him. Cal was in the middle, afraid of something he didn't understand.

"Are you hungry or just thirsty?" Cal asked.

"Don't I look full of gaping holes?"

"I'll buy you a meal at Waldorf's."

"Hey, why not? Lead the way."

They walked toward the restaurant at the corner of Tremont and Boylston. The snow squall stopped, and the sun came out. Pigeons on the sidewalk fluttered out of their way, and a mangy white dog with one eye jogged across the Common toward them, then urinated against a green waste barrel tied to a young maple sapling with rubberized wire holding it to a wooden stake.

"Here comes Julius," the man said. "Hey Julius! Hey! Here boy! He's too smart to listen to me."

"How do you know his name?"

"I know him. You get all your information from questions?"

"You have to start somewhere."

"No brother, if you're going to talk 'have,' you have to *be* somewhere."

Inside the Waldorf restaurant, they took trays and stood in line. Cal ordered pancakes and orange juice, and the man ordered eggs, home fries, toast, and coffee. They took their food to a table in the corner.

They ate in silence, and Cal finally said, "So!"

"So we were out there in the great city of Boston, and now we're in here in the great Waldorf restaurant."

"You came to me, I didn't go to you. What's your story?"

"Thanks for the breakfast, brother."

"At least explain 'bemuse.'"

"That was the bait."

"You said you wanted a beer."

"If I asked you for food money, you'd have turned me down, afraid I'd spend it on what your mother called 'drink.'"

"How do you know my mother?"

"I don't. Am I right or wrong?"

"Yeah, my mother called it 'drink.' And yeah, I'd have turned you down. So how did you know 'bemuse' would interest me?"

"These are pretty good home fries, but the coffee's lousy. You seminary types have all got something tucked in an invisible bag, but the bag is only invisible to you."

"And we're bemused by what's in the bag?"

"Pretty good pun for a seminarian."

"I don't get the pun. You mean we think we've got it in the bag?"

"We're just fucking around. I hate these places with the baked bean eaters gumming their strawberry jello, and I'm out of here, but I'll tell you where 'bemuse' comes from. Let's start with your biggest problem as a theology student: the miracles of the *New Testament*. You start with a historical figure, Jesus of Nazareth, who becomes in the hands of his biographers, divine. OK?"

Cal nodded, trying to figure out where this man came from, and who he was.

"Never mind how I know, just concentrate on what I'm saying. "Jesus becomes famous for his teachings, and after he's dead the things he said are written down and circulated. Within the next hundred years, stories of Jesus' life appear, including miracles, and his resurrection from the dead. Now you got problems, right?"

"How so?"

"Don't try to shit me. You're a theology student. You got problems."

"Yeah, I have problems."

"When you're a little kid your family goes to church every Sunday. You got no problems with Jesus raising people from the dead. On Easter you think it's the nuts when Jesus meets his girlfriend outside the tomb. You believe that when you die you go to heaven. Then you grow up some night in the front seat of a car with your girlfriend. You think about your cock all the time. You go off to college and take a course in botany or zoology. You find out that Goldilocks didn't create the world in seven days. You decide that maybe God is some kind of process. You take a course in poetry and another girlfriend finds you. The old minister at home begins to talk to you on vacations about the rest of your life. You don't dare tell him you don't believe in miracles, or resurrections. You don't dare tell him you found out that 600 Jewish zealots were crucified in Palestine the same month that Jesus was. You don't dare tell him that you know there were fistfights in the Church Councils when the books of the *New Testament* were voted in, that the *Book of Revelation* made it by one vote. Shall I keep going?"

"Actually I didn't find out some of that until I got to seminary."

"Oats and peas. One day you find yourself studying for the ministry and nobody knows a goddam thing about Jesus. You read Albert Schweitzer's *Quest for the Historical Jesus* and you find out that a hundred theories are out there and nobody knows. You figure out that when Jesus died, his followers didn't want to go home; all his cronies had gotten used to the good life, eating in rich men's homes; all those women in the campaign were too excited by the candidate to go back to work when the election was over. The Disciples hide Jesus' body, they invent the idea of the Second Coming to stall for time. The bridge clubs meet every week to talk about Jesus coming back. How am I doing?"

"I'm fascinated. Keep going."

"You're fascinated, shit. You're sitting there with no clothes on. But I'll finish it up before I beat it. Maybe you didn't read Schweitzer. Maybe you didn't read anybody. Maybe it wasn't like that for you. But it was like something like that. So I'll tell you where 'bemuse' came from. Schweitzer uses the word when he describes the early followers of Jesus after the death. Schweitzer says they were 'bemused' with the idea of Jesus coming back. You're a theologian, you know the term 'Parousia,' the Second Coming. They knew it didn't make sense, but they wanted something, they needed something, so they became 'bemused' with the idea that they didn't have to go it alone.

"They were 'taken,' they were 'rapt' in their own invention. And what they really were, was befogged. That's the history of the Church. People who have no answers, so they assume whatever it takes to bemuse themselves. And on that I'll excuse myself and hit another establishment that I know in the vicinity."

"And so I'm befogged?"

"You said it, I didn't. So long Kimosabe."

"So you just ride off onto the plains?"

"Is that what you ask when your girlfriends leave you? Buck up, kid."

He left his tray and walked out the door. Cal watched him turn left at the corner and head for Washington Street and the Combat Zone. Cal hadn't dared to ask him how he got the bruises on his face.

CHAPTER TWENTY FOUR

▼

Cal looked at his watch as he maneuvered the waxing machine from the janitorial closet at the far end of the refectory. It was almost one o'clock in the morning, and he had hot-mopped the floor in forty-five minutes, but there was plenty of wax left to work up a shine. Joe should be home soon from his weekend church in Braintree. Cal had left a note on his dormitory room door.

Untangling the extension cord, Cal walked with it across the vacant room and plugged it into the wall near the doorway that led into the lounge with the divans and the grand piano. The lounge lights were out and the furniture was cast in shadows. Beyond the semi-darkness, Cal could see the lighted corridors through the pingpong room and the mailroom. Joe would come from the bottom floor elevator into the mailroom. All the rooms were empty and quiet. Cal was exhausted and yearned to go to bed, but this weekly job was his work scholarship, and he had to do it. Paul Bennington would check first thing Monday morning. Cal knew that if he bagged it, Paul might let it go, but Cal didn't want to test it. The one Sunday night he didn't do the job, when he stayed in Clare's darkened living room in Newton until three in the morning, Paul's only reprimand had been to call to him from his open office door when Cal was getting his mail from his combination box: "Late night last night?"

Cal needed to talk to Joe. He started the polisher and balanced it as it spun, and it crawled itself across the refectory floor. For an hour, Cal maneuvered the heavy machine back and forth, and the soft hiss of the rotating brush created a new and shiny dark surface. Cal went through the motions.

Later, he turned off the refectory lights and walked through the darkened lounge to the empty mailroom and the elevator. Cal pressed the up button and saw the arrow in its counter clockwise descent. When the door opened, Joe stood there smiling.

"I just got your note. I had a flat tire."

"Good weekend?"

"Pretty good. What's up?"

"Let's sit in the lounge. You want a coke?"

"Sure."

One, then another bottle clinked into the receiver slot of the coke machine, and Cal and Joe sat in the darkened lounge.

"So you guys went to the Common this morning. How did Jack do?"

"I met this guy, Joe."

Cal told Joe what happened that morning.

"He's an ex-minister."

"How do you know that?"

"I don't. I'm guessing. What bothers you about him?"

"I don't know. He seemed so reckless, so all together. He's read a hell of a lot. His face was a mess."

"There are some smart drunks who live in city parks."

"I think we should try to find him."

"What the hell for? You think you're going to save him? These kinds of guys have been long gone and back. He'll convert you before you convert him."

"I want to find out who he is."

"Why do you need me? He sounds like he knows what he's doing. Do you know what you're doing?"

"No, I don't know what I'm doing. I'm just trying to find out what I'm doing. Maybe if I find out more about this guy I can find out more about myself."

"You can find out everything about this guy and you won't find out anything about this guy or yourself."

"Will you help me find him? If I go into the Combat Zone alone I might not come out."

"That's a little dramatic, buddy, but I'll make a deal. I'll go down with you for a day and we can check out some places, ask around and stuff. In the meantime you come out to my church with me for a weekend, stay with me on the rounds, help with the service and stuff. OK?"

"Deal."

Joe slid down at the end of the long divan and worked on his Coca Cola.

"It's kind of nice here in the dark without anyone else around. So what else is new? How's Clare?"

"Who's Clare?"

"I know. Then how's Miss Green?"

"Phenomenal. She listens."

"Sounds right to me."

"You should try it, Joe. It changes your life."

"You mean taste it a little bit to see how it feels?"

"No, I mean, . . . I guess you have to be sick to understand."

"Hell, everybody's sick. You don't think I'm sick? I'm sick, boy, believe me. Maybe I ought to see her. Everybody in my church ought to see her. Hell, she could have clients for life."

"She already does. If you needed to see her, you'd know, I guess."

They talked for another hour and drank two more cokes. The next morning, Cal slept in and cut his *Old Testament* class.

CHAPTER TWENTY-FIVE

▼

Joe pulled his 1950 Plymouth sedan over to the side of the road and parked between two large maple trees. "There she is," he said.

"It's the same church I grew up in," Cal said.

"The houses in the Forest of Arden all look the same."

"Only way you could tell them apart would be in the dark."

"By their fruits ye shall know them?"

"I guess. Sweet fruits. Janet Remy, the smell of her perfume. She appeared in the church one day when I was sweeping the sanctuary floor, and after a couple minutes I knew she liked me. Then, every week, ten minutes after I'd put the lights out in the sanctuary, she'd be sitting in the seventh pew, center aisle. I'd come in from the back room and she would have entered from the downstairs back door, crossed through the basement in the dark, climbed the stairs, and sat down. She was like clockwork."

"The perks for a teen-age church janitor."

"If it hadn't been for Bonny White, I'd never have touched Janet. Remember Bonny? You were right. I never saw her again. I knew Janet liked me when she came in the church, and I didn't want her to get mad at me like Bonny did, so I touched her on the breasts right away and she put her hand on my crotch. She could feel my boner so she unbuttoned my fly and then jerked me off. She came back every week, but we never really did it."

"We won't go in tonight, I just wanted you to see it from the outside."

"Remember that song after the war about the lights coming on again all over the world? We had our own joke about the lights coming on when it was still dark in the church. The only soft spot was the rug in front of the altar. Then we'd feel our way down stairs and out through the basement. I bet you have the same pictures of Jesus in the Temple and the Good Samaritan in your basement."

"All in brown. No trees on the hillsides, a lot of sheep on the roads. The Holy Land always looks dry and dead in those brown Biblical pictures."

"I haven't thought about Janet for a long time. She used to open her legs and pretend she was gargling, with her hands cupped around my face. Then she'd take care of me quickly."

"Bonny did you some good after all."

"Janet always made me laugh when I had a hard on, and we always did the same thing. I felt guilty afterward but she felt so good about what we did that part of me just seemed to melt. She'd talk in the back of her throat, softly. One night she said, while she was doing it, in that throaty voice, 'Come unto me, Cal boy who labors and is heavy laden, and I will give you a fat bambino--later.' I started to laugh because of the way she said it, but all I could think of was my mother. One time she did it so hard that it hurt me. That's when I knew something was wrong. I told you about what I did when I was at the University. God I was crazy."

There was a long silence. Joe waited for Cal to continue, but Cal said, "That's all. I just needed to say it."

"You lucked out, man, be grateful. Listen, I've got to make one pastoral call tonight. Then we can watch the end of the ball game on TV. Come with me, OK? I want you to meet old Tom Sewall. He's eighty something and he doesn't come to church much, but he's a great guy. He played minor league ball and he's great company."

"Just the smell of a church basement gives me the creeps."

"It's easier if it's your own church. I don't notice the pictures anymore. I don't even smell the smells.

"The idea of having my own church would be like being sent to prison."

As Joe and Cal entered Tom Sewall's house he called from the kitchen, "Back here!" He saw Joe and said, "Don't mind me, I'm doing the work of the Lord. Physician, heal thy feet and all that. You're late. I saved some fried fish there on the stove, but maybe you don't want to eat fish while I'm doing a little surgery here to stay young."

"Tom, this is Cal. He's my buddy from the seminary."

"Hi Tom."

"Sit if you're a mind to, or else you can watch the game in the living room, through that door. It might be on already. What time is it? It's on Channel seven."

Tom had his shoes off and was sitting on a kitchen chair with his right bare foot propped up on another chair in front of him and one of his toes was bleeding. Cal could see the long yellow toenails on the other bare foot on the floor, curled and fang-like.

"Sorry about this. I don't like it any more than you probably do, but I'll be goddamned if I'm going to have old man's toes. I've been fighting these bastards for two years and I'm going to fight them for the rest of my life if I have to, but I'm gaining on 'em. There's nothing worse than an old man's feet. They're the signs of death. Yellow goddamned rot."

Cal sat in a corner chair. Joe walked over to Tom and watched Tom work with a small knife. "Is that your fishing knife Tom?"

"Yup. Damn sharp too. Don't worry, it's sterilized, and I got good blood. It's nothing that a doctor couldn't do, but a doctor wouldn't do it. He'd squeeze some salve on them every week for a year, and still wouldn't fix it. I clean them up and they heal within a couple days. Once the yellow spots appear, it means there's dead skin underneath the nail and you have to dig the whole thing out. If you don't get the yellow spots, the nail will grow over and six months later the whole nail is dead again."

"Everybody's feet get old, Tom."

"Yeah, well mine aren't going to. I don't mind you not wanting any part of this. It's disgusting and un-pretty. It's a goddam private enterprise but it's got to be done. It's like doing the dirty work with the cemetery office when someone in the family dies. Everyone's home eating soup and crying but someone's got to get underneath the public folderol and deal with it."

"You're bleeding pretty bad there on that toe, Tom."

"I can goddamn see that I'm bleeding, and I want you to know that I enjoy it. You're looking at good red blood, young fella, and that yellow crusty rotten piece of toenail on the floor there is not attached to me anymore. If I have to have ten bleeding stubs, so be it. I'm not going to be leprous and pretend I'm healthy. I'm about done, and I'll have me a Crofts ale and watch the game. If they hurt tomorra I'll soak them in hot water so they won't infect. I'd be damned if I'd watch anybody do this, but suit yourself."

"No, I'm just sitting here making sure you're still kicking, so to speak. I wanted Cal to meet you."

"I won't be doing much kicking with these feet for a couple days. I couldn't dropkick a grape with this foot when I'm done with it. I do this about every four months. 'Cal, aye'? Is that for Caleb?"

"That's what my mother says. She told me it was my grandmother's favorite name because Caleb and Joshua were the only two to enter the Promised Land."

"So you were named by your maternal grandmother. That's a good sign. Young women usually pick names out of a hat."

"No, sir, it was my father's mother. My mother took kindly to her. She didn't get on with her own mother. Most people think it's for Calvin because of Coolidge. Then when I got to seminary they all thought it was after John Calvin. The hat that people wear with the nickname 'Cal' is not very big, once you get past Caligula."

"There's a thought. But you got more options that than, boy. There's Caliban, from the *Tempest*. Then there's Calisto, but she was a nymph. How about Callisthenes, the chronicler of Alexander the Great? Or Caliope, the muse of epic poetry? You got more handles to trace than you've thought about, it appears. Me, I prefer Calvados. You know that one?"

"No sir. Joe said you were a baseball player. You sure know a lot of history for a ball player."

"Don't be naive, boy. If you want flavor in your life, find something that does as much for you as salt does. Everyone's got a lot of handles they don't want to face up to. It just takes a little research that's all. All the John Calvin boys got you pegged, huh? Everyone's got a little Caligula in him, and everyone's got a little Caliope. Depends how you want to go. Me, I told you, I'm a Calvados man. Good brandy. Made from apples. Comes from Normandy in France. You know what brandy is, boy?"

"It's very strong alcohol, sir."

"Hell it's better than that, it's wine distilled to its finest concentration and taste. Have you read the *Odyssey*?"

"No sir."

"You seminary boys don't read much these days, do you? Here, I'll save you boys from the rest of this. I'll do the other foot tomorra."

Tom hobbled over to the stove, took the dustpan and brush hanging on a nail by a string, and swept up the yellow, gnarled chunks of toenails and dumped them into the wastebasket.

"Now I'm going to scrub up until I'm all perfumy, then I'll join you in the living room and watch that ball game."

CHAPTER TWENTY-SIX

▼

Cal woke early the next morning. The sun filled the room with the late spring light. He studied the crack in the ceiling and the yellow stains around it. The ceiling looked like a flaky hand with a mysterious lifeline in it. When he was a boy he would lie in bed on Saturday morning and the whole day would be his to invent, except for his clarinet lesson at ten. He had plenty of time before that. The other boys would be in Maes's field by eight-thirty and he could play for a whole hour. Then he would run home for his clarinet and ride his bike to the old high school in Mapleton Center and a half-hour lesson in the girls' coatroom of the dingy basement where Mr. St. Romaine had set up two music stands and two chairs.

Cal carried a folded dollar in his right front pocket and Mr. St. Romaine thumped time with his pencil on the top of the metal music stand. He muffled his impatience with Cal's unpreparedness and kept tapping with the pencil. Then Cal gave him the dollar and Mr. St. Romaine told him to practice longer the following week. Cal pushed his bicycle through the dark basement and up the steps to the open front door of the old school and pedaled home.

Passing the pick-up game still in progress, Sonny St. Fleur yelled, "You're late, Cal, Hurry up. We're short a player."

"I'll be right back," Cal called and rode his bike into the garage beside the two lilac trees in back of his house, left his black clarinet case in the basket of his bicycle and ran back to Maes's Field where the game was still going on. He had nothing to do for the rest of the day. "Who's calling the plays," he asked inside the huddle.

Later, the boys lay around in a group on the banking across from St. Fleur's house talking about the afternoon before them. "Who's going to the show?" Buddy Thomasen asked. Cal was going. Ray was going. Irving was going. Tommy Remis was going but he wasn't walking through the woods because his mother had to pick him up afterward so he was going to get a ride early with his father, to get a haircut. They agreed to meet at Ray's house at 12:30 and walk through the woods to Oak Street and then past the foundry to Mapleton Center. The show started at the Capital Theater at 1:30.

When Joe yelled, "Coffee, sailor!" Cal was still looking at the bedroom ceiling, walking through the woods past the historical marker denoting the Indian Stockade in the middle of the Mapleville woods. Cal called out to Joe that he would be right down. He wondered where that Saturday lifeline on New England ceilings was taking him. When he opened the door of his bedroom in the old parsonage he could smell Joe's coffee downstairs. Then he could smell bacon.

"I'm almost ready to eat again after watching old Tom operate on his feet last night."

"Tom would rather have bleeding toes than rotting ones. Not too aesthetic, but a noble battle for an eighty year old ex-ballplayer."

"I hope I'm not going to find out that he's your Sunday school Superintendent *too*."

"Hardly. That's another story. Tom barely shows up in church twice a year. He's sworn off coming about five times. Then some bright and sunny Sunday morning he shows up in his one black suit with a rose or a daisy or a black-eyed Susan in his lapel. I ask him what the special occasion is and he just says, "That's for me to know and you to find out. You just preach the Gospel today, my boy, none of that arsonist Paul talk about the fiery pit."

"He doesn't like Saint Paul I take it."

"He's no saint to Tom. Tom calls him Saul. He says the so-called conversion was just an excuse to keep throwing stones at more people who didn't agree with him. Tom says hell talk is embarrassing to Jesus, makes Him look bad. Tom would throw out all Paul's letters and the Fourth Gospel. He says Jesus didn't go around talking like a fool."

"Where did an old ball player like him discover the *Odyssey*?"

"Tom reads everything. He says we're all illiterate. He says he wants to reconvene the Council of Chalcedon so he can nominate *All the King's*

Men as part of the Canon. You ought to hear him when he gets going about the fist fights on 'the floor of the Convention' when the fourth century bishops debated the *Book of Revelation*."

"He knows what happened at Chalcedon?"

"He says the one vote margin was a stuffed ballot in the box."

"Why don't you get him to preach some time?"

"I would except that the whole Official Board would resign. He's insulted them all, one by one, over the years. They'd kill him if they thought they could get away with it. About three months ago he challenged Bill Porter to a duel and expected me to be his second."

"Over what?"

"Mary Magdalene, what else? Bill was raking leaves on the church lawn and Tom stopped by and said something about the day being as nice as Mary Magdalene's lips on the mouth of sweet Jesus. Bill thought at first that Tom was kidding, but when the joke expanded into Tom's version of why Mary Magdalen always traveled with Jesus's mother, Bill realized he was serious and swung the rake at Tom's head. I came out of the vestry just as Tom picked up a rock. Before I got them separated, Tom said that Bill didn't have anything to worry about if he killed Tom, all Bill had to do was steal the body and claim that Tom was resurrected and the congregation would believe him, they were so gullible. Bill has come to church every Sunday, both services, waiting for Tom to show so he can file charges before the Official Board."

"Tom stopped coming?"

"He'll pick his spot. He'll show up some Sunday with a peony in his lapel and think they'll be no trouble. You want eggs with the bacon?"

"Sure, great. So this is what it's like to have your own church? I thought it was all teenage pregnancies and the annual visit of the bishop."

"Tom flavors the job. I don't care if he comes to services or not. He's read everything and he gives me half my ideas for sermons. When he does come he lets me know I'm a well-read preacher. Having a church is really just what we saw as kids in the church except you know that no problem is ever really solved. If other people's problems can help diminish your own, you know you're in the right profession. That sounds selfish, but it's how it is. If they complicate your own problems, you know you're not. The key is, suspending moral judgment. What people believe doesn't really matter. Everything goes bad eventually, and the only answer is still in the *Book of Job*."

"'I will love the Lord though he slay me?'"

"Whatever else there is, it comes down to that."

"But why you, Joe? All this is so frigging squalid. The musty smells in the church, this old barn of a house, the ordinary lives, twenty-five people in the pews on Sunday when you worked four hours writing a sermon for forty bucks a week?"

"Six hours."

"Where is it all going for you?"

"Where does any life go? I can't explain it so it makes sense, but there's meaning at the heart of life and the thing is to find it. Pain and suffering and loss blur it, but it's there, and the Church is as good a place as any to probe for it. For some, it's the best place. There's no hierarchy of vocations. People just make decisions to point their lives in some particular direction."

"But they blur the line between faith and hope."

"Sure, but when something simplifies, it usually clarifies. Maybe hope is faith. When I was in China two years ago on that Student Movement tour, I met an old Buddhist nun in a temple on a mountain near Kunming. She weighed about sixty pounds and was about four and a half feet tall when she stood up. She was sitting on a little stool near this huge grinning golden Buddha, occasionally rapping a bell with a stick. I asked my Chinese guide to translate if the old nun would talk to me, and the old nun agreed. She told me that she had been in the temple for sixty years, ever since she was fifteen. She said that she didn't regret one moment of it, and that she knew if she had stayed in the world of power and things, she would have awakened some day to find that it had all been a dream. That's pretty good, Cal, *power* and *things*."

"That rests your case, I guess."

"It overstates the case, but when she said it, the bell she rapped, sounded inside of me. The only trouble is, to switch images, whoever placed the eggs in the bushes for the hunt, hid some of them almost too well. I know you think my decision to enter the ministry was easy, but it was never a question of whether to look for all the eggs, it was which forest I was going to look in. I know there're other eggs in other forests. But right now I'm living in the forest of the Church. I spend most of my energy trying to stay neutral, not so much with people, but inside myself. The good thing about Tom is that I never have to think about judging. Tom doesn't pretend, he's just Tom, and I love him for that. The pretenders disqualify themselves; you don't even have to sidestep them."

"Great eggs."

"More toast?"

"Sure. What's on for the rest of the day?"

"I can wrap up my sermon in a couple hours. Then I have to meet with the Ladies Aid steering committee for the Arbor Day Supper. That'll take me a half-hour. Then the Men's Group is making a new lawn this afternoon at the church and we should put in an hour there. I should make about four calls on some back-sliders, visit an octogenarian at a rest home, then a Youth Fellowship play rehearsal for an hour after supper. You can pick one or more, hang out by yourself, or go visit Tom."

"Tom's probably healed himself by now. I'll do it all except the Ladies Aid and the backsliders."

Joe went to his study to write his sermon and Cal went for a walk. The street was lined with maple trees and the lawns were sprouting dandelions. Next door to Joe's parsonage, four young girls were jumping rope on the sidewalk. Cal walked around them as one of the girls called "Pepper!" and the little jumper jumped faster as the swinging clothesline slapped faster on the cement. Two houses further, Cal passed the mailman.

"Morning," he said.

"Morning."

Cal kept walking, crossing streets.

He remembered Harold Ricks, the mailman when he was a boy. Mr. Ricks arrived twice a day, once in the late morning and once in mid-afternoon. He carried a soft pliable leather pack draped over his shoulder, and held several letters from it in his left hand from which he picked one or two at each house. He walked up the front steps and placed the letters carefully in the black tin envelope-shaped box at eye level on the right side of each front door. Sometimes he fingered through his mailbag for a magazine. Mr. Ricks always called Cal by his first name, softly and respectfully.

One time Cal overheard his mother talking about "Harold's drinking problem," and after that Cal always tried to discern if Mr. Ricks had been drinking, but he never could. One day, the Lynn Item *said that Mr. Ricks' wife had been beaten to death by his son-in-law. Two years later, Mr. Ricks came to church one Sunday morning. Cal was in the vestibule, leaving after Sunday service, with his mother and father and heard Mr. Ricks say to John Finney, the minister. "Pastor, I came to church for a reason this morning."*

"Yes, Harold," John Finney smiled, "Why's that?"

"Because I wanted to hear what you had to say." Mr. Ricks laughed.

Everyone in the vestibule laughed because they were all glad to see Mr. Ricks. He came every Sunday after that, even after the church changed ministers twice.

Cal passed a corner drugstore and looked in the window at a mobile made of World War II airplanes dangling on strings. Beyond the slowly turning planes he could see old-fashioned leather covered stools before an ice cream counter. He went inside and ordered a vanilla ice cream on a sugar cone from a teenage boy wearing a white paper hat.

"Jimmies?" asked the boy.

"Sure."

The boy opened the heavy lid over the tub of vanilla ice cream and with both hands scraped out a round ball of hard vanilla ice cream. He dropped it on top of the sugar cone and tapped it with the end of the scooper.

"You want two scoops?" he asked.

"No, one's OK."

"Twenty cents," the boy said, handing Cal the cone.

Cal gave him a dollar and the boy pushed down a key on an old-fashioned cash register, ringing a bell as the drawer came out. The boy pressed three quarters and a nickel between his forefinger and thumb and handed them to Cal, who bit into the cone and held his bite-full of ice cream in the center of his mouth until it melted. He walked over to the candy racks and studied the candy. When Cal had been a little boy, Skybars were his favorite, but they seemed smaller now. Then he saw the Butterfingers in their orange wrappers. Most of the old fashioned candy was there, Milky Ways, Necco Wafers, Milk Duds, Mr. Goodbars, Hershey bars with almonds, Baby Ruths, but no Peppermint Patties. He scanned the rows looking for a Powerhouse but couldn't find one.

CHAPTER TWENTY-SEVEN

▼

Walking along the tree-lined sidewalk, Cal finished his cone except for the final bite. Cal liked maple trees best, and he walked along, holding the tiny end of the cone in his fingers. When he realized that he was avoiding stepping on the divider lines in the sidewalk, he made a conscious effort to step on the lines if they came naturally under his walking pace, stepping through sunlight and shadow on the way to old Tom's house. This walk reminded him of the street he lived on when he was growing up just a few miles north of Boston.

At that time, this South Shore of Boston had seemed like another world, far from his own, but now he thought that these maple trees must be the cousins of those along his own Pine Ridge Avenue. *Before the hurricane of '38, he climbed out on the piazza roof from his bedroom window and sat among the branches arching out from the big maple tree in front of his house. He could see the whole neighborhood from the roof. He remembered calling to his dog Pickles from the roof and then ducking back in the branches so the dog, looking around, couldn't see him.*

On this street far away, Cal still held the uneaten end of his ice cream cone with the last drops of the ice cream melted in the bottom. *Cal could see his dog Pickles patiently waiting beside Cal in the back seat of the car for the last bite of Cal's cone as they drove home from Maine on Sunday afternoons in summer. Cal always held the last piece carefully for Pickles so he wouldn't spill any bits of cone on the back seat, even holding his other hand under Pickles' mouth as he chewed. If any pieces fell into Cal's hand, he would hold out his hand for Pickles to lap after he had swallowed the rest of the cone. Everyone in the car ate their cones in silence except Pickles, who made a lot of noise chewing.*

Soon they would be slowing down on route 1 in Salisbury Beach because of the southbound traffic. Then they would cross the bridge in Newburyport, and soon pass the insane asylum on the top of the hill in Danvers. Sometimes Cal's father would turn on the radio and they would listen to a late Sunday afternoon church service. Cal wondered why his father and mother didn't talk to one another in the car, but he knew it was better than the arguing he would hear at home. They never argued at the lake, not once, in all of Cal's childhood.

When Cal reached old Tom's house he had forgotten eating the last bite of his ice cream cone. Cal found old Tom in his front yard repairing the lattice of his rose arbor.

"You made it through another night," Tom said as Cal walked over to him.

"You too I see."

"Oh yes, yes sir, another day in the world of the roses."

"My mother had a rose bush like that in front of our house."

"American Beauty Rose. You can't beat it."

"It seemed like ours bloomed all summer."

Tom was wiring two pieces of lattice together with a pair of pliers. "She's a beauty all right, well named. But you have to give her a few shoulders to lean on so's she can do her job. It's the nice thing about nature—inevitability. Just be yourself. I guess we don't really need this prop, she'd do just as well crawling around the ground, but it's a nice privilege to show her off, don't you think?"

"I'm all for it. Can I help?"

"Sure. Hold this little gizmo here against this other one and I'll wrap her. There you go. Tell me, Mr. Calypso, while we're doing her majesty this little service on a lovely Saturday morning, how you managed to get yourself in the preaching business."

Tom sensed that Cal had something on his mind and Cal knew that he knew it. "I don't know, Tom, I guess the same way we come to be talking about it so quick."

"I'll tell you right off the bat, son, Joe has told me some things about you. You don't have to worry none about it. I knew I'd like you even before you got here, so I just thought I'd make it easy for you if you wanted to chew it around a little. You sure don't have to talk about anything with me. So feel easy."

"I do, Tom. I've been talking about it with this woman three times a week. I've been seeing her for a year and a half now."

"Sounds like a good deal to me."

"No, I mean she's an older woman, a Jungian psychiatrist from Peter Bent Brigham Hospital. But I don't really talk about the ministry any more with her, I talk about my mother mostly, and my dreams at night."

"Still sounds like a good deal to me, if you can afford it."

"She only charges me five bucks an hour because I'm a ministerial student. I guess it's her contribution to the Church. She goes to the Church of the Advent in Boston, and goes on retreats and stuff for her vacations."

Tom gave Cal instructions for the lattice as they talked. "Here my boy, hold this small piece right here and I'm going to split this other piece with my knife, then we'll join them. Yeah, that's right, that's good."

"Do I smell baked beans cooking, Tom?"

"I hope so. They were white little stones when I put them to soak in the pot last night, but they ought to be getting on to it in the oven by now. Smelling them is a good sign. They were white-ripe for the baking at nine this morning. Stick around later and you can prove or disprove me a respectable bean cooker."

For the next hour, Cal sketched for Tom the story of his life growing up in the church, then his years at the University with Joannie, then the story of Clare. They finished mending the lattice and went around to the back of the house and put in the stakes for Tom's young tomatoes. Tom listened without comment, except "sure" now and then, and nodding every once in a while that he understood.

"Stop me when you've had enough, Tom."

"Keep a-going until *you've* had enough. I've got a strong constitution, strong enough for a good story anyway."

"That's probably it. Once anyone says the word "enough," it's his own signal to stop. I'm not going to solve the problem anyway, so I oughtn't to keep laying it on people."

"Hell boy, I'm not people, and if you can talk about it, you sure as the sun can act on the talking. Timing's the thing, though, isn't it, what move to make and when to make it? Makes life interesting. There's a time to talk and a time to stop talking, and neither one of them has anything to do with doing. That's a time all in itself. *Deuteronomy* 1.1, 2.2, and 3.3. The main thing is to make it count without trying too hard so's you spoil it."

"I used to feel on the inside of the Church, Tom, but I never felt the Church inside of me. I just said that, but I don't even know if I know what I mean by it. All of a sudden it just came out of me."

"Sounded right, too. You drink beer?"

"Actually, once in a while I do."

"You fussy?"

"No way."

"Can of Ballantine OK?"

"Lovely."

"Let's sit ourselves down on these back steps here and you wait a second and I'll go get the material to do the honors with." Tom pronounced "ma-ter-i-al" with the accent on each of the syllables, and opened one of the bulkhead doors and disappeared down the steps into his cellar. When he reappeared, he had two golden cans of Ballantine beer and a metal can-opener. "These ought to do the trick for a while anyway."

Tom sat beside Cal on the back steps and pierced the top of one of the cans with the triangular can opener. Some of the beer came out of the can in a *whoosh*, and the suds dripped off Tom's hand as he gave Cal the can. He opened the other can with another *whoosh* and tipped his can against Cal's can and said, "Here's to the first one."

"Here's to it."

Tom took a long swallow and said, "Man, that's a reward for a working man, I'll tell the world."

"It sure is. Tom, you were a ball player, you've been out there in the world and know what it's like. I think I'm afraid to go out there. I was afraid to go in the army because I thought I'd get killed in a tank. We had R.O.T.C. at the University, and I was headed for the tank corps. My father and my cousins were in the world wars, and I convinced myself that it was my turn to get killed. One of my fraternity brothers got killed early in Korea and I've got a first cousin who won the Silver Star in a tank battle with the Chinese, and he was killed too. I think about that all the time."

"Consider yourself lucky. There's no outside or inside the real world. Everybody's there, one way or another. You have the same problem we all have, son, it's called being human. We're all scared, we all feel guilty. I know that doesn't help, I'm just saying it to hear myself say it. I was in the Second War. I sat it out in a palm tree in the Solomon Islands, reading Conrad, Tolstoi, and Stendhal, occasionally talking on a short wave radio. I'm telling you this because we're drinking beer and the therapy session is over for today. When you drink together, you forget the non-directive stuff and just swap stories."

"I feel as if my sessions with this woman are the only things I've got. It's a lifeline for me, and if I hold on long enough, I'll be at the other end of it. I just don't want the church to be waiting for me at the other end."

"How about breaking the rules for another beer?"

"I'm ready. When Joe gets back, I'll be primed to do the duty tour with him all the way to the play rehearsal."

Tom disappeared and reappeared again from the cellar, sitting down and *whooshing* two more cans of Ballantine.

"Here's to the top and the bottom."

"Here's to them."

They sat in silence, drinking their beers and hearing the faint sounds of the Red Sox game in the neighbor's back yard.

"Did you ever read Conrad?" Tom asked.

"I read *Heart of Darkness,* but there was too much darkness."

"It's a bit grave, but he's a master. I don't know if you're a reading man or not, but if you're inclined to the muse, dip into *The Secret Sharer.* It's all there, the whole kit and caboodle."

"OK, I'll find it."

"I was on a ship once, Cal. Once you're on a ship, and all that seemingly endless inside gets outside, you're on the way somewhere not on your itinerary, and the rest of your life is part of the voyage. A port is a port is a port, as the large lady in Paris said. Listen to me spout the literary talk."

"It's good talk, Tom. I'm knocked over. Joe didn't tell me that you've done everything and you're a hell of a good guy, but I should have known. Joe seems open to everybody and everything, but deep down he's fussy.

I can sure see why he hangs out here a little bit. You're probably why he stays in this church."

"Actually, I doubt that, but flattery is the great embalmer, and I'm enjoying getting embalmed right now."

"So am I. Who's this pallbearer coming around the mountain? Hey Joe!"

Joe Stearns was carrying a bag of groceries, and smiling. "Am I too late for the fun?"

"Depends on how much fun you want to bring to the old folks home and the play rehearsal, it seems to me. But I'm still in for it all. Tom's been priming me with *Deuteronomy*. He knows it by heart."

"Hi ya, Joe, it'll take more than two Ballantines to kill the pain. Are you with us, or what?"

"I've got some hamburger and some rolls here, and I figured we could test your baked beans," Joe said. One beer oughtn't to throw off my timing for the Old Folks Home."

"All *right*," Tom said and disappeared again down the bulkhead steps.

CHAPTER TWENTY-EIGHT

▼

Joe turned off the ignition in the parking lot of the nursing home and his motor sputtered and coughed and died.

"I need a tune-up I guess. Are you up for this? It won't be like visiting Tom."

"As I said, I'm in. I'm not exactly a stranger to these places. Dr. Waylord sent me out to two of them last semester in the Ministry of the Church course. Like Tom it ain't going to be, I know. Let me have another one of those Lifesavers. You don't need a beer breath buddy while you're talking your way through the valley of the shadow of death."

"Cheer up, my man, the way is lined with those who need our ministrations. Let's go in and ministrate."

The Stanislaus Home for the Aged was a turn of the century wedding cake house, a layered, wooden structure with a cupola on the top with a wood railing. Vines grew up one side and on the front, gone-by forsythia and large white bushes starting to bloom.

"What is this, Bridal Wreath?" Cal asked as they walked up the steps. "A white wedding cake house and Bridal Wreath growing up the sides. All we need is Jesus floating down from heaven in a bridal gown."

"No. Orange blossom."

"We had one in my front yard when I was a kid. I used to catch honeybees in it. I'd clamp them in an empty mayonnaise jar while they were sucking honey, then I'd punch holes in the cover and listen to them buzzing around inside the jar."

Entering the house, Joe said, "I thought you were going to tell me about all the orange blossom you drank with Joannie at the University on Saturday nights at the frat."

"I wish I *had* drunk some of that orange blossom. I was such a prissy little teetotler in college, Joannie and I would spend the whole evening upstairs in my room making out."

"Mabel Hallowell is in the room with the closed door over there. She's got asthma and she's got cataracts, but she's a great old lady." Joe rapped three times on her door.

"Come on in. Allee allee in free!"

Joe opened the door and led Cal in. Mabel was sitting in a rocking chair in front of an open window, rocking slowly, one hand over a copy of *Liberty* magazine and a large magnifying glass in her lap, the other hand clutching a white rumpled handkerchief.

"It's Joe Stearns, Mabel. I brought a friend, Cal Newsome."

"Can he sing? Can you sing young man? You don't have a harmonica with you, do you?"

"Yes ma'am, I can hold a tune a little, no ma'am I don't have a harmonica."

"I'm not nutty, you don't have to be afraid of me. I like a little action around me, that's all. Tell him I'm not an old nut, Joe."

"She's not an old nut, Cal."

"Good. That's what I like about you Joe Stearns, you don't act like those other ghoulish morons who come Bible packing around here as if everybody in the place was dead and buried. The only trouble with this place is the smell. If they could ease up on that almond disinfectant and use some good old-fashioned lemon ammonia, this place would be a darn sight nicer. Do you think I'm an old crab, Joe?"

"She's not an old crab, Cal."

"Come on, both of you, over here where I can get this glass on you and see what you look like in the light. There, that's a little better. You both look the same to me, isn't that awful? Joe, why can't they cut about six layers of old potato skin off these eyes of mine so's I can see something?"

"I've asked them about an operation for the cataracts, Mabel, and they tell me that the problem is more than cataracts. The doctor who did the eye exam for you last February says that it's a high risk, low percentage chance for any eyesight at all after the operation. Maybe I can get them to schedule another exam with a different doctor."

"Oh Lord, would you do that, Joe? It'd give me some pleasure to be able to really read again, instead of thumbing through magazines looking at the pictures in the ads. If it fails, it fails. What the Sam Hill difference does it make if it fails anyway? If I'm gone I won't know the difference. I'm nobody's fool on that one. Ask them, Joe. They'll listen to you more than they do me. They think I'm a quack because that's all I do when they're in here. I just quack quack at them and they can't wait to get out of here. I scare them half to death. Tell me about your friend here, what's his name, Hal?"

"They call me Cal, Mrs. Hallowell. I'm a student at the same seminary as Joe. I grew up with Joe up north of Boston and I'm visiting with him this weekend."

"It's nice to see some good young people in the church these days. Heaven knows it needs them. All those rickety old men with bad breath talking baloney, I don't want them creeping around me like the floor was made of soda crackers. The church needs some life blood in it. You got a girlfriend?"

"Sort of."

"*Sort* of? Oh boy, Joe, where did you get this guy? Oh don't mind me, I'm just kidding you. What's the point of life if you can't kid? I had a boyfriend once, after Arthur died, and I guess you'd call him a 'sort of.' I better not get into it. I'll bet she's a nice girl, Cal, and you just don't mind me. I have to find things to talk about when Joe comes to see me so he won't start preaching to me. Isn't that right, Joe?"

"You're the boss, Mabel. I carry an accommodating portfolio and you're my favorite client."

"Well I love you too dear, and you know I do. But it would be nice to sing a little. We used to sing after supper when I was a little girl and I miss it so. We would all stand around the piano and my older brother would play the old hymns and it would do us a lot of good. My favorite hymn is 'Are Ye Able,' and it's always been. The first preacher I ever knew taught us that hymn in that little Methodist Church down on the Cape in Chatham. I've known the words by heart ever since I was six. You know how it goes, Joe, you start and I'll join in. Come on, Cal, if you don't know the words, just hum along."

Joe suggested that they might close the window but Mabel said, "Never you mind closing the window. Anybody that hears our singing it'll do them good. Close the window, my land, Joe Stearns, is that your idea of spreading the Gospel?"

Joe grinned and registered with his eyes that he'd been counter-commanded and began, "Are ye able, said the Master, to be crucified with me? . . ." and Cal joined in, occasionally singing the bass accompaniment.

"Why, *you know* something about singing, Cal. That was certainly head of the line. Where did you learn to sing the low accompaniment like that?"

"Well, I sang in the choir at our little Methodist church when I was growing up, and now our seminary has a singing group called The Sacred Singers, and we go on tour to Florida every January and sing at churches in the South."

"Well, it's a mighty nice voice.

They sang "Love Lifted Me" and "Rock of Ages" and "The Old Rugged Cross" and it was time to leave.

"This has done me a world of good, Joe. Thank you, and thank you, Cal. Please come back, Cal, and maybe next time I can see you better. At least my hearing's good, and today, hearing was almost as good as seeing. God love you both."

When Joe and Cal closed the door, Mabel was already sitting quietly, looking out the open window, watching what she saw as the outlines of two little girls playing hopscotch on the sidewalk.

Chapter Twenty-Nine

▼

Joe pulled out of the parking lot and headed down the main street of the town.

"Saturday afternoons in New England are great, aren't they? Ever since I was a kid, I loved Saturdays. Look at these trees, smell the air, it's great. It sure beats being dead. It's impossible to talk about, but when I visit these people who've moved through life and are waiting to die, I end up nowhere in my thinking. It just comes back to life and being alive. Do you know what I mean?"

Cal was looking out the car window at the passing houses.

"We've visited two of your old people and the God thing has never come up. No Jesus, no Church, no Bible, no God."

"Oh they come up all the time. It's come up with Tom and Mabel too, but they didn't want anything from me when we talked about it, and I got the message early that if they wanted any praying or Bible reading or cheer uptitude with Jesus, they'd let me know. That's Tom's term, 'cheer uptitude with Jesus.'"

"Tom ought to be a bishop."

"The second time I visited Mabel she told me she didn't know what she believed about God but she had no illusions about an afterlife. What she said was something like, 'When it starts to be over, it's all over.' I asked her if she knew who Yogi Berra is, and you know what she said? 'That little man hits bad pitches further than the ones straight down the middle. He's funny because both sides of his doubletalk are true.'"

"Where'd she get the baseball lingo? 'Straight down the middle' is not your average old lady talk."

"Her only son was a sports information director at a college in Providence before he got killed in a car accident. Maybe she got it from him. Maybe it's just living in New England with all the Red Sox and Braves talk in the air. When her son came home from the war he used to sit in an easy chair in the living room and listen to Jim Britt do both ends of the Sunday doubleheader at Fenway Park, without leaving the chair. He'd have the radio loud with the windows open and she could hear it 'plain as day' out in the yard when she was working in her garden. She always says 'plain as day' when she reminisces. But no talk about Jesus."

"She listen to the games now?"

"She likes Gowdy. One day she said to me, 'That Mel Allen fella who does the Yankees is the best of all of them. He makes me feel like I'm sitting right in the ballpark. If we had any preachers like him, I'd still go to church on Sunday.'"

"I'll bet Allen *could* read the 23rd Psalm pretty good."

"One time I heard him do the Casey at the Bat poem and it gave me the chills. It was marvelous."

"Britt was good but he'd drive me crazy when Doerr or York would be up and they'd hit one in the air to left and Britt would yell, 'It's a long drive to left field. . .' and there would be a pause and he'd say 'and the left fielder backs up and takes it with his back to the wall.'"

"Can you imagine being dead, Joe?"

"No, can you?"

"When I try to, the first thing that comes into my mind is not being here, right this minute, with the sun shining and the daisies in bloom, and going out in the yard at night just before dark and listening to the frogs or the crickets in the summer or the whipporwhill down the lake, and then the next thing I know I'm thinking back to when my grandfather died, and what he's missed, but then I think of the Egyptians and then millions of years, and nothing but nothing for millions of years to come. I can't imagine it. The deadness of eternity with no consciousness or anything, and a kind of lonesomeness or terror comes over me. I haven't believed in eternal life since I was a sophomore in high school when I took a chemistry course and we studied atoms and molecular structure.

"When I first got to seminary I thought Jesus rose from the dead. I remember arguing with Hendricks about the Prayer of Confession where it says we are not worthy to gather up the crumbs from under the table, and I said we *were* worthy, and he said we weren't. We argued about original sin, and then about the flesh, whether it's evil or not, and I said to him something about Jesus' body being raised from the dead, and he said to me, I remember his exact words, 'My dear boy, do you not know the difference between the resurrection of the body and the resuscitation of the flesh?'

"Remember I asked you about it last year? By the time I read Schweitzer for Roth's course, I knew the resurrection scenes were myths. I still don't know what resurrection of the body means if it doesn't mean the same as resuscitation of the flesh. Did you ever preach on this?"

"I preach Easter sermons, but they're not explicative, and especially not of the controversial texts. If anyone in the congregation asks me what I think, and they really push me after I try to find out what they think, I tell them, but I don't try to defend it, and I don't try to change their minds. It always comes down to a mystery, because we don't really know, and faith is unarguable anyway."

"It's a good thing that the Christian congregations of the world cannot plug into seminary bull sessions and hear their theological students argue about everything they're supposed to believe as a matter of course."

"If people really wanted to learn about the original contexts of the historical arguments about theology, it'd be a good thing. They'd realize that ultimately you can't *know*, and that would strengthen their faith, but almost no one wants to know. They're scared of death like most of us, and they're scared of a lot of life. When they discuss questions of faith they get angry because they *really* don't know, and most of the time can't get straight answers from those of us who are supposed to know. So the discussions turn into arguments, and the arguments turn into fights, just like they do in our dorm."

"Thank God for Mabel and Tom."

"Even if there isn't one. There isn't a single thing I do in this parish that I'd do differently if there were no God. Mabel and Tom are terrific, but the believers around here are *also*, most of them. If you hang in with me tomorrow, I have to do some parish visits in homes, and you'll meet the believers. Some of them are quick and some slow. Some of them are naive and some are dumb as nails. Some are backbiters and some are backsliders, but I like most of them. I'd like to ship out a couple on a slow boat to China with Jo Stafford to improve their dispositions, but on the whole they're package deals like the rest of us. Friends know that. It's what Jesus meant when he said we should forgive each other seventy times seven. The grudge-holders just choose to be shunned. Hell, I'm preaching to you, old buddy."

"Can Tom cook those hamburgers without cremating them?"

"Yeah, he's a good cook. He's got the old batch knack for cooking simple stuff. He bakes great bread, but only every other week. This week we get beans with salt pork and onions. He'll be stir-frying big white leeks for the hamburgers, and he drapes them over the meat like white velvet so they hang out from the sides of sesame seed buns."

"I'm ready."

"After that we'll hit that play rehearsal, and you'll meet someone you already know."

"How would I know someone? You've been holding out on me. *Have* you been holding out on me?"

"I've been holding out on you. Sort of."

"What do you mean sort of? You've got a woman down here, someone I know, someone from school. Whoa! Am I ready for this?"

"You will be after the rare beef and the beautiful white leeks."

CHAPTER THIRTY

▼

"ARMY ACQUIRES ONE HALF OF ALL AVAILABLE BUTTER: Shortage Will Get Worse Next Year," *Daily Evening Item*, May 21, 1946

In the spring of his twelfth year, Cal was invited to the Rainbow Girls' Dance. Fran Burnside was a tall gangly redhead who sat in the seventh seat on the far right aisle in Miss January's home room. Her father owned the company in Revere that ran the stoneworks. The Burnsides lived on Sigourney Avenue off Main Street a couple blocks from the foundry, and it was one of the nicest houses in town. Fran must have watched him from across the room because, although they had never talked at school, she called him on the phone one afternoon after school in March to invite him to the dance.

When he hung up the phone after Cal's mother had said he could go, and reminded him to say 'thank you' at the end of the conversation, she said, "If she said 'semi-formal' it means you have to buy her a corsage."

"What's a corsage?"

"It's a flower, or several small flowers, and the girl wears it on her dress. You have to find out from her what kind of a dress she will wear so you can tell the florist."

"She said something about it but I didn't know what she meant. She said the name of a flower for her wrist. I never heard the name of it before."

"Well, she wants a wrist corsage, and you'll have to ask her again the kind of flower that she wants."

"We can get it from Zawicki the florist down in the flats, can't we?"

"Yes, we'll have to call him and find out how much he charges."

"The name of the flower was a foreign word."

"Well, it was probably either a camellia or a gardenia. One is white and smells lovely and the other is pink or red and doesn't smell at all."

"I think it was a gardenia."

"You can ask her at school tomorrow. We have plenty of time. We have a month."

"Do I wear a tuxedo?"

"No, you just wear your suit, that's why it's called 'semi-formal.' It would be called 'black tie' if it were formal. You won't go to a black tie dance for a long time, if you *ever* do. School dances are for the girls to wear evening gowns to show off, not for the boys. I never got to go to one when I was in school. Fran Burnside is a lucky girl."

When Cal's father came home from work that night, Cal's mother told him about Cal's invitation. Cal's father asked Cal how he was going to get there.

"Her father is going to pick me up and take us to the Happy Valley Country Club in Peabody, and then afterwards we're going to Chickland out on Route 1. Then they'll bring me home."

"Pretty fancy" was all that his father said during supper.

Later that evening, Cal's father was sitting in his living room chair beside the radio, waiting for Gabriel Heater to come on with the news, and he asked Cal, "How come you don't go to Chickland before the dance instead of after it?"

"I don't know," Cal said.

"That's the way they do, Lem," Cal's mother said. She was knitting, across the room.

"Who's going to pay for the meal?" Cal's father asked.

"The kids say Mr. Burnside is rich. He'll probably pay for everything," Cal said.

"Lem, we'll give him some money and he can offer to pay," Cal's mother said. And that was what they did.

A month later, on the afternoon of the dance, Cal watched his mother sprinkle water with starch in it on his freshly washed white shirt. She dipped her fingers into the basin and shook the drops onto the shirt, then rolled up the shirt and put it on the end of the ironing board while she ironed the pants of Cal's wool suit. She soaked a white piece of cloth in water from the faucet and then wrung out the cloth before she spread it over each pant leg on the ironing board, ironing it as the damp cloth hissed and dried under the iron.

"How come you don't put starch into it too, like the shirt?"

"Pretty soon you're going to have to do this yourself, Cal, so watch. If you starched the suit it would make you look like you were standing in a box. The thing is to make it look neat and nicely pressed. If I didn't use the damp cloth it would make the suit look shiny and cheap, and it might burn the pants. The dampness in the cloth takes out the wrinkles because the iron makes steam."

When she finished ironing the suit, she unfolded the shirt in which the dampness had spread evenly, and carefully ironed it, starting with the back stretched over the end of the ironing board, then the front, then each arm, then lastly the collar. She put it on a metal coat hanger and hung it with his suit over the knob of the dining room door.

"Get your necktie, Cal, with the dark flowers on it, and I'll iron it now while the iron is still hot."

"I want to wear the one with the football on it."

"No Cal, not tonight, not at a semi-formal dance. Trust me, the flower tie is better. When your father comes home, we'll drive over to Zawicki's and get the gardenias."

Later, Cal waited in the muggy greenhouse while Mr. Zawicki carefully wound together the two stems with their evergreen leaves surrounding two white gardenias, then poked a long pin with a white nippled end through the white ribbon separating the flowers."

"Your best girl won't need this long pin to tie these ribbon, but it look nice anyway."

He delicately placed the corsage in a box with soft green paper and held it up for Cal to smell.

"Nice, huh?"

The perfume of the gardenia was very powerful, and Cal never forgot the smell. The petals were soft creamy white, and they looked rich and special, as if the branches that made them grew far away from any other kind of trees. The leaves were dark evergreen.

"It's strong. It's a nice smell. How much, Mr. Zawicki?"

"Dollar and a half. Zawicki does good work. Make sure she don't touch the white petals or they go brown. Come back next time."

Out in the car, Cal said to his mother, "You should smell it. It's like perfume."

"Yes, they're lovely. They say if you touch the petals, they'll turn brown. I never had one."

"Mr. Zawicki said that. He said to tell Fran."

"I'm sure that Fran knows."

At seven o'clock Mr. Burnside beeped the horn of his Packard car in front of Cal's house. Fran and her cousin were sitting in the back seat trying to keep their puffy evening dresses from blocking their view of the front seat. Mr. Burnside tipped his felt hat when Cal's mother waved from the front door, then drove to North Mapleton to pick up Billy Warden. They continued on to the Happy Valley Country Club in Peabody, a great stone edifice with a stone archway they had to drive beneath. After the winding drive through the golf course and up the circular driveway to the glass front doors, Cal recognized the clubhouse from the previous January when he skied past it one Sunday with Buddy Thomason and Alden Sahl. Cal never thought he would one day be inside.

Fran looked at the gardenias when Cal got into the car, and said "Thank you, they're perfect. I'll save them in the box till we get inside because I don't want to bruise them."

When she reappeared from the girls' room inside the clubhouse ballroom, she was wearing the gardenias on her wrist.

"See," she said, "they're gorgeous. Smell."

She held her wrist to Cal's nose. "Don't touch," they'll turn brown."

"I know," Cal said.

During the evening as they danced, Cal could smell the gardenias. Fran had tied the white-ribboned corsage on her left hand and the flowers were behind Cal's head when they danced. Fran told him that she was going to save them in her refrigerator when she got home. After the orchestra played "Good Night Ladies" at eleven o'clock, they left the dance floor. Fran came back from the girls' room with her same green corsage box and Cal wondered how she found it again. He also wondered what it was like inside the girls' room if they had places to store boxes.

Mr. Burnside was waiting in the Packard, smoking a cigarette. He drove them to Chickland on Route 1 where they all ordered a chicken dinner while he waited in the Packard and smoked more cigarettes. Cal burned his tongue on the banana fritters and got a stomachache and had to go to the boys' room to wait for the stomach gas to pass, and everybody kidded him about spending so much time in the boys' room. Later, when Mr. Burnside paid for the dinners, Cal saw him unroll a wad of fifty-dollar bills that he carried in his left front pocket. Cal estimated that there were twenty or thirty of them. He had never seen that much money before.

At quarter to one in the morning, when Mr. Burnside dropped off Cal at home, Cal's mother was waiting up for him in the living room.

"Boy, are they rich," Cal said as he came through the cellar door to the kitchen and then into the living room.

"Did you have a nice time, Cal?"

"Yeah, it was OK. I burned my tongue on banana fritters. You should see the fifty-dollar bills Mr. Burnside has in his pocket all the time."

"Did Fran like her gardenias?"

"Yeah, she liked them. She knew about the brown spots if you touch them. We were careful, we didn't touch them. She's going to save them in her ice box."

"Well, you've been to your first formal dance. They'll be more, I'm sure. You better go up now. I'll see you in the morning."

"Semi-formal, you mean."

"Yes, I mean semi-formal."

"Night, ma."

"Night, Cal."

CHAPTER THIRTY-ONE

▼

"We should have done the dishes for Tom," Cal said as Joe shifted into second gear and eased the car into the town traffic.

"Not enough time," Joe said, "Besides, Tom gets a kick out of shaming the 'Handyman of the Boss,' as he calls me. It's ironic because he doesn't believe in God, so we have fun with it. Don't sweat the dishes. Tom says only women worry about dishes."

"A Tom-ism."

"Yeah. He's got theories about men and women, and about old maids and bachelors. He says women use non-essentials to avoid the essentials, but men use essentials to avoid having any fun."

"Except for him."

"Sure, except for him. Everybody has to have theories. They keep you from getting programmed. Tom says if you're going to get through your forties and fifties, you have to start getting eccentric. A dash of ornery behavior keeps you on the edge of things and you don't get sucked into the dullness of the world. So I say, what difference does it make what anyone really believes? If you believe in something, it only means that you hope it's true. What you hope for sketches the lines of your own cariacature."

"And that's true for the Church?"

"Maybe so. It's just Tom's theory pushed further. We hope the world is going to keep being the way we thought it was when we were kids. The more we find out about it the more we see that it really is the way it always was but that there are other things we didn't know were there. The trouble with most people is that when unexpected things keep popping up, they think the new things take the place of the old things, but they don't. It's why carnal knowledge is so attractive and so deadly for some people."

"What do you mean 'deadly'?"

"We're there, so you get the nutshell summary now or the full price of admission later."

"The nutshell, and along with it, where are we, and who's the mystery woman?"

Joe turned into a narrow driveway alongside an old and unused movie house called "The Coliseum," eased twenty-five yards further and stopped in a parking lot among several other cars.

"OK, Stearns Axiom #1: Falling in love is an alchemical reaction.

"#2: Carnal love negotiates the up-river swim.

"#3: The conservatives in the Church have always hated the Gnostics and the Alchemists because they don't need Jesus to be God. Now let's go. Susan is already wondering what's keeping us."

"Susan *Bur*well? You're kidding."

"We'll see. Let's go."

Cal followed Joe through a door illuminated by a single light bulb, then through a passageway brightened by another single light bulb. At a curtained wall, they turned left into a series of higher curtains and the back of a lighted stage where a group of teenage actors and actresses were listening to a voice coming from darkened seats in front of the stage.

"Hey, it's the Rev," a boy exclaimed.

Teenagers surrounded Joe, who peered across several stage bulbs, then called, "Hello, anybody out there?"

A woman's voice with a southern accent called from the semi-darkness: "You're late, oh holy one. I see you got a furlough for your cell mate." Susan Burwell became visible and managed to appear upright on the stage after a slow motion, almost graceful, jump.

"Not bad," Joe said. "Nice transition."

"I practice when no one's around. Welcome to the Congregational Players rehearsal. Hi Cal. I see you're still upright after eating this guy's meals for a day."

"Yeah, he's initiating me into the pastoral life. The food's the best part of it."

"He must have taken you to Tom's for dinner. How were the leeks?"

"Nice. You're familiar with the drill."

Susan pretended to sock Joe on his left upper arm and said, "Hey man, glad you're here, you and Cal can be the critical eyes that spot the chinks in the armor." She turned to Cal: "It's a farce about a minister who gets hit on the head with a softball at a church picnic and doesn't know who he is for awhile, embarrassing himself in the process, but in the end it turns out all right, of course. All the stay-at-homes who think Joe is such a stiff fill the church on Christmas Eve because he's human after all. Harmony and success and all that."

"I thought all churches were always full on Christmas Eve."

"Well, they are, but this is a play. Funny plays are not supposed to be real, right Joe?"

"Thus saith the Directoress," Joe said, smiling.

A young actress called out, "Miss *Bur*welllll! Our re*hearsal!* We've got dates."

"OK Jenny, of course. Let's take it from when these two interlopers appeared. Come on, you two, join me in the pit."

The rehearsal lasted for another hour, and Joe and Cal followed Susan to her apartment a couple blocks from Joe's church. Inside the car, Cal said, "It feels like you two guys really know each other, everything's so easy. You sound almost married. You're catching me off guard. You got an axiom for this, Joe, one I can understand?"

Joe thought for awhile, then turned off the ignition: "Stearn's Zen Afterthought: When walking toward sex, do not let lead foot get too far behind. When walking after sex, make sure back foot stays attentive."

CHAPTER THIRTY-TWO

▼

The worship service began at eleven on Sunday morning. The choir stood at the back during the prelude, played on the old pump organ by Mrs. Sweatser who began playing the organ in her late teens, fifty years before. Her hands were still supple and efficient, and she played a simple old Scots melody to begin the service. In the silence that followed, Joe sat with his head tilted forward and his eyes closed in the high-backed chair behind the pulpit. After several seconds, Joe began to sing a cappella the *De Profundis*. Joe had a good baritone voice and sang the ancient melody full-toned and clean.

Cal, who was participating with Joe in the service, was moved, and he sat immobile, looking at the unpainted ceiling timbers, as Joe sang the powerful words of the 130th Psalm: "Out of the depths, O Lord, do I cry unto Thee; O Lord, hear my voice." When he finished, Cal stood and announced the call to worship that he had heard so many times in the wooden Methodist church where he and Joe grew up: "The hour cometh, and now is, when all true worshippers shall gather...."

Mrs. Sweatser pumped the organ bellows and laid out the beat of "The Church's One Foundation" as the ten-person choir in red robes marched down the aisle. Susan sang the soprano lead, and Cal watched her, as she finished singing the hymn, shake her hair so that it fell down over her shoulders, then look to the front of the church where Joe stood tall in the pulpit. *She's in love*, Cal thought, Joe's gone and done it.

Cal wondered what was going through her mind. He wondered if they were sleeping together. If he asked, Joe would tell him, but he had heard Joe say too many times that you don't get information by asking questions. What difference does it make? Of course they're sleeping together, they're just being shrewd about it. Or is the word "secretive," or "careful," or "classy." Maybe the word was "wise," or "self-protective." Cal decided that the best way to describe it is "considerate." *They don't suck others into their intimacies, they don't burden the rest of the world with their needs. But how can they be so relaxed in their knowledge of each other that they don't need the approval of the rest of the world?*

Cal watched Susan watch Joe as he gave the church announcements with a touch of wit and pleasure, and then began the morning pastoral prayer. Susan kept her eyes on Joe for several seconds and then bowed her head. She looked peaceful and unburdened as Joe prayed. Cal and Joe had learned from jowly Doc Harmer that the pastoral prayer was the most difficult thing to perform effectively in the church service, that almost all ministers did it badly because the function of the prayer was to lift the congregation into the presence of God, not give a mini-sermon. Don't judge, don't castigate, don't beg. Above all, don't give God information. *Where does that leave you,* Cal wondered. He had heard prayers that moved him, but he couldn't remember what they said. *That's the trick,* he thought. *If the words do their job, they're secondary to the feeling of the moment.* Cal's problem was how to open himself up, how to lay bare his feelings in front of others and not tell God things He already knew. *If God was God, He already knew. That made sense.* But Cal didn't think he believed in God. *Where did that leave him? Where did it leave the congregation?* Joe was still praying. Susan's head was still bowed, motionless. What was Joe saying? Cal was not listening to Joe's words, but he was now caught by the tone of Joe's voice. Joe was talking softly and straight, as usual. Cal listened.

". . . *We have come together to place this day before you, to gather the light of these mid-day hours so that it shines on the distractions of our lives and clarifies the path, that the thicket be un-gnarled, the valley to the oasis be un-shadowed. We ask that our own rhetoric be simplified so that our desires may be made clear to ourselves. We pray for the elegance of simplicity in our lives, we pray for openness to the riches of the Gospel, we pray that the words of our mouths lead to the uncertainty of our dreams,*

*that our motives be chaste, that our passions be honorable, that we may
enlarge the quiet places in our hearts to include those who truly need us,
that our visions of Jesus' life be clarified every hour, that these emanations
from our mouths mirror the deepest feelings of our hearts. We ask for the
grace to be singular in our devotion to what is revealing of the spiritual
nature of all things, that we recognize the truths inherent in the brevity of
life. We ask the grace to forgive each other seventy times seven, to honor our
parents and respect our neighbors, to bow down in our hearts at the very
name of Jesus. Amen."*

Cal felt Joe's invitation to the still waters, and he was moved. He
looked at Susan who did not raise her head for many seconds, not until
Joe announced the final hymn.

As the choir filed in front of him down the nave during the singing
of the last two stanzas of "Crown Him with Many Crowns," Cal waited
until Joe motioned for him to follow the last choir member, then Joe filed
out behind Cal. Joe's voice rang clear above the congregational singing,
and Cal listened carefully to the words as he looked straight ahead and
focused on the outside light he could see through the open church
doors:

*Crown him the Lord of life Who triumphed o'er the grave;
Who rose victorious to the strife For those He came to save:
His glories now we sing, Who died and rose on high;
Who died eternal life to bring, And lives that death may die.*

Cal was thinking about what Joe said in the pastoral prayer about the
truth of the brevity of life. As Cal tried to imagine being dead, the idea
slid away from him. Outside, the sun was shining in a blue sky. One of
the young actresses from the night before came up to him and told him it
was nice that he could share the service with them. She had long chestnut
hair, woven loosely with its own thick strands and knotted below her
shoulders. Cal caught a vague smell of her perfume, subtle and delicate.
Oh Death, where is thy sting? O Death, where is thy victory? Cal was
nodding at her, shaking her hand, thanking her, but he was thinking of
eternal nothingness, millions and millions of years of nothingness, an
unending forever of nothingness.

Cal wanted to talk to Joe about death. He felt an urgency, as if
something was dying right now inside him, but Susan was standing
beside them, asking Cal if he would join Joe and her for Sunday dinner

at her apartment. Cal thanked her and said he had to get back to Boston and do some work before he went to his Youth Group that evening. He asked her for a raincheck and she said, "Of course, Cal, next time." Cal walked to his car.

CHAPTER THIRTYTHREE

▼

"REDS INVADE SOUTH KOREA; U.S. SPEARHEADS U.N. ACTION, *Daily Evening Item*, June 25, 1950.

After Dr. Woodside passed back the exams at the end of zoology class, Cal filed out of the lecture hall and started up Butterfield Hill to his dorm. It was a cold November afternoon, almost dark already at four o'clock. He recognized the small hunched-over form carrying a heavy load of books in front of him as Dave Reagan, and Cal hurried to catch up with him.

"Geez, it's cold, huh Dave?"

"Feels like snow."

"I know it. This frigging hill will be harder to climb tomorrow."

They walked in silence. The hill was vacant before them, and the lights of the dorm were beginning to be visible.

"How'd you do on the exam, Dave?"

"I did OK. You?"

"I did OK last time, but I screwed up and drew the central nervous system instead of the autonomic and got an 87. On today's I got a C. How about you?"

"I got a 92."

"That's the only A. Wow, that's great."

"Thanks."

"Are you pre-med?"

"Yeah, if I can keep up my grades."

"Yeah, me too. Are you taking German or French?"

"Spanish. I had some in high school."

"I got Fischer in German. He's pretty good. Who you got in zoo lab?"

"Miss Bromfield."

"She OK?"

"Yeah, she's good."

"I got Libnitz. He's a grad student. You still on the frog?"

"I finished dissecting mine yesterday."

"I got another week."

Cal felt his lab kit in his coat pocket. He was carrying his German book, his English essay book, and his trigonometry book, all in one hand against his side, and his hand was cold.   He held the warm lab kit and switched his books to his warm hand. He wondered if he would really do it.

"I'm going into Lakebourne. See you, Dave,"

"I'm in Hammerton. So long."

"I know. So long."

Cal entered the south side of Lakebourne Hall and walked down the corridor to the north end. It was warm inside the building. Charley Finney's door was open and Cal said, "Hey Charlie," and kept walking.

"Hey, Cal. How's it going? You want to play pitch tonight?"

Cal called, "Can't tonight, let's play tomorrow night."

Most of the doors in the vicinity of his room at the north end of the hallway were open. This was the freshman football wing of Lakebourne Hall. Fuzzy Grillo and Gigi Romer were lying on their beds talking in the next room to Cal's. Across the hall, Moose Greenville and Mike D'Agostino and Duke Romney were playing cards. Moose saw Cal as he was unlocking his door.

"Geez, the Calpal is back from class. What time is it? I'm late. They can't get along without me. I'm out of here." Moose grabbed his coat and ran out the side door. He worked in the kitchen of the refectory in the basement of Dramington dorm next door, as part of his football scholarship.

Cal entered his room and turned on the lights. He put his books on his bed. He left the lab kit in his coat pocket and hung his coat in the closet. His roommate Becker wouldn't be back until almost midnight.

Cal closed his door, pressing the lock button. Fuzzy Grillo banged on his wall and called out when he heard the door close:

"You got a girl in there? What's with the closed door."

Cal rapped back on the wall.

"I'm going to take a nap, Fuzzhead. Rap when you go to eat."

"OK."

Cal lay on his bed and thought about it. Laundry pickup would be tomorrow morning, so he could get rid of the sheets if there was any blood. Becker wouldn't walk in on him because he stayed in the greenhouse until eleven thirty every night. Cal was afraid to go to the infirmary. Dr. Sutcliff would think he was crazy. Maybe he wouldn't. Cal couldn't take the chance. Two weeks before, Cal had been shaving when Lew Alters came in and took a leak in the urinal beside the shaving sink in the bathroom. As Lew was urinating he picked up on a conversation they had the night before:

"Remember that word I couldn't think of? It's *peristalsis*. If you're lying down eating, it's what the throat does to get the food down into the stomach."

As Lew finished urinating, Cal glanced over and saw him pull back the foreskin on his penis, then shake the last drops of urine. When Cal saw the foreskin move smoothly all the way back and expose the head of the penis, Cal was amazed to see how easy it was supposed to work. He had never been able to pull back the skin of his penis. Somehow it was either grown together where it shouldn't be or something else was the matter, but something was wrong.

In his room Cal tried to pull back his foreskin, but it hurt. Ignoring the pain, he forced it, then released. Then with the thumbs and forefingers of both hands, he again forced back the foreskin, exposing half the head of his penis, then further. Two places where the surface skin seemed to be grafted together, pulled apart, without blood. Cal forced the foreskin further back until the head was exposed for the first time, hurting him because the foreskin was still attached too far forward, directly at the tip of the V on the underside of the head. Retracting the foreskin pulled the head downward, and the further back he forced it, the more pain he felt. He released the foreskin and thought for several minutes. He did not want the shame of an operation.

The main thing would be infection, that and the cut. He wondered if he could actually cut himself at the attachment underneath the head, allowing the foreskin to slide back without pulling down the head. Then in his mind *he was alone in the boat in the isolated narrows of the middle lake, casting his long white plug into deep water, reeling the plug to the side of the boat, seeing the plug fall away from the ligature, sinking slowly out of sight to the bottom of the lake. He took off his clothes. The sun was warm on the seat of the boat as he dropped his clothes in a pile. He put one leg over the side and then slipped into the water. Dog paddling to stay afloat, he looked around the lake and could see no one. Deep water frightened him, but he didn't want to give up his new fishing plug. He ducked his head and started down toward the dark bottom of the lake. Several feet below the surface he still couldn't see the bottom, then something about the bottom of the lake frightened him and he surfaced, hanging on to the side of the boat, his heart pounding.*

As Cal lay on his bed in his dormitory room, the banging on his wall started again, then Fuzzy was calling to him and there was simultaneous banging on his door. Mike D'Agostino was thumping with the side of his hand.

"Come on, Cal, it's eat hour. Let's go. Get off the nap crap. You can beat your meat later. Hey, let's go."

Cal opened his door as Mike pounded on it.

"OK, OK I'm in. Let's go."

Mike was three inches shorter than Cal, and his square, powerful shoulders hitched up and down as he faked a punch at Cal's midriff, moving his feet in a quick soft shoe routine. Mike was jowly with a dark five o'clock shadow and a receding hairline. "Wake up, cod eyes," he said, "or forever hold thy piece. Do you get it? P- I- E- C- E. Codpiece. You know what a codpiece is? It's what you hold in your hand in the dark."

"D'Agostino, you got fullback mouth. You're spoiling my dinner," Romer said.

Six football players filed out the side door of Lakebourne Hall, then across the walkway and into Dramington House next door. None of them wore jackets and they yelled to one another to hurry up as they filed through the big door to the descending steps into the warm cafeteria.

"I'm going to tell the coach you're an English major and you don't even know Shakespeare," Mike said. "It's not surprising you Mapleton guys don't get my literary references, *whereas* if you went to Everett High, where the couth guys originate, you'd be more on the ball."

"Jesus Mike, every English class is reading *The Tempest*. I was named after Caliban, don't you know that?"

"Hey, is that true?"

"Really, Mike, really. Scout's honor."

"Imagine that! Old Horsepiss Calbuddy!"

Across from the receiving line, three students in white jackets and white billowy hats waited with large spoons before trays of mashed potatoes, Salisbury steaks, carrots and peas, and white rolls.

Mike swept his hand by the trays: "I'd be much obliged, honored servers of the people, to have three of each." He winked at Cal and whispered, "Watch me get an extra steak out of this."

The first two servers, co-eds, looked at each other, debating what to do, as the third, a tall thin boy with long sideburns, looked down at the rolls and shook his head. The first girl picked the top plate off a pile, heaped on a large dollop of mashed potato and passed it to the second girl, who added an ample sized Salisbury steak. The tall boy scooped on carrots and peas, added two rolls and handed Mike the full plate.

The three servers watched Mike silently. Mike held the plate in mid air, and looked at Cal for several seconds. As Mike deliberated, the first co-ed said, "We're only allowed to give one serving. We know that you play football, and you need a lot of food. We'd like to give you the whole tray." The boy with the sideburns stared down at the crowded rolls in the tray before him.

Mike nodded his head a little bit and looked at Cal who raised his eyebrows and furrowed his brow, suggesting that it was up to Mike. The first co-ed said, "Maybe if you'd like to come back later when we've served everyone else. . . ."

Mike tightened the skin over his jaw and protruded his upper lip, nodding his head in acquiescence, and just at the moment that Mike had decided to compromise, the tall boy looked up at him and said, "Just because you're a goddamn football player doesn't mean that you own the fucking place."

Mike stared at the tall boy. "Hey!" he said softly. "Hey!—Ichabod Cranesville! You want to breathe through your fuckin ears?"

Several things happened at once. Cal motioned to the co-eds to get the tall boy out of there, but before they could move, the tall boy scooped an over-full portion of peas and carrots in his large spoon and riveted them into Mike's face. Mike leaned over the food trays and pushed his full plate at the tall boy's face but the tall boy ducked aside and the plate hit his shoulder, spilling mashed potatoes and Salisbury steak and peas and carrots over the counter and the trays of food. The football players in front of Mike quickly turned and formed a semi-circle around Mike, preventing students rushing in from the occupied tables to enter the small narrow space of the serving line.

One of the co-eds rushed inside the kitchen for help while the other one tugged at the tall boy to get him away from Mike who was reaching across the food trays to grab him. Moose Grillo appeared from inside the kitchen.

The tall boy pulled away from the co-ed and round-housed his skinny fist into Mike's eye, cutting the skin on Mike's cheekbone. Mike, in his fury, swung and missed several times, aiming at the tall thin boy's head. The boy's small fist, reaching across the shiny metal trays of the food bar, kept probing into Mike's face, lacerating it. Moose embraced the tall thin boy from behind.

Cal embraced Mike with a shoulder lock and powered him against the opposite wall: "The kid's not worth it, Mike, he's zero, leave it. Come on baby, leave it, we'll get him later if you want."

"The fucking animal doesn't even cut his fingernails," Mike said. I've probably got rabies, the little prick-fucking weasel face."

"It's OK Mike, let's get out of here. Let's go downtown to Barsilotti's. Screw this place. Come on, baby, let's go." Cal motioned to Fuzzy and Moose and Lew to come with him, and they followed Mike and Cal out of the cafeteria and back into Lakebourne Hall.

"Whad'ya do that for?" Mike complained to Cal as they stood in the hall outside Cal's room. "That fucking bean sprout had long finger nails. . . . little bitch-cat."

"It's OK, Mike. One of those girls is in my zoology class. She's a nice girl. She was scared. Come on, let's go downtown and get something to eat. Moose'll take care of that kid. If coach finds out about this we'll be dead. I'll talk to her tomorrow. I'll smooth it over. The beanpole doesn't count. You could hurt him."

"Whaddayamean he doesn't count? You want me to worry about his fucking weight or his fucking sick grandmother? He's a fucking asshole is what he is. I'm going to kill the fucking little prick when I get my hands on him."

Fuzzy touched Mike on the shoulder: "Mike, we just called Frankinetti's, they've got two tables for us. We ordered pizzas all around. We'll have a few beers. Let's go bubba."

It was a half mile walk to town. They were going to hitch a ride but no cars came by. The night was dry and cold. Maple trees hung overhead along Lincoln Avenue like arms penciled on a winter canvas. Turn-of-the-century houses with high, lighted downstairs rooms lined the quiet avenue all the way to town.

Frankinetti's neon sign flickered over the quiet main street. Inside, the six football players ate pizzas, drank beer, and Mike flirted with the waitress who was a towny. Cal was the only one who didn't order a beer. Mike told the waitress she looked like she had strong wrists. Lew and Fuzzy tried to talk Mike into walking back to the dorm but he wanted another beer. He asked the waitress if she did thigh exercises. She said, "You guys would be fun if you had a sense of humor."

Mike asked Cal what she meant by that. Cal said she was just very intelligent, that's all. Mike said, "You're a good shit, Caliban old Mapleton bean, but you're a fuckin nut, you know that?"

By nine o'clock, everyone but Cal had drunk five beers, and they were noisy. Mike was drunk. Cal said, "I'm going back to the dorm. I've got an exam tomorrow."

Fuzzy said, "I'm going too." They all left except Mike.

As they were going out the door, Mike yelled, Hey, Calcock, give my regards to your old Trunkblow."

The last anyone ever heard of Mike, he was standing out on route 9 at midnight trying to hitch a ride home to Everett.

CHAPTER THIRTY-FOUR

▼

"TWO PUERTO RICAN FANATICS FAIL IN ATTEMPT TO ASSASSINATE PRESIDENT TRUMAN," *Daily Evening Item,* Nov. 3, 1950

Back in his room, Cal undressed. *It's not so funny about the name Caliban,* he thought. *It never occurred to me until Mike said it. There is something grotesque about me. Only a crazy would do what I'm going to do.*

Becker would be back in an hour. Cal was worried about infection. He put on his bathrobe and took the scalpel from his zoology lab kit. Down the hall, he held the blade under the faucet in the boys' bathroom. The steaming hot water burned his hand and Cal hoped that it was hot enough to sterilize the blade.

Sitting on his bed, he pushed back the foreskin of his penis as far as he could, pulling the head painfully down, and drew the scalpel quickly across the taut gnarly skin where it had grown together, releasing the head so that it extended normally from the barrel of the penis. After the streak of ice-cold pain, Cal felt no discomfort, but blood gushed from the cut. There was so much blood on his penis that the foreskin slipped back easily over the cut, then Cal wrapped several folds of his extra pillowcase around his penis and hoped the bleeding would stop.

Later, when Becker entered the room, Cal pretended to be asleep, but he lay awake a long time, afraid to un-wrap the blood stained cloth. He knew he could never tell anyone what he had done. He was still picturing the foreskin of Lew's penis sliding easily back after Lew urinated, and he fell asleep wondering if his own penis was now OK. He woke in the night and remembered immediately what he had done. He was amazed that he had done it, but he had had to, something had been really wrong.

Cal woke again at first light, and lay with his face to the wall, waiting for Becker to dress and leave for breakfast and his eight o'clock class. When the door finally closed, Cal peeled the red stained pillowcase from his body. The bleeding had stopped, and both sheets were stained with blood. In the shower, Cal let the warm water pour onto his head and face for a long time, finally getting the nerve to pull back the foreskin of his penis and gently bathe the cut with warm water. The foreskin slid smoothly back and forth. Then the bleeding began again, but not heavy, and he prayed that he would not get an infection and have to explain to the infirmary people what he had done to himself.

He stripped the sheets from his bed, folded them into his old pillowcase, and dressed for class. He wondered what the laundry man would think when he found the bloody sheets. When he left the room at 8:45, he placed the pillowcase containing the sheets outside his door so that the blood couldn't be seen by his dorm friends. The wound did not infect, and Cal never told anyone about the event.

CHAPTER THIRTY-FIVE

▼

Standing next to his illegally parked car behind the School of Theology, Cal looked at the dark windows of the vacant church history classroom in front of him. A streetlight on Fielding Drive reflected in one classroom window, and behind his back he could hear cars passing. As he unlocked his car, Cal looked up at the top floor row of dormitory windows and spotted his own darkened room. Only three windows were lighted in the whole dormitory, three students who had no Sunday evening church duties, studying. Cal remembered his recurring dream about this parking lot. *He couldn't find his car, so he walked over a bridge where nothing was familiar. The football field on the Cambridge shore was gone. There were no connecting roads to his hometown ten miles away.*

Cal got in his old Plymouth and pressed the starter. The battery whined and grew weaker in the late November cold, and he took his foot off the starter. On the third try the car whined weakly but started, and Cal backed away from the darkened building. He crossed through the regular parking lot, turned left then right, onto Memorial Avenue.

As he approached the light at the Harvard Bridge, it changed to red. He pushed the gearshift into neutral and waited. It was raining again. It seemed as if it rained every Sunday night as he drove to meet his Youth Group at the Presbyterian Church in Wellesley. The light changed and Cal headed up Memorial toward Brighton, thinking of Clare. Each time he drove this route he thought of Clare. Almost two years ago tonight she turned up at the church with another girl from Endicott Junior College.

Cal showed his Montana slides for the program, including pictures of himself stripped to the waist, chain sawing switch track ties for the Great Northern Railroad. Clare introduced herself at the end of the meeting and told Cal that the pictures were great. He had intercourse with her three weeks later, on the living room floor of her house in Wellesley, her parents asleep upstairs. When he saw Miss Green the following day, he was in a black guilt. She said, "What do you want me to do for you?"

Cal didn't answer. He felt that Miss Green was exasperated with him. Finally he said, "Just make it all clear to me." She looked at him and waited, and Cal knew that the life he had buried would be a long time coming clear.

Cal's worn wipers merely blurred his windshield, and it became difficult for him to see the road clearly. He debated whether to stop and wipe the windshield with his hand but he was afraid he'd make it worse and he kept driving, through Brighton, into Chestnut Hill. He passed the last MTA stop near Boston College, entered Newton and crossed into Wellesley. He had no program for the evening. The group would be bored with the planning session. He knew it was a fake program. He wondered where Clare was. Sometimes he fantasized that she'd turn up on Sunday night as if nothing had happened, still available. *Who are you kidding?*

Cal's inner voice talked roughly to him, exploiting every weakness he despised in himself. The voice lacerated Cal the theology student, *the goody goody boy who threw his Bible in the bushes on the way to sixth grade Wednesday Bible Class after school when he saw Carrie Wormstead approaching him on Pine Ridge Avenue.* Cal thought of Carrie as he drove through the rain. *Carrie must have seen him throw away his Bible. The next week she came to Bible class with Norma Brophy, and in the basement of the church at the end, the missionary woman from the hills of Kentucky asked all the children to close their eyes and raise their hand if they hadn't accepted Jesus Christ as their personal savior. Cal didn't know what that meant so he raised his hand. When he opened his eyes, the missionary woman asked Cal and Carrie, who was the only other one to raise her hand, to remain behind after the others left. In the back room behind the altar, Cal and Carrie had to repeat the words of the missionary woman that they accepted Jesus Christ as their personal Savior. Afterwards, Cal still didn't know what a personal savior was. He didn't ask the missionary woman because he knew she would keep him longer to talk about it and he wanted to get out of there.*

Outside, walking down the stairs together, Carrie asked Cal to teach her how to play football. The next afternoon he made Carrie tackle him running at her in the high grass across from MacWilliams' house, and he was amazed when she hit him head on at the knees several times. Cal himself did not like to tackle head on. Carrie was very brave. Cal did not give her any more lessons. Carrie's mother died of breast cancer the following spring. In Cal's senior year in high school, Fred Goodfellow told him that boys from Salem used to come to Carrie's house in the afternoon after school. Sometimes Carrie smoked cigarettes. She was always polite to Cal. The voice inside Cal hated the boy who decided Carrie was off limits.

In Wellesley, the rain turned to sleet and began to freeze on Cal's windshield. He rolled down his window a couple inches and turned the heat of his defroster as high as it would go. Before he arrived at the church, the sleet became snow and he had to stop twice and scrape the windshield.

When he drove into the church parking lot, four cars were already there, three together and one by itself. They were already covered by the white snow.

Inside the recreation room of the granite Presbyterian Church, two separate groups of young people were standing, talking quietly among themselves. When Cal entered, the first group of co-eds and young men waved and walked over to him: "Hey, Mr. Newsome, you made it. We didn't know if you'd come. We're supposed to get a big storm."

"Wouldn't miss it for the world. I've got a whole drawer of perfect attendance pins," Cal said, laying his coat on a chair against the wall, and ruffling the snow from his hair.

"Is that all we get for coming?" a tall girl wearing a short skirt and bangs said, smiling.

"Name your price, I aim to please," Cal said as four more students entered and walked over, exclaiming over the weather.

Cal pointed to a group of three young men who had remained by themselves, and said, "We've got some new people, great. Did you meet them?"

A young woman with high cheekbones and freckles, dressed in slacks and a sweater, with her scarf still wrapped around her neck, said, "We thought we'd wait for you. We know them, they're locals."

"Hey, that's great," Cal said. "Introduce me, Deborah." But Cal knew then that something new was entering his life. He smiled his best fake smile, and felt tiny muscles tighten in his chin and around his eyes.

Deborah untied and again tied her scarf, saying, "You do it, Regina, I used to know one of them a couple years ago."

"Sure, OK gang, come on Mr. Newsome, what the heck, we're all one big happy family, I'll do the honors," and Cal, still smiling, followed her to the three young men standing by the small stage with their winter jackets unzipped and their hats tucked in their back pants pockets.

"Hey guys, welcome," Cal said, extending his hand to each of them. "I'm Cal Newsome, and sort of in charge of this motley crew."

A short burly fellow with slicked-back blonde hair, wearing a heavy pullover jacket, extended his arm without taking a step and grasped Cal's hand. "I'm Jerry."

"Hi Jerry," Cal said and extended his hand to another short young man with a thin moustache and bright darting eyes.

"I'm Nate. Glad to meetcha." The word "meetcha" came out with a slight lisp, and Nathan looked up at the third fellow, and said, "This here is Vinnie. He used to know someone who used to come here, so we thought we'd drop over and see what's going on. We heard it was a good group with some things happening. Is that OK?"

"It sure is OK," Cal exclaimed, extending his hand to Vinnie, the tallest. Vinnie had deep brown eyes that looked at you, then away from you, then back at you, and a square jaw that barely moved when he talked, as if he had bad teeth and was hiding them.

Vinnie took half of Cal's hand in a way that prevented Cal from getting a firm grip, and nodded, smiling at Cal, as if he were making a connection. "Yeah, I used to know someone," he said.

"Great. Who was it?" Cal asked. "Maybe he'll start coming again." Cal knew exactly who Vinnie was looking for and he wondered how this was all going to play out."

"Maybe he will," Vinnie said, looking at Cal, looking at the floor, looking back at Cal again and smiling. Vinnie's teeth were as perfect as a Hollywood star's teeth after dental surgery.

Five more young people had arrived, stamping the snow from their shoes and throwing their wet coats on chairs.

"Come on over and meet the rest of the group," Cal said, urging the three musketeers to enter the civilized world of religion and culture and urbanity, but they weren't buying into urbanity tonight, or any night. Cal recognized Vinnie from Clare's description.

"We already know Gina here," Jerry said. "We knew her from before. Hey Geen, how's it going?"

"Hello Gerald. Hello Nathan. Hello Vincent." Regina curtsied to each. "We're honored by your visit. We hope you stay. We serve refreshments later."

"Come on Geen," Jerry said, a little too pleadingly, "Don't wise off on us, we're being respectable."

"We going to play spin the bottle, Gina?" Vinnie did his looking at and away thing with his eyes, and grinned at her. "Remember the good old days?"

"I remember, champ. Yes, we do that later too, only it's a grown up version," Regina said.

"Hey, whoa, no kidding?" Nate exclaimed.

Vinnie elbowed Nate hard enough to knock him off balance: "Don't play the fool for the queen, Nate. Lean Regeen the queen. She's smarter than us. In *her* kissing games, you don't touch."

"Not smarter Vinnie, only wiser. There's a time and a place, and in our circle, we do hold hands," Regina said.

Cal had been motioning for the rest of the young people to come over and join him and Regina and the musketeers, and they did. A short young man still wearing his earmuffs called out to Cal, "Mr. Newsome, it's supposed to snow harder, and all night. Maybe we should sleep here—does the church have blankets?"

"We'll check that out in a minute, Billy. Right now I want everyone to meet Nate and Vinnie and Jerry. Some of you know them. Make yourselves known to them while we draw straws for the piano-playing duty tonight. Is Millie here? OK, over there. Where's Rose Small? Not here. Sandra Braun? OK. Sandra, whose turn, you or Millie?"

Each Sunday night, before the main Youth League program, usually a movie or a speaker, Cal arranged for one of the young members to conduct a short worship service. Cal wanted it kept short enough to cover the basics, a prayer, a five-minute talk or reading, two verses of hymns at the beginning and end.

Cal was grateful for the service tonight because it gave him time to think, and he was also grateful for the snowstorm. Maybe he could escape the planning session. For the next few minutes, as Deborah conducted the service, Cal puzzled what to do about Vinnie and his boys. They were sitting directly behind Cal at the back of the group. Cal didn't want any trouble, but he knew that these guys could turn out to be bullies. He didn't want to be embarrassed in front of his Youth Group, and he didn't want to fight.

Growing up in his own neighborhood, Cal fought easily with Sonny St. Fleur and Frank Kendall when tauntings led to fists. He even got into a fight with Danny McIntyre from Maple Hills when Cal knocked to the ice Danny's younger brother Raymond in a hockey game on Hyacinth Pond when he was twelve. Yet when Cal went to the Junior High School in Mapleton Center, he backed down whenever challenged to any form of wrestling at lunchtime in the schoolyard. He remembered with shame the day Steve DeAngelo from Maple Hills started play-boxing with Cal as he was eating one of the sandwiches his mother had made that morning. Cal was sitting on the cement wall in front of the entrance to the auditorium, next to Roger Howland and Richie Brantley, when DeAngelo walked over from the hot dog cart on Autumn Street.

Steve always bought his lunch. His father owned a night club on route 1, and Steve smoked cigarettes. He was barrel-chested and big-toothed, with unkempt black hair down over his ears. He also played fullback on one of the seventh grade scrub football teams that played on the high school field at Bly Stadium on Saturday mornings. Steve often teased Cal about his ineffectual tackling.

"Hey Newsome," Steve called, as he approached Cal. Steve had yellow mustard on his upper lip from his hot dog. "How about a little friendly tackling practice?"

"No thanks, I got my good clothes on," Cal said, with a hollowness growing in his stomach.

Steve knew that Cal would back down, and it egged him on. Cal's reluctance to engage Steve in any sort of contest made Steve more aggressive. "C'mon," he said, how about a little wrestling match?"

"I'm eating my lunch, DeAngelo."

Richie Brantley said, "Leave him alone, DeAngelo, go bother someone else."

"Go bother someone else!" Steve said it in a singsong voice. "Who the hell asked you, Brantley? Fuck off."

Brantley said, "Fuck off yourself, DeAngelo. Pick on someone your own size. Pick on me."

"Aw," Steve said, "Cal's just my size, aren't you Cally Wally?" DeAngelo assumed a boxing stance, tilting his head to one side and patting Cal lightly on the cheek with his open palm. Come on, Newsome, show me something." He slapped Cal a little harder.

Cal said, "Cut it out, DeAngelo, I don't want to fight." Other seventh graders were watching, and Cal was embarrassed. He wanted to dive into DeAngelo and smash his mustardy mouth with his fist, but something inside him wouldn't let him do it. He couldn't take the risk. Someone would tell his mother. He might break something and he'd be held accountable. It would be his fault. He would be shamed.

Richie Brantley stepped between them and led Cal away from the group. Brantley and Howland walked Cal around the schoolyard. "God I hate Steve when he's like that." Brantley played on the same football team with Steve. "He doesn't have to be like that."

"I should have slugged him," Cal said. "I just didn't want to." Tears of shame and self-pity formed in Cal's eyes.

In the worship service, Deborah was reading from Kahlil Gibran's *Jesus the Son of Man:*

Take your harps and let me sing.
Beat your strings, the silver and the gold;
For I would sing the dauntless Man
Who slew the dragon of the valley,
Then gazèd down with pity
Upon the thing He had slain.

Behind him, Cal heard one of the musketeers giggle and say, "Beat your strings, Holy fuck." Another said "Shhhhh."

The minister, Rev. Breastburn, had entered from the door leading to the sanctuary, and was standing several feet away from Cal, just within Cal's line of vision, and Cal looked over and acknowledged him.

Breastburn was looking at Cal and acknowledged him in return, holding up one finger, as if to speak to Cal. Cal was sure that he had heard the remark, and wanted to speak to him about it.

They walked to the back of the room and Breastburn told Cal that the storm was getting worse: "I'm wondering, Cal, if you might consider dismissing the group early so everyone can get back home safely. The forecast is changing every half-hour. Now they're talking about a real old-fashioned Nor'easter. School closings for tomorrow are already being announced. What do you think?"

"Yeah, sure, I think so. I mean we ought to call it off, probably right now. No sense to wait. We're ready to do business tonight but all that can wait. We've got a pretty good turnout on a snowy night, but if we can get them here tonight, we sure can do it next time too. Thanks for coming in and telling me, I didn't hear the radio at all today. I spent the weekend in Braintree with Joe Stearns at his church, and I wasn't thinking about the weather. Thanks a lot. I'll do it right now. Deborah's at the end right now, and we can sing a hymn and call it off for tonight."

"I see you've got some new people here tonight, Cal. It's nice to see different styles and backgrounds here. You're obviously bringing our young people together. Keep up the good work. I'll be getting back to my study now." Breastburn made as if to tiptoe out of the room, back into the sanctuary.

The pompous prick, Cal thought. Back to his television set is what he means. Cal was certain Breastburn had heard the remark but was too chickenshit to mention it. Breastburn was everything Cal detested about the Church, and he hated himself for being one third in and two-thirds out of Breastburn's churchy life. Cal knew that he himself was a materialist, indulged his own carnality, used and tortured women, was unclean in spirit, and he was now hating and fearing Breastburn and hating and fearing these three thugs ten feet away from him.

He waved his arm to catch Deborah's eye.

"Yes, Mr. Newsome?" she called.

"Deborah, thank you," he said, then to everyone, "I just want to say that Reverend Breastburn has just advised me that the storm is getting even worse than all of us and the weather bureau expected, and that the best thing might be to call off tonight's program. I urge all of you to get in your cars and go straight home. The plow's are out in full force and it ought to be safe for a while yet. Thank you all for coming, and see you next week. I'll check my calendar and see who's in charge of the worship service and be in touch with you during the week. God bless."

As coats were retrieved and put on, and the young people left for their cars, calling shouts of goodbye to Cal and other friends, the three musketeers lingered, obviously waiting to talk to Cal.

Cal played it out with his cheerful good-bye to each departing student, knowing he couldn't avoid whatever it was that the rest of the evening promised for him.

Regina, however, smelled the three rats that were ready to slip into the empty barn, and she lingered close to Cal as he pretended to gather his papers and straighten out the temporary lectern: "Mr. Newsome, how about if I stick around until these creeps leave? They're not hanging around to be baptized. I know them from another life."

As Cal was saying, "No, Gina, it's under control—get yourself home," they were standing next to him.

"I got a question for you, Rev." It was Vinnie, who looked directly at Cal, at Regina, and back at Cal. "Something struck me, what you said, so I thought I'd ask you about it, OK?"

Cal nodded. "Sure."

"Yeah, good. Well, it probably sounds kinda funny, but I remember, when I was in school the teacher always told us if you don't know, look it up. Right?"

"Right. But Regina was just leaving and I don't want her to miss her bus, so. . ."

"Hey Rev, there's no buses, hold your water, we'll take care of the queen. She's ridden in our bus before, so she's comfortable, right Geen?"

"You guys are so full of shit." Regina was almost as tall as Vinnie and she looked him in the eyes. "What do you want Vinnie? Spill it before your breath starts a fire in a decent place."

"Touchy baby! Such language from a queen! I heard you got lady bodyguards, Rev, now I see it's the actual." He moved closer to Regina.

"Quit talking like one of the Gangbusters, Vinnie. You sound like an idiot. Actually, you are an idiot." Regina reached out to push Vinnie away from her.

"OK sweetcrotch, if you want to disabuse baby face of the myths about the counter culture, it suits me. If the apprentice reverend doesn't want the first question, we can give him the second."

"No," Cal said, "Let's have the first question. I'm curious."

"I'll bet you are, pureboy, I'll bet you are. I'd just like you to define a word you used, that's all, you with your happy talk, juicing up to the black jackets before the prayer hour. Mr. Fellowship and his 'motley' crew. Is that what they teach you in the seminary these days? Words like 'motley'? They ought to call it the "*semen-airy*," but I'll get to that in a minute. No, I changed my mind, I'll let that go. But I'll tell you something baby boy, you don't greet the representatives of the other side with throwaway talk like 'This is a motley crew.' Don't talk cocktail hour cliché bullshit. 'Motley' means different kinds of colors, but it also means clowns. It's fancy-face talk and it's bullshit. Let me make it clear. I don't give a flying fuck how you talk, but you're what I thought you were, a fake, and it pisses me off that you faked out Clare. Where is she, you piss ant?"

"So that's it," Cal said.

"Yeah, that's it, and you knew it was it before you tried to breeze us, but you didn't have the balls to talk straight to yourself."

Regina shouted, "For heaven's sake Vinnie, what do you think to gain by this? Clare hasn't been here for weeks. You're acting like a henchman of the mafia. This is a church!"

"Where is she, Pureface?"

"I don't know. I haven't seen her for weeks myself."

"Vincent," Regina shouted, "Leave this place now or I'll go and get Reverend Breastburn."

"Reverend Breastburn, huh? That's good. That's his real name? Boy, this is right out of a book."

Regina began to walk toward the sanctuary door and Vinnie said, "Take her, Jerry."

Regina started to run and Jerry tackled her into the first row of chairs.

"Just be yourself, OK Geen?" Jerry said to Regina. She had hit her head and a thin stream of blood crawled out of her hairline, down her forehead. She touched her forehead and saw the blood on her fingers: "Nice, Jerry old childhood buddy, really nice!"

"I'm sorry Gina, but we got to stick together here. It may be a long night." Jerry said it loud enough for all to hear.

"What do you guys want?" Cal shouted.

"Keep it down, Pureface, or you'll find out sooner than later," Vinnie said. "It's good and simple, just like the Amish. You're supposed to know about these things. You've heard of Intercourse, haven't you? Theology students are supposed to know their geography: Intercourse, Pennsylvania, right down the street from Bird in Hand. I used to live in that vicinity. I know all about Intercourse and Bird in Hand. I think you know all about them too, Pureface."

"I want you guys to leave Regina alone and get out of this church," Cal said.

"There's a storm outside, haven't you heard, Pureface? Stop talking like a goddamn Boy Scout."

Regina was standing up, holding her wrist against her forehead. Jerry stood next to her. "Don't touch me again, you creep," she said.

"I'm not touching you, Gina, just don't make with the feet, OK?

"I can outrun you any day of the week, and you know it."

"But you got to open that door before you get through it, and you won't make it. Old Firechest is in another country drinking pineapple juice and watching Ed Sullivan."

"Cut the crap talk," Vinnie said. "We're going. You can come without the mouth, Gina, or we'll shut your mouth, you choose."

"What do you think you're going to do, just walk out of here with the two of us?" Cal pleaded, "This is a civilized community. We can identify you, unless you kill us. Are you going to kill us? For God's sake man, tell me what you want."

"Maybe to the questions, Pureface. I asked you where Clare is. Tell me or we go out and have a snowball fight in the parking lot."

"I'm not lying to you. I haven't seen her for weeks. She won't see me. She broke up with me. I'd tell you where she is if I knew. I've got no reason not to."

"Yeah, maybe, but I don't like this room. I prefer snowstorms. Jerry, you escort Gina. Gina, you can put on your coat like a good girl or you can freeze your ass, it's up to you. Same for you, Pureface. Let's go."

Regina and Cal put on their coats and walked out to the parking lot. The snow was coming down in silver dollars, and the two cars were covered by two inches of snow.

"Last chance, Pureface, where is she?" Vinnie asked.

"On my word of honor, I don't know," Cal said. Gina was standing next to him, and she looked dazed. She put her hand out to Cal to steady herself. "Tell him, Mr. Newsome, what have you got to lose," she said.

"I would, but I don't know," Cal said. He visualized what it would be like to butt Vinnie with his head and start a free for all, but the image passed. He didn't think that they would hurt Regina, but he was afraid. The voice said, *what are you afraid of? Hit the bastard. Let go for the first time in your life!* But Cal didn't do it. He waited, and was ashamed.

"You make me sick," Vinnie said. "You won't even fight for the queen here. And she's a good skirt. She's got balls. You're a fucking eunuch. You can have your fucking church and your youth groupies, but I'm going to find Clare, and if I ever find out that you're sucking around her again, you won't enjoy what I'm going to do, I guarantee it. Regina, I can see you don't have a car. You want to come with us? We'll take you home, or you can stay with this queer. Whatever you say. Which?"

"I'll stay," Regina said quietly. "You're a bunch of pigs."

"Whatever," Vinnie said, and walked to his car. Jerry and Nate followed him.

CHAPTER THIRTY-SIX

▼

"MILLION CHINESE DEAD FROM CHOLERA AND FAMINE; PRESIDENT
ROOSEVELT ELECTED TO UNPRECENTED FOURTH TERM," *Daily Evening
Item,* Nov. 7, 1944

With each run of the toboggan, the long sloping hill became snow-
packed and faster, and as the boys grinned and tried to upset the balance
of the long leather-seated toboggan-sled, the girls shrieked and counter-
balanced their weights to keep it stable. At the bottom of each run and
during the deep snow staggerings back up the hill, there were snow fights
and pulled scarves and tacklings, and a few stolen wet kisses.

"We saw you Betty," Fran Burnside shouted to her cousin in a teasing,
sing song voice, "Wait'll Paul hears about this."

"You didn't see anything," Betty shouted back in the same singsong
tone, biting a mouthful of snow from the pile in her hand and throwing
it in Fran's direction. "Besides, Paul doesn't exist any more and we can
forget about *him.* As she said "*him,*" she pushed a mitten full of snow in
Billy Warden's face and started running. Billy stumbled after her in the
deep snow and fell down. He couldn't catch Betty until she fell down and
pretended she was stuck in the snow. He tugged on her arm until she got
up and they hiked up the hill together.

Cal and his eighth grade friends were alone on the state reservation
in Melrose on a Saturday afternoon in February. Fran's father had driven
them there after a lunch at the Burnside's house on Sigourney Street.
They had unloaded the long toboggan from the top of Mr. Burnside's

Packard beach wagon, and been left together for the rest of the afternoon. They were all excited to be together and to be in an isolated area where they didn't have to contend with skiers and children on sleds. They had already made several trips down the hill, and some of the thrill had worn off. They began to realize that they were tired.

Fran and Cal followed Betty and Billy up the hill. By now everyone had paired off. There were four couples, but only six people could fit on the toboggan at one time. Fran turned to Cal and said, "Betty likes Billy. Isn't this grand? I wish we could stay here and camp out all winter."

"And your father would bring us meals and a big tent, right?"

"Sure he would. Why not? He does everything for me. He even stays married to my mother for me."

Cal pretended he didn't hear what she said.

"What time is your father coming to pick us up? I just remembered that my mother told me to be home by five o'clock. I'll get in trouble if I'm not."

"I shocked you, didn't I? I'm sorry, it just slipped out. Come on, Cal, don't go home. Don't be a kill-joy, we're going to have a party at my house tonight. You can call your mother when we get home."

"Gee, I can't Fran, remember I asked you when we'd be home when you called me?"

"I didn't know your mother was so strict. My mother says stuff like that all the time, but she doesn't mean it when the time comes. What're another few hours? *I* know. I *scared* you when I said that about my father and my mother. Never mind me when I say that stuff. My mother drinks is all, and my father hates to be around her. It's all bubbullshubbit."

"What's that?"

"You never heard it? It's just a way of talking in code. Betty and I call it pig Latin, but we don't know if that's what pig Latin is. Do you know?"

"No, *I* don't know. What's *bubbullshubbit* mean?

"Just take out all the ubb syllables, and what's left?"

Cal thought about it. "Yeah, I get it. Pretty good."

"My mother doesn't let us swear but she can't figure out the code. She can't figure anything out. She thinks Betty and I talk in riddles."

"Betty's your cousin, isn't she? Billy told me."

"Lubbets gubbo obbuvubber thubbe hubbillub abbund nubbevubber cubbomubbe bubbacubbuk."

"I'm slow, Fran. Can you say it again?"

"Sure. Lubbets gubbo obbuvubber thubbe hubblillub abbund nubbevubber cubbomubbe bubbacubbuk."

They heard shouts, and the toboggan was coming straight at them. Marilyn Branfield and Nickie Serino were calling to them: "Clear the way! We're coming through!" Fran and Cal jumped aside and tossed palmsfull of snow at them as they went by.

Cal was embarrassed not to be able to decipher what Fran had said: "I'm slow, Fran, I'll have to study it on paper."

"It's OK. Just as well. I was only kidding anyway."

"When *is* your father coming?"

"Just before dark. Probably around four."

"That's swell. I'll have plenty of time to get home if he'll give me a ride."

"Of course he'll give you a **ride**, Cal, do you think he'd make you walk home? But not at four, OK? Promise."

Cal was too embarrassed to answer, so he made two lightly packed snowballs, tossed one up in the air so that it would come down on Fran, and as she watched it he threw the other, hitting her on the shoulder.

"Hey, that's a dirty trick," she laughed, "but it's pretty good. I'll get you for that." She ran at Cal and tried to grapple him to the ground. Cal kept his balance and gently threw her down twice before she said, "You're too strong. I know when I'm beat. Let's help Nicky and Marilyn pull the toboggan up the hill."

By three-thirty it was snowing again, and the toboggan track slowed down as the flakes fell. By four o'clock, another couple inches of snow had accumulated, and the hill was getting too slippery to walk up. Everyone was tired. They sat in close pairs at the top of the hill overlooking the road.

"My father will be here any minute," Fran said.

By four-thirty the wind picked up and the hill on which they sat seemed to be at the center of a blizzard. The eight tobogganers sat with their faces shielded by crossed arms.

"Maybe he got stuck," Jimmy Hunt said.

"I hope he told someone we're here," Marilyn Branfield said.

"He's not stuck and a lot of people know we're here," Fran said.

"Like who?" Candace Worthington asked.

"Like her mother," Betty said.

"Yeah, like my mother," Fran said, unconvincingly. "But Phoebe knows where we are, I'll bet a million dollars."

"Who's Phoebe?" Billy asked.

"Phoebe Barclay," Fran said. She's my father's secretary. She knows every minute where he is."

"I'm freezing, Francis," Betty said. "I'm getting off this hill. It'll be less windy down by the road."

"I'll go with you," Billy said.

"C'mon, let's all go," Jimmy said.

Billy pushed the empty toboggan before them and it picked up speed as it continued to the bottom of the hill, crashing into a green waste barrel at the *cul de sac* where Mr. Burnside had dropped them off. When they reached the toboggan, Billy examined it and said it wasn't damaged.

"That's all we'd need," Betty said.

"Come on Bet, buck up," Fran said. "It'll be nice and warm at home and we'll all feel good."

"I am going to be cold for three days," Betty said.

At five o'clock the wind suddenly quieted down and the snow became large wet flakes. Within a few minutes it was raining. Then the rain stopped. Lightning and a loud crack of thunder were followed by another lightning bolt and a louder crack of thunder.

"What a freako day," Billy said.

"That's one word for it," Betty said. "I can think of another."

"Betty!" Fran said.

"It's five-twenty," Candace said. "Let's all think *Phoebe*, real hard."

"Come on everybody, say *Phoebe, Phoebe*," Nickie said.

All but Fran chanted *Phoebe, Phoebe*, together.

"I don't know what to say, guys, I'm sorry," Fran said.

"Don't say anything," Billy said, "Here he comes. There're the headlights, just making the turn."

"Good old dad," Betty said.

"Betty, I'm going to tell Aunt Chris," Fran said.

"Oh god, tell her, she'll be glad to hear it, I'm sure."

"Well, be human."

"Human? That's what I want to be. You call this human? If Phoebe's in that car, I'll die."

They all watched the headlights coming closer, and stood waiting like large wet dolls in a Roman pantomime.

The long Packard beach wagon came to a stop before them, and the driver's window rolled down. Mr. Burnside grinned at them and said, "Taxi?"

"What's the fare, Mr. Burnside?" Jimmy Hunt asked. "We might have to wait for the bus. In the meantime, we'll load the toboggan on top."

Fran was standing beside the open window, studying her father's face, wondering whether to say anything. She decided not to, and opened the first back door and told Betty and Candace to get in. Then she followed them. Betty went around the car and got in the front seat with Mr. Burnside.

"Afternoon, Betty," he said. "You're going to join me up front? That's my girl."

"You're welcome." Betty pushed over next to Mr. Burnside and glanced over to see if the flask was in the open pocket of the driver's door. She couldn't see it. "Since Phoebe isn't here, I thought I'd keep us on schedule by riding shotgun with you."

Fran reached over and drilled Betty in the shoulder with her finger. Betty absorbed the blow, which hurt, without a word.

"Phoebe?" Ben Burnside said. He turned his head to Betty. "You have Phoebe on your mind?"

"It's nothing daddy," Fran said from the first back seat, "We were just having some fun while we were waiting. I told everybody not to worry about you picking us up because Phoebe would know where we were. I explained that Phoebe is your appointments secretary, and she was very efficient."

"Thank you Elizabeth, my own," Ben Burnside said, looking at Betty. "Are we all square on that, my good sister's daughter?"

"I didn't mean anything, Uncle Ben, I'm just cold. We were freezing before you got here."

The boys were piling into the second back seat. Billy said, "Raise the mainsail, Captain, the anchor's up and the gear's stowed. We're shipshape except the wind seems to have died."

"Very well, Ensign Warden, thank you. As for you, Quartermaster Hunt, we seemed to have changed vehicles. We've reduced the fare because the buses do not run on this line. Do you approve?"

"I approve sir, humbly and heartily. Let's get the hell out of here, sir," Jimmy called out from the back of the beach-wagon.

Ben Burnside chuckled and maneuvered the beach wagon out of the *cul de sac*, onto the winding road leading out of the state reservation.

Cal had pushed in next to Betty in the front seat and sat in silence. He knew he was in trouble but he didn't want to appear to give Mr. Burnside orders.

"I presume the destination is Sigourney Street," he said, stopping for a red light at the intersection of route 1 in Mapleton.

"We're pretty wet on the outside daddy," Fran said, "and mummy's preparing dinner, so that would be great."

Cal knew that he had to speak up: "Mr. Burnside, sir, I apologize for bringing it up, and I apologize that you have to go out of your way, but I have a problem. I have to be home as soon as possible, if it's convenient, sir. Could you drop me off maybe? I would like very much to go to Sigourney Street, but I have to be home tonight. I promised my mother I would be home, and I don't want to let her down, Sir."

"That's no problem, son. We are now the Mapleville Express. I'll just make a left turn here and then a right and we can glide down Beechnut Street and get you home in elegant Mapleville in a jiffy."

"Gee, thanks."

"Not at all."

Fran remained silent in the back seat.

Eight minutes later, the beach wagon stopped in front of Cal's home on Pine Ridge Avenue.

"Thank you Mr. Burnside. Thanks for driving me home. Thanks Fran, I had a great time. So long everybody. See you in school on Monday."

Everyone said goodbye, and Ben Burnside slid the shift, grinding it a little, into first gear and drove off.

Cal ran up the driveway. He saw that his father's car was not there. There were no lights in the living room. He opened the cellar door to the landing and the stairs that led up to the kitchen, and was met by his mother and his aunt coming down. They had their coats on.

"You're late," his mother said, brushing past him.

"We waited an hour," his aunt said, also brushing past him.

"Where are you going?" Cal asked.

"We're going to Sassone's for dinner and we're going to the show. We've got fifteen minutes to get to the bus."

"Can I go?"

"No you can't go," his mother said. "Judith and I have planned this for a month. It was going to be a surprise for your birthday next week. You said you'd be back. We don't have time for you to change."

"Where's daddy?"

"He's at the annual meeting at the shop. He'll be late."

"It'll take me five minutes!"

"Maybe you'll try harder next time to get home when I tell you," his mother said. They were hurrying down the driveway.

Cal couldn't believe that they were really going to leave him. But they were gone. His mother never did anything like this before. He stood on the landing in his wet clothes. They were going to the show in Lynn and he was left alone on Saturday night. He took off his overshoes and mounted the four steps, turned the doorknob and entered the empty kitchen. The light was on but the room was very quiet. There was no supper. He was alone in the house.

CHAPTER THIRTY-SEVEN

▼

"FIRE AT RINGLING BROS. BARNUM & BAILEY CIRCUS IN HARTFORD, CONNECTICUT KILLS 107, *Daily Evening Item*, July 6, 1944.

Cal took off his mackinaw and his snow pants and carried them into the back pantry and hung them on a hook. *They left me alone.*

Cal opened the door to the cupboard and took out the Aunt Jemima pancake batter. He opened the Frigidaire and took out a bottle of MacAdams milk and an egg and the white coffee cup half full of bacon grease. He opened the oven door and took out the iron frying pan his Uncle Nate called a spider. He emptied one cup of flour, one cup of milk, a half-teaspoon of salt, and a pinch of baking powder between his fingers into a red glass bowl. He broke the egg on the side of the bowl and dropped it in. He heated two tablespoons of bacon fat, one at a time, in a large stainless steel spoon and emptied the spoon into the mixture. Then he beat everything together with the spoon.

Cal took a wooden match from the box on the wall beside the big stove with the kerosene burners, lit the gas stove next to it, and placed the iron frying pan over the blue flames. He scooped and then shook two more tablespoons of bacon fat into the skillet and watched it melt and then begin to sputter and spit, turned the gas jet to medium and scooped three separate portions of batter into the skillet. The batter was thick, but it spread into round, flat cakes that began to rise slightly. Two of the pancakes merged before the batter cooked. Bubbles formed on the edges, then in the middle of the pancakes. Cal turned the gas jet to low, then eased a metal spatula under the pancakes and turned them over. The edges of the pancakes sizzled, and little wisps of steam rose from the collapsing bubbles as the last of the uncooked batter in the center of the pancakes cooked through, then Cal slid each one onto a plate with the spatula. He made nine pancakes, finishing the batter. He put the batter bowl in the sink and filled it with water to soak.

Cal sat at the kitchen table and ate the pancakes in stacks of three, several times pouring Log Cabin maple syrup over the top of each pile. He drank a glass of milk as he ate the pancakes. When he was finished eating, he drew hot water in the sink and washed and dried the dishes and put them away. Then he didn't know what to do. Nothing good was on the radio until Gangbusters came on at eight and then Inner Sanctum at nine.

Cal was still angry and hurt. He moved one of the kitchen chairs over to the dish and glass cupboard and stood on it, reaching his hand to the back of the top shelf where he felt the tiny whiskey glass. He went to the Frigidaire in the pantry and got the Pale Dry ginger ale bottle. It was two thirds full. He sat at the kitchen table and poured himself a shot of ginger ale. He threw it down, then another. Cal pretended to get drunk, to let it all go, say the hell with it all, punish them, throwing his life to abandon. He would show them. He drank ten straight shots of pale dry ginger ale.

He sat at the kitchen table, bored. They could have waited five minutes. *Then they would have all missed the 6:20 bus.* They could have told him they were going to take him to the show. Cal thought of throwing a chair across the room. He wanted to be reckless. He wanted to show his mother and aunt that he meant business, that they couldn't just leave him out of things. He wanted to break something valuable and hurt them, show them that they couldn't trifle with him. But that would get him in trouble.

Cal remembered his rabbit. He hadn't thought of the rabbit for weeks. "Maybe it's dead," he thought. "Poor Bingo. I better check."

Cal got his wet mackinaw from the pantry and put it on. He took the flashlight from the commode drawer in the dining room and sat on the first step above the cellar door landing, putting on his overshoes. He walked along the driveway and slipped between the lilacs and the side of the garage to the rabbit coop. He shone the light into the cage.

Bingo was huddled in the corner of his coop, his head buried against his shoulder. The coop was empty of food. The wooden partitions next to the wire floor had been gnawed. One place had been gnawed two inches deep. Cal shone the light to Bingo's feet. His toenails were an inch long. Holding the flashlight, Cal's hand was freezing. Cal reached in the cage to pat Bingo. When he touched the rabbit, it jumped. Cal felt the bony backbone with no flesh underneath the skin. Bingo did not open his eyes.

Cal went back into the house and opened the Frigidaire. The vegetable tray contained half a bunch of celery and several slightly wizened carrots without the tops. He looked in the bottom drawer and found four potatoes. Cal took the celery, the carrots, and the potatoes and went back to the rabbit cage where Bingo was still huddled in the corner with closed eyes. Cal put the food next to Bingo but he didn't move. He took a potato and held it up to Bingo's nose and mouth. Bingo began to gnaw the potato as Cal held it for him. Bingo's long front teeth protruded like fangs. When Cal put the potato down on the wire floor of the cage, Bingo remained stationary, huddled in the corner. Cal tried again with the potato, and realized that he was freezing cold himself. He tried to bend Bingo's head down to the mound of fresh vegetables, but Bingo wouldn't move. Cal tried a carrot and Bingo gnawed, but he wouldn't follow the carrot down to the bottom of the cage if Cal took it away from Bingo's mouth. Cal tried the celery. Cal was freezing cold and he closed the door to Bingo's cage and went back into the house.

If Bingo dies, it's my fault. I haven't fed him and he's alone and he's going to die. Cal wondered what movie his mother and sister went to see.

Cal looked at the clock on the wall in the kitchen. It was seven-twenty. Nothing's on except the Answer Man, Cal thought.

Cal looked around the living room for the *Lynn Item* but he couldn't find it. He flicked on the front porch light and opened the front door. The folded paper was on the floor of the porch. Back in the living room, Cal spread the paper on the living room rug and knelt down, turning the pages until he came to the funnies. He scanned down to "Dickie Dare." Dickie and Dan were in a diving bell on the ocean floor. Bad men with breathing masks were swimming close, intent on cutting their air hose. Dickie could see a huge octopus through the window, its tentacles winding around the diving bell. He would have to wait until tomorrow to find out what happened. Cal moved his eyes up to Terry and the Pirates. Chinese men naked to the waist with ropes around their necks were wading in the dark to a cabin cruiser. Two bald Orientals with scarves around their necks, holding machetes, stood on the prow of the boat. Terry and three men in white clothes watched from trees in the swamp, pistols in their hands.

Cal turned the pages of the paper. He found the daily serial about Eddie Rickenbacker on the raft in the Pacific Ocean. Cal started to read. A seagull landed on Eddie's head and he slowly reached up and grabbed it. Eddie and the other pilot ate the sea gull raw. It was all the food they had for 54 days. They even swallowed the seagull's blood because they knew it was good for them. Then it rained and they soaked their shirts and squeezed the water into their mouths.

Cal checked the clock in the kitchen and it was already five past eight. He turned on the radio and moved the dial to *Gangbusters*. The man telling the story had a deep voice, and he told about two detectives who were trapped in a warehouse on the waterfront after they discovered a gang who had kidnapped a man from a bank. Cal listened to the sounds of creaking boards and men running on wooden planks and guns going off, and got scared. He turned off the living room lights so no one outside the house could see him sitting in the big stuffed chair next to the radio. When he turned off the lights, he thought he heard a sound upstairs. He wished his father would come home.

When *Gangbusters* ended, Cal thought about going to bed but he was afraid to go upstairs. He turned the station to *Inner Sanctum*, but as soon as he heard the creaking door at the beginning he got scared and crawled behind the couch. He stayed there in the dark all through the program, wondering why somebody didn't come home.

The next thing he knew, he heard his mother's voice. "Caleb! Caleb! Wake up! What on earth are you doing behind this couch? We've been looking for you for fifteen minutes. Why didn't you go to bed? Do you hear me, wake up! Wake UP, you foolish boy. This is what you get, you hear me?"

When he awoke in the morning, he wondered what day it was. Then he remembered the night before, and that it was Sunday. I have to go to Sunday school, he thought.

Cal dressed and quietly opened the door to the hall and listened. No one was up yet. He walked carefully on the sides of the stairs so they wouldn't creak, put on his almost-dry mackinaw, and went out to Bingo's cage. He looked in and Bingo was stretched out along the back of the cage behind the pile of celery and carrots and potatoes. He looked asleep. Cal opened the door to the cage and reached in to feel Bingo. He was cold and stiff.

A week later Cal told his mother that Bingo had frozen to death.

"The poor little thing," she said.

"Yeah, I know, Cal said.

CHAPTER THIRTY-EIGHT

▼

The snow fell heavily as Cal and Regina stood and watched the three young men disappear into their Chevrolet convertible. Un-melted flakes turned Cal's and Regina's hair white as the snow on their faces melted, and water formed on their eyebrows and dripped from their chins, and they waited.

"They can't possibly leave without wiping some of that snow off their windshield," Regina said. "Then again, they're capable of anything."

Their Chevrolet battery groaned for several seconds and the motor started.

"Let's go back in," Cal said. "We should have that cut on your head checked."

"By Breastburn? I don't think so."

"No, but I can look at it."

"Not until they leave."

"The Chevrolet idled for a minute and the headlights came on. The car backed up and turned. Huge falling snowflakes glistened in the headlights, then the car stopped and the headlights went out.

"Oh oh," Cal said, "They changed their mind. Come on, let's go back inside."

"Wait, this'll be interesting. Vinnie will be furious. I bet I know what's happening."

"What?"

"I've worked on cars since I was in junior high. They blew a fuse."

"How do you know that?"

"They must have turned on their windshield wipers with all that snow on the windshield and the wipers couldn't move, so the fuse burned out. They're going to need a fuse and a flashlight or they'll be in this parking lot all night."

"Can't they work the wipers by hand?"

"In this snow? Not unless Vinnie sits Jerry on the hood. He better have an extra fuse. Watch."

Both doors of the Chevrolet opened at once, and Vinnie and Jerry began rubbing their arms up and down against the side windows, trying to brush away as much snow as possible. Jerry lifted the windshield wipers away from the windshield and brushed his arms across the snow-covered glass.

"I've got a flashlight in my car," Cal said.

"Try offering it to Vinnie and I won't predict what he'll tell you to do with it."

"Probably."

"You want odds?"

The lights of the car brightened again and the Chevrolet eased through the snow out of the parking lot and disappeared.

"C'mon," Cal said, taking Regina's arm. "Let's look at your head. They'll have a hard time finding an open gas station tonight."

"Let's hope so. Why don't we just bag the going back in and go to Howard Johnson's or some place where it's quiet."

"I could take you to Newton-Wellesley Hospital to emergency out-patient, just to make sure."

"That's very nice, Mr. Newsome, but you can feel my head if you want. I've got a bump, that's no lie, but the bleeding stopped, and I'm not going to die. I'm OK, trust me. Jerry got the worst of that tackle, believe me."

"He didn't look hurt to me."

"He's got a lot of pride. I kneed him square in the balls a split second after we hit the chairs. Sorry about the language, but I got him. This hasn't been my most successful religious night."

"Let's see if my car will start."

"Right on."

"Pray for my battery."

"Not you too. I was really afraid Nickie's car wouldn't start."

"That wasn't Vinnie's Chevvy?"

"It could be. Nickie owes Vinnie enough, but Vinnie prefers to ride in other people's cars."

"You know a lot about those guys."

"I ought to. I told you I used to run with them."

Cal was intrigued by Regina, and he was both attracted and intimidated by her openness. "Howard Johnson's it is," Cal said. He unlocked his car and opened the door for Regina.

She said, "I'll get the windows."

"Wait, I got a brush." He searched on the floor in front of the back seat until he touched the yellow plastic bristles under the front seat.

He crawled back outside to give the brush to Regina but she had already scraped the snow from the front windshield with her bare hand. "Get the back," she said. "This is OK."

After three tries, Cal's car started. "Do I dare to turn on the wipers?" he asked.

"Give them a whirl, I got most of it."

The wipers brushed back and forth easily. Cal pulled out onto Romandale Avenue and drove past the church. "Bye Bye Breastburn," he said.

"Do I hear a little irony in your lyrics?"

"Well, just about as much, I guess, as you could fully appreciate."

"We don't have to go to Howard Johnson's, you know."

Cal didn't answer for several minutes. The snow was still falling heavily, and the road was visible ahead for only fifty yards. The tires of Cal's car were slipping at twenty-five miles an hour.

"I don't know if I can get back to school tonight or not," Cal said.

"You can stay at my house. My mother is a good woman and a good sport."

"I'm supposed to wax and buff the cafeteria floor before tomorrow morning."

"Excuses, excuses."

"Yeah, I know. I'm not very courageous, am I?"

"I don't know, aren't you? That's not the word I would have used."

"What word *would* you use?" Cal turned at the route 30 cut-off and headed slowly down Fairchild Street. Howard Johnson's was five blocks away.

"This is a little bit incredible, you know, I'm not the Lucy type in Charlie Brown, but it's hard to believe that you and I are alone together and we're talking like normal people. How did this happen?" Regina said.

"I don't know. Why is it incredible? We're just here. We got up this morning and ate breakfast and did stuff and I drove out here and you came to Youth League and we're here."

"Boy, your view of fate isn't mine. Do you know how many times I've fantasized about something like this?"

"What do you mean 'something'?"

"'Something' is close enough. I'm glad to be here."

Cal pulled into the Howard Johnson's parking lot. "Now we're here too," he said.

"It may be my imagination, but it looks a little dark inside."

"I'll check. Be right back."

Regina looked at Cal, watching him pretend that he didn't know that Howard Johnson's was closed. Cal waded through the snow, which was now three or four inches deep, and tried the locked door. He waded back to the car and sat back in his seat.

"Well," he said, "Howard Johnson's is closed for the night. Can you believe it?"

"I'm flabbergasted."

"You're making fun of me. Let's get back to 'something.'"

"Now? In Howard Johnson's parking lot while it's snowing? Mr. Newsome, you don't know where you're going to sleep tonight?"

"I'm not very practical, I guess."

"As I said, that's not the word I'd use, Mr. Newsome."

"So, are you going to tell me the word you would use?"

"May I suggest something?"

"Sure."

"Tomorrow morning's headline: COUPLE FOUND DEAD IN HOWARD JOHNSON PARKING LOT. You know, carbon monoxide and all that?"

"If I take you home, and your mother sees your head, she'll think we run a pretty rough program at the Church."

"Ah, my mother."

"I know what I want to do."

"But?"

"I'm very shy."

"I forgot my violin, Mr. Newsome—I apologize for that. It was flip."

"I deserved it. I'm Cal, I'm not Mr. Newsome, or Reverend Newsome, or any Newsome. And you're right, I'm faking a little."

"Mr. Newsome, I mean 'Cal,' if you want, life doesn't have to be complicated. You walked around Clare for weeks. We all watched it. It was so painful."

"You all watched it? Everyone knew?"

"No, not everyone, just some of us. Actually, a couple of us, Debbie and me, mostly me."

They sat quietly for several minutes and Cal started the engine and pulled out of the Howard Johnson parking lot.

CHAPTER THIRTY-NINE

▼

"PRESIDENT ROOSEVELT DIES SUDDENLY AT WARM SPRINGS, GEORGIA," *Daily Evening Item,* April 12, 1945.

Cal's mother parked in Market Square in front of Lynn City Hall and told Cal she had to do some errands while he went to his dentist appointment with Dr. Treadwell across the square, and she would meet him there. After that she wanted to talk to him before they went to pick up his father at the River Works. It was mid-Friday afternoon and Cal knew what her errands were, because they were always the same. She would walk down Market Street and go into Kresge's five and ten cents store and buy a quarter pound of Spanish peanuts, then go in the Lynn Five and Ten Cents Savings bank and weigh herself on the big scale at the back of the bank before she deposited money from Cal's father's weekly salary envelope. Then she would shop at J.B. Blood's Market on Commercial Street, always a pound of hamburger, two pounds of corned beef, and sometimes a pint of raw oysters. She would get a can of Spam and the rest of the stuff at the Co-op store in Mapleville at the bottom of Spruce Avenue.

Cal thought about his mother. He crossed the square, opened the heavy glass door with the square brass handles, and stepped onto the smooth marble floor of the entranceway. He walked slowly up the marble stairs. He didn't know what she wanted to talk to him about, but it wasn't good, whatever it was. Whenever she said she wanted to talk to him about something, it was bad news because she had been thinking about it. It must be something she was thinking about in the car on the way to Lynn, and had decided to face him with it. He had done something wrong, he was sure of it, but he didn't know what it was.

Walking up the stairs of the Bellview Building to Dr. Treadwell's office on the third floor, the smell distracted him from whatever he had done wrong. He hated the building because it smelled like the dentist office. Treadwell would use the drill today. He would dig out the temporary filling and drill some more, and it would hurt. There was nothing Cal could do about it, and he kept climbing the stairs. His mother told him that one time Dr. Treadwell pulled a live nerve out of her front tooth when she was a young girl and she fainted in the chair.

Cal opened the opaque glass door with Dr. Treadwell's name in black, OLIVER TREADWELL, D.D.S., into a large room with several chairs and a small table piled with out of date magazines, and sat down. He could see Dr. Treadwell in a smaller room, looking up from somebody's mouth, nodding to him. Cal sat down and tried to think of something he had done wrong.

Later, as Treadwell was lightly tamping a warm temporary filling he had just squeezed into Cal's molar cavity, he looked up and nodded and Cal knew that his mother was in the waiting room. After Treadwell's assistant unclasped the cloth napkin around his neck and pushed the tray aside, Cal slowly spun out of the chair and walked over and waited beside his mother while she paid the bill at the assistant's desk. They walked down the marble stairs together and Cal asked her if she did all the errands. She said she did.

In the front seat of the '38 Buick, Cal's mother looked out for several moments through the window on her side and then turned to him.

"Your father says I shouldn't say anything to you about this, Cal, but I want to know something. I want you to tell me the truth."

"OK," Cal said. He was thinking hard, running over possibilities in his mind, but he couldn't think what he might have done wrong.

"Twice within the last month, there's been a large spot on your pajamas that feels dried and crusty, as if you've been blowing your nose there."

Before she could continue, Cal said quickly, "That's what it is, I blew my nose because I didn't have a handkerchief."

"I know there are natural things that happen to a boy when he reaches your age, but there are other things that could happen that are not natural. I know you are a good boy and I am not accusing you of anything, but these spots were on the bottoms of your pajamas. I don't want to make something out of nothing. . ."

"That's what it is ma, it's nothing. I told you, I just blew my nose. I should have used a handkerchief. It won't happen again."

"I asked your father if he had talked to you about certain things that you should know about and he said he did. Did he? Do you know what I'm referring to?"

"I do, ma. He did. It's all taken care of." Cal was thinking about the conversation six months ago with his father:

"Do they teach you at school about men and women stuff?"

Cal lied and said, "Sure."

"If you ever want to know anything, just ask me." Cal's father was embarrassed as he said it. Cal was embarrassed for him.

In the car in front of the Lynn City Hall, she said, "So you already know about what could happen between young men and women?"

"I do, ma."

"I don't mind your knowing just as long as you never do anything of that kind."

Cal nodded that he understood.

"Now let's go get your father. He needn't know about this conversation."

She turned on the ignition key and stepped on the starter, and the engine of the '38 Buick fired immediately.

CHAPTER FORTY

▼

Cal came back to the car and told Regina that it was room forty-five. "Be sure to lock the door on your side of the car."

"I'll wait and go in the side door in five or six minutes," Regina said.

Inside the Radial Motel near the hospital mall, Cal turned on the lights on either side of the double bed, the standing light in the corner of the room, the desk light, and the lamp on the table. He turned off the hall light, then turned it on again. He turned on the bathroom light, then turned it out. He picked his coat off the bed and tried to hang it up in the closet. He was so nervous that he couldn't get the hanger out of the metal coupling, and had to wrap his coat around the hanger as it dangled from the rod arm.

He lay down on the bed and wondered what he had gotten himself into. He was very excited and very scared. He got up off the bed and sat in the chair under the standing lamp. He picked up the *Radial Enterprises National Magazine* from the table and began to thumb through it, stopping at a photo of a New England farmhouse in Vermont. It was summer. Maple trees hung over a country mailbox, and rolling hills were soft in the distance. An old man and an old woman were in an old-fashioned two-seater swing watching a little boy and a little girl play croquet on the velvet lawn.

There was a knock on the door and Cal hurried to open it.

"Sorry, I should have left it open," Cal said.

"At least you opened it. I envisioned bumming a ride home from a squad car at the hospital. Thank you." Regina smiled.

Cal walked to a chair and sat down. She easily unhooked a coat hanger next to Cal's jacket, tucked it into the arms of her coat and re-hooked it in the metal jacket attached to the rod arm.

"What will your mother do?"

"You mean 'think.'"

"Both. Should you call her?"

"Sure. I'll do it right now." She picked up the phone.

"Do you want me to go in the bathroom?"

"Not on my account, or my mother's, but don't let me stop you if you have to—I'm sorry again, I don't mean to be flip, I do it when I get nervous." She dialed.

"You're nervous?"

"Of course I'm nervous. You think I'm Marlene Dietrich? Mama? This is Gina. I'm snowed in at the minister's house. Reverend Breastburn made a big bowl of popcorn and opened a case of beer. Sure you can come if you can get here. Yes. No. Yes, of course I'm kidding. Yes. No. *Extremely* dry. Yes. Deborah. Yes. Thanks, mama. Tomorrow. Bye."

"She sounded great."

"She is. You'll never know how great. My father doesn't know what he missed."

"He's gone?"

"These many years, as the novelist wrote. This is awkward for you, isn't it? I can sleep on the floor, you know."

"No, I, of course not, I mean, you're very attractive to me and I'm not very good in these situations. I hope you'll be patient with me, Regina, I, basically am very scared that I'll screw up."

"You have this feeling that you shouldn't be here. And tomorrow you're going to feel that you shouldn't have been here. So nothing that happens or doesn't happen here is going to be any good or have any meaning or be any fun. You're trapped if you stay and trapped if you go."

"Women who see through me have always scared me. I can't believe you know about Clare. Did everyone in the group know about us?"

"I don't know. We didn't talk about it. None of the girls that I know of came to Youth Group to get in bed with you, but it did fascinate Debbie and me, and if they did know, it probably made you more attractive. The boys probably didn't know. They were too busy trying to get in bed with the rest of us."

"I never understood how girls younger than me always seemed to know more about the way things work than I did, but it's true. You're way ahead of me."

"Be careful of what you're attracted to. You might end up with one of us. Is that why you broke up with Clare?"

"She broke up with me."

"I always liked her. She's got balls. Should I apologize again?"

"No."

"Would you be offended if I lay down on the bed? Maybe pulled the top spread over me? I'm cold. It's not a line."

"Of course. I'm sorry, I. . ."

"Let's make a deal. I won't apologize any more and you won't be sorry any more, and we'll all be unapologetic and un-sorry together in a little crooked bed."

"Good. OK. *Very* good. Geez, it's very unique being with you, I mean, I don't know how we . . . but I'm very glad . . . it's my first time in a motel, I'm just very nervous, I don't know what the hell I'm doing, I don't know where Clare is, I wasn't bull-crapping Vinnie, I don't know what I'm doing in theological school except that I'm a nut case, some of my friends are in Korea, I can't be myself with women without dropping into a black hole for a month, I can't even admit being in love with a woman without torturing her. You know what I've been doing? I'm like a serial killer. I go from woman to woman, rejecting each one, not for the next one but for the one before, but since I've already fouled up with that one, I can't have the one before so I torture myself as well. I'm more of a jerk to talk about it."

"At least you warned me so I won't get in line."

"I hate that Breastburn. I grew up in a little church."

"As the song says, 'the weather outside is frightful.'"

"And I'm not being too delightful. Why can't I just 'let it snow, let it snow, let it snow'?"

"I'll tell you what, Mr. Cal, we seem to be stuck with each other for this snowy night in history, so why don't you just get in bed, on or beneath the covers, take your pick, and we'll just try to be understanding of each other. I mean, relax and be friends, and talk or not talk. There's nothing wrong with chaste relationships. Believe me, I have no expectations. So far, this has been without a doubt the most interesting night of my life, so whatever happens from now on, whatever it is, will be added unto it. Isn't that the phrase Jesus used, 'added unto'?"

"Don't remind me." Cal climbed between the sheets. "Do you mind if I take off my pants? I'll keep my underpants on. But I perspire like crazy if I wear clothes in a sleeping bag and I'm sure that this will be the same."

"I'll consider it. No, I'm kidding. I'll tell you what. Would you mind terribly if I did the same? Whole deal, same reason, with gratitude added unto that this is not a sleeping bag."

Cal worked off his pants under the sheets and threw them onto the chair next to the bed. Under the covers, Regina worked her dress up over her head and dropped it next to the bed. From beneath the sheets, Regina pulled the bedclothes up under her chin and lay with her head on her pillow. "Lord of mercy," she said, "this is the most comfortable I've been in all my years. That's what my aunt Hazel used to say when she lay down on the couch after Christmas dinner."

Cal half sat, half reclined against the backboard of the bed with his pillow behind his head and shoulders, the bedclothes pulled up to his waist.

"How are you at bedtime stories?" Regina asked.

"I never told one."

"Remember what Daisy said in *The Great Gatsby?*"

"You read that book?"

"In my senior year in high school. We had this English teacher who thought Fitzgerald was the living end. She brought flowers to class the day after he died, and she spent the whole class reading out loud his short story called 'The Birthday Party.' At the end, grown adults were standing on someone's front lawn throwing a child's birthday cake at each other. I never could figure out why she read that story that day. She thought it was so sad and so beautiful. I thought it was pathetic. But I loved *Gatsby*, even though Daisy was a dip."

"Daisy said, 'What are we going to do this afternoon, and tomorrow, and for the rest of our lives?'"

"It's dumb, but it's great that she could at least say it."

"What was the word you said you would use to describe me?"

"It's silly and we've gone past it. Years have passed since then. Can we turn out some of these lights? We can always leave one on if you need it. You're going to get a crick in your back if you don't either sit up or lie down."

"Do you want me to get the lights?"

"Do you want *me* to?"

Cal would have liked that. He was curious to know what she looked like under the covers. He was beginning to relax. He grinned at Regina: "No, I will."

"Shall I pull the covers over my head?"

"Suit yourself, *compadre*." Cal went from light to light, turning each off, then sat on the edge of the bed, took off his shirt and T shirt, and got between the covers on his side of the bed.

"Thank you. This is nice."

"Yes it is nice." They lay there in the darkness and the silence. After a while he said, "You got me out of a jam tonight."

"I didn't get you out of anything, Mr. Newsome, sir, Cal, whatever. *Compadre*, I guess. They just left us there. There's probably some unfinished business brewing."

"You mean I'm a target."

"Vinnie's smart as hell, he really is. He's probably a genius. His IQ is enormous. But he's got a temper to match. And he's frightfully strong. He can rip telephone books and stuff like that. He really can. I've seen him do it. He'll end up in a penitentiary somewhere, it's in his genes. Obviously you know about him and Clare."

"Clare told me about him, but just enough to keep it straight between us."

"He's always been a bully, but he sure is attractive. It took a lot of us a long time to give up the bad for the good."

"What's attractive about him?"

"All the corny things. He's brave, handsome, attentive in his own way, *that* stuff. And he's all male. Not too reverent though, but that's attractive too. He's just one hundred and ten percent Vinnie."

"What's the bad like?"

"I'll tell you. When you forgive somebody seventy times seven, seventy times eight seems more than enough. Seventy times nine is close to unbearable. Seventy times ten, you wake up at the bottom of Niagara Falls and feel it's a miracle that you're alive, and you know you'll never get back up the falls again so you just drift down the river and keep going."

"He sounds dangerous."

"Everyone is dangerous. That's what you find out down river."

"Am I dangerous?"

"Of course you're dangerous. Why do you think you're afraid of yourself?"

"Is that your word to describe me?"

"I've been teasing you, haven't I? No, that's not the word, Mr. Sometimes Cal, but if I tell you the word I think of when I think about you, and I've thought a lot about you the last two years, you have to understand that it's my own word for my own private reasons, and most people don't even use the word, and it won't make any sense to you, and you just have to let me have it for myself. It's not a bad word, it's not a significant word, it's not even an important word. But you're curious about it, and it's not fair to tease you with it, or to try to fib you after all this."

"I'm almost afraid for you to tell me, after all this. But tell me. I can take it."

"It's very innocent, actually. Probably even silly. The word is 'bemused.' It just came to me. I've never even used it, but it popped into my head one day and I looked it up. Most of the words in the dictionary definition fit you perfectly: 'engrossed,' 'distracted,' 'preoccupied.' One dictionary said 'stupefied,' but you're not stupefied, so that's not accurate. Are you offended?"

Cal was stunned. It was the same word that the man on the Boston Common with the navy pea jacket used when he taunted Cal during Jack's sermon.

"Wow," he said quietly.

"You're not upset are you?"

"It's OK, no, no. 'Bemused,' huh? Until recently I never heard anyone use that word, and twice within the last . . . it's just the exact word that someone else used about me recently. Some of my dorm friends were preaching on Boston Common a couple months ago, and this bum came up to me and worked to get my attention. When I tried to ignore him he asked me if I was 'bemused.' Actually, this guy wasn't a bum, at least he hadn't been a bum all his life, and he knew about theology and things about the Church. He was amazing. I bought him some food and he disparaged everything about the Church, and me to boot, and he was very compelling. I didn't want him to leave, but he did. He was physically messed up, cuts all over his face and stuff. But he knew what he was talking about. I'd like to find him and talk to him again. It's very mysterious, and it's all tied together with me and the Church and my feelings and who I am."

"And I stumbled into all this?"

"I'm the one who stumbled."

"You haven't been accused of anything, you know. You're intense, but your intensity is attractive, that's all."

"I hurt people, and I hate myself for it."

"You're not hurting *me*, so let yourself off if our being here right now starts to get to you. I got myself here, not you. I'm a grown person and you've been nice to me."

"So far, I don't owe you anything."

"What do you mean 'owe me'? How could you owe me? I don't get it."

"If anything happened between us, I mean."

"This is what I get for staying after church in a snowstorm and getting tackled into a church chair? Do you always analyze everything?"

"I didn't used to."

"Didn't you like yourself better when you didn't?"

"Not afterward."

"Are we talking about the same thing?"

"Sex is very powerful."

"Am I leading you on?"

"In the discussion?"

"How about if I just listen for awhile and you do the talking. Just try to say what it is that you feel like saying. I was getting relaxed for a minute there but now I'm, whoa, wide awake. Mr. Newsome, Cal Reverend, *compadre*, whatever, I still don't know what to call you, you are a talker. No, not in the discussion, in the bed, because I don't want to be, if I am, and I don't want you to do anything you don't want to do, and I don't want you to think I think that sex has anything to do with hurting anyone, but mostly I don't want you to think that my saying that is leading you on. And even more, mostly I don't want to stop you from talking if you want to talk about something. Talking about hurting people is one thing, and talking about sex is one thing, but confusing the two in order to talk around sex is a game. See, I can do it too, but what's the point?"

"I think I'm in over my head. I was excited to do this. Those guys scared me, but you made me feel I'd get out of it. Then when Howard Johnson's was closed it was like the whole town, even the world, was closed. Nobody knew where I was but you, and you were safe for me. I didn't think about consequences. It was like tomorrow was a year away. I wouldn't be waxing the cafeteria floor tonight, I wouldn't be going to *Old Testament* class tomorrow morning, I wouldn't be seeing Miss Green tomorrow afternoon. Miss Green is just something else I do, she's not my girlfriend. Call me Cal."

"I'm not saying a word."

"I would like to touch you but I feel like a little boy and I'm not supposed to. How's the bump on your head?"

Regina didn't reply.

"Regina?"

"It's fine."

"I thought you were really hurt when you crashed into those chairs."

After several seconds Cal again said, "Regina?"

"You don't think I was?"

"You're very quiet in bed."

"I'm a deep sleeper, just like one of the seven dwarfs."

"I didn't know they were deep sleepers."

"Yup."

"If I stopped talking, would you go to sleep."

"Sure I would, wouldn't you?"

"I hate to give up this moment."

"It is nice."

"If I talk about sex, will you think I'm trying to seduce you?"

"I can't help you on that one. I don't know what I'll think. Why you want to analyze something you haven't done yet is beyond me."

"I wonder why we're attracted to some people and not others?"

"Curiosity."

"Miss Green told me it's because the other person is us."

"If I'm attracted to you, you're really me?"

"Everyone is both male and female. The male is attracted to the male part of the female to complete the female part of himself."

"You believe that?"

"It makes sense, doesn't it?"

"Do you remember that radio program when we were little kids, 'I Love a Mystery'?"

"It came on at 7:30 on Thursday nights, right after 'Fu Manchu.'"

"It was my favorite program."

"Mine was 'Let's Pretend,' ten o'clock on Saturday morning."

"That figures. I don't think you're listening to me."

"Yes I am. I liked 'I Love a Mystery,' too. Radio was so great when I was a kid. I used to have to go to bed at 8:30, and I always asked to stay up longer. My mother let me on the weekends."

"I bet if we both were quiet and listened to the dark, we'd be right back in the same bedroom we were in as kids, and we'd think about things we did then, and picture what might happen tomorrow, and we'd fall asleep happy. Then we'd wake up, changed just a little bit forever."

"Sure, why not? Cal reached over and touched Regina's face lightly and said, "Night Gina."

"Night, Cal."

They both lay in the darkness on their backs, not saying a word for a long time, neither one knew how long. Cal fell asleep first. He slept soundly for several hours, and opened his eyes. He was lying on his side, facing Regina's side of the bed, but she wasn't there. The light was on in the bathroom and the bathroom door was open. He heard her draw water from the sink faucet into a glass, then after a few seconds he heard her put the glass down. She came out of the bathroom and started to walk toward the bed. She had taken off her panties but she was still wearing her bra. He had never noticed her breasts before, and she was perfectly shaped, larger than he would have thought. Cal was immediately tumescent. Halfway to the bed, she stopped. He closed his eyes immediately but she had seen his face. She turned back to the bathroom and snapped off the light. A few seconds later he could feel the bed move slightly as she got back in.

"I see that you're awake," she said. Did you sleep well?"

Cal feigned sleep for a while but he knew she had seen him. He didn't know what to say. "You're gorgeous," he said.

"I thought you were asleep. You snore, did you know that?"

"I'm embarrassed. No one ever told me. No one ever could have, I guess."

"Don't be. I knew that you were at peace."

"When I was a kid, the leaders snored in the lodge at Boy Scout camp and it was gross."

"It depends on who it is, I guess. My mother snores once in a while. I don't mind it."

"Not your father? No, I remember, he's been gone for a long time."

"My father's been gone for a lifetime."

"I want to touch you." Simultaneously, they tentatively slid their hands across the bed. She touched his upper arm just as the knuckle of his little finger grazed her bra and he found the warm skin of her stomach.

"Sorry," he said.

"For what?"

Regina felt his shoulder and the muscles of his upper arm, and her hand went to his neck. Her hand was warm and gentle and Cal was uncomfortable in his jockey shorts, stretched by his bulging penis. He moved his hand upward so that the back of all his fingers touched Regina's full bra.

"Is that OK?" he asked.

"Yes," she said, "Is this OK?" and moved her hand downward.

"Oh yeah, yes, yes it is." Cal moved closer to her and reached, cupping her full breast. With her other hand, she had removed her bra."

"You are so lovely," he said.

"And so are you, my friend. So, finally, are you."

CHAPTER FORTY-ONE

▼

Cal was lying on his bed, reading *Sweet Thursday* when Travis entered the room. "Big news man, the Supreme Court voted unanimously to desegregate the schools. Phil Whately and Hafy Brown are going crazy in the Library. Miss Jansan is pretending she can't hear them."

Cal laid the book on his chest. "What's it mean?"

"Comes the revolution, brother. The whole Court, even Warren, struck down the separate but equal clause. Old Faubus and Wallace'll be ankle deep in shit as soon as the first applications are filed."

"Applications for what?"

"State universities in Alabama and Arkansas, Mississippi, Georgia, South Carolina, the whole South. Eisenhower's got to hold the line."

"Eisenhower? What do you mean, hold the line?"

There was a knock on the door. "Come in," Travis called.

Jim Toffert stuck his head in and said "Gentlemen."

"Come on in Jim, what's up?"

"Thank you. It's not safe anywhere in the building. Lordy lordy, you'd think it was the Second Coming. Those Baptist colored boys of yours are on a rampage."

"What do you mean 'ours'? And Phil and Hafy aren't Baptists."

"You know perfectly well what I mean. They might as well be. They're flailing their arms and shouting."

"It's a big day for the good guys, Jimbo. Get used to it."

"Oh posh. You liberals think the Supreme Court is the Roman Forum. They're just a tired old bunch of Unitarians re-writing Emerson. Next year they'll name the Supreme Court building, 'Brook Farm.'"

"I didn't know Episcopalians read American literature," Cal said. "I'm impressed."

"Well at least the nineteenth century didn't breed atheists like that rubbishy Steinbeck that you're always talking about."

Cal held up his book so that Toffert could see the cover.

"Oh my God, Caleb Newsome, you're impossible. What drivel."

"Don't you believe in good-hearted prostitutes, Jim? Jesus and the woman at the well? Christian compassion for the poor in spirit?"

Toffert shuddered and his jowels shook. "Jesus, Mary, and Joseph. You would test the patience of a saint."

"Jim boy, I hate to ask this, and I don't want to seem unfriendly, but did you initiate this conversation for a reason?"

"Of course I did, you imbecile. I come in Christian charity to extend the hand of fellowship to you two slimeballs. Dr. Loyalton is retiring in the spring and the Dean in his wisdom has appointed me and George Burlson to organize the event. We are soliciting, in order: ideas, bodies, and money, and we are hoping you two will make Christian contributions in all three categories."

"Cal said, "I'm shocked that you are soliciting bodies, Jimbo."

"Ugh! On that typical note, I depart, Newsome. I do know, however, that your body in spite of yourself is a temple of the Savior, and your wayward mind is in some mystical way detached from it. As usual, I forgive you, but I will continue to detest you and to pray each night for your soul. Goodbye, you two atheist gentlemen." Toffert closed the door behind him, firmly, not quite energetic enough to consider it a slam.

"I think he likes you," Travis said.

"Thanks. Did you know that Dr. Loyalton is retiring?"

"You ought to go to chapel more often. The Dean announced it two weeks ago. Joe said to tell you he was available to hit the Combat Zone this afternoon if you wanted. I think that's what he said. Does it make sense?"

"Yeah it does. Thanks. Did you ever read this book, Trav?"

"Which one?"

"This one, *Sweet Thursday*."

"No, I read *Cannery Row*, though. He's a great writer."

"Listen to this. It's about a guy named Doc who fell in love with a working girl."

"A working girl?"

"A prostitute. Listen:

They say of an amputee that he remembers his leg. Well, I remember this girl. I am not whole without her. I am not alive without her. When she was with me I was more alive than I have ever been, and not only when she was pleasant either. Even when we were fighting I was whole. At the time, I didn't realize how important it was but I do now. I am not a dope. I know that if I should win her I'll have many horrible times. Over and over, I'll wish that I had never seen her. But I also know that if I fail I'll never be a whole man. I'll live a half-gray life, and I'll mourn for my lost girl every hour of the rest of my life.

"Pretty good."

"I'm not finished. Listen!"

"I've got a class. I've got to go."

"No listen. I'm almost finished. It's really great:

As thoughtful reptiles you will wonder, 'Why not wait? Look further! There are better fish in the sea!' But you are not involved. Let me tell you that to me not only are there no better fish, there are no other fish in the sea at all.

"Cal, I'm out the door."

"Wait. Just one sentence. Listen:

The sea is lonely without this fish. Put that in your pipe and smoke it.

"Isn't that great?"

"Yeah it is, it's great. If I see Joe, shall I tell him anything?"

"I'll meet him after his *Psalms* class."

"Got it. Bye."

Cal went back to *Sweet Thursday:*

He took off his clothes and had a shower and scrubbed himself until his skin was soap-burned and red. He brushed his teeth until his gums bled.

CHAPTER FORTY-TWO

▼

Joe and Cal left the dorm and walked along the snow-cleared sidewalk to the Chapel Terrace where they crossed to the trolley middle of Memorial Avenue. They could see the orange MTA streetcar with its black insect-like antenna moving under the wires toward them down the slight incline from the Bay State Bridge.

"Who's that sharp Negro who came down the elevator with us?" Cal asked. "I see him every once in a while and he's always dressed to kill."

"One of DeFranco's Th.D. students. His name is King. I think he's got a church in Jamaica Plain."

"They must pay him pretty good to wear those white starched shirts all the time. He's certainly got the name for it."

"Try *Martin Luther* King."

"Wow. You have to wonder about parents who name their kids like that and they still end up in the ministry."

"How about John Wesley Lord who ends up a bishop in the Methodist Church?"

"I wonder if he'd made bishop if his name were Axel Grease."

"Remember the rag man's name when we were kids?"

"Lipshitz. Remember Mary Malarky in high school?"

"You have to get out from under a name."

"Remember the radio show, 'Just Plain Bill'?"

"It came on in the morning at 10:45, just after 'Young Doctor Malone.'"

"No, it was just after 'David Harum.' 'Young Doctor Malone' was before 'Ma Perkins.'"

The streetcar arrived and others got on. Cal and Joe talked, not noticing the driver staring at them: "Are you getting on or what? I can come back later if you want."

Joe quickly stepped in and dropped a quarter and a dime in the fare box and moved down the aisle and sat down. Cal dropped two dimes in the box and tried to hand the driver fifteen pennies.

"What's that?" the conductor asked, looking at Cal's hand.

Cal said, "Pennies. I don't have the right change."

"We don't take pennies."

"It's all I have."

The driver pressed the button to close the doors, stepped on the silent pedal, and looked straight ahead, moving the car along the tracks toward the Kenmore underground tunnel. He did not look at Cal.

Cal was embarrassed. Everyone in the front part of the car was watching him.

"What'll I do with these?" Cal asked the driver.

"What do you want to do with them?"

"I'd like you to take them so I can sit down."

"You do, huh? You're a beaut, you know that?"

"Why are you doing this? This is a public transportation system."

"And you're the public, right? Don't they teach you any rules in this college here? You're a college student, right?"

"Do you want this money or not?" Cal extended his hand with the pennies.

The driver looked straight ahead as the train sloped downward into the tunnel leading to Kenmore station, then extended the open palm of his right hand toward Cal. "Count them into my hand."

"Here, take them," Cal said, dropping the fifteen pennies into the driver's open palm, or so he thought. The driver had pulled back his hand and the pennies splashed onto the floor.

"I said 'count 'em.' Are you deaf as well as dumb? Now pick'em up or get off'n this car."

Everyone in the car could hear the argument, and the car went silent. As it moved into the brightly lit Kenmore Station, Cal started to walk back toward Joe, and the driver said, "Hey bud! You're off this car."

All eyes were on Cal. He sat down next to Joe.

"What's up?" Joe said.

"He wouldn't take fifteen pennies and he wants me to pick them up off the floor."

"You gave him pennies?"

"I just wanted to get rid of them. No big deal."

"I've got change, why didn't you ask me? MTA drivers are not happy people. Here, go put this in the box." Joe held out a dime and a nickel.

The streetcar had stopped and some of the passengers had moved out through the open doors.

"He's got the money. It's on the floor. He told me to count the pennies into his hand and I dumped them but he pulled his hand away. The hell with him, Joe."

"HEY BUD!" the conductor called from the front of the car. "You can sit there and we can wait until security comes, or you can get your ass out of here now."

A lady sitting behind the driver said, "This was unnecessary, driver. You were gratuitously rude to him and I'm going to report you." She was wearing a large green hat, and when she finished her speech, she tilted her head as if to punctuate her indignation and the hat bumped against the window, tilting the hat. She pulled it back into its proper position.

"Yeah, OK lady, let's hear it for the educated youth of America. You can tell the security guard. He'll be here in fifteen minutes. But talk English to him, OK?"

"Let's go, driver, fight your personal fights later!" People began to shout, some to the driver, others to Cal. "Pay the fifteen cents for Christ's sake, like everybody else!"

"Move the goddamn car!"

Joe suggested they get off and wait for another car. "If we wait for the security guard, this place will go berserk. You might win but it'll cost us the next three hours. Let's go."

Joe and Cal got up and left through the middle doors. As the driver closed the doors he called, "Bye girls."

The lady with the green hat said to the driver, "You're very common."

"That I am, lady, that I am."

As the streetcar silently moved away from them towards Copley Square station, Cal said, "Jesus, that was so humiliating. I'm sorry, Joe."

"No sweat. We'll get another car, that's all."

They waited in silence for a minute. "Nothing was at stake and I still got sucked in," Cal said. "It didn't have to happen. I didn't have to give him the pennies. But I hate being the good little boy again."

"Let yourself off the hook. It's too easy to be a judge, even of yourself."

"You never press your advantage, Joe. Thanks."

"What advantage? We're all little boys, we're all jerks, we're all the guy driving the streetcar. We're all in it together."

"I don't feel in it, Joe. I feel out of it. When I was standing there with the pennies on the floor and the driver ordering me out of the streetcar, I felt like a little kid. I feel the same way when I'm wearing a robe in a pulpit. I'm no shepherd taking care of his sheep. It comes down to this all the time. Something always happens like this. Something combustible in me leaks out and I light a match. 'Physician heal thyself,' as Tom says, but I'm in the wrong profession. I still see myself walking down a hospital corridor in a white jacket, going into rooms to heal people. In churches I only smell the basement with those brown pictures of boy Jesus with the glow around his head lecturing the rabbis. You give up your afternoon to go with me on a wild goose chase into the Combat Zone to find some guy who's dead."

"Maybe he's not dead. Maybe we'll find him."

The single headlight of the next subway car appeared in the tunnel. When the doors opened, they entered. Three stops later they got out at Boylston Street and walked up the stairs to the corner of the Boston Common. The wind blew and the ash trees whipped above their heads.

"There aren't many bums around this time of year," Cal said.

"You said he's not a bum."

"I don't think he is, but he looked like one."

"What's the game plan?"

"I don't have one. We can either ask around here or go into a few places on Washington Street and see if anyone knows him."

"OK. Why don't we just case the Common. We might come across a few guys full of anti-freeze. Then we can hit the Zone."

They angled into the wind. The Common was vacant except for an older, elegantly dressed woman heading to Beacon Hill, and a middle-aged man in a long raccoon coat and a Russian fur hat, walking an Irish wolfhound.

"We picked the wrong day, Joe, probably the wrong life," Cal said.

"Naw," Joe said. "You never know. That's what my right end at Bowdoin said when I asked him in the huddle if he could get free down and deep, 'you never know.'"

"Could he?"

"He caught twelve for touchdowns our senior year, all more than 30 yards."

"Football seems a hundred years ago, almost like it never happened."

"Not for me. It still happens every day. I remember the guys and the things they said and did. I loved it so much."

"Me too. I loved it too much. I still have dreams that I'm back there. In my dream I'm always recovering from an injury and don't know if I can play again. It's never an ordinary injury though, but a broken hip or something. It's weird."

"Like after wrestling all night with an angel?"

Cal looked at Joe, and Joe smiled at him, and they headed across the Common.

"Let's follow that gray squirrel," Joe said.

"He's huge, look at those hind legs. Did you ever eat squirrel, Joe?"

"No, but I read about hunting squirrels somewhere, I think it was in Hemingway. Yeah, it was in a short story and the boy tells his father he knows where there are black squirrels. The father and the mother don't get along and the father says he'll go there with the boy. Something like that, it's terrific."

The gray squirrel scampered across the frozen snow to a heavy clump of bushes and disappeared. Then two more squirrels came out of the bushes and raced toward a large begonia tree. Their claws ripped into the bark as they climbed and disappeared in the upper limbs.

"There goes our leader," Joe said.

"I'd like to read that story," Cal said.

"I've got it in the dorm."

"This is a dead end deal, Joe," Cal said. "It was a dumb idea. Let's head over to the swan pond and we can get the Arlington Street subway back to the dorm."

"Hey, we don't get out enough in the middle of the week. This is fun. We've got time, let's cut over and see what's happening on Washington Street."

Chapter Forty-Three

As they walked, Cal said, "My dad used to take me squirrel hunting. The first time was a Saturday morning in the woods across from where we lived in Mapleville. I saw him leaving the house with his single shot .12 gauge shotgun and he said I could go with him. We went bird hunting on the path to the valley and down into Black Swamp but we didn't see anything. Coming back through the lower end of the valley he held out his hand for me, behind him, to stop. I was so excited when he raised his gun, and it seemed like a minute before he fired, then he lowered his gun and said, 'I got him.'

"I asked, 'What is it?' but my dad didn't say anything and we walked about twenty-five yards to a big oak tree where the squirrel was lying on the ground. My dad said, 'He was just playing around the base of the tree,' and he let me carry the squirrel home by the tail. He skinned it in the kitchen sink and said I could have the skin. He showed me how to scrape off the fat and salt the hide and nail it to a board. We put the board in the garage, then in the spring I took it off the board and kept it in my room, but the heat melted some of the skin where I didn't get the fat off and my mother made me throw it away."

"My father always talked about taking me duck hunting, but he never did."

"My father went duck hunting in Ipswich once with the plant managers from the General Electric. He came home with a black duck and told my mother to soak it in salt water, and she did and it rotted."

"Remember the day we saw the wood ducks fly across the Rezzie?"

"No, when?"

"When Frank Kendall killed the wood duck when we looked for crayfish in the Rezzy?"

"Geez, I'd forgotten that. I wonder where Frank and Buddy and Eddie are now? You know, I've thought about that black duck. If my mother had just cooked the damn duck instead of complaining about the smell, it probably would have been OK to eat. They fought about everything."

"I heard that Frank and Eddie both got married. Eddie still lives in Mapleville. Frank lives in Peabody, I think. Buddy's somewhere in Pennsylvania."

"It's strange Joe, they never fought at the lake. Of all the times we went down there, weekends all through late spring, summer and early fall, the first two weeks in August every year, they never had one argument. The lake was Eden for me, it was my real home growing up. Most of my time was spent in Mapleville where everything revolved around that little white church, but my real life was at the lake. I remember waking up in the morning and seeing the second hand tongue and groove wood roof above me and feeling safe. Then lying in the dark at night before I went to sleep, listening to the rain on the outside tar paper."

They came to the intersection of Stuart and Washington Streets.

"Home Sweet Home," Joe said.

"We're there, all right."

"Let's check those two customers down there. They don't look like the mayor and the vice-mayor."

"Boston has a vice mayor?"

"More than one, my boy."

"Should we give them money?"

"We'll see. Let me go first."

They walked to two men in animated conversation. One was pointing his finger at the other, who was laughing and pushing the air with his hand.

"Excuse me, gentlemen," Joe said. "Do you know a fellow who wears a navy pea jacket and army fatigues?"

"Who invited you?" said the one with the pointing finger.

"We need some information and we thought you might help us," Joe said.

"Fuck you," said the one who had been laughing. He concentrated on lifting an inch long burned-out cigarette to his lips, but his hand trembled and when he couldn't get a puff, he threw it away. "You got a cigarette, friend?" he asked Joe. His eyes blurred and he blinked, waiting for Joe's answer.

"I'm sorry, I don't have a cigarette," Joe said.

"Hey," the finger pointer said, re-pointing his finger at Joe, "are you a joke or what?"

"I don't think I'm a joke."

"Well I think you're a joke." He dropped his hand and then lifted it again and pointed his finger at Joe's chest. "You live around here?" He started to choke, bent over and coughed up something and spit it on the sidewalk. He stared at Joe. "Are you still here. Go back to Beacon Hill, or wherever the fuck you came from. Go look for your pisscoat navy pimp over there."

Cal said, "Let's go, Joe."

As they left, Joe said, "So long gentlemen."

"Fuck you, Beacon piss-brains," the finger pointer called, then bent over coughing.

They walked away. "Nice," Cal said. "My turn next."

"Let's ask a bartender," Joe said.

"Where? These are all movie houses and sex joints."

They were standing in front of "Barnaby's Specialty Shoppe."

"Let's go in and ask," Joe said.

Inside, they edged around two men reading magazines. At the counter, a Chinese man watched them approach.

"Where can we get a beer?" Joe asked.

"That all you want?" the Chinese man answered, smiling.

"Yeah, that's sort of all we want," Joe said. "We're actually looking for someone, but a beer would go fine right now."

"You're looking for someone special, maybe? I can help you, very sure. Would you like step into back room?"

Cal said, "The man we're looking for wears a black navy pea jacket and army fatigues."

"Oh, I see. Which one of you Dick Tracy?"

"No, we're priests, sort of. We met this fellow on the Boston Common a few months ago, and we'd like to help him."

"Sort of Priests? Yes, OK. I will ask colleagues. Perhaps you come back next week?"

"Sure," Cal said, "about the beer? Any bars around here?"

"Priests drink beer, that pretty good. Sure, three blocks down take right. On corner there's restaurant with bar, run by Chinese. You want introduction? He knows special people also."

"No, we'll just tell them we talked to you. Thanks a lot," Cal said.

"Sure."

Outside, Cal said, "You want someone special maybe? You want big tits, medium tits, economy size tits?"

"Everyone wants to be helpful. You want to follow it up?"

"I'm on your time, Joe."

"Let's hit it, and if we strike out, we can come back next week."

"Or next year, or never. This was a crazy idea of mine, Joe."

"Who knows, what have we lost? And look at the new friends we've made."

They walked the three blocks and turned right. A young woman in a short leather skirt and jacket stepped out of a doorway and blocked their way. "Hey boys, want some fun?" She opened her leather jacket with both hands and her large bare breasts jiggled as she shook her shoulders. "I can do the two of you at the same time. I'm very very good."

"Thanks for the offer," Joe said, "but we have to meet somebody. Maybe some other time." As Joe passed her on one side, Cal tried to pass her on the other. She leaned into Cal and lifted up her bare breast with the cup of her hand.

"Suck this big boy, see what you're missing."

Cal turned sideways to avoid brushing up against her and walked on.

"What are you, a couple of queers?" she said just loud enough for them to hear, and stepped back into her doorway.

They kept walking. "She wasn't bad looking," Cal said.

"She was a knockout," Joe said.

"How does a girl get into this crap?" Cal said.

"Why didn't you ask her? She'd love to tell you."

Outside the Chinese bar, Cal said, "What do you think? This looks like a grundgy enough place."

"Why not, we came this far. I'll do this one."

Inside, low hanging shade lanterns with dim light bulbs created shadows on the walls. A bald Caucasian with long sideburns stood behind the bar, chewing gum. Joe and Cal sat down on the bar stools.

"What'll it be tonight, gentlemen?" The bartender nodded to someone behind them.

"A couple of draft beers," Joe said.

"Just bottles."

"Dawson's ale," Cal said.

"Carlings Black Label," the bartender said.

"That'll be fine," Joe said.

"Glasses?"

"Sure, glasses, thanks."

The bartender set up two tall glasses, reached into a case behind the counter, opened the bottles with a towel covering his hand, poured two inches of beer into each glass and set the bottles next to the glasses. "That all?"

"Yeah, that's good. Thanks," Joe said. "Well actually, we're trying to locate someone."

The bartender looked at Joe for a few seconds, then turned and went down the bar and adjusted one of several bottles lined up against the mirror. He turned and nodded again at someone behind Joe. He polished the mirror briefly and came back to Joe. Two men got up from a booth directly behind Joe and disappeared into the back of the restaurant.

"You fellows got any I.D.?"

"We're not policemen," Joe said. "We're only looking for a friend."

"And this friend is looking for you, right?"

"Well, he's not looking for us, but he'd be willing to talk to us."

"You're sure of that."

"We're pretty sure."

"And you're not cops, and this is all on the level. Why'd you pick us?"

"Really by accident. We asked a Chinese fellow in Barnaby's up the street if there was a bar around here where we could get a beer and he sent us here."

"I don't know anybody who comes in here, I make it a point. Maybe you ought to finish your beers and look someplace else."

"He wears a navy pea jacket and army fatigues."

The bartender walked away and began to wash dishes at a sink behind the bar. He turned two wet glasses upside down to drain on a towel.

Joe said, "Maybe we could leave a name and address in case he comes in sometime in the next couple months."

The bartender looked up and looked down again. Then he walked over to Joe and Cal and said, "That'll be eighty cents for the beers."

Joe got the change from his pocket, and Cal wrote his name and address on a back of a ticket stub in his wallet and put it on the bar.

Outside, Cal said, "I left my name just in case. What do you think? Do you think he knows the guy?"

"It's a huge long-shot. The guy really could be dead by now, or in Dallas. If you want to pursue it, your only chance is in the warm weather when there are other guys hanging out on the Common. Did you see those guys go into the back room?"

"Yeah. It's a good thing it's still light out. I'm sorry, Joe."

"Hey, we got a reminder of how the other half lives, didn't we? Nothing's ever wasted. Here's Chinatown, let's find a place we've never been before and order some Sichuan. I could drink a whole pot of chrysanthemum tea. You can tell me about your new flame."

CHAPTER FORTY-FOUR

▼

"GENERAL JAMES DOOLITLE FLIERS BOMB TOKYO," *Daily Evening Item,*
April 18, 1942

It was a warm Saturday evening in late summer. Cal's mother opened
the screen door of the porch and called for him to come in the house.

"It's my turn next, mama. Please? Bruce's mother said *he* could."

George Gray was giving rides to the neighborhood kids on his goat
cart. Jane and Joanne had ridden up to St. Fleur's house and back, sitting
on the little red cart pulled by George's goat, and Mariette was now
on her way back, holding the reins and steering the goat while George
walked behind the cart. She was in front of Hoods, two houses down the
street. Cal and Bruce were next in line.

In the spring and summer, George kept his goat in the field behind
his barn, next to North's house, and Cal was afraid of the goat because
it had butted him in the stomach one afternoon when his father had
walked over with Cal's Uncle Nate to show him the goat. Cal was
standing between his father and Uncle Nate when the goat jumped
forward with its head down and caught Cal in the stomach, knocking
him backwards to the ground. Cal couldn't breathe for several seconds,
but he didn't cry because he didn't want to show that he had been hurt
by the neighborhood goat. On this early summer evening, George held
the goat's muzzle as each rider got into the cart.

"Please, mama?" Cal pleaded.

"It's seven-thirty, Cal, and you've got to have your bath."

"I will, mama, just ten minutes more. Please?"

"All right. Ten minutes. You'll come in without me coming out to get you?"

"I will, mama. I'll be right in."

Mariette got out of the cart, and after George led the goat in a half circle, Cal got in. George said, "You want me to go with you like the girls, or d'you want to go by yourself?"

"By myself," Cal said.

"OK, just let him go. When you want to turn around, tug the reins, but not too hard."

Cal rode down the street past Teddington's house and Grant's house and Hood's house. He was very excited, being pulled by the goat. He passed Mackin's house. When he reached St. Fleur's house, Ronnie was sitting on the front steps, watching. His fingers were at his mouth.

Sometimes Cal and Ronnie played together with the other boys, but they had also had two fistfights. Ronnie had a disease that had hardened his fingers into stumps. His fingernails were like claws. Sometimes the skin on his hands cracked. Buddy Thomason was two years older and he told Cal that he shouldn't fight with Ronnie because of his hands, but Cal didn't think it was fair. Ronnie was always challenging Cal and hitting him with his hard stumpy hands. Ronnie went to a special school in Swampscott, and he liked to sit in the street and dig tar out of the macadam road with his fingernails and chew it. "Hey Cal," he called, "Lemme take a turn."

"I can't, I've got to get home."

Cal was nervous and pulled hard on the reins to turn the goat around. The goat pulled against the reins and kept going straight ahead. Cal pulled harder and the goat started to run. Cal got scared and let him go. At Maes's house, the goat slowed to a walk.

By the time Cal got the goat turned around and past Ronnie, who yelled to him that he was a mama's boy, and home again, he was a half hour late.

Inside the front door, he passed his father reading the *Lynn Item* in his big stuffed blue chair. His father said, "Your mother's drawing your bath, she's mad. You better have a good reason."

"I couldn't turn the goat around," Cal said. "Will you read to me?"

"Better ask your mother."

In the bathroom, Cal's mother had drawn four inches of warm water in the bathtub. "It's probably cold," she said, "but I can't draw any more because the cesspool will overflow. It's your own fault. It's the last time I'm going to let you stay out longer. You don't keep your word."

"I couldn't turn the goat around, mama, I didn't do it on purpose."

Cal undressed and held onto the edge of the bathtub and stepped into the four inches of lukewarm water and sat down. He shivered. His mother rubbed soap on a green washcloth and washed him all over. She didn't talk. When she was finished, he climbed out and stood in front of the sink, waiting for her to wipe him off. There were no towels on the rack.

"I'll get a towel," she said.

While he was waiting he looked in the mirror. He could see only his eyes and the top of his wet hair. He had a strong feeling in his penis and he looked down at it. It was big. He jiggled his hips and flopped his penis up and down. It felt good. He kept doing it. His mother came through the doorway with a towel and his pajamas, and saw him.

"You dirty little gutter boy," she said. She wiped him with the towel, hard, biting her lip. Cal's erection subsided. His mother handed him his pajamas and told him to get into bed.

"Can daddy read to me? He said he would. Just for five minutes?"

"It's up to him, I suppose," she said, and went down the hall toward her bedroom.

Cal got the book he wanted from his room and took it to his father, now asleep in his chair. The book had a yellow jacket, but the cover inside was red: *The Good Shepherd and the 100th Sheep.* Cal said, "Daddy?" and he woke up and looked at Cal.

"Are you ready?"

Cal crawled into his father's lap and his father began to read. In the story, a shepherd counted his sheep at the end of the day and one was missing. He could count only ninety-nine sheep, so the shepherd went looking. A lamb had fallen off the side of the mountain, and the shepherd looked over the edge and saw the lamb lying on a shelf of rock several feet down the sheer side of a crevice. The shepherd reached with his long crook and pulled the lamb to safety. The shepherd carried the lamb in his arms back to the flock.

When his father finished reading, Cal pretended to be asleep. His father carried him upstairs, tucked him under the bed covers and kissed him on the forehead. Cal never opened his eyes, and he could smell the faint shaving cologne his father used. He liked it very much. His father left Cal's bedroom and Cal could hear him walking down the stairs.

CHAPTER FORTY-FIVE

▼

Cal got off the elevator on the third floor and entered the School of Theology Library. He walked past the book repair room, glancing in to see if Angelica was at her desk. She was wetting a piece of paper in her mouth. Cal almost turned around to enter the room and talk to her, but decided to keep going. He passed the main desk and could see Miss Jansan in her office talking to Jake Foster. Her head was bobbing up and down and she was smiling her hostile smile. Cal passed the stacks and walked toward the study tables at the back. James Breed was sitting alone at the farthest table with his back to the river, reading.

Angelica Stone had been on the cover of *Life Magazine,* and she fascinated Cal. She had brown eyes and blonde hair that hung in curves around the sides of her face. She was easy to talk to. A year ago when Cal came to the seminary he was given a work scholarship in the library, and on his first day pasting date sheets inside the front covers of repaired books, Miss Jansan told him about Angelica having been on the cover of *Life.* Miss Jansan was very proud that a good girl could be a cover girl. Angelica later told Cal the photo had been taken when she was a student at Sewanee. A United Nations diplomat from Africa gave a speech there and the two of them were photographed up close. Cal looked up the copy in the library stacks and admired the photo.

Angelica was married to Cordell Bottomly from Kentucky. Whenever Cal talked to Angelica he tried to imagine Bottomly screwing her.

"Hello James. How's it going?"

"Right well. Caleb, isn't it?"

"Cal."

"Cal it is."

"Am I interrupting you? I took a chance on you being here today. You said you were here mid-morning on some weekdays."

"Yes, I mean no, you are not interrupting me, just brushing up on my Gibbon. The scholars these days make fun of him, but I think he's pretty solid. I meant yes I am here sometimes in the morning. I like to get out of that room, you know. It's not so steamy here, and the river's right by, of course."

"You're right about it not being steamy in here, anything but. It's drier than dry, if you don't mind my cynicism, but the river *is* nice. I see those shells and I always wish I were out there instead of in here."

"Quite. I sit this way because if I could see the river my mind would go wandering off down the stream, I'm afraid. Have a seat, please."

"Thanks. I'm fascinated by a couple of things you said to me the day we had lunch downstairs. Could I open that subject again?"

"The *Gnostic Gospels*, I take it. I've been thinking about our chat and wondered if I should have, how do you say it over here, shot off my mouth like that. May I presume on you to do me a bit of a favor along those lines?"

"Just before we left the table that day I sensed that you probably didn't want me to go to the newspapers, or Dr. Jansan here. No, I'm kidding. Am I right?"

"The ideas are free, of course, in the sense that they've been lost for a very long time and now have been found, but as long as the manuscripts haven't been published, they're liable to create a bit of a stir. As a guest here, I'd prefer not to have my name associated with something that's bound to cut away a bit at some of the Jesus myths, especially when I haven't performed a shred of the actual work, you know, my scholarship money from England and all that."

"You have my word that I won't say anything about you, or England."

"England would rather leave a trail to me, wouldn't it?"

"So there actually is a manuscript?"

"Actually, many. Two friends of mine in Wales have gotten onto a team of rather sophisticated language scholars who are grinding away at these rather remarkable Gnostic documents. It's all years away from publication, maybe decades. A huge amount of related reading and collation has to be done, but the revolutionary thing is there, and the project is within their grasp."

"That day at lunch you told me that Jesus was a Cynic philosopher."

"Yes, I didn't mean to shock you. You rather jumped when I said it."

"I was excited, not just for theological reasons. My personal theology, as Professor DeFranco calls such a concept, has changed since I got here, and I have ambivalent feelings about being here at all. If it weren't for some stuff going on in my personal life right now, I'd probably be out of here."

"Does Jesus the Cynic philosopher help you to stay in or encourage you to leave?"

"Neither, I guess. I'm here because I don't seem to be able to quit. But when I graduate I doubt if I'll take a church."

"You're not ordained, I take it."

"I'm supposed to be this spring. I can't believe I'm going to do it."

"But you intend to? I'm sorry, I don't mean to push. This is none of my business. You see where Jesus the Cynic philosopher leads us?"

"Don't be. Jesus didn't get me here and he won't get me out of here. I have so many things I want to ask you. Are there any miracles in these gospels or is that a secret?"

"No, there are not."

"Screw miracles, then. Everyone around here tries to explain the miracles."

"Someday you'll be able to say 'screw,' as you Americans put it, a lot of things in the four Gospels. It is quite exciting. It puts another focus on the Christian religion.

"The miracles are a sore spot with me. When I first got here, I was enamored of all the rational explanations, but now they're merely part of the fraud. Maybe 'fraud' is wrong, I don't know. The professors here are good men. Dr. Roth is really great. His history classes are the highlight of the week for me. The Indian, Chakravarty, is wonderful."

"I don't know about him."

"He was Tagore's secretary when Tagore won the Nobel Prize. Chakravarty was with Ghandi on the Salt March to the Sea. He teaches world religions. He's also a poet, with ten books of poems in Bengali. He gave a lecture last week on the Buddha that had the whole class wide-eyed for an hour and a half."

I'll have to pursue him before I go back."

"I'll introduce you, if you like. He's a Hindu, but around here it doesn't make any difference. The magic word here, you probably already know, is 'ecumenicity.'"

"Yes, I'm sitting in on a course taught by Bergstrom, the Swedish theologian."

"How is he?"

"He's actually quite keen, but a bit stuffy near the end of class. Not really dry, but pressing, perhaps."

"I was so eager to talk to you, and I've taken up most of your time with drivel."

"Not so. I was relieved to learn a bit about you. I see so few people, living in my little room on the Fenway that I rather gushed that day at lunch and now I feel better about it."

"Sitting on facts that will revolutionize Christian history would make anybody impatient to talk about it."

"It's probably my small room more than it is my friends' research. My hunch is that when the news breaks and they publish their book it will be barely recognized in Christian circles. Theologians will seize upon it, but the counter weight of orthodoxy will brand it as heretical and drag it away from serious scrutiny. The business of Christianity is rather caught up in the administration of the church by officialdom and in the daily anxieties of the communicants. It will be like stepping into a lake from shore with one's shoes on. The little ripple in the lake is infinitesimal, and the owner of the shoe merely has a wet shoe to deal with. One can remove it and dry it, or one can leave it to dry by itself. It's private, as you say. In the most extreme of cases, the wet shoe could cause pneumonia and death, or merely a change of socks. It could lead to a new pair of shoes, perhaps a whole new wardrobe, maybe a change in one's life."

"You said the other day that there might never have been a Jesus."

"Yes, I remember. I must have been very lonesome to have admitted it. Undoubtedly there was no Bethlehem, no Nazareth, no Crucifixion, no Resurrection. There isn't a fact known about Jesus, only the Sayings."

"Not even a Crucifixion?"

"No real evidence for it. Only the Fourth Gospel, written in Ephesus, and in Greek, a hundred and thirty years after the supposed event. Paul talks about Christ crucified, and He may have been, but there's no evidence. Since the Gospel writers invented everything else, they surely invented the Crucifixion as a world-shaking event. During the Roman occupation at the time of Herod, six hundred crucified Zealots lined the road outside Jerusalem. Jesus may have been one of them. Paul's theology of Christ crucified works whether there was a Jesus Crucifixion or not."

"Schweitzer says, 'He comes to us as one unknown.'"

"It depends on who or what He is, doesn't it? If you take the whole idea of Jesus, as traditional Christians have become familiar with Him, with all the trappings of the miracles and the Resurrection that personify Jesus' character, and you then put them together with a ransom theology in which Christ dies for our sins, obviously that whole package comes to us from an unknown past. It has the ring of humanist mystery to it, to say nothing of the literal belief in a personal Savior. Some people, remember, think of Jesus as an actual living person. Others may think of him as codified church dogma and everything that goes with that, but it is a powerful thing.

"The force of personal belief is enormous in one's life. If you don't have it or you don't need it or you don't want it, that's something else. The history of the world is full of physicists and chemists and artists who prefer the whole enterprise without Jesus or religion. One has to merely stay out of the line of fire of the dogmatists and the religious bureaucrats. If you put yourself in or get trapped in the way of an active Inquisition, you'll get mowed down by a relentless, unmerciful, anti-human power. Christians, along with some Muslims and other sectarian extremists, have been some of the greatest blood let-ers in history. There now, I've made a speech in the library of a respectable institution."

"You think Schweitzer's sentimental?"

"Certainly his hospital in Lambarene was not sentimental, nor the Bach he played on his organ, nor the faith that directed him to his African mission and his life's work. Nor even the scholarship of *The Historical Jesus*. But maybe his idea of Jesus was sentimental. I have thought about it. His book has a very moving conclusion. It is what faith in Jesus means. I'm even tempted to say faith in the risen Jesus, but then again, I don't believe in any form of the Resurrection."

"By 'risen' you mean spiritually elevated or intensified."

"Perhaps, I don't know what I would have meant if I had actually said it. I only said that I might have said it."

"You mean 'might have' in the sense that it could have occurred to you."

"I mean that if I were honest, and probably because of my own background in a little village church in Wales, the phrase occurred to me, so in another context I would have been comfortable with it."

"But not here."

"Not in this time and place, no."

"So Jesus the Cynic philosopher who had a physical relationship with Mary Magdalene hasn't changed your theology."

"It's modified it. It's opened it up. It hasn't changed my emotional receptiveness to the rituals and familiarities of the Church."

"You can sing the hymns when you don't believe the theology of the words and still be moved."

"Oh dear me, yes. Can't you?"

"Can you take the sacrament and believe?"

No, but I can take it and feel renewed."

"You can accept the magic of it."

"It's not magic, it's transformation. It comes from within. It's instrumental, not initiating."

"Forgive me for grilling you, James. I know you didn't bargain for this when we talked that day at lunch."

"It's quite all right. It surely beats Gibbon."

"May I ask you one more question along these lines?"

"Fire away."

"What if a minister or a priest administers the sacrament to someone who is unconscious, does it affect the person who is not aware of it?"

"Hypothetically, you mean? I'm hardly the expert, you know."

"I'm just curious what you think. We've had this discussion in bull sessions upstairs. My liberal friends think that the receptor isn't changed, the priest may or may not be changed depending on his feelings about what he's doing when he's performing the sacrament, yet the ritual itself preserves some vital link, some traditional communal connection, even some symbolic elevation of spiritual potential. Even the way I've expressed it, I've probably shaded it away from spirituality."

"I think something of the same myself, actually. Sometimes consciousness is an elusive thing, coma and all that. The discussion goes immediately to the unconscious, you know. Certainly the priest, as you call him, is the least significant party to the sacramental occasion."

"Dr. Roth is famous for saying that the character of the priest does not determine the validity of the sacrament. If the priest is drunk, the baby is still baptized."

"Quite."

"Are there other things I could learn about these gospels?"

"Implications perhaps."

"Can we talk again?"

"If you like."

"Could I bring my friend, Joe? He has a church in Braintree."

"Does he live there, then?"

"No, he lives here in the dorm, but he goes there on weekends."

"Perhaps some evening. I'd like to get out and about a little, and I've heard a bit about your Chinatown."

"We go there to eat all the time. That would be great."

"Do you fellows have a telephone upstairs?"

"Yes, there's one on each of the top three floors. Joe's on the 5th floor and I'm on the 6th."

"How about if I ring you up some time? I'll be out of town for a week or so, so I'm not exactly sure when it will be, but I'll get on to it, you can be sure."

"Well, back to your Gibbon, thanks a lot."

"Cheerio."

When Cal passed the book repair room on his way out, he looked in, but Angelica wasn't there.

CHAPTER FORTY-SIX

▼

Back on the sixth floor, Cal found a note scotch-taped to his door. Jack Ward wanted to talk to him, but no hurry. Cal decided to cut his Ministry of the Church class and go see Jack. His weekly class report on the Youth Group was still on his desk, unfinished, and there wasn't much point to facing Dr. Warren again without it. Cal was tired of being forgiven. But neither did he want to write the report, and he had left it to see James Screed in the library. Cal didn't want to write anything about Sunday night's snowstorm. He hadn't used a condom with Regina.

Cal knocked on Jack's door, and it opened.

"You got my note. Thanks. Come on in. Have you got a couple minutes?"

"More."

Cal sat by the window, and he could see Memorial Avenue below. Two MTA streetcars were passing each other, going in opposite directions with their bug-like antennae fingering the silent overhead wires.

"Do you think spring will come this year?" Cal asked Jack, staring down into the blackened snow frozen above the curbs. "The snow is still halfway up to the parking meters."

"It's a great life, Cal. Sometimes it seems as if life stops in this place, and sometimes it's speeded up so fast you can't keep up. I'm trying to finish three papers and every time I sit down to work on one of them I just dog paddle around in a circle. That goddamned Perkins has already turned in both his *New Testament* and *Psalms* papers."

"Does he have a work study? I never hear him talk about one."

"He's got a high school group at the big Presbyterian church in Brookline. It goes like clockwork."

"High school girls are safe, I guess."

"All girls are safe with Ben. All his sex is in his head. It's calculus with him."

"He's probably sleeping with the minister's wife. Guys like Ben are sleepers sometimes."

"One way or another. He sure gets his nine hours every night. He sleeps the sleep of the innocent."

"I wish I did."

"Don't tell me you got problems, Cal."

"No, not really, just the big problem."

"You're OK?"

"Yeah, I'm OK. Or I will be when I get this thing finished with Miss Green."

"That's still going on, huh?"

"Three times a week."

"Maybe I ought to do something like that."

"Don't if you don't have to."

"That's what my minister at home told me when I thought about coming here."

"*That* worked out for you, didn't it?"

"Sometimes I think it did. Right now I don't know."

Jack got up from where he was sitting on the edge of his bed and went to the window: "You have a better view in your room than I do. All I can see are cars and people going somewhere else."

"I watch rowers in little thin boats go up and down the river."

Cal knew that Jack wanted to tell him something, so he waited. He felt close to Jack at this moment, and he wanted to tell him about Regina, but he knew it was against the rules. He also knew that he should save it for Miss Green.

Jack looked at Cal and then at the street below.

"Thanks for not pushing me," Jack said.

Cal did not reply, and also watched the street below.

Jack smiled, seeing several seminarians they both knew, crossing to the streetcar stop in the middle of Memorial Avenue: "Did you get an A from Winston?"

All the third year seminarians had taken Paul Winston's course in Pastoral Counseling, so Cal and Jack knew the non-directive techniques of Carl Rogers, the psychologist.

"Yeah."

"Me too. It works." Jack waited several more seconds. I think I knocked up a girl in my choir."

Cal was thinking of Regina in bed. "But you're not sure."

Jack stared down into the street. "She's two weeks overdue."

Cal touched the seam of dried blood at Regina's hairline and marveled at how the morning light glistened on her hair. Regina kissed him on the chest as he gently dabbed the blood with the tip of a warm washcloth. She said "Thank you for doing this."

"I don't know whether I'm in love with her or not," Jack said. "We're good friends. She goes to Simmons College. We only screwed once before."

Cal looked at Jack, his dejected face and receding hairline. Jack was a small man, un-athletic, intense. He wore glasses. In addition to his church job in Belmont, he was the assistant to Rex Rehnquist who played the chapel organ. The veins in Jack's neck stood out when he was playing spirited hymns. After he volunteered to preach on Boston Common that day in the fall, he told Cal that he did it because he was going to be a choir director, not a preacher, but he wanted to prove to himself that he could do it.

Cal was still thinking of Regina. *She sat on the bed and said, "Just for now, let's not pretend we didn't do it. I'm glad we did. We can pretend later if you want. But please don't ever think that you owe me anything. Believe me, it was free, even though I'll probably now have to choose one special name for you."*

Cal said to Regina, "I wish I had used a safe."

"You didn't have one. I made the choice. We have a good chance to be OK. I'm not going to second guess myself."

"You're making it easy for me."

I"m not trying to. I"m trying to make it easy for myself.

"You got more than you bargained for when you came to Youth Group last night."

"I didn't make any bargains, and I'm trying not to make one now, either with the devil or myself. You could help if you'd let yourself go free."

"Allee allee in free? I heard a nice old woman use that phrase last month. I hadn't heard it since I was a kid."

"If you take yourself hostage in this, you'll be making a mistake."

"That's the kind of thing my therapist thinks."

"I don't know what a therapist does. My mother told me to trust myself and take the consequences."

"Your mother sounds like a therapist."

"My mother is a manager at the big Y. She's done it all alone. She's wonderful."

"She sure sounds like a straight talker."

"She's a straight everything. She goes to church but she's straight in spite of it."

"I know I'd like her."

"She knows that Breastburn is a fake, but she knows that Breastburn's not the Church, and he isn't important. She doesn't say he's a fake, just that he's a squash pie."

"She said that?"

"Yeah, that's what she calls him. She says he's afraid of his own shadow. She tried to talk to him once about my father but he perspired the whole time, and she never went back to see him."

"It's better than his making a pass at her."

"Poo. She could have handled him with her little finger. No one seduces my mother unless she wants them to."

"She told you that?"

"My mother's had two affairs and I met both men. One of them was a nice guy."

The lock turned in the door and Perkins came into the room carrying books in one arm and a grocery bag in the other. His glasses were fogged and he didn't recognize Cal until he put the armful down and took off his glasses and wiped them. Cal and Jack waited for him to speak. "Am I interrupting?" he said.

"Yes," Jack said.

"Shall I go back out?"

"Do you want to?"

"No, but I'm willing. I'll take an apple to the lounge. If you enjoy the guilt, as you obviously will or you wouldn't shun me, thus creating Christian regret for wounding your neighbor roomie in Christ, you may intensify said by munching on your Christian neighbor's apples while he is absent one from you brothers. Get it? Garden of Eden, original sin, absent one from the other?"

"Jesus, Perkins, don't go," Jack said. "We can't afford to deprive ourselves of your wit and wisdom. Sure, I'll have an apple. You want one, Cal?"

"No thanks, I've got to get downtown."

"I'll walk you to the elevator," Jack said.

Walking down the corridor, Cal asked Jack if he wanted to continue their conversation later.

"No, there's nothing else to talk about. I just wanted to tell someone. Just get it off my chest, you know?"

"Yeah, I know."

"Thanks a lot, Cal. I'll tell you how it turns out, or doesn't."

Cal rode down the elevator.

CHAPTER FORTY-SEVEN

▼

"ALLIES SINK, DAMAGE 23 JAP SHIPS IN INVASION FLEET OFF NEW GUINEA," *Daily Evening Item*, March 18, 1942

It was the middle of the night, and Cal was sitting on the edge of his bed. His eyes were open and he was talking to his mother and father, but part of him was still asleep. His father asked him where he was and Cal said, "I'm here," but he felt as if he were in dark space on the edge of the world. He started to cry and his mother said "Cal, wake up!" Cal looked at her and stopped crying. He nodded that he was awake, but he wasn't.

Cal's father frowned, studying Cal. He said, "There's something wrong with him." Cal's mother bit her lip and didn't say anything. Cal was still in dark space, now falling. In the darkness, he heard his father say "Jesus Christ," and with his eyes wide open, he shivered.

His mother said, "Cal, wake up!" and Cal looked at her and nodded. Cal's father said, "Has he been like this before?" Cal's mother said, "Once, but he just got back in bed and went to sleep."

Cal's father said, "Call Dr. Kneale tomorrow." Cal drowsed and closed his eyes. He looked as if he was asleep but then opened his eyes wide and started to cry. Cal's father said, "Jesus, he's sound asleep." After Cal finally went to sleep, his mother sat on the edge of his bed for a long time, then pulled the string of the ceiling light and left the bedroom.

The next morning, Cal's mother asked him if he remembered sitting on his bed, crying. Cal said he remembered falling off the earth and everybody looking at him. Cal said, "Daddy seemed mad at me."

Later that day, Cal asked his mother where his Captain Marvel comic books were, and she said, "I'm going to keep them for awhile."

CHAPTER FORTY-EIGHT

▼

It was raining when the subway car disappeared underground a hundred yards before Kenmore Square. Cal had an outside seat near the middle of the car. In Kenmore station, the car filled up. Cal thought of Eugene O'Neill. *Long Day's Journey into Night* had opened the week before on Broadway. Professor Konigsbauer had told the Art and Religion class that O'Neill died in the Kenmore Hotel where he lived alone.

At Copley, Cal watched two co-eds enter the car and move along the aisle to stand in front of him, holding the ceiling straps and conversing animatedly. He tried not to listen to the *he said this* and *I said that* conversation. One of the girls was tall and thin, and she had big breasts. When the subway car lurched on an underground curve, her right arm hanging from the ceiling strap pushed against her breast, and Cal could see a lot of cleavage in the open V of her dress. She had white teeth, and her hair was wet from the rain and curled along the hairline on her forehead. "God, I didn't know how to get rid of him," she said. Cal got an erection. The fast moving subway car lurched again as it turned into the Arlington Street station and the girl leaned into Cal. Her breast touched his face and he could smell her perfume. She said, "Oops, I'm sorry," and giggled, casting a sideways look at the other girl, who pretended that she didn't see what had happened.

Cal flushed and said, "It's OK, my pleasure." She looked at him, glanced away, and then looked at him again. Cal knew that at that moment he could have said something else, and made a gesture of some sort to prolong the interaction, but he couldn't think of anything. He asked her forgiveness with an apologetic smile. She smiled back. At the Tremont stop, the girl looked at him again, giving him one last chance, then disappeared into the lighted subway station.

Cal left the Arlington Street station and crossed to the Public Garden. The rain had stopped and a cold wind was blowing. He was ten minutes early for his appointment with Miss Green so he decided to walk slowly through the Garden instead of following straight along Arlington to the big brownstone house on the corner of Beacon and then up the stairs to her apartment on the third floor. The swan pond had been winter-drained, and several beer cans spotted the mud between the rain puddles. Cal walked the edge of the drained pond. He and Clare had taken a ride on a swan boat here last spring. Then they walked up Beacon Hill to the St. Gauden's bas-relief sculpture of Shaw's Negro Regiment across from the State House, and then over to the Union Oyster House where they ate raw little neck clams and fish chowder and Johnny cake. Later they walked back to Copley Square and went to Storyville to hear Burl Ives.

Cal walked past the statue of Washington on his horse. Part of the horse's mane was still wet from the rain. Black and white pigeon shit spotted Washington's sword handle.

At the monument to the doctor who first used ether as an anaesthetic, he re-read the familiar inscription and once again remembered as a child stepping up onto the edge of the kitchen chair to look into the kitchen mirror, tipping the top edge of the chair-back against his open mouth. When Dr. Kneale told Cal to breathe into the ether cone so he could sew the cut across Cal's tongue, he then asked Cal to count out loud to ten. At the number seven, Cal said through the cone over his nose and mouth, "I want to start over." The next thing he knew, he was throwing up, hanging over the couch in his living room at home, into the basin his mother had placed on the floor beside him. The vomit smelled and tasted like rotten tomatoes.

Cal crossed Arlington Street to the brownstone house where he climbed the three flights of stairs and knocked on Miss Green's door. He waited for her "Come in," but he heard nothing and knocked again. After several more seconds Miss Green opened the door partially and looked at him and said, "Yes?" She was smiling but looked surprised.

Cal said, "Am I too late?"

Miss Green said, "I believe this is Tuesday."

Cal was so embarrassed that he couldn't think of anything to say. He made a face as if to say how dumb he was, and then he said, "I guess I was in a hurry."

"I guess you were." Miss Green laughed.

"See you tomorrow," Cal said.

"See you tomorrow." Miss Green quietly closed the door.

Cal knew that she was with another patient, and he felt left out as he walked down the stairs. He opened the front door and walked along the sidewalk. This was the first time that he had not felt better after leaving the brownstone building. He crossed Commonwealth.

Cal thought to himself, *the truth shall make me free.* He walked down Boylston to Tremont and crossed over to the Common. He was cutting another class. The wind had died down and a fat pigeon, walking in front of him, nodding its head, stopped to peck at a Snickers wrapper, then backed up a few steps with the wrapper in its beak, its beady eyes pointing nowhere and everywhere, watching Cal as he passed. Cal said to himself, *I'm wandering around with the pigeons.*

Cal passed the Park Street Church and went into the Granary Burying Ground. His mother's ancestor, Mary Chilton, was buried here. Alone in the graveyard, he walked past the monument to Franklin's parents. At the furthest row of gravestones, he turned along the right lane and stood before the fourth grave, marked by an upright slate with barely legible writing on it. The skull on the upper portion of the slate was clear. Cal wondered if the bones of Mary Chilton were still in the ground or had turned to dust. He tried again to imagine being dead, but it slipped away from him. The gravestone said that the particles of dust beneath it had believed on the Lord Jesus Christ and the Resurrection.

Cal wondered where he himself would be buried. He did not want to be cremated. He wanted his body in plain view at his funeral. He would think of something appropriate to be inscribed on his gravestone, but it would not be religious. Maybe just $E = MC^2$. Maybe Mendel's law. The voice inside Cal's head said *How about Keats' "Ode to Autumn"?* Cal said to the voice, *How about the eighteen steps in the proof that a parallelogram has two sets of equal sides?* The voice said, *How about Rilke's "Torso of an Archaic Apollo"?*

Cal had not seen the two young people enter the graveyard, and only became aware of them as they passed behind him. Cal heard the girl say, "I love the sayings, they're so hopeful and creepy at the same time."

Cal could see out of the corner of his eye that they were holding hands. They looked like high school students.

The boy laughed and tugged the girl along. "*You're* creepy," he said.

The girl lent herself to the boy's tugging. She said, "But I'm hopeful *too*, aren't I?"

Cal watched them pass out of earshot, then turned and walked slowly out of the graveyard.

When the subway car had stopped on the way downtown in the Kenmore station, Cal had remembered Eugene O'Neill dying alone in the Hotel Kenmore, a block from Fenway Park, and he now wondered if O'Neill heard the Fenway fans during Red Sox games. Then he wondered why he thought of that. He tried to imagine O'Neill writing *Long Day's Journey into Night* on spring days when the noise rose from the park because Jackie Jenson had hit a home run into the left field net or over the net into Lansdowne Street.

CHAPTER FORTY-NINE

▼

Cal stood outside Fielding Drive and rang the bell for Howard
Konigsbauer's apartment. The buzzer clicked within the lock of the large
glass door and Cal pushed it open and heard the elevator descending to
him.

At the fifth floor, Konigsbauer's apartment door was ajar. As Cal was
about to knock, Konigsbauer's eyes appeared in the opening, and the
door opened.

"I thought it might be you," Konigsbauer said, smiling.

"Thanks for sending down the elevator."

"Of course. I'm so glad you could come."

Konigsbauer lived in a five-room apartment across from the New
India House, adjacent to the home of the President of Zion University.
From the apartment living room, Cal could see the Charles River to the
left of New India House, beyond Charles River Drive.

"You can see the river," Cal said. "That's nice."

"It *is* nice," Konigsbauer said.

"I can see it from my dorm window too."

"I understand that the river side is quieter than the streetcar side."

"I'd rather watch the shells than the streetcars."

"Of course you would."

"It's nice of you to look at my poems. They're not much."

"Of course they are much. Your poem in *Kairos* was splendid. I'm
very excited about your work. And I have something I want to ask you
later, related to that."

"I just brought two. I wrote one of them last year, and the other one this week. They're just sort of nature poems. I hope they're not corny."

"They are not corny, you can be assured, and I know that from your whole demeanor. You are certainly anything but a sentimental person, unlike, as I am sure you are aware, many of the young men in the seminary."

"Well, maybe. Most of them are pretty good guys, I guess. But I know what you mean."

"The Church needs more young men like you. Of all the ninnies I've known in the Methodist Church in my day, I could write a book. The ones like you are a very small number."

"I think I'm more interested in writing than in preaching, thanks to your class."

"Yes, I want you to tell me about the class, how I can make it better. I'm interested to hear what you really think."

"I think it's great. That assignment at the Museum of Fine Arts was really good. Just looking at one thing and writing about it really made me concentrate on the detail."

"You liked that, did you?"

"I really did."

"I have more ideas along those lines. In New York, perhaps, some stage plays. Would you like that?"

"Wow, yeah. I've never seen a Broadway play. You mean a bunch of us go down and stay in the city?"

"Why not? I think I can get a little money out of the Dean. If not, the only cost is gas for the car, maybe parking, and that's a pittance. We could stay at a friend of mine's apartment, if you boys don't mind sleeping on the floor."

"Count me in. The only thing is the guys with weekend church stuff."

"Why not go mid-week? What're a couple days of missed classes. I know that fussbudget Roth won't like it, but he'll recover if we don't make too much of it."

"He doesn't take attendance anyway."

"You mean he just presumes that everyone's there? Pooh!"

Cal took a folded paper from his pocket and opened it. "Well, these are my poems."

Konigsbauer looked at him 'meaningfully,' as Joe jokingly described the look later when Cal related the evening, and Konigsbauer said, "I have an idea." He went into another room and returned with a book. "I'd like to read you something before we do your poems, just to get us in the mood."

"Swell," Cal said.

Konigsbauer sat on the couch next to Cal and began to read. Cal could not see the cover with the title of the book, but it was a long thin book with a blue dust jacket and white writing.

"It rained last night. . . " Konigsbauer began.

Cal was immediately moved. He felt the loneliness behind the words, and the mood became his own mood, and he was captivated

Konigsbauer read several pages from Walter Benton's *This Is My Beloved.* Cal felt as if the poet were talking directly to him. Later, Cal would read the lines and regard them as sentimental, especially after hearing Joe call it "slush-mush," but on this particular evening he was affected deeply. Konigsbauer knew that Cal was moved, and he was pleased.

"I had a hunch that you might like this," he said. "I have something even better that I will show you some other time, if you like."

"Sure."

"Now let's look at your poems. These, I take it, will become grist for *Kairos's* mill?"

"I don't know. Maybe, if they're good enough. Grapple saw one of them and likes it. I haven't shown anyone else the one about the shadows in the river yet."

"So I'm the first audience. How splendid." Konigsbauer read the two poems, then read them again.

"Oh I like these, the images are poignant, and you show that you are able to work both in form and free verse. Quite good, yes, I like them."

"I actually wrote the one about the falling leaf to a girl, in a letter. Or I started it in a letter, then stopped and worked on the poem, then copied the rest of it in the letter."

Konigsbauer read out loud two of the stanzas:

among the grass the shadows grow
and brooding insects shun the light,
for now, wind-won, they fall below,

these carved colors freed from flight.

This leaf I saved for you tonight has freed itself
from red trees tall,
And send it not because it's new, but simply this:
I saw it fall.
"She must have been impressed."

"I don't know. She was, I guess. I hope so."

"You hope so. You *know* so. Don't try to hide your talent under a bushel."

"I'd like to get a lot better. There's a lot I have to read."

"Yes, by all means, read. But reading won't make you a better poet, by a drat. Do you know the German poet, Rainer Maria Rilke?"

"Actually, I've read a lot of Rilke. My friend Joe Stearns put me on to him. I think he's a genius. He and Keats are my favorite poets. Joe says they bite the bullet for him, and they do for me too."

"They bite the bullet, eh? That's pretty good. Where is this Stearns fellow hiding himself? I don't think I know of him."

"He spends all his weekends at his church in Braintree, and he studies a lot. We grew up together. He was a great football player in college. He played for Bowdoin. "

"You played too, I take it."

"Yes sir, I played at the university out in the western part of the state."

"That's quite interesting. I'm impressed that two football players know Rilke. Do you know his *Letters to a Young Poet*?"

"No sir."

"How about if I get a copy for you, and you come back next week at the same time. If you have any more poems, you can bring them."

"I probably won't, I'm not writing much these days."

"Any special reason, or just in the scheme of things."

"Just in the scheme of things, I guess."

"Well, you come back anyway, and we'll read some things together. I like you, and I want us to be friends."

"OK, I'll be here. Thanks a lot."

"And I do have something else to talk to you about, but perhaps I'll save it until we do the New York trip and see how everything goes."

Konigsbauer stood up and Cal shook his hand and thanked him and went down on the elevator. Cal walked the few steps to the corner of Fielding Drive and crossed the parking lot in back of the Communication College. He cut behind the married theological students' apartments and passed the entrance to the University refectory. He could see inside the open double door several students sitting at tables. The evening meal had been finished long ago and the place was almost empty. He wouldn't know anyone there.

Cal walked up the steps to the Chapel plaza and crossed to his dormitory. He was wondering about Howard Konigsbauer. *He was very open-minded. He actually said that the perfect conclusion to a man kissing a woman was sexual intercourse, and that he couldn't think of anything more perfect. Then he showed Cal a photograph of Rodin's sculpture of Le Baiser, "The Kiss." It was very erotic.*

Inside the dormitory he went to the elevator and waited for it to come up from the mailroom. When the door opened, Isaiah Rankins was inside, and they rode up together. Isaiah carried a shiny black cane with a pearl knob handle, and he wore a long black silk cape that was white on the inside. His face shone like ebony but he didn't make eye contact. Cal had never seen him without his cape and cane. He had actually never seen Isaiah except when walking to and from the elevator or standing inside the elevator. He had never had a conversation with Isaiah.

"Hi Isaiah."

"Hello."

"Nice night."

"It is indeed."

"How're things going at your church?"

"Fine, thank you."

"It's in Dorchester, isn't it?"

"Yes it is."

Isaiah's eyes were big and round with touches of light brown in the corners of the whites. When he glanced at you he smiled, and when he smiled he looked amused.

He had hit the #4 button and the elevator stopped,
"No library tonight, huh Isaiah?"
"Not tonight."
"Good night."
"Good night."
The elevator door closed and Cal rode alone up to the sixth floor.

CHAPTER FIFTY

On a Saturday morning in late March, Cal and Regina walked along a path in the woods of Cal's hometown. The path took them along the shore of a large reservoir of water.

"Where are we going?" Regina asked.

"The coves go way back in," Cal said, "where we used to fish and swim. No one could see us from the highway."

"I love it in here where there's no wind," Regina said.

"It's nice."

"I could worship just the Saturday morning sun in the spring."

"People do."

"No, they do it all year, I mean just spring itself."

Fifteen minutes later they stepped out on a ledge along the shore of the final cove. Four ducks exploded from the other side of the cove, streamlining over the water until they disappeared from view.

"They scared me," Regina said.

"I saw them before they took off, but I was looking for them."

"They go so fast. What good eyes you have, grandma."

"The years go by faster. Everything is the same except how it felt then."

"And now are you going to tell me where we are, and why you finally telephoned me, Mr. News?"

"We could go further in, like over there where the ducks came from, but we'd lose the sun."

"It's lovely here on the ledge."

Cal and Regina sat down beside each other on a great elephant back ledge, and Regina leaned her head back to catch the full rays of the sun on her face.

"Talk," she said.

"Yeah, I know." Cal stared across the water to the other side of the cove. After a few minutes of silence, Regina leaned back further on the warm ledge, her eyes closed.

"I waited six weeks, I can wait more," she said.

"At first I didn't call because I thought I'd see you every week at the Youth Group, then after that one time you came I figured out that you weren't coming any more. I understood that OK, I knew it was my move. Then it got easier because I didn't have to talk about it or even not talk about it. I didn't have to do anything. But I was talking about it with Miss Green. I told you I was seeing a therapist."

"I remember Miss Green."

"Yeah, well, it's not a good thing to make decisions when you're in the middle of therapy. I mean, like big decisions."

"So what big decisions are you talking about, specifically?"

"Well, I know, there are actually no big decisions, but I *felt* like I would be making big decisions, just by seeing you, you know?"

"No, but go ahead."

"Well, I've been going through this thing about Clare, and it's still sort of unresolved, maybe not for her, but for me. I mean, as long as I'm unsettled in my mind about Clare, I'm off balance is maybe one way to put it."

"Talk about 'unsettled.'"

"Yeah, you picked the right word, I guess. You're like Miss Green."

"Anybody can listen to anybody, if they want to. There's no trick to it."

"My problem is I don't know what I want. I don't want to go into the ministry and be a preacher. I don't even want to stay inside the church in any way, like teaching or administration, but I don't know what else to do. I had lousy grades in college and I probably can't get into graduate school. I want a girlfriend but I don't treat girls well. I wanted Clare but I was afraid of her, or I was afraid of myself with her. I understand why she won't see me. I did the same thing with my girlfriend at college. Now you."

"Elaborate, Mr. News, on that last topic, will you?"

"I want to see Clare again, Gina, just to resolve things, whatever that means. I don't even know where she is. She was in that bad accident, and I know I'm mostly responsible for that, and she wouldn't see me. Then when she did, she got mad at me and broke it off again. If I see her again and we get back together, where would that leave you?"

"Did I miss something? How did I get left anywhere? Outside of that shared snowstorm, we barely know each other. Aren't you presuming something that might possibly not be the real deal?"

"I don't mean to. I just want to come clean with you. I want to see Clare again, and I want to see you."

"No one else can live your life for you, Mr. News. Before I came out here with you today, my mother asked me what was up with you. I said I didn't know, and I really didn't, but I expected something like this."

"Are you disappointed?"

"Are you? It's a beautiful spring Saturday morning. When I was a little girl, Saturday mornings were magical, especially in the spring. The sky was so blue, the air so clear, everything fresh and brisk, and the leaves on the ground smelling of damp earth and that wonderful spring smell in the air. It was a little bit like walking in here on the path, as if we were going someplace important and when we got there we would be someplace separate from ourselves and just the best place to be, not anybody knowing we were here. Are you disappointed, Mr. News?"

"You sound angry."

"First, I'm disappointed, then I'm angry, and it's a good thing that I'm not pregnant because then you might think I'm bitter."

"I was afraid to ask. I'm glad you're not pregnant."

"So am I, Mr. Old News. But what exactly did you have planned for this morning besides wanting me to hold your hand because you want to fix it up with Clare again. Actually, it's OK, it's still Saturday morning and somebody else has deep feelings. It's still spring, the sun is still out and the muck beneath the old leaves is drying. I'm neutral. You want to dig around in the muck some more, go ahead. I'm happy to worship the spring sun while I listen. I'm serious. I wasn't going to tell you this, because I didn't think it would come to anything, but since you're going to risk getting your head knocked in again, I will also. Vinnie knows where Clare is, and he doesn't like you. Part of Vinnie is dangerous, but another part of Vinnie is real. He's not afraid of anything, that's for sure, and at least he goes after what he thinks is his."

"He thinks Clare is his?"

"Sure he thinks Clare is his."

"Does he call you?"

"He called me once."

"Did he mention me?"

"If I answer that, next you'll be telling me that I sound exasperated. You seem to think you get information from asking questions. What *did* you have planned? Tell me that, Mr. Old News, just tell me straight."

"I suppose it doesn't matter."

"It does if getting your head knocked in matters. I don't intend to try to save you from Vinnie and I don't intend to try to save you from Clare. In another place, in another time, saving you from yourself, I might have joined in this thing. Right now I want to fish."

"I didn't bring any gear."

"Ah, Mr. Old News, I did. I brought a fishing line and two squiggly worms I found under the leaves in our back yard before you picked me up this morning. You said on the phone that we might go fishing, so naive me wanted to be ready. I thought you'd bring a fancy pole or something, and I just wanted to do it the way I did when Mr. Sadoski my old neighbor took me fishing at Walden Pond one Saturday morning in spring when I was ten."

"You've fished Walden? That's really something. I was there once, but I didn't fish."

Regina took the coiled fishing line with its sinker and hook from her paper bag, and a piece of cellophane wrap from her coat pocket. When she opened two folds of cellophane, Cal could see the brownish pink worms. "What do you mean 'something,' me or the worms?"

"You and the worms and the sun on the ledge and the calm cove, and you fishing."

"Don't forget the ducks flying and the leaves drying and the willows weeping. It beats that other guy who was here with me ten minutes ago."

Regina edged closer to the water and began to push one of the worms onto the hook, following the curve so that half the worm covered half the hook. The end of the worm squirmed in the air.

"I'll bet you're even going to spit on the worm," Cal said.

"You bet I'm going to spit on the worm. What do you think I am, an amateur?"

She spat in the direction of the squirming worm but missed. She held the baited hook closer to her lips and spat again. "There," she said, tossing the hook and sinker fifteen feet out into the water.

Cal sat down on the ledge next to her. "I remember," he said, "one Saturday morning when I was about eleven. I got up early, before anybody else in the house, and got my kite and my father's deep sea drop-line from the garage. We lived about two hundred yards from the Lynn line where Pine Ridge Avenue becomes a dirt road that curves along the edge of some woods where there were two huge boulders. We called them First Rock and Second Rock. I took my kite and climbed First Rock and let the wind take the kite into the air. As the line pulled out, the salty tar smell from the unraveling line got stronger. I had brought extra cloth strips in case the tail wouldn't be heavy enough to hold the kite in the wind, and when it started wobbling and dipping, I hauled it back in and tied on two more pieces of cloth tail. Then I let the kite way out, to the end of the line.

"I flew it for about a half-hour. When I hauled it back in, it was wet with dew. Then I went home and ate my breakfast at the kitchen table. It was only seven o'clock in the morning, and still no one was up. I always ate Wheaties in my red Bobby Benson cowboy dish."

"I had a bite, just a nibble."

"Is he still there?"

"No, I don't think so. Then what happened?"

"I was being very quiet. It was as if I had just performed a secret magic rite, and I wanted to leave the house before anyone came downstairs and broke the spell. I took a nickel from the little brown pocketbook my mother kept for me in the comb tray fastened to the cupboard next to the kitchen sink. I wasn't supposed to ever touch the pocketbook money because it was for when my mother took me to Revere Beach for a day at the beginning of summer. But I only took the nickel, and it was the only time I ever took money from that brown pocketbook."

"There! I've got him! Oh oh, I think he's gone. That was a good bite. He really banged it, but when I tried to set the hook, I lost him. Maybe I yanked it too hard."

"I don't think so. The hook probably was just in the wrong position."

"I better check my bait."

Cal watched Regina retrieve her line, re-bait the hook, spit on the worm, and cast out again. When the baited hook and the sinker hit the water and descended, Regina said, "Now, go on with your story. I love it."

"I went out to the garage again and quietly opened the swing door to get my bike. I had gotten it about two months before and I was very proud of it and careful not to scratch it. I had saved up my money to buy a Columbia bike and had seen one advertised in the *Lynn Item*. The store was in Salem and we had driven over in my father's old Buick. When I saw this blue and white bike, I fell in love with it, and although it didn't have a Columbia label on the front, the store man said that the bike was made by the Columbia Company.

"I had eighteen-and-a-half dollars saved for the bike and my mother said she'd put in the other five, and we drove home with my hands out the back window holding the bike to the running board of the car. I remember how the wind blew my hair and how kids along the road watched me holding this beautiful blue and white bike as we drove by. Anyway, I got the bike out of the garage and rode down Pine Ridge Avenue toward Wilfred Berry's house. I knew that Leger's store opened at 7:30, but I wasn't allowed to call for Wilfred until 8:00. Any more bites?"

"Not yet. Go on."

"I didn't have a watch, but I knew it was still early because no one was up except Cappy Hood. I had seen him carrying out his trash barrel when I passed his house. Cappy was the MacAdams milkman and I really liked him. Later when I played football in high school, Cappy was my greatest supporter. On this morning, he waved at me when I went by on my bike. I rode all the way to the end of Pine Ridge Avenue where it joins Hayes, past Wilfred Berry's house on the corner. The only other person I saw the whole way was old Jimmy MacDowell, out for a walk. He was Protestant Irish with a little lilt to his speech and he went to our church. He wore a cap with a wide brimmed visor and he always put his forefinger to his cap to simulate tipping it instead of saying hello.

"I passed Wilfred's house and went down Hayes to Beechnut Street that ran along the reservoir. You couldn't see the reservoir, though, because there was a pine grove between Beechnut Street and the water. Mr. Leger's store was about two hundred yards down Beechnut Street, and I leaned my bike against his front steps and went in. He came out from the kitchen and said hello. I asked him what time it was and he said 7:45. I said that I would be back in fifteen minutes with Wilfred because we were going to buy a Whoopie Pie. He said 'All right,' and went back into his kitchen. I sat on the front steps of the store and waited for what I thought was ten minutes, watching the cars go by. Not too many cars went by because it was early Saturday morning."

"Wait! There it is, he's nibbling." Regina yanked the line and yelled, "I got him. He's big." She brought the line in slowly, alternating her hands, which were being jerked every which way by the submerged fish.

"Bring him in slowly. What do you think it is, a bass?"

"How do I know? It's not a flatfish, I can tell you that."

Regina pulled the fish to within several feet of the ledge where it suddenly broke water and made a big splash, submerged again and pulled so hard that Regina had to give up two steps on the ledge as she held the line, both arms against her body, making a hard fist with the line wrapped around it, backing up a step, then another.

"It's a huge pickerel," Cal shouted. He wanted to help but he didn't know what to do except watch. If he touched the line and she lost the fish, he would feel responsible.

Regina backed up another step, then another, dragging the squirming and slithering pickerel out of the water and onto the ledge, the whole length of its body arching back and forth, flopping, scraping itself on the ledge with the sound of a razor slapping against a leather strop.

Cal threw himself between the flopping fish and the water, cradling his hands and pushing the pickerel further up the ledge to safety. Regina kept backing up and hauled the pickerel into the woods. She stood still, blinking her eyes.

"You did it," Cal said. "Nice going. He's a beauty."

"My mother loves pickerel," she said.

"She really does?"

"No, I'm kidding. She's never heard of a pickerel. She'll die when she sees it."

"It must be twenty inches."

"I hope it's big enough to keep because it sure is big enough for me."

"Oh it's legal all right. It's just that we're not."

"Who's not legal?"

"Us. We don't have fishing licenses."

"I thought you said this was a reservoir, and you fished here."

"We were never legal."

"No fishing, no license. Two illegals make a legal, right?"

"Right. The only problem will be getting it into the car when we get back out to where we parked. Are you sure you want it?"

"Of course I want it. You think I'm going to arm wrestle this baby out of his lair and his life and then just leave him. Old Mr. Sadoski said, 'We catch it, we clean it, we eat it, we give life to death.' But we need some kind of a bag or some newspapers to wrap him in."

"I've got this morning's *Boston Herald* in the car."

"Right now, Mr. Old News, Good News, New News, I want to sit by the water and drink in the morning sun again and listen to the end of your story. We can wrap this creature in swaddling clothes later. On MacDuff."

"You are very literary today."

"Because it's Saturday, the sixth day. The sixth day is always when you break out the books. You can't be literary on the seventh day because God is watching for stuff like that. God does not like the *literati* on the seventh day, or fishermen either, for that matter. Didn't Jesus say something by a lake, like 'Gather ye fishes while ye may?' I know that it was a Saturday because all the boat people were off work for the weekend."

"That was Suckling and it was rosebuds."

"Yeah, Suckling, that's it. Whoa, am I worked up! My heart is still pounding."

The big pickerel flopped again in the bushes. Cal went to drag it out of the sun and it was no longer attached to the line. "He worked the hook out of his jaw."

"Good for him. I'll deal with him later. He's not going anywhere. Come on, your story."

Cal sat down next to Regina in the sun. "The story's almost finished anyway. Where did I leave off?"

"The cars are going by Mr. Leger's store. Get to the Whoopie Pie. What in the world is a Whoopie Pie?"

"OK, to the Whoopie Pie."

"No, don't skip, just don't forget it."

"How can I forget it? It's my life story. The cars are going by and I'm watching them. Ten minutes maybe, and I get on my bike and ride to Bancroft's house on the corner and walk up Hayes to Wilfred's house."

"I love that name, Wilfred Berry. Was that his real name?"

"Sure it was his real name. So I'm standing over my bike, calling for Wilfred outside his back door. I call two or three times and his mother opens the back door and says he's just getting up and would I like to come in while he has his breakfast. So I push down the kickstand on my bike and go in the back door behind Mrs. Berry and sit at the kitchen table."

"Was Mrs. Berry fat?"

"Round."

"I love it. What was Mr. Berry like?"

"He wasn't there but he was round too. I'd seen him before. He was a lot to look at. Wilfred walks into the kitchen rubbing his eyes. He had blonde curly hair and big ears that stuck out, and blue eyes. His eyes were full of sleep seeds and his mother sent him to the bathroom to wash his face. By this time I felt as if I'd been up half the night, and I was actually starved again, but I was not hungry for any more cereal."

"Just the Whoopie Pie."

"Yeah, just the Whoopie Pie. So when Wilfred's mother goes out of the room, he's eating his cereal with one of those small spoons, and I tell him to hurry up and finish eating because we're going to Leger's store to get a Whoopie Pie. The last time we had done it, Wilfred had gotten the nickel from his father."

"From old round Berry."

"How? Wilfred said to me, 'I don't have any money.' I said I had a nickel. He said 'Really?' I said hurry up before he had to do chores or something. He said 'I did them yesterday.'"

"So you rode your bikes to Leger's store."

"Right."

"And you bought the Whoopie Pie and sat on the front steps and ate it and watched the cars go by."

"Right. You got the whole story."

"Come on. That's not the whole story. It can't be."

"No, actually we broke the Whoopie Pie in half."

"If you don't tell me what a Whoopie Pie is, you'll be in trouble."

"All's it is, it's a double chocolate bun, sort of, with whipped cream in between."

"What do you mean, 'sort of'?"

"Well it's a chocolate bun, but it's bigger, like an inflated chocolate pancake. It's really good."

"That's not really the end of the story, is it?"

"No, we went back to Wilfred's house and got fishing lines like you have there. Wilfred always had two of them, and we rode our bikes to the path we walked in on today, and pushed our bikes right here to this ledge. It was a day just like today, and we sat on this ledge in the sun, away from the wind, and we had the rest of the day before us, and our whole lives, and we lay in the sun out of the wind with our lines in the water and fished and talked."

"What did you talk about?"

"I have no idea."

"It doesn't matter, does it?"

"No. I just remember the morning sun back here in the cove where nobody knew we were, and a mystery fish was somewhere out there in the water down deeper than we could see.

"Did you catch any that day?"

"No, we never had a bite."

"Somehow, that's even better."

"Somehow, but I don't know why."

"I do."

"You're one up on me, I guess."

"It's simple. It's only what happens. Anything else, your whole life would have been different."

"You believe that?"

"I do."

As they walked back to the car, Regina gripped her pickerel with her right thumb and forefinger in the V of its gills, the tail dragging in the leaves as she walked. When they nearly reached the end of the path, Regina cut into the woods and came out where the car was parked beside the road. Cal had opened the back door of his Plymouth and spread newspapers on the floor. Regina laid the pickerel on the open *Boston Herald* and turned the page to cover it. She wiped her hands on the business page, crumpled it into a ball, and dropped it into the back.

Cal drove north on Beechnut Street and turned right, just before the overpass, onto route 1. Soon they were in Lynnfield, and then they were driving west on route 128.

CHAPTER FIFTY-ONE

▼

"MURDER OF YOUNG LYNN WOMAN, FRANCES COCHRAN, STIRS NEW ENGLAND: Mutilated and Sexually Ravaged Body Found in Thicket on Danvers Road," *Daily Evening Item*, July 17, 1941

On a warm summer night, lying in the double bed at the back of the darkened camp on the shore of the lake, Cal could barely hear the adult voices on the screened-in porch, but he knew they were talking about the Francis Cochran murder. He held his breath so that he could hear better, until he had to breathe. Then he inhaled deeply and listened again. After a while they were talking louder, and he didn't have to hold his breath. He could now distinguish most of the voices except Mrs. Banway and his mother, who whispered. Edna Brewster's voice was scratchy, and Cal heard her say that they found motor oil in her lungs. Cal was scared and thrilled to be hearing this. He knew this wasn't for his ears, as his mother would say.

The adults had just come in from hornpouting, and they had been drinking beer, except for Cal's mother, and they had at first tried to be quiet so as to not wake Cal. His mother didn't know that from the porch Cal had watched them in the anchored rowboats just off shore with the kerosene lanterns on the seats, and had gotten back into bed after the boats tied up at the dock and a flashlight moved away from the fish table where the men were cleaning the fish. The women were coming up to the camp. The Banways and the Brewsters were his parents' closest friends, and they had driven from Mapleville to spend Saturday night and Sunday at the lake.

Earlier, from the porch, watching the lanterns on the water, Cal wished he was in one of the boats, joining in the fun on the lake, close to grownups fishing in the dark. Standing alone on the porch, he was not afraid, even though he didn't want to go to bed inside the dark camp. He wasn't afraid of the dark when he was on the lake, not even when the bats flew close to his head, and he wasn't afraid of the woods either. He just didn't like being in the camp alone in the dark.

On the lake, someone had shouted, and then everyone laughed. Mrs. Brewster said, "Come on Lem, you take it off for me," and everyone laughed again. Cal liked hearing the voices coming up from the water. He knew they were having fun catching the hornpout.

Now, in his bed, Cal listened. He hadn't known that his mother knew about a murder in Peabody. Somebody said something he couldn't hear. It was mostly the women talking. Mrs. Brewster said that part of a tree branch was jammed down her throat. Then Cal heard Mrs. Banway say, "They say everything comes in threes. I wonder who will be next. First the Lindbergh baby, then Francis Cochran."

Cal had already heard his mother and father talking about the Lindbergh baby. Cal shivered. He knew about the dead baby.

On the porch, the summer night voices were talking about a ladder. Cal pictured a ladder up against his own house, someone coming across the porch roof and into his room after dark.

Now Cal was afraid to listen to the voices, but he was more afraid not to listen. He wanted to know everything. The more frightened he got, the more he wanted to know. He couldn't help it. The word "murder" sent electricity through his veins. It would be inconceivable to murder someone, but someone might murder him. Not here at the lake. Cal felt safe in his bed, in the dark, his parents on the porch.

The pauses became longer between the talk on the porch. Cal looked up toward the roof of the camp and the darkness. He couldn't see them but he knew the wooden boards were there. Tomorrow night the ceiling would be white again, and he would wake up the next day at home. Cal loved this darkness in the camp when he was in his bed, but now he was getting sleepy. He loved the close feeling of the grownups sitting together on the porch in the quietness, liking each other, enjoying the darkness of the summer night, speaking after long pauses. Then a beer can was opened, and Cal liked the sound of the snap-squish, then another, and it was quiet again.

Cal thought of his new floating plug, a "jitterbug" that made a bubbling noise when it moved on the surface of the water, its black and green spots like a frog. Uncle Orion read out loud what it said on the top of the little box it came in: "See dope on back." His father and Uncle Nate laughed.

Cal remembered the water snake coiled on the rocks in the sun in front of the fish table, then how his dog Pickles picked up the flopping pickerel in his mouth and dropped it overboard and his father laughed in the light mist and the cove was dark green. His father was jiggling the frog along the water with his long yellow bamboo pole, then two days later the long yellow pole was floating in the middle of the lake, moving in a circle because Cal had left the pole in the boat overnight with the dead frog still on the hook in the water.

When Cal's mother came inside the camp and lighted the kerosene lamp hanging over the round table in the middle of the room, Cal was asleep in the corner double bed.

CHAPTER FIFTY-TWO

▼

The bells in the Chapel tower rang five, then six, then seven o'clock, early evening. Cal lay on his bed in his room reading *East of Eden.* He had saved it for the last of Steinbeck's books to read. The main character's name was also Caleb. Cal hadn't gone to class for two days, leaving the room only to eat and to go downtown to see Miss Green. Jake Foster had told him at the last *Kairos* board meeting that Hollywood was making a movie of the book and that James Dean was going to play the lead. Cal didn't know who James Dean was, and Jake said that he was a brilliant young actor, and as Cal read the book he pictured himself playing the role of Caleb.

As Caleb in the story talked to Lee, the Chinese house servant, Cal imagined himself talking to Lee. Cal had come to the part where Lee explained the Hebrew word *timshel,* "thou mayest," and tried to convince the younger brother that he could change as a person if he wanted to, but Cal now remembered what Foster had said: "It's a great book but not as good as *The Grapes of Wrath*. And Steinbeck mistranslated *timshel*." Cal now would have to ask Foster what he meant by that. Cal didn't know whether *East of Eden* was better than *The Grapes of Wrath*. It didn't matter. Cal didn't want the book to end. He would stay in his room, reading. In the book, Caleb and his brother Aaron had a fistfight and Aaron ran from the house. The chapter ended. Cal looked at his watch. It was five minutes to eight.

Cal closed the book and went to the window and stared into the dark, then opened the window and the cold spring breeze made him narrow his eyes. He listened for the last coxswain shouts on the Charles River, but he could hear only the rush of the cars on Fielding Drive. Cal realized that he was hungry and decided that he would walk over to Beacon Street and eat at Schrafts, or maybe Chinese next door. He took his coat, walked to the end of the hallway and pressed the elevator button. Jim Toffert rode down with him to the fourth floor. "Why don't you heathens ever come to Thursday night chapel?" he snarled in his subtly amused and pompous way.

"Lighten up, Jimbo," Cal said as Toffert waddled out of the elevator.

Crossing Memorial Avenue at St. Catherine Street, he met Joe Lober, Foster, and Truckee coming back from dinner. "It's too late, Cal, they just ran out," Truckee called from the other side of the street.

"I already ate," Cal called back. "I'm going over to preach tonight at the Unitarian Church."

"Give Burntcock my best," Truckee yelled and waved.

Cal crossed the bridge over the railroad tracks and then was in Brookline walking under the linden trees. He was glad to be alone tonight. He felt as if his life had stopped in the middle of a strange new calm, while everything else was moving around it. Ordination loomed ahead of him in May like a spectre.

Cal hadn't called his parents, ten miles away, in months. School was a ball of loose ends, reading novels, cutting class, planning a trip to New York with Konigsbauer, another all-nighter next week on the verityper with *Kairos*, a summer job, next year, and then there was his life. And the voice inside him said *and that's not all, kid, by a long shot.*

I know, there's Clare, and behind Clare, there's Joannie.

If you're going to play, why not deal yourself the whole deck?

Miss Green's got to be finished with, sometime. I can't force it. I've got to let it happen.

Just don't leave anybody out.

She's on the edges. She's not asking for anything. She's not part of this.

You don't tell Miss Green that.

I'm still working through my mother.

Bravo. Good for you.

If I get this thing straightened out between me and my mother, the rest of my life will fall into line. Miss Green, my mother, Joannie, Clare—

Is that all?

No, that's not all. There's a lot more. All the names of all the females inside of me, mostly Regina. . . .

Then what?

Here's Beacon Street.

Cal looked at the menu inside the window at Schrafts. The special was baked scallops in lobster sauce. He looked at the price: $3.75. He pushed through the glass door and sat at a booth. The waitress came over and said, "Hi." She was wearing a short black dress with a round lace apron at her waist. A ringlet of brown hair curled under each ear. She asked Cal if he was ready.

"Are you still serving breakfast?"

"Why not?"

"I'll have bacon and eggs with English muffins and a large glass of tomato juice."

"Be right out." She went into the kitchen.

When the waitress brought his bacon and eggs, Cal asked her how the scallops were. She said "Really good."

"When I came in, I was going to get them."

"Why didn't you?"

"I don't know. I like eggs, I guess."

"Me too, but I had the scallops."

While Cal was walking back to the dormitory, it started to rain lightly, more of a heavy mist. As he walked under each street lamp, he noticed the circular configurations of tree branches reflecting the light. He was passing under giant spidery bullseyes in the cold spring mist. As he passed the Boston city line, it occurred to him that it was Thursday night. Chapel starts at nine o'clock. Why not?

Cal found Travis studying in the room and told him he was going to chapel.

"Sure 'nuff, man," Travis said, "I'll go. What time is it?"

"Five till."

"Let's go." He turned his book upside down, still open. "Man, this is the greatest book I ever read."

"Which?"

"*Ten Days That Shook the World*, man. I got the chills. Comes the revolution, brother."

"Bishop Moore will love that."

"Wouldn't he now?"

They took the elevator to the second floor and entered the small chapel. Jack was playing the prelude: "The Church's One Foundation." Cal counted thirteen theology students and D.R.E. candidates, including Cripswell and Lovell and Jim Toffert. He nudged Travis. "There's Susan."

Travis nodded.

"I think Toffert's going to do the service. No wonder he goaded me today."

When Jack finished, Toffert stepped to the small lectern and intoned the invocation:

The hour cometh and now is when all true worshippers
shall gather and bow down at the blessed name of Jesus.
Come into his temple and open your hearts. Sing his praises,
lay your past on the altar of the Lord. This is the night
of the Redeemer. Amen.

Everyone sang "Holy, Holy, Holy" and said the Nicene Creed. Toffert led them in the prayer of St. Chrysostom, which he had passed out beforehand on typed carbon copies. Cripswell turned around and handed his copy to Cal and Travis, then turned around and looked on with Lovell.

For the meditation, Toffert read "An Exhortation" from the Book of Common Prayer, which lasted for ten minutes. Toffert read slowly and majestically:

Examine your lives and conduct by the rule of God's commandments, that you may perceive wherein you have offended in what you have done or left undone, whether in thought, word, or deed. And acknowledge your sins before Almighty god, with full purpose of amendment of life, being ready to make restitution for all injuries and wrongs done by you to others; and also being ready to forgive those who have offended you, in order that you yourselves may be forgiven. And then being reconciled with one another, come to the banquet of that most heavenly Food. And if in your preparation, you need help and counsel, then go and open your grief to a discreet and understanding priest, and confess your sins, that you may receive the benefit of absolution, and spiritual counsel and advice; to the removal of scruple and doubt, the assurance of pardon, and the strengthening of your faith. . . .

Cal whispered to Travis: "Where's that from? It's not from the Methodist Hymnal."

Travis put his hand over his mouth and whispered back: "From the Anglican *Book of Common Prayer*. He's a high Anglican, man."

They sang another hymn and Toffert gave the benediction:

Almighty God, with whom still live the spirits of those who die in the Lord, and with whom the souls of the faithful are in joy and felicity: We give you heartfelt thanks for the good examples of all your servants, who, having finished their course in faith, now find rest and refreshment. May we, with all who have died in the true faith of your holy Name, have perfect fulfillment and bliss in your eternal and everlasting glory; through Jesus Christ our Lord. Amen.

Cal elbowed Travis. Travis leaned his head toward Cal's lips. Cal said, "That's a funeral committal prayer. That pompous pimp."

"It's his joke. Look at the smirk on Cripswell's face. They think we're dead, man. Don't let on we know. They think we don't know the *Book of Common Prayer*."

"I'm going to wait for Susan. I haven't seen her to talk to since I went to Tom's for the weekend a couple months ago."

"I'll see you in the room. You want to play ping pong later?"

"That'll be great. See you." Cal turned to Jim Toffert, who was also leaving. "Nice service, Jim. Thank you."

"You're welcome, silly boy. But pardon my being dumbstruck. I expect perfect attendance from now on." Toffert made the sign of the Cross.

Susan Burwell had also waited for Cal, each waiting for the other to be alone. Cal smiled at Susan and said, "Hi Susan, long time no talk."

"I'm so glad to see you, Cal. This is really strange. I was going to call you right now, before I went home. Now you're here."

"Oh oh, what'd I do?"

Susan shook her head. "Have you talked to Joe within the last two weeks?"

"Sure, we had dinner in Chinatown last week with a visiting grad student from Ireland, and I had dinner with him two nights ago at Simione's in Cambridge. What's up?"

"He didn't *tell* you anything, then, did he?"

"About you and him?

"No, about him."

"We talked about me, mostly, as usual."

"Cal, I've got to talk to you."

"Sure. Let's go back in the chapel."

Cal opened the chapel door and followed Susan. They sat in the closest pew inside the door. Susan put her hand on Cal's and said, "Cal, Joe's sick."

"How sick?"

"He might have leukemia. Cal, we were talking about getting married next year, after second ordination."

Cal looked away, then looked back at Susan. "Jesus."

"If he hasn't told you, he hasn't told anybody."

"Not even Tom."

"No, I asked Tom last Sunday, and he hadn't."

"So you told Tom?"

"Yes, I did. Did I do the right thing, Cal?"

"Yeah, you did."

"Joe found out three weeks ago. He kept it to himself for a week before he told me."

"Who did the lab work?"

"Mass Medical."

"Shall I tell him that I know?"

"I don't know."

"I better not. He probably doesn't want to tell me until he's sure."

"He's sure. The doctors say there's an outside chance that it's not, but Joe says he's sure."

"What'll we do?"

"I don't know. Thank you for telling me, Susan. I'll walk you back to your apartment."

"I knew you'd ask, and I was going to say no, that I wanted to walk back alone, but I changed my mind. It would be nice. I'd like you to."

Outside it was still raining and misty. Cal walked Susan to her apartment behind Kenmore Square and then walked back to the dormitory. At midnight, Cal and Travis went down to the recreation room and played three games of pingpong. Travis won all three games by lopsided scores.

CHAPTER FIFTY-THREE

▼

Cal's mother came in from the kitchen and set a platter with four grilled chunks of tenderloin of venison on the dining room table: "There. You're going to be the judge, Joe. You have to tell us honestly whether you think this is deer meat or we just went out and bought some beef to fool you."

"Do I get to taste it first, Mrs. Newsome, or do I have to tell by the looks? It sure looks like beef."

"Guess, Joe, and if you guess wrong, we get to eat yours," Cal said.

"Don't pay any mind to him, Joe. You go ahead and eat. I'm just bragging beforehand. I had a little taste in the kitchen."

"If it's that good, I'm going to get in a little bragging myself," Cal's father said. "Anybody can cook deer meat right, it's the hanging that makes the difference."

"Sounds like an execution, dad."

"That's right. It's the perfect execution. Two weeks at the end of a rope is the minimum and four weeks is the maximum. All depends on the weather, the colder the longer."

"Listen to him," Cal's mother said. "To hear him talk you'd think blood-rare and well done is the same. I'd sure as like to have two weeks to four weeks to decide when to turn the grill off instead of two to four minutes."

"Score two points for mum, dad."

Cal and his parents watched Joe cut a piece of venison steak and put it in his mouth. Joe smiled as he chewed, and after a few seconds said, "It's marvelous Mrs. Newsome. Whatever you both did, it sure is good meat. If I didn't know it was venison, I'd have to say it was prime tenderloin of beef."

"That's because I got all the wild moisture out of it," Cal's father said. The hanging dries it out. That deer dressed out at 194 pounds and by the time we took it to the locker it was down to 175 or so. But you cooked it really good, mum."

"This is just like Thanksgiving, Mrs. Newsome, with the mashed potatoes and gravy and all these vegetables."

"It's all from last summer's garden, Joe. I put up the pole beans and the peas, and we have a whole coffin full of sand and carrots in the cellar."

"She even made a pecan pie," Cal's father said, pronouncing it 'pee can.' "I was wondering who was coming for supper and then I saw her making that pie and I knew it was Cal. The only time I get fed like this is when Cal comes home."

"That's a story if I ever heard it. But we have to do something special for when we're all together. That means you too, Joe. We're so excited about the ordination coming up, and Worcester's not that far so we can drive out there. And the doctor says that Cal's father can go. He just can't drive, but I can, so we'll be there early. It's not every day that I get the chance to see my son and his best friend ordained ministers of the Church."

"It's not that big a thing, mum."

"It is so a big thing to be able to marry people and baptize their children."

"What's the difference, exactly, between a deacon and an elder?" Cal's father asked.

"It's like an inoculation and a booster shot, Mr. Newsome," Joe said. After the inoculation, you're certified to do everything a regular parish minister does except officiate at the Holy Communion. After the booster shot, you get to do that."

"What about burying people?" Cal's father asked.

"Deacons can do it," Cal said.

"What on earth did you ask that for, Lem?"

"Actually, anyone can do it," Joe said. "It's one of those common sense things, I guess. Even the Catholic Church allows anyone to give the last rites of the Church."

"Just checking," Cal's father said. "There's no point to die not knowing whose going to do the honors if you can find out beforehand."

"Lem, . . ." Cal's mother began.

"What's up dad? What did the doctor say?"

"Daddy, nothing's going to happen to you. The doctor said. . . . This is supposed to be a celebration," Cal's mother said.

"He said 'maybe.' It *is* a celebration. These upcoming deacons here, they know the score about heart attacks. They're professionals. They know about dying. Right guys?"

"Right," Joe said.

"Right, Cal?" his father said, looking directly at Cal.

"Yes, . . . that's right," Cal said, "we're professionals."

"Let's go for a walk," Cal's mother said. "It's a quarter of seven. We've got just time before dark. The doctor says we all need exercise, and we haven't walked the neighborhood since you went off to college, Cal.

It was a cool spring night, although spring wouldn't officially arrive for another week. The day before, it rained and the wind blew all day, but now it was quiet, and the smell of the wet ground was in the air. The four of them walked up Grant Avenue past houses whose occupants were now strangers to Cal and Joe.

"I wonder where the Bucchieri's live now," Cal said. "Remember when Johnny Bucchieri kicked the field goal in the post season game against Salem and Mapleton won, 3-0?"

"Snow was piled all around the field, and the coach sent the players out in the second half wearing sneakers," Joe said.

"Buzz Grayson was a smart coach," Cal's father said. "Nashua, Vermont got the best high school coach in the business."

"Johnny kicked that field goal in his sneakers," Joe said.

"There's Old Man Brault's house," Cal said. I took that path into the woods a hundred times to get to Oak Street. I wonder if the stockade sign is still there in the middle of the woods."

"It is," Cal's father said. "At least it was last year. I went out squirrel hunting for old time's sake, and it was right on the path as always. I heard from Ray Maes that they're going to put a road through and build houses next summer."

"I remember the day Old Man Brault died," Cal said, "a taxi driver dropped him off at the top of Pierce hill because it was the town line.

He thought Brault was drunk and pushed him out of the cab right onto York's lawn. But he was dead. In back of his house it always smelled of urine. I don't know how he got through the winters."

"You remember the darndest things, Cal," his mother said.

"I remember everything, mama, see those swings in the school playground? I remember the day Dickie Grella faked showing me the magnifying glass and burned my wrist. See that lamp post, I remember the last day we played *Buck Buck, How Many Fingers Up?* with Ralphie and Ray and Duck Grain. I remember the day Duck pushed me down in a football game during recess and I hit my head on a stone and Miss Shoreham made me stand in front of the class while she dabbed alcohol on my head to clean the cut."

They walked past the house where Cal was born, and reminisced about the hurricane of 1938. They passed the lot where the little white church had been where Cal and Joe went to Sunday school. Someone had set it on fire and it burned down. They talked about ministers John Finney, Emory Roberts, and Phil Pitcher, students from the School of Sacred Thought where Cal and Joe were now studying. Cal said, "Remember the Ladies' Aid variety show when you read the long poem you wrote, mama? 'This is for Pitcher, the minister Phil, who rides his bike all over the hill.'"

"Gorry day, you do remember everything. Phil Pitcher used to show up every Monday noon at my front door asking me if I had a warmed-over plate of beans from Saturday night. And I always did, God love him."

They passed the house where Joe lived as a boy, before his parents moved to Mapleton Center. "Remember the day we looked for crawfish, Joe and those guys came by with the wood duck?"

"I do now."

It was dark when they arrived back at the house.

Driving the ten miles back to Boston, Joe and Cal were quiet. Instead of going past the reservoir on Beechnut Street to route 1, Cal drove down Oak Street to Mapleton Center, through East Mapleton to the Revere Road. As they passed the drive-in theater, Cal said, "I remember seeing *Wuthering Heights* here in the back seat of Mrs. North's car when I was seven. I can still hear Cathy's voice calling into the wind, "Heathcliff, Heathcliff. . .."

"I only read the book, but I can hear her too," Joe said.

Neither spoke until Cal parked behind the dormitory next to the trash barrels. Joe said he was going to walk for a while along the river before going up to his room.

"Thanks Cal, for the evening. The deer steak was swell. Night."

"Night, Joe."

Cal entered the dormitory through the back door.

CHAPTER FIFTY-FOUR

▼

"It's the second act, you see, where a real playwright delivers, not the first act or the third act, but the second act." Professor Ehrensperger spoke with pride and alacrity as he led his small band of seminarians along the edge of Central Park, toward the zoo. He was visibly happy, more so than Cal had ever seen him. The day before, when Cal had arrived at Konigsbauer's apartment before the others, to drive to New York City, Konigsbauer had asked Cal if he would be interested in driving down to North Carolina with him in late April. He had a speech to make at Chapel Hill on religion and art. Cal said that he would.

"This is not Williams's greatest play, mind you, but it is crafted. Williams is a craftsman. He knows the theater inside out." Cal wanted to ask Konigsbauer why the second act was more important than the first, but he didn't. He didn't know why.

They were passing a pretzel stand and the smell of the roasting onion pretzels drew Konigsbauer to order six from the vendor: "Let's really do New York," he said, passing out the pretzels. "How can you walk Central Park after a matinee in spring and not eat a roasted pretzel? On to the zoo, men, to see the polar bears, and then we'll get a cab to the Russian Tea Room for a quick bite and then on to Lunt and Fontaine for the evening."

As they walked along Fifth Avenue, they divided into twos, Konigsbauer talking to Grapple up ahead, followed by Foster and Jack Ward, and then Cal and Perkins. Cal said, "What's this about second acts?"

"If the first act is any good, it's a hard act to follow, I guess."

"Why are we going to see the polar bears?"

"Six different reasons. Look around and count us."

"Nothing makes sense until it's in print, does it?"

"What's good about live theater is that the audience can be on stage and in the dark at the same time. It's perfect for Howard because he likes things both ways as long as they're on the up and up. Forgive the pun."

"Do you think he's both ways?"

"I'm going to make a point of not finding out."

"Williams has it both ways with Brick and Skipper."

"Sure, it's not about what he calls 'mendacity,' it's about acting. The second act is simply follow up and declaration. They're football players. Skipper can't get it up for Maggie the cat. So everybody punishes everybody. He who is without self-pity casts the first gallstone. I'd rather needle Ward than let him think I take him seriously."

"Do you?"

"Of course. He's my best friend."

"None of this matters, does it?"

"Sure, everything matters."

"Let me ask you a question, do you think Antolini in *The Catcher in the Rye* is a flit?"

"Of course not, do you?"

"No."

"Affection is very difficult."

"Yes."

"Konigsbauer gave me Rilke's *Letters to a Young Poet*. Have you read it?"

"No."

"Rilke says sex and experiencing art are so close in pain and ecstasy that they are two forms of the same thing."

"The same what?"

"He says 'yearning and joy,' I think. No, 'yearning and delight.'"

"We're at the zoo. You don't get to see the polar bear until you pass through the gates."

Konigsbauer bought six tickets and they filed past the cages of monkeys. Ward called back, "Hey Perkins, there's your cousin, the one with the red ass."

"I resist the temptation to incriminate you with a question, Jack my boy," Perkins called back.

They watched the male peacock strutting with his feathers preened and spread. At the polar bear compound, Konigsbauer said, "I'm always thrilled when I see these beautifully muscular pure white animals. All the myths of savagery are here, yet they appear so benign and peaceful." The bears were nowhere to be seen. "Let's go in where we can see inside the little pond."

Down in the lower passageway, on the other side of a glass wall, a large polar bear was lying in a rock crevice next to the edge of the man-made pond. "There he is," Konigsbauer said. "Gracious, he looks so efficiently powerful."

"It reminds me," Ben began.

"Whatever is occurring to you, don't say it, Perkins," Ward said. "We're all enjoying ourselves."

"What did Deborah Kerr say to the polar bear as he opened his jaws to devour her?"

"OK Benjamin, I'll bite," Konigsbauer said, "What did she say?"

"When you speak about this later, and you will, be kind to me."

"Boo, hiss, Perkins, we all liked the play last night, remember?"

"I rather like that, Benjamin," Konigsbauer laughed, "It's a touch smutty, but clever." The ending of the play *is* a bit affected."

"What did Anthony Perkins say to the polar bear. . ."

Before Ben could finish his sentence, Ward threw a six-inch piece of baked pretzel at him, catching Ben on the forehead and deflecting against the thick glass of the viewing wall. Everyone was solicitous of Ben, who brushed off the solicitudes with protestations of knighthood in the presence of a spoilsport. "I accept your sympathy," Ben said, "Now let us move on to tea with the Russians."

"Cabs will be scarce right now, but let's give it a try," Konigsbauer said.

As they walked back to Fifth Avenue to hail a cab, Cal said to Ben, "You think he liked the second act this afternoon because of Brick and Skipper?"

"Of course. Did you read what Canby said in the *Times* last Sunday? He talked about the second act and he quoted Williams from a phone interview before the opening. Williams is really good. He said two things:

first that the bird he was 'trying to catch in the net of the play is not the solution to the psychological problem of one man, but the interplay of five different people in the thundercloud of a crisis.' I memorized it because I knew I was going to see the play. I listened carefully. In the second act, Brick disavows what he calls 'sodomy,' but he also says that 'one or two times we . . .' and he doesn't finish the sentence. Williams leaves it up in the air. Brick clearly is straight. Skipper is probably homosexual, but we don't know. The fact that he can't screw Maggie is not proof of anything. The ambiguity leaves the question of homosexuality itself up in the air, and Williams shifts the question of Brick's and Skipper's relationship to the censuring of the gossips and the liars, not the normality or immorality of Brick and Skipper."

"You mean he begs the question artfully?"

"I think he dramatizes the subject artfully."

"Yeah, I think so too. That still leaves us Konigsbauer."

"Konigsbauer will always be with us. So will Brick and Skipper and Maggie and Big Daddy."

"*Cat* is a better play than *Tea and Sympathy.*"

"Sure, *Cat*'s a real play. *Tea and Sympathy* is melodrama."

Konigsbauer hailed a cab and directed Perkins, Ward, Foster, and Grapple to get in. He told the driver to take them to the Russian Tea Room and gave Grapple a ten to cover the cost.

"Cal and I'll be right along," he said to Grapple.

Inside their own taxi, Konigsbauer said, "Well Cal, welcome to New York City. What do you think of this world of plays, plays, plays?"

"Burl Ives knocked me out this afternoon."

"When the curtain comes up, the rest of the world goes away, doesn't it? I've been enthralled with the theater all my life. Acting is everything. Wait until you see these two old pros tonight. Then we'll have to go out and splurge someplace afterwards. Can you stand the pace?"

"I'm keeping up so far."

"Here's the Russian Tea Room. Have you been here before?"

"I've only been in New York City once before, on our senior football trip to Washington, D.C. in high school. It's all new to me."

CHAPTER FIFTY-FIVE

▼

Cal drove to Braintree to see Tom. He pulled into Tom's driveway and could hear a baseball game through the open living room window. When he called Tom's name, Tom yelled, "Come on in, the back door's open."

"It's the goddamn right-handed pitching as usual," Tom said as Cal came in and sat down in the big chair opposite Tom, who was sitting by the standup radio. "Give me another Parnell and I could take those Yankees myself in the stretch come summer."

"I believe you."

"You know I'm full of beans is what you know. And spring training was invented for retirees. What brings you down here the first week of spring? You ought to be sailing on the Charles with your girlfriend. That is, if you know how to turn one of them little things around. They say they're tippy. I'll stick to a troopship myself, but without German subs, I've had my fill of them. You think I've lost my mind, don't you? Rattling around from right-handers to girl sailors to German submarines. Don't make a hell of a lot of sense, do I? You might's well speak up, I'm getting older by the minute."

Cal smiled at Tom, and sank into his chair, as if he were letting the air out of himself. "I'd rather be here right now, old buddy, than anywhere."

"Well, just take off your shoes. I'll get us a couple of Carling's Black Labels and we'll tolerate this lousy baseball game until it self-destructs, and then go bowling. What do you say?"

"I vote for the shoes off, the Black Labels, and the bowling."

"I hear you, my man. The game's off." Tom turned off the radio. "You either want to talk about something or you want to nap, and you didn't come down here to nap. I'll get the Carlings and then let's have it." Tom brought two opened beers from the kitchen.

"Cheers."

"Cheers."

They clinked bottles.

"Has Joe been around, Tom?"

"That's a nice girl he's got there, and I admire his intelligence to occupy her in his spare time. I trust you know about her."

"I know Susan. She's terrific. I've gotten to know her better lately, but she told me something I didn't want to know."

Tom looked at Cal and didn't say anything. "You want to tell me or are we going to keep going around this thing?"

"What are we going to do about Joe, Tom? Susan told me."

"I was just making sure. I promised her. What the hell *is* there to do? Some things aren't supposed to happen, and when they do, there's no beginning and no end of anything. Life gets jangled from wake-up to sleep, and dreams get screwier."

"Joe hasn't talked to you?"

"Not a cotton-picking word. I just don't see as much of him."

"So no one else knows?"

"Not unless human nature has changed in the last month. There's not a word brewing anywhere, no expressions have changed, and nobody's catching eyes in the room, not that I've been in many churchy rooms lately."

"Joe's been my best friend for almost twenty years, Tom. I don't know what to do. I don't know what I'll do without him. I can't imagine my life without Joe. We grew up together. We played football together. I went to seminary because Joe did. I took him home to dinner at my folks' house the other night, and we ate some of the deer that we shot last fall down the lake. He never said a word about being sick. You couldn't tell anything was wrong. He might die, but he's acting like nothing's changed."

Tom looked at his beer and drank from the bottle. He looked at Cal and nodded his head. He took another drink from the bottle. "You know, if you keep drinking this stuff, the level in the bottle drops." Tom rubbed his several-day whiskers with his palm and squeezed his chin with his thumb and forefinger. He looked at Cal and nodded his head again. "I hear you, boy."

"Joe and I are getting ordained in two months, Tom."

"That might be worth getting worked up about."

"I don't believe in the biblical God, I don't believe Jesus existed, I don't believe in life after death. I've got three women on my mind and I'm living the celibate life."

"Well, if you're gonna be a preacher, I'd say you fit the mold pretty good. And if you're not gonna be a preacher, you'd make a good doctor, lawyer, or Indian chief. No club I ever heard of that's worth more'n a dime's gonna blackball you for that puny confession. Hell, you got to do better'n that, son, if you're gonna pound into yourself some real nails."

"I go to a psychiatrist three times a week. I've been doing it for almost three years."

"I take a shit every day. Been doing it for sixty five years."

"Joe might die, Tom."

"That's the hell of it."

"When I was a kid I used to have this sort of wide-awake dream that I was falling off the edge of the world. It was all part of my mother's and father's fighting. I was all torn up. My mother used to cry and wail in the night, and I could hear it through the wall of my bedroom. In one argument, my father took the butcher knife up to his bedroom. They had started to fight after Sunday dinner. I said 'please daddy, don't' and he walked past me with the knife in his hands and that bitter look on his face, and climbed the stairs. I should have run from the house. I should have gotten the hell out of there, but I huddled in the corner and listened to them."

"I'll bet he didn't do anything with the knife."

"I found the knife a couple days later in the garden below the bedroom window."

"The worst part for him was what to do with the knife if he didn't do it. He must have suffered, knowing it wasn't worth it."

"When he went past me up the stairs I pleaded with my mother to ask him for the knife. She just said, 'He won't do anything with it.'"

"The hardest part is not being able to save someone else."

"Now they're nice old people who go to high school hockey games together and watch Arthur Godfrey and the Wednesday night fights. And Joe has to go and die."

"I sure as hell hope not. There're only two things: he will or he won't, and you can't save him. And I can't and Susan can't. We don't have to like it. I'm not one of those Job 'I love Him though he slay me' people. It's got nothing to do with love, and it's come to me in my old age that it might have something to do with, not justice, but the lack of value judgments. That idea holds out against favoritism. Materialists get sucked into value judgments because they keep adding up how much everybody else has got. If you start and end with nothing, and you know that life isn't fair, and death takes us all, maybe there's some comfort in the fact that all the bastards out there die too. We know nothing about time, friend. Unending space is incomprehensible because we think in a time frame. We're so bemused with our own lives, adding up our days like glassies in our sugar bags, we can only conceive of divine justice instead of opportunity. It's sad when good people die. It's awful. But remember, the bastards also die.

"We watch as our toenails rot, the veins on our calves stand out, the hair on our ears grows faster, the warning signals when we take a leak get worse. Everyone faces it. Death is God. The nitrogen cycle is God. Think of that boy wonder, John Keats. I've lived almost three of his life spans, and what did he do in his 26 years? Think of that other wonderful boy, Mozart. Everybody's got his own lists of unfair deaths. The really unfair thing would be for someone to be passing out bar chits for eternal life. The hell with Job and loving the killer. If Joe goes down, I'll go down with him as far as I can go, and then I'll see him off. None of that justice talk means a goddamned thing."

"Being here right now means something, Tom."

"That's another story. This doesn't have anything to do with justice. This is the other side of justice. This is living. This is drinking beer and yammering like a couple of blue jays at the world in spring."

"But it's part of Joe's dying."

"No, it's part of our dying. And if we don't know it, we might as well be dead."

"It's a hard point. You're the third person who used the word 'bemused' to me recently."

"It's just another fancy word. We've got to make a decision here. We're right on the verge of talking crap, and if we have another brew and keep talking, we'll be talking crap as sure as we're sitting here, and we don't want to do that, agreed?"

"Agreed."

"How are you, really, at candlepins?"

"I'm good. I used to set them up for a nickel a string at the pool room in Mapleton Center when I was in the ninth grade. Every four strings and I could bowl a string mysef. I averaged in the nineties when I was in high school. My high was 123 when I bowled a guy for money one day when I was in college."

"I know a place. Let's go."

Chapter Fifty Six

▼

Cal dropped off books by Edgar Brightman and Borden Parker Bowne at the main desk of the library and looked for Angelica as he passed her office doorway. She was at her desk re-covering a book. Cal stopped and said, "Hi Angelica."

"Well hello there," she said, smiling, "How're you doing these days?"

Cal walked over to her desk and said, "Pretty well. Just dropping off a couple of books before heading south."

"Heading south? Lucky guy. I'd like to be heading south with you, but duty calls. Dr. Jansan likes to keep the sweatshop going during spring break. She says it's the only time the men with churches get the chance to catch up on their school work. What draws you toward the warm country?"

"Konigsbauer's giving a talk at Chapel Hill and he asked me to help him drive. He says that North Carolina's nice this time of year."

"It's heavenly. It'll be green and green and green, and the flowers will be in full bloom. Think of us transplanted southerners up here with our fingers crossed hoping it won't snow again."

"I sure will. So long, Angelica."

"Bye now. Say hello to Dr. Konigsbauer for me. He sure is a nice man."

Cal got on the elevator and rode it down to the first floor. As he got off, Martin Luther King got on.

"Morning," Cal said.

"Good morning," King said, and the door closed as he was pressing the button to go up.

He's probably headed for DeFranco's office, Cal thought. *Good luck to him. I'd rather be going to North Carolina.*

Cal crossed the chapel plaza, descended the steps and cut behind the Communication College to the parking lot where Konigsbauer parked his new Dodge sedan. He had timed it perfectly, for there was Konigsbauer carrying his suitcase, walking over from Memorial Avenue.

"Good man," Konigsbauer called, "right on time, bright and early." He cocked his head to one side and blinked as he smiled.

"So's yourself," Cal called.

"You know the car so you might as well drive."

Cal got behind the wheel and started the engine.

"Let's make this a good trip," Konigsbauer said, "I'm very excited and I hope you are. Why don't you get us over to the Fenway and Huntington Avenue and we can go out route 9 and connect to route 20."

"Sure thing," Cal said.

Konigsbauer read the *New York Times* as Cal drove, making periodic comments on world events as Cal passed the Museum of Fine Arts, the tennis stadium in Brookline, and Framingham Teacher's College.

"Hungary is trouble," Konigsbauer said. "Nagy will not last, and they will want us to fight the Russians. It will be nothing but trouble." He read and turned each page, occasionally saying "Silliness!" and "Good! It serves them right!"

Cal drove in silence. Later, he said, "Route 20 to New York coming up."

Without looking up, Konigsbauer said, "That's the one." After a few minutes, he said, "*Teahouse of the August Moon* is opening with Brando this week. We'll have to catch it on the way back."

Route 20 became the Merritt Parkway in Connecticut. Cal's thoughts drifted from Clare to Joe, Regina, ordination, the summer, next fall. What would he do with his life? Cal thought of Vinnie, Joannie, his mother and father, Miss Green, and Tom. He remembered bowling last Saturday night.

Konigsbauer said he felt sleepy and would take a nap. He put his head back and closed his eyes. Pretty soon his mouth was open.

Good old Tom, Cal thought. He was going to hit that punk. Cal pictured the scene in the bowling alley as if it were a movie playing before his eyes. *The punk lobs the ball each time he releases it and the ball bounces twice before it starts rolling clean down the waxed alley. The punk's buddy is making nines, tens, and spares. The punk is loud. He yells "prick of misery" and "mother fucker" when he throws gutter balls. He starts throwing harder and his buddy laughs at him, egging him on. They have a bottle in the punk's jacket, and they take swigs between turns. Tom is bowling well but is unnerved by the lobbed balls and the cursing. Tom is totaling the final box of the second string and the punk throws another gutter ball and comes back to sit down and says, "This is a lousy fucking alley." He says it loud enough to be heard by people bowling in the next lane. They have two little girls about ten years old.*

Tom tells Cal that he is behind by six pins and he'd better pick it up if he wants to win. Tom is trying not to get involved in the punk's behavior. The punk looks over at Tom who shakes his head at the punk's comment, and the punk says, "What are you shaking your head at, mother fucker?"

"Lobbing the ball doesn't help your game any," Tom says, "and it doesn't do the lanes any good either."

"HEY!" the punk yells at Tom. "HEY!"

People in the surrounding lanes stop bowling and look at the punk.

Tom says softly, "You've got my attention, if that's what you want."

"HEY! METHUSALEH CAN TALK!"

The punk's buddy says to the punk, "Hey Jack, the manager's coming over. Tone it down. Forget the old buggar. We're not finished bowling."

The manager of the bowling alley stands behind the curved seats and says, "Is there a problem here?"

The punk says, "No way. No problem, right Methusaleh?"

The manager says, "This is a family recreation facility. We'd appreciate it if everyone cooperated with the nice tone we try to set in here."

"Yeah, that's good," the punk says. "We're family bowlers. Methusaleh here, he's act-u-al-ly my great-grandfather, and everything's hunky-dory in the family, right grampa?"

The manager says to Tom, "Is everything OK, sir?"

"Sure, it's OK."

The manager leaves and the punk takes a swig from their bottle and puts the bottle back in the folds of his jacket on the seat. The punk looks at his buddy and giggles. The punk's buddy smiles and shakes his head. He says, "Come on, Jack, let's bowl one more and get out of here."

The punk says to Tom, "What do you say, Methusaleh, you want to bowl another string for old time family's sake? You know, just for the family, in the family, of the family?"

Tom looks at the punk but doesn't answer him.

The punk says, "What are you, chickenshit? Hey Jewel, the old fart's chickenshit. Won't bowl another one for the family."

Jewel says, "Come on Jack, you're up first. Let's go."

The punk shakes his head and goes to the ball rack and picks up a ball, hefts it, puts it down, and picks up another.

Tom says, "Fifty bucks!"

The punk looks over at Tom and says "Fifty bucks what?"

Tom says, "Fifty bucks. One string. Put up or shut up. Us two against you two."

The punk laughs: "Are you shitting me? My buddy Jewel here will cream your ass."

"Fifty bucks on the table, yes or no?"

The punk goes over to talk to Jewel. Cal says, "Geez Tom, you got the fifty bucks to lose? That other guy's good. He's been knocking down spares all night."

"He'll wilt. All you got to do is make eights and nines steady. They're half loaded, they'll press."

Jewel reaches into his dungarees pocket, and the punk comes over to Tom. "See this bill? It goes under the last ball for safe keeping." The punk goes to the ball return rack and places the fifty dollar bill under the last ball. He comes back and says, "Where's yours?"

Tom takes out his wallet and gets a twenty, two tens, a five, and five ones and adds them to the bill under the black bowling ball snug against the post. The punk says, "Why don't we alternate lanes to make sure everything's even."

"You're not bouncing your balls down this lane," Tom said, "I'm not bowling any pock-marked alley. You want to do this or you want to argue about rules?"

The punk thinks about that for a minute and says, "OK, bowl your own fucking lane. You guys are dead either way."

Jewel goes to the rack and picks up a ball for each hand. He says to Tom, "Total score, one string, right Mac?"

"Loser pays the night's tab."

Jewel ruminates on that. "Yeah, OK, Loser pays the night's tab."

Jewel approaches the lane, holds up both balls to sight the head pin and throws a strike. With his next two balls he makes a spare and sits down.

While Jewel was bowling his two frames, Tom made a ten and a spare.

"Nice and easy," Tom says, "Keep looking at the head pin, Cal, and slide up to the line. They'll go down. Never mind the punk."

"It's not the punk I'm worried about, it's the other guy. He's very good."

"We'll see. Just concentrate on the head pin."

Cal steps up for his first two frames and picks up his ball. In the next lane, the punk throws a gutter ball, then knocks down eight and misses the remaining two. Cal hits the head pin straight on and cleans out the middle four pins, leaving three on either side in a line. He throws his second ball down the middle and misses. He ends up with a seven. The punk gets five and Cal gets nine.

Jewel makes a six on his spare and settles for an eight, then strikes. Tom makes two spares. The punk makes a four and a five. Cal knocks down seven, then spares. The punk makes a three and a ten. Cal makes two eights.

Between frames, Tom says, "Keep hitting the head pin. Roll 'em nice and easy. It's pretty even."

After four frames, the punk and Jewel have 89, Tom and Cal have 94.

In the fifth frame, the punk throws a strike, but after a gutter ball makes only four. Cal gets a spare in the sixth frame. Jewel makes two spares. Tom makes three tens and a spare. At the end of eight frames, the punk and Jewel lead by seven.

Tom says, "The punk isn't talking now."

"He isn't tipping the bottle either."

In the ninth frame, Jewel spares, and Tom strikes. Jewel just misses the sixth pin on his extra ball and gets a three. Tom spares on his strike. Jewel finishes at 148, Tom at 142. The punk goes to the line and makes a seven. Cal makes a nine and a seven, finishing at 86. The punk has three more balls. He and Jewel are down fifteen. The punk picks up the ball next to the one covering the hundred dollars, walks over to Tom and Cal and says "Fuck you guys, watch this."

Jewel says just loud enough for the punk to hear, "Roll it slow, Jack. Easy, man."

The punk rolls the ball evenly off his fingertips and hits the left side of the head pin. Nine pins go down, leaving number ten with wood in front of it. Now they're only down six. The punk rolls at the dead wood and spares. Down five.

Tom whispers to Cal, "I'll bet you a quarter he blows it."

Driving down the Merritt Parkway, thinking of Tom in the last frame of the bowling bet, Cal looks over at Konigsbauer, sleeping. Cal thinks of Tom's world, how trustworthy it is despite its risks. But it has loyalties. Loyalties and risks are there in Konigsbauer's world too, along with all the value judgments. Who wants you to be a minister, Cal?

Cal sees the punk approach the line needing six pins to win. All he has to do is hit the head pin. The punk makes a trial slide toward the line to test his form. He looks over at Jewel and smiles. Then he looks at Tom and gives Tom the finger. He takes three steps and slides, releasing the ball perfectly, coming in from the right side of the lane. The release is perfect. No lobbing the ball this time. The ball heads directly at the head pin, coming straight across from the side, then the ball is heading for the number two pin. The angle is too much. The ball hits the number eight pin and three pins drop immediately. A fourth has been wounded and it totters, then falls. Four pins.

The punk stands at the line, staring down the alley. Jewel tears off the tally sheets at their table. The punk walks back to his coat and puts it over his arm, careful to keep the bottle hid. He looks over at Tom and says, "This is your night, man. How about next week? We'll double it."

Tom says, "No thanks."

The punk says, "I didn't think so. You know we'd kick your ass."

"Maybe so," Tom says.

Cal hands Jewel the tally sheets from his and Tom's table. Jewel and the punk go to the front desk to pay the tab. Tom summons the waitress and orders a couple cokes. Jewel and the punk leave the building while Tom and Cal sip their cokes.

"What do you think?" Tom asks.

"I didn't know you had fifty bucks."

"I didn't. I put up the money for my oil bill tomorrow."

"How many times you ever bowled 142 before?"

"Never."

"I didn't help you much."

"All's we needed was 86. You hit it just right."

"You were great, Tom."

"I shot my mouth off is what I did."

"You delivered. I shot my mouth off about my 123, but I didn't deliver."

"The punk failed is what happened. We fool with those guys again and they probably would kick ass."

"I wish Joe had been here."

"I'll tell you something, Cal. If Joe wasn't dying, we wouldn't have had to do this, remember that."

CHAPTER FIFTY-SEVEN

▼

"At 11:54 of December 29th, the first flight of 18 twin-engine bombers of the [Japanese] 14th Heavy Bombardment Regiment, covered by 19 fighters, approached Corregidor at a height of 15,000 feet and in regular V formation," *The Siege of Corregidor*, 6, Louis Moreton, http://Corregidor.org

"Why is Daddy reading about a corridor?" Cal asked his mother as she combed his hair in front of the kitchen sink. She dipped the long brown comb in the glass of sugared water and coursed it through his hair as she looked over at Cal's father at the kitchen table where he was reading the *Boston Post*.

"Corregidor, not corridor," his father said without looking up.

"It's an island in the Phillipines," Cal's mother said. "Last night Gabriel Heater said that yesterday the Japs took all the American soldiers prisoner."

"Does that mean we're going to lose the war?" Cal asked.

"I've got to go to work Sal," Cal's father said, putting down the newspaper and leaving the table. "No, it sure doesn't," he said to Cal on his way out the back door. "The war's just starting. Those Nips—wait until Uncle Sam gets going. General MacArthur says we'll be back, then we'll see what Tojo says."

"Who's Tojo?" Cal asked his mother after his father left.

"One of the Japanese leaders."

"Why does dad have to work on a Saturday?" Cal sat at the kitchen table eating Wheaties. The box was propped in front of him against the sugar bowl, and he was reading the comic strip on the back of the box.

"Because we have to win the war before you grow up. What are you going to do today, after you dig your part of the garden?"

"Do I have to?"

"Remember what you said when you wanted us to buy the Victory Garden seeds from school. You said you'd have your own garden."

"It's too early to plant onions. Johnny and me are going out in the woods. How can the G.E. help win the war?"

"Johnny and I. It's not too early to dig. You can't do it all in one day. The General Electric makes things for the soldiers. Even your father does. He's the boss in building 63 where they make the big engines for the ships. They call them turbines. He's already made the turbines for the *Wasp* and the *Hornet*."

"What are those?"

"Aircraft carriers."

"I thought the Japs sunk them all at Pearl Harbor."

"I don't know, Cal. Maybe they did. But we have to have more. I'm going down to the Co-op to shop for some things this morning. If I don't get back before noon, you can heat up a can of Campbell's soup."

"I don't want tomato."

"You don't have to have tomato."

"Do we have any chicken gumbo?"

"I think so. Look in the cupboard and check."

"Do I have to have a glass of milk?"

"I bought some more of that coffee syrup you like. You can make a coffee milkshake."

"George Gray is going to let the snakes go in the field this afternoon."

"My Lord, what's he going to do that for? What snakes, anyway?"

"He and Dwight's got blacksnakes in cages in their barn. They caught 'em with loops on poles out in the woods under rocks and stuff."

"What did they catch them for if they're going to let them go? They'll be all over the neighborhood. Some times I think that George Gray is crazy, and Dwight is not much better. Johnny's going to grow up to be just like them. You better watch your Ps and Qs with him. If he wasn't younger than you I'd see to it that you played with somebody else. Do you understand what I'm saying?"

"Johnny's fun, mama. He isn't bad."

"What I'm saying is that you're older than Johnny and I expect you to make the decisions. Whose idea was it to start the fire under Gray's front porch last spring, yours or Johnny's?"

"Johnny's, but we won't do anything like that again. We're just going out to Pirate's Glen and dig around."

"You stay out of that cave, mind you, or I'll know the reason why."

"Are you mad at me, mama?"

"No, I'm not mad, I've just got things on my mind, so go on and go if you're going. And put on your sweater."

"It's warm out, mama. It's May. The sun's out. I'll get all sweaty."

"You heard me, what's it going to be?"

"I'll wear the sweater." Cal got his sweater off the clothes hook on the way down to the landing and the cellar door.

"Bye, mama."

Cal went down the street to Johnny's house, walked around back and called for him. His mother opened the back door and said, "He's coming."

They walked through the field between Thomason's and North's house, crossed Grant and walked the old cow path beside Barn Hill, then down to Appleton's Pond, past Slide Rock, and followed the piggery road to the base of Pirate's Glen. They walked up the open slopes where they skied in the winter, to the top where the oak trees surrounded the opening between the base of the granite boulder and the earth.

From the top of the Glen they could see in the distance, Avery Graham's farm, North's house and the top of Barn Hill. Johnny said, "Let's go into the cave."

"I'm not supposed to," Cal said.

"I'm not supposed to either, so what? Who'll know?"

"I never been inside before."

"Me neither."

"How'll we see where we are?"

"I brought kitchen matches."

"How many?"

Johnny took the matches out of his pocket and counted. "Seven."

"You go first."

Johnny sat down and edged his way down the moist leaves to the opening. Then he slid on his back and wriggled feet-first into the cave, turning his head sideways to get through the opening. Johnny called, "I'm inside." His voice sounded hollow.

"What's in there?"

"I can't get a match going. It's too dark to see. It's OK in here. There's room. I can touch the ceiling over my head. It's wet. Are you coming?"

"I'm coming. Wait a minute."

"For what?"

"I'm taking my sweater off. I don't want to get it dirty."

Cal slid down to the opening, wondering what it would be like not to be able to get out again. Cal was afraid to squeeze into the cave, but now that Johnny was in there he was almost afraid not to. He turned his head sideways to fit through the low passage, and then he was inside.

"Where are you?" Cal said. "I'm inside."

"I'm here," Johnny said, Cal reached and touched him. "It's a room."

"Do you think there's treasure here?"

"I got five matches left."

"I almost didn't get in."

"Everything's wet."

"Are the matches dry?"

"They're in my pocket."

"Strike two together on the tips."

Cal could hear Johnny trying to strike the wooden matches together.

"I broke one in half," Johnny said. "I can't find the end with the tip."

"Just feel around with your fingers. You have to hold them way down at the end near the tips."

"I'll burn myself if it lights."

"No you won't. As soon as you hear the click, move your fingers."

"I found it. The end is wet."

"Get another one."

Cal could hear Johnny scraping the match tips together. Then Cal heard the click of the igniting phosphorus. The two matches blazed.

"Hold them straight up, Johnny, they'll burn longer. Give me one."

Johnny handed Cal one of the wooden matches.

"Get out the other ones before these burn down," Cal said.

Johnny handed Cal one of the two dry matches. The lighted match burned down to its last half-inch and Cal ignited his second match just as the first one almost burned his fingers, and he dropped it. "Don't light yours yet," Cal said, "it'll give us more time."

"We won't be able to light it."

"Wait'll this burns down and we'll light it from this one."

They were sitting in a small room with an uneven granite ceiling four feet high in its deepest spot. From the opening to the end measured around twelve feet. The floor was rocks and dirt. Each wooden match burned for about twelve seconds.

"Light it now." Johnny held the tip of his final match into the flickering light of Cal's burned-down match and the phosphorus flared. Johnny held up the light and they took one last look inside the cave.

They sat in the darkness for a little while.

"It's not bad in here," Johnny said.

"We should of brought a candle."

"We could bring some girls in here and play strip poker."

"Who would come in here? Not Joanne, not even Esther."

"Maybe Joanne."

"Let's go. I'm getting cold."

Outside, the sun was shining, and the first budding leaves had turned the woods from a reddish blur to red-yellow and yellow-green. "Let's go over to Slide Rock," Johnny said.

"What time do you think it is?"

"Who knows?"

"Let's cut around on the top of the Valley." They walked along the ridge path. "When is George going to do the snakes?"

"When everybody shows up."

"Who's everybody?"

"All the big guys are bringing their girlfriends."

"Like who?"

"Alfy Meserve, Normy Broding, Charley Johansen, those guys."

"Is Normy going to bring Jacqueline? She's really pretty."

"Best tits on the hill."

"Says who?"

"Me."

"Wouldn't you like to know?"

They walked to the top of Slide Rock where they could see the houses along Grant Avenue and Graham's electric fence that ringed the field across from North's house.

"Let's slide down."

"I'll rip my pants. We need some cardboard."

Johnny started to slide down the face of the smooth granite boulder, using his feet out in front of him to slow his speed. He called from the bottom, "Come on, it's fun."

"My mother will kill me if I rip my pants."

"Mine didn't tear, come on."

"Let's see if Dwight's in the field yet."

"Come on down and we can check the dump by the pond on the way. Maybe a snake is sunning there."

Cal walked and climbed down the side of the great rock and they walked along the road to Appleton's little cow pond. Appleton had thrown trash in an old cellar hole across from the pond and it was now sprouting briars and sumac.

They stood at the edge of the old dump and looked for a sunning blacksnake.

"Let's go in a little ways," Johnny said.

They pushed aside a clump of sumac and stood on some old rotten boxes.

"Look, right there," Johnny said.

"Jesus," Cal said, "it's a huge one."

"I'll bet he's six feet."

"What'll we do?"

We have to get a pole with a loop. We can make one but he might not be here when we get back."

The snake was ebony black, coiled and unmoving in the sun on a flat rock in the middle of the old dump.

"My stomach's all jumpy." Cal said. "Big snakes scare me."

"That's why they're fun."

"Let's go back."

Johnny tossed a big rock near the sunning snake and the snake slithered off the rock and disappeared.

"Why'd you do that?"

"Why not? They move like hell."

Cal and Johnny circled the pond, climbed the ravine, and walked the pasture road by the field with the electric fence.

"Want to touch the fence?" Johnny asked.

"It's live. You'll get a shock."

"It's only a couple volts. It just goes up to your wrist. I'll do it if you do it."

"I'm not doing it."

"We can do it together. You hold on to my wrist and I'll touch it."

"Not me. You touch it all you want. I'm not touching it."

"Watch."

"You're crazy."

Johnny closed his fist around the wire for two seconds and pulled his hand away and smiled.

"Did you feel it?"

"Course I felt it." Johnny gave Cal a little shove. "Why didn't you do it?"

"What did it feel like?"

"Like an electric shock. What do you think?"

"I just didn't want to do it."

"Look! Everybody's in the field."

CHAPTER FIFTY-EIGHT

▼

Cal and Johnny crossed Fairmount Avenue and walked toward the group of older kids. Dwight and George Gray carried clothesline poles and walked in a circle around several large blacksnakes slithering in the grass. When a snake headed toward one of the older girls, she cried out and Dwight or George caught the snake in the Y at the end of his pole and flipped it back into the circle. The snake landed with a heavy thump on the ground and headed again toward the ring of spectators, trying to escape.

The snakes fascinated Cal and he imagined one biting him. He stared at their slithering speed and liked the thumping sound when Dwight flipped one and it hit the ground. The older girls clutched their boyfriends when the snakes came toward them. The older boys laughed. Cal wondered how Dwight and George would get the snakes back into the cages. He counted eight of them, and one was at least six feet. Dwight and George were quick with the poles, grinning as they controlled the agitated and frightened snakes. The event lasted for half an hour, and then the two snake handlers opened the four cages half filled with straw.

One by one, Dwight pinned down each snake's head with the end of his clothesline pole, then grasped the snake just below the head with his fingers of one hand and inserted it with both hands into a cage. Twice, snakes slithered out as the second snake was dropped into the cage. Cal shivered, thinking of two snakes touching each other.

As Dwight picked up the snakes with his hands, two of the older girls, Madeleine Burke and Shelly Wisnooski, oohed and aahed. But Jacqueline

Hamilton just watched. Her eyes blazed as the muscular snakes rippled in Dwight's hands. Shelly tightened her jaw and squeezed Jim Meserve's arm. A few minutes later, Normy Broding called 'Thanks' to the Gray brothers, and the three couples walked down Fairmount Avenue in the warm May sun under the budding maple trees.

George disappeared into the barn. He never had a girlfriend and he never married.   Dwight married his first girlfriend in England after the war, and brought her home. Cal never saw a blacksnake again.

CHAPTER FIFTY-NINE

▼

On the outskirts of New York City, Konigsbauer said yes he would, he loved being read to, so he took the wheel in Darien, and Cal read to him from Rilke's *Letters to a Young Poet* as the car moved through New York City, the Holland Tunnel, the Pulaski Skyway, and into New Jersey.

"It's such a grand book," Konigsbauer said. "He was Rodin's secretary for a time, you know."

"Wow," Cal said.

"Such a fortuitous artistic relationship."

"It's hard to picture Rilke as a secretary."

"He was young. He was learning all the things that would make him a great poet. He lived the great questions, just as he says in your *Letters* there. There's a marvelous passage somewhere, I think it's in the *Malte Laurids Brigge*, where he says a poet must live a lifetime to write anything really good. One must know about animals and how flowers open, one must sit in an open window by the dying, one must be able to think back on nights of travel and have memories of many nights of love, all different. And then one must be able to forget the memories and have patience until they come again as verses. It's quite extraordinary."

"My favorite poem is the one about the half-statue of Apollo. The last line says, 'You must change your life.'"

"I'm impressed, Cal. You know that one? '*Du muszt dein Leben ändern.*' It's the only poem I know that ends with a command. That's some trick."

"The real trick is *how* to change your life."

"Ah, but don't you think that writing it *is* doing it, even if it's only slightly? Once a writer creates a great line, the line seems inevitable, but to create that seeming inevitability, the writer has had to discover something deep in himself that can be accounted for only as a result of undergoing some change. The writer is transformed as he allows the insight, or the articulation, or the creation as it were, of the insight. I mean by 'allow,' being open to it. It seems easy to have said it once it's been said. That's the way with all great lines.

"Think of 'the multitudinous seas incarnadine,' or 'magic casements opening o'er perilous seas,' or 'to be or not to be.' At the instant the line occurred to Rilke it *did* change his life. Don't ask me how, but it did. It must have. All the genius of both Rodin and Rilke are in that poem. If the line had occurred to him before he wrestled his way around the impact of the sculpture and through the poem, he wouldn't have had to write the poem, but something was lurking in the tension of the experience Rilke was feeling in the presence of the half-Apollo. Something to do with a remnant, or an uncovering of the past, or discovery itself as the artistic process, something external that was becoming internal as the poem progressed, something godlike, or Apollo-like, something terrible in its realization."

"That's what Rilke must have meant when he said 'terrible in its beauty.'"

"Exactly, exactly."

"Wasn't Apollo the god of light?"

"Much more. He was the god of divine distance. Rilke chose Apollo for a reason. Rilke was not a Christian, he didn't believe in immanence or transcendence, but a kind of monism where life and death, time and space are all one. Apollo was a god who made men aware of their guilt and purified them of it. Only Zeus and his mother could stand him. He also loved poetry and music. And something that might interest you especially, he had trouble with women."

"How do you mean?"

Konigsbauer pulled the car into a Jersey Turnpike restaurant and gas station. "I've got to use the men's room, and we might as well get gas here. Are you hungry?"

"Sure."

"We'll get a sandwich and then you can drive and I'll tell you about Apollo's women."

A half-hour later, Cal was driving towards Philadelphia. When he saw the spring's first forsythia bushes, they blazed as yellow as in his childhood, the green trees in bloom and flocks of birds swarming and unraveling and swarming again.

"Will it be warm in North Carolina?" Cal asked.

"Have you ever smelled a real gardenia?"

"Once, a long time ago. I know about the petals turning brown if you touch them. They're supposed to be like Jesus coming out of the tomb. Tell me about Apollo's girlfriends."

"You're changing metaphors, young man. 'Touch me not' is the Impatiens flower. You're a gardener too?"

"They supposedly mistook Jesus for the gardener when he walked out of the tomb."

"Oh I love it. How did you ever find your way into seminary, Cal?"

"Don't ask *me*, Professor Konigsbauer, I just woke up one day and I had a roommate from Georgia, and I could watch the shells and their crews rowing up and down the Charles River."

"Call me Howard, Cal. The Church needs poets, God knows. If you can stomach the Church, it needs you. I like you for that reason. You're quite Apollonian yourself, do you know that?"

"I don't know what to say to that. My best friend is dying, my father's at the edge of dying, I'm hanging on to a rope with a psychiatrist, and I'm driving south to North Carolina in the spring. That doesn't sound very Apollonian to me."

"Everybody's got questions, Cal. The only answers are the ones we live into. I know that sounds literary. But art and religion are the same thing, finally. I heard what you said a little while ago about Jesus and crap. You may be right. Just don't stop asking the questions, don't stop being dissatisfied with the answers. You may not find the right answers or even any answers right away, but someday the sky will clear for you, I promise you. Even if you think you are making decisions, later you will discover that what you thought were decisions were actually gropings in certain directions that seemed at the time to offer openings. We feel our ways through life and then make up the reasons why we acted. Rilke had a sad childhood but he never said later that he became a poet to express himself or to deal with his sadness. He just wrote the poems. I tell you, Cal, you may not feel like a poet, but you are one. Write poems, never mind if you think they are bad or not. Listen to Rilke, write your memories, describe the everyday objects of your life, and don't indulge in self-pity. I can help you in this. I see something in you. Trust me."

Later, they were nearing Philadelphia when Cal said, "I heard you. I'm sorry not to be more responsive. I feel frozen. I'm just beginning to know about art. Nobody in my family ever knew about these things. All I ever wanted to do was play football. Now I feel lost."

"You're lonesome, like every one else."

"I don't feel like everyone else. I don't feel like Apollo either. Are you going to tell me about his girlfriends?"

"Yes, here's the city of brotherly love. The Walt Whitman Bridge is just over there. We will pass right by it. Apollo is at the heart of Whitman. All the other gods were afraid of Apollo because he was mysterious and came from Asia. He took the form of a dolphin and leaped onto a Cretan ship and took command, killed the female dragon that guarded Pytho, and re-named it Delphi. He chose an old woman whom he named Pythia to be his temple oracle.

"Oh yes, his girlfriends. You're putting me to the test here. I can remember three, there may have been more."

"How can you remember all this stuff?"

"Well, I have been a believer of sorts all my life."

"In the Greek gods?"

"In art. I began at Vanderbilt as a student of architecture. I migrated to Yale Divinity School, . . ."

"I didn't know you were a minister."

"Hold on. I left the Divinity School after one year to study Greek Classics, and after another year switched to Professor Baker's Drama Workshop. Thus I found myself as a half-ministerial student with a jack-of-all-trades arts background. I worked for the Board of Education of the Presbyterian Church, then founded *intent* magazine and edited it for ten years before coming to Zion."

"So you got the Greek at Yale."

"I got the Greek at Yale. Apollo's big three were Daphne, Coronis, and another C, let me remember, oh yes, Cassandra, the wily one. Apollo always had his hands full."

"Cassandra yelled a lot, didn't she?"

"She was the daughter of the king of Troy, Priam. She wouldn't have anything to do with Apollo, so he punished her by making her give true prophecies that no one would believe."

"That's terrific."

"You like that? Coronis was unfaithful to Apollo, so his twin, Artemis, shot her."

"Good."

"Daphne tried to get away from Apollo and he turned her into a laurel bush."

"His numbers are about as good as mine."

"See, I knew you were Apollonian."

Cal and Konigsbauer stayed that night outside of Washington, D.C., then drove the following day to Chapel Hill. The campus was blooming like high summer in New England. In the following three days, Cal dined with university dignitaries, including the university president and his staff, and church officials, including a bishop and ministers of the largest churches in Chapel Hill. Cal also met several co-eds at a church reception, including one who had long nut-brown hair and large brown eyes with long lashes. She had a Southern drawl which she exaggerated for Cal's benefit, was deeply tanned, and her body smelled vaguely of vanilla. When Cal first saw her he thought of Johnny Gray who would have described her breasts with a football metaphor.

She was the daughter of an Atlanta drugstore mogul, and was elusive with Cal. Konigsbauer introduced him as a theology student from Zion seminary and Cal fell immediately under her power, which amused her. He asked several times to see her, and succeeded in two walks and a benign movie date. When Cal walked her home from church on Sunday, he stayed so long that the family were forced to take him with them to the Country Club for Sunday dinner. By the pool, with the mother and father drinking martinis, she recounted to Cal swimming dates with southern boys when she shot beer cans from river logs with a .22 rifle. Cal couldn't decide if they were naked or not, and he was intimidated. For their movie date she wore a fresh gardenia behind her ear, and it intoxicated Cal. Later, she laughed at him as she turned her head away from his attempted kiss. He left Chapel Hill feeling like a ministerial leper.

They drove home by way of Knoxville, where they attended a minor league baseball game with friends of Konigsbauer from the Board of Education of the Presbyterian Church, the new editor of *intent* magazine and his young wife. The editor, Konigsbauer's successor, seemed gawky and naive, and his wife worldly, informed, and attractive. The home baseball team won the game on a three run homer in the last of the ninth inning, and it seemed to Cal that everything was working well for everyone else.

On the last night of their homeward journey, outside Baltimore, Konigsbauer and Cal talked from their separate beds after retiring for the night. Cal talked about Joe and about Miss Green, and Konigsbauer listened. Because he was so quiet, Cal thought him tired or asleep, and decided to finish their conversation. He said, "At least I know I have hope. Good night Howard."

In the darkness, Howard said, "Good night, Cal."

What seemed like several minutes passed, and Cal was thinking of the girl with the gardenia behind her ear, sitting naked on a river log, shooting beer cans, when all of a sudden Konigsbauer jumped up from his bed, and stood over Cal saying, "I must do this, I must." He took Cal's head in both his hands and kissed Cal on the forehead, returned to his bed and said, "I was so moved when you spoke of hope like that. It is so courageous."

Cal shivered and slid down further under the covers, pulling the sheet over his face in a spasm of revulsion. He couldn't say anything. He didn't want to hurt Howard, but he didn't want anything like it to ever happen again. He knew that Howard was attracted to him, but he hadn't thought Howard would ever touch him. He also suspected that Howatd's gesture was innocent, merely a little out of control, but the kissing had so revolted Cal that he would have to say something about it tomorrow, and he dreaded it.

The next morning, leaving the restaurant next to the motel, Cal said, "Howard, I don't want to hurt your feelings, but please don't do anything like that again."

Howard said, "I think you misunderstood."

"I understood, and I know you were only being nice to me, but I'm not used to that sort of expression of friendship, and I'd rather you didn't do it anymore."

"I still think you misunderstood," Harold said.

CHAPTER SIXTY

▼

The bell rang to end class and Cal headed for the back door to avoid Dr. Candle, whom he owed a paper on Psychology and Religion. The double-header started at one-thirty and he was already a half-hour late. Joe wasn't in class. Neither was Susan. Jack Ward was waiting for Cal outside the door.

"Hey Jack, you want to go to the ball game? They're playing the White Sox. We can make the third or fourth inning of the first game."

"Can't. I told Grapple I'd help him with *Kairos*. But everything's OK with you know what. Just wanted you to know. Thanks a lot."

"Great. You don't need that. Tell Grapple I'll do the verityper tonight. Williams is playing today, I'm out of here for the afternoon. You don't know where Joe is, do you?"

"I haven't seen him for a week. He's got my Schweitzer book, I think. You haven't got it, have you?"

"No, I've got my own. I'll see you tonight."

"I'm going to my church, that's why I'm helping Grapple this afternoon."

Cal jogged down Memorial Avenue past the Communication College, then crossed near Temple Immanuel and into Kenmore Square. The temperature was in the low seventies and Cal was sweating as he waited at the lights, then crossed by the Kenmore Hotel and jogged over the bridge above the railroad tracks and down Lansdown Street where he bought a sausage grinder. As he paid his dollar he heard a roar from the crowd and looked up to see a baseball rolling down the net over the left field wall. The fans were still noisy when he jogged up the ramp into the centerfield bleachers. Cal looked out over the green grass of Fenway Park and felt warm inside.

"Who hit it?" he asked a portly man sitting in the first seat next to the ramp.

"Jenson, two on," he said.

Cal looked around the half-filled bleachers. People were still coming in. The first game was a makeup game from a rainout, and Cal knew that the workers from the seven to three shift would arrive before the end of the first game. In the deepest part of the park where the left field wall joins the centerfield seats he sat down and bit a mouthful of his Italian sausage. "Who's up?" he asked two teenage boys in front of him.

"Piersall."

Cal couldn't read the scoreboard on the Green Monster because of the angle but he could make out the small balls and strikes board under the sky view boxes. The count was three and one. People yelled "Come on, Jimmy," and "You can do it, Jimmy." Cal took another bite of his Italian sausage and chewed. He felt safe in the ballpark. The players on the field stood in their positions, waiting. Baseball was a beautiful game to watch alone if you had something on your mind. The ball became the center of all things.

Cal relaxed into the leisurely pace of the game and the feeling of the warm afternoon. The pitcher fired the ball toward the plate and Piersall swung. As the ball sailed toward centerfield, Minnie Minoso backpedaled and caught it a few feet in front of the wall.

Cal wondered where Joe was, what he was thinking, if he was really dying. Cal had seen him twice after returning from Knoxville, but Joe still hadn't mentioned the leukemia. Maybe he and Susan had gone off someplace.

Between innings, Cal concentrated on Ted Williams jogging to left field and throwing the practice ball to Piersall, who threw it to Jackie Jenson, who threw it back to Piersall, who threw it back to Williams, who threw the ball toward the dugout and walked to the wall to talk to the man inside the scoreboard. Jenson talked to the pitchers in the bullpen. Someone in the stands yelled to Piersall, standing with his hands on his hips, looking in at home plate, "Hey Jimmy, how's your wife?" Piersall turned around to face the centerfield crowd and extended his arms in a circle in front of his stomach and puffed out his cheeks. Then he grinned at the crowd. The fans knew that Piersall's wife was pregnant with their sixth child. Someone yelled, "Way to go, Jimmy!"

Cal bought a bag of peanuts from a vendor. The first Chicago batter hit a line drive down the right field line and Jenson chased it at full speed, extending his gloved hand. He caught the ball as it was entering the stands by the foul pole. The crowd roared and Jenson threw the ball to Dale Goodman, the first baseman, tipping his hat as he jogged back to his position. Men in the bleachers were still yelling to Piersall. Somebody asked him about his psychiatrist. Piersall didn't turn around. A fight started behind Cal and he turned around to watch. Ten rows behind him, someone looked familiar, and Cal almost waved to him. Several ushers started up the stairway toward the fight. Cal couldn't place the person and turned around to look again. The man was drinking a beer. He was wearing a t-shirt with the sleeves cut off at the shoulders, and a sailor hat. Then Cal remembered him.

Cal debated with himself what to do. He saw the ushers guide a drunken fan down the aisle and disappear down the exit ramp. Should he go up and sit next to him or should he try to get his attention and ask permission from a distance to talk to him? Cal turned to see if he was still there, and he was. What was there about this derelict that unnerved Cal? The inner voice said, *What are you afraid of? If you want to talk to him, go talk to him.*

Cal turned around to look again but he was gone. Cal panicked for several seconds, then spotted him walking down the aisle toward the exit ramp. When the man disappeared, Cal moved quickly across the empty seats. Going down the ramp, Cal spotted him walking slowly across the under-stadium and followed him from a distance until he entered the men's room. Cal waited for several minutes and the man came out. He was walking toward Cal and then got in line to buy a beer. Cal walked over and stood in the line next to him.

"I'll be damned, Albert Schweitzer himself," the man said when he saw Cal, "and having a beer, no less."

They were face to face.

"I tried to find you after we met that Sunday on the Common."

"I heard."

"I wanted to talk to you again."

"You're a real crusader, aren't you?"

"You seem to know things, and I'm curious about you."

Cal's line moved faster and the man said, "You want a beer or not? You're keeping the guy waiting."

"Oh, sorry, no, go ahead, I changed my mind." Cal moved aside.

The man put a dollar on the beer counter. Cal waited. The man took his two beers and started up the ramp.

"Can we talk?" Cal asked, following him.

"What'll it take for me to quietly drink my beer and watch the game?"

"We could meet afterward."

"No way. I'm busy after the game."

"Just a few minutes."

"You're something else. I didn't come here to watch these two games with you, Buster Brown, so say what you have to say and then the word for you is amscray. If you can't do it in less than five minutes I'll make sure you get tossed out of the park if I have to get tossed out with you."

Cal said "OK," and followed him to the highest row in the center field bleachers. No one was within ten yards of where he sat. Cal sat down beside him.

"It's nice here," Cal said. "I've been waiting all week for this. For the game, I mean."

"I come to see Williams hit. Nothing else."

"I like everything, the park, the Green Monster, the sun."

"The park's a park. Grass is grass. The rest of them are crazy. Piersall's crazy. Jenson's a wimp. His wife fucks other guys and all he does is cry about it. Williams has got balls. He knows what he's doing."

"He's a great hitter."

"The hell he is. He's the greatest hitter of all time. If he was as mean as Cobb he'd be the greatest player of all time. Is that what you want from me, you want to talk baseball with me?"

"You were in the Church. You gave it up. Why?"

"You need a shrink."

"I've got one."

"Take my advice. Save it for him."

"It's a she."

"Lucky you."

The man watched the game and drank his beer. Suddenly he said, "I can't do anything for you, you know. When I saw you on the Common that day, I was pissed off at all you theological types. Never mind the reason. Reasons are bullshit. I'm working on not being pissed off, it takes too much energy."

"You're not a bum. You don't talk like a bum."

"Don't kid yourself, I'm a bum, but I'll tell you a secret. If you want answers, don't ask questions. Once you figure that out, you can be a bum too. That's what you want, isn't it?"

Cal pretended to watch the ball game. He said, "I don't want to be a bum."

"But you want what you think comes with it, right?"

"You're a writer, aren't you?"

"I'm an ex-sailor and a dish washer and a drunk."

"You're not really a drunk."

"You don't want me to be a drunk. Give it up."

"What's after that?"

"I can't help you."

"Square one, I guess."

"Every goddamned day, buddy. See Williams talking to the guy in the scoreboard? He doesn't give a shit about those other guys."

"Do you write every day? How do you live?"

"The interview is over. I'm being straight with you. You're fucked both ways until you accept it."

"What's both ways mean?"

"You got me all riled up again. You theological boys are so full of 'finding yourself' and 'fulfillment' and the 'whole personality' that the other side of the wall never occurs to you."

"My best friend's dying of leukemia."

"What else is new?"

"That's it?"

"We're all dying of leukemia."

"I don't know what to do."

"Do? What do you mean 'do'? What's 'do'? The man said die now and you're quit for this year."

"I just finished reading all of Steinbeck."

"Congratulations."

"What do you write?"

"When Williams hit that single a minute ago, I didn't even know the count. I can't help you. I'm trying to get along. If you found out anything about me, all you'd have is a case history. You're dying friend is a case history, the world is jammed with case histories. You don't get it."

"Just one thing. Tell me about 'bemused.' I've been thinking about it ever since you said it. I went back to Schweitzer again. What you said is true. I've been bemused with the church. Tell me how you recognized that in me."

"Will you go away and stay away?"

"Yes."

"Look at that. They say that Williams is slow. Did you see that stride going around third? He beat that throw by five feet."

"The relay was slow."

"Slow my ass. You don't know anything about baseball either. OK. Listen, I know about bemused because it's the state of this fucking civilization. We live in a bemusement park in America. We're hypnotized by big boats and glitzy broads. We're bemused, distracted, sedated. For two thousand years, the Jesus people have been stupefied by rhetoric and symbols, rhetoric that turns out to be doubletalk and symbols that remind everyone of their deaths."

"There's nothing good in the Church?"

"Fuck you and the question. If there is, find it. All Jesus ever said was pay the price, give it up, and they made rhetoric out of it and started a business. I'm going to get another beer. Don't be here when I get back."

"Thanks for talking to me."

"Don't be here."

He brushed past Cal and walked down the steps toward the exit ramp to the beer stand. Cal moved to the third row in back of the bullpen. He left in the middle of the second game. He never checked to see if the man was still sitting in the sun.

CHAPTER SIXTY-ONE

▼

"ALLIES STORM INLAND: Paratroopers Land in France; Eisenhower Asks Only Victory," *Daily Evening Item*, June 6, 1944

Cal was excited as he closed the door to the band room and walked through the dark basement of the high school. He loved going to the Thursday night wrestling matches with his father and his Uncle Orion. Tonight the masked Superman was wrestling The Angel, Maurice Tillet, once the world champion. Cal's father said his arms hung down to the floor.

Cal left his clarinet in the mechanical drawing room where the band members kept their instruments. He would bring it home tomorrow. He wanted to stop off at Handy's and play pool with Nick and Roger. He would have to do scout's pace to get home by five-thirty.

Cal went in the boy's room to take a leak. He stood before the slate wall with the water draining down from the perforated copper pipe, and urinated. Every time he came into this basement room with its cement floor and wooden stalls with the swinging doors, he remembered one school morning when he had a basement pass, Barry Westford standing here drinking from a whiskey bottle, holding it straight up, gulping. Cal had walked in on Barry, alone in the boy's room, and Cal stared. Barry said, "What the hell are you looking at?" Cal ran out of the boy's room. When he told Roger at lunch, Roger said, "Do you know how sad Barry must be to do that?" Cal had not thought of that. He had thought Barry was bad.

Cal walked through the dark basement cement corridor of the old high school, through the boy's dark coatroom, and then climbed the dark stairs to the front exit of the school. The sports page of the *Lynn Item* said Superman wore a red wool mask down to his shoulders and he would wear it until somebody defeated him. Two weeks before, Superman pinned a huge Negro with a shaved head. Cal wondered if the wool mask scratched his shoulders and face when he got sweaty. The idea made Cal shiver.

Cal walked past the Warner Theater. A Boston Blackie movie was playing on Saturday, and another episode of the Green Hornet. Cal crossed the railroad tracks and went down the stairs to the Rat Hole, everyone's nickname for Handy's Pool Emporium.

Inside, one of the four bowling alleys was lighted and two young men were bowling. Across the low ceilinged room, green shaded lights dangled over the four pool tables beyond the last bowling alley. As Cal passed behind the bowlers, he saw a fast-thrown bowling ball hit three deadwood pins in front of an upright candlepin and careen off the set-up boy sitting above on the railing. He held his shoulder and yelled for the bowler to quit throwing so hard. Rusty Burnell, the bowler, yelled back, "Quit crying and set up the fucking pins!" He was with Hal Crumpy, the set-up kid's cousin. They lived in Maple Hills.

Cal could see his friends playing pool on the third and fourth tables, but he stopped to watch the money game at the first table. Jack Edgehill, Neil Bowman, and Kenny Goodman were playing Three, Five, and Eight for quarters, and Cal stood away from the table and watched the colorful balls clicking and rolling smoothly over the bright green cloth, rebounding off the tight banks and dropping quietly into the invisible leather pockets.

Cal knew the game. The shooters had to sink all eight balls in sequence, and the three, five, and eight balls each paid a quarter. If the money balls dropped while shooting one of the other balls, the players would have to pay the shooter again, and the money balls would be spotted back on the table until they dropped in sequence. Each time a shooter sank a money ball, the other players would step from the darkness and place their quarters on the edge of the table.

Cal loved the darkness and the silence and the skill of the players. Edgehill was a small dark man in his thirties who was always in the pool hall, except on Saturdays during high school football games when he would be in charge of moving the first down chains. Goodman was the high school goalie on the hockey team and Cal thought he was a wiseguy. Neil was the second string quarterback on the football team and the number one pitcher on the baseball team. Each could put english on the cue ball and make great position shots with unbreakable composure.

Waiting their turns, they stood back from the table, holding their cue sticks, butt end on the floor, as if they were palace guards at parade rest. Axel Hendricks, the short fat manager who wore a red vest, would press the quarters from the table's edge into his palm with his thumb, keep one for the house and give the shooter the other three when he finished his turn. The only emotion from the players came when a shooter unexpectedly sank a money ball while also sinking a ball in sequence. One or more of the non-shooters would bang the butt of his cue stick on the wooden floor. Each one, while studying his shot before shooting, would pick up, without looking at it, from the edge of the table a small square piece of blue chalk and turn the tip end of the cue stick into the rounded depression in the chalk, and without taking his eyes off the cue ball would take his shot.

Cal watched Edgehill sink the black eight, and Axel again racked the eight colored balls. Nick was waving to Cal to come to the fourth table, but Cal seemed hypnotized by the quiet, professional ritual and the clean and smooth colors deciding the fate of money. Cal envied each of the players' skill, and he coveted the quarters. He didn't know where Edgehill or the older boys got their money, although he knew that Kenny's father owned the paper company on Water Street near the marshes in East Mapleton.

Edgehill sank the brown seven and the red three on the break. Axel spotted the three. Then Edgehill sank the yellow one ball in the side pocket and the blue two in the corner. He couldn't see the three so he softly one-banked the cue ball so that it slowly rolled toward the three and came to a stop directly against it. The men and boys watching the game murmured approval of Edgehill's skill. Kenny approached his shot, saying, "Thanks for the leave, Edgehill."

Nick stood beside Cal and whispered, "You going to play or what?"

"Yeah, I'm coming, but I've only got twenty cents and I have to leave at five."

They moved to the last table. Cal said "Hi" to Bobby Forti and Frankie Robinson.

Nick said to Cal, "They want to play us. I'll back you one game, maybe you'll get lucky. I did, last Saturday night, at midnight."

"Congratulations." Cal said.

"These guys are fish."

"What about Roger?"

"He's going to play one ball with Hank Grady."

"Today?"

"Yeah, right here, table three, four-thirty. What's wrong with that?"

"Nothing. Grady is just a big jerk, that's all. He quit football after three days. He's a grandstander. I didn't know he played pool. Roger told me last week that Grady dated Gail Yardley for the Senior Prom. Where is Roger, anyway? I thought I saw him when I came in."

Forti yelled, "If you guys aren't going to play, we'll use the table by ourselves."

"Yeah, we're going to play. Get a cue, Cal. Roger's watching the first table. He was standing right next to you, asshole. Grady took Gail to the prom, all right."

Forti broke, sending the cue ball into the racked set of balls, and the game began. Cal looked at the clock. He had forty minutes before he had to start home. "What do you mean he took her to the prom, all right?"

"He said he fucked her three times."

"What do you mean he said? Who said he said? I don't believe that. She's a really nice girl."

"Nice girls fuck, dimhead."

"Grady is a big dumb fake."

"Nice girls fuck big dumb fakes. It's your turn."

Cal said, "Five ball in the corner pocket." He missed and Robinson sank the shot and ran the table.

"It's a good thing we're playing for nickels, Mrs. Grundy," Nick said. What do you look so hurt about?"

"Here he comes now, the son of a bitch."

"He's harmless, for chrissake. Roger will clean his pipes."

Hank Grady walked up to them and said, "Hello fellows. How's your game going?"

"It's going good," Nick said.

"OK," Cal said.

"Where's Roger?"

"Right behind you," Nick said.

"Oh Hello Roger, I hope I can give you a game. I'm pretty rusty at pool these days."

Cal looked at Hank and imagined him screwing Gail with the front of her evening gown up in the air above the back seat of some car. He wondered how he kept getting her to do it. Cal tried to figure out how much time in between screwing and whether they did it in the school parking lot or in a field somewhere or out in front of Gail's house. Cal remembered that when he was in the seventh grade, he met her one day in the passageway between the high school and the junior high school on his way to the boys' room and was embarrassed to be alone with her. Gail said, "It's my boyfriend! How are you?" Cal blushed. She was very beautiful. Cal tried to imagine her screwing Hank Grady. Cal was very hurt.

Hank and Roger were still playing one ball when Cal left the pool hall at five-fifteen. Cal had made sixty-five cents and he felt rich. He would be late unless he got a couple rides so he stuck out his thumb on Main Street, jogging between cars. When he got to Mr. Brandy's barbershop a car stopped and a man drove him to the old mill below Appleton Street at the Mapleton River Bridge. "Thanks a lot," Cal said, and started jogging as the car headed toward North Mapleton. He ran a couple hundred yards and a car stopped for him at the base of Oak Hill. Cal was going to cut through the woods but the man was going to Swampscott by Beechnut Street, and drove Call all the way to the store on Beechnut. Cal jogged the rest of the way and made it home by five-thirty five. His father drove in the yard ten minutes later.

All through supper, Cal thought about Gail screwing Hank in the back seat of a car. Nick had said it was true. Hank bragged about it and Eddie Robinson asked Shirley Lipscomb who said they did it three times. Gail must have bragged too. Cal thought you had to get a girl hot before she would do it. He knew the girl didn't want to do it but got hot and couldn't help it.

That night, Cal sat in the Lynn Arena with his father and Uncle Orion and watched the wrestlers. They circled and grappled each other to the canvas mat. The referee separated them and they locked arms and shoulders and legs and grunted and sweated and rolled on the mat until one of them pinned the shoulders of the other so that he couldn't move for three seconds. The referee slammed his hand on the mat three times and held up the right hand of the man on top.

Cal's father bought him a bag of peanuts, and he ate the Hershey bar his mother had given him to bring. The arena was clouded with smoke, and the bright lights over the wrestling ring made the wrestlers seem very big and strong. When the time came for the main bout of the evening, the announcer went to the center of the ring and introduced the undefeated Superman. He strode around the ring and doubled his fist into the air. The audience cheered a little, but they were so curious about his identity that they wanted him unmasked. The referee shouted into the microphone that the match would be decided by two out of three falls. Cal's Uncle Orion told him that the challenger, Maurice Tillet, was a Frenchman who had once been the heavyweight wrestling champion of the world. He was short and stocky and had a huge bald head with elephant ears. His long arms dangled to the floor from great wide shoulders.

"Why do they call him the Angel?" Cal asked his Uncle Orion.

"Maybe he looks like one with those arms," his uncle laughed.

The arena quieted when the bell rang and the two men faced each other. Superman seemed tall in his red wool helmet-mask and blue tights. He unhooked his red cape and tossed it to his corner. The Angel crouched and approached Superman, cupping his hand around Superman's neck. Superman bolted his left arm upward and flung the Angel's hand away. The Angel laughed and stalked Superman.

Cal's heart pounded as the two giants grappled and separated, grappled and separated, and the crowd yelled encouragement. After several minutes, the Angel got an arm-hold on Superman and flipped him over his head and came up on top of Superman with most of his weight on Superman's shoulders. Several times the referee slammed his open palm twice on the mat, but each time Superman got free before the third count. Finally, Superman rolled the Angel and pinned him in a flash. Bang! Bang! Bang! It happened very quickly. First fall to Superman who got up and strode around the ring with his arms in the air.

The Angel sat on the canvas for several minutes, feeling his shoulder, as if it had been injured. The referee signaled for them to resume wrestling, but the Angel protested that he needed more time. The referee encouraged the Angel to get up and wrestle, but the Angel protested and stayed on the mat, feeling his shoulder. Finally, the referee brought the microphone into the ring and began an announcement:

"Ladies and Gentlemen, because the challenger, the world renowned Angel, the former heavyweight champion of the world, can no longer continue, the match is awarded . . ."

At this point, the Angel jumped to his feet and rushed at Superman who was standing in his corner. The referee threw the microphone to someone at ringside and tried to separate the two wrestlers who were grappling in Superman's corner. All three of them went down on the mat and the referee crawled away as the combatants tangled and rolled on the floor.

Within an instant, the Angel held Superman in a hammerlock, and the referee quickly knelt on the mat and slammed his palm three times. Superman's handlers rushed to the center of the ring, claiming a foul. People cheered loudly. The Angel stood in his corner laughing at Superman, who stalked around the ring, gesturing at the Angel and raising his fist in the air.

After several minutes the referee persuaded Superman to return to his corner, then announced the third and final fall of the match. The crowd yelled for the Angel to unmask Superman. The wrestlers engaged in the center of the ring and the Angel once again cupped his hand around Superman's neck. When Superman attempted to arm-lift the Angel's hand away, the Angel dropped to one knee and reached with his long left arm to grab Superman's right leg. Superman tried to step back but went down. The Angel was on top of him in a flash, and within seconds the bout was over. The crowd yelled for the unmasking, but Superman stepped through the ropes to leave the ring, gesturing to the crowd that the fight was unfair, that the Angel had not earned the right to unmask him. The crowd stood and booed. Superman re-entered the ring, defying the crowd with arm and hand gestures, making disparaging gestures toward the Angel. As he turned his back to the Angel and began to leave the ring again, the Angel grabbed him in an arm lock from behind. The crowd roared its approval.

"Pull off his mask, Angel!" men in the crowd shouted. "Rip it off."

Caught with his head between the ropes and held in an arm lock by the former champion, Superman was seemingly helpless and the crowd was on its feet. The Angel pulled the red and black wool hood from Superman's head and the unmasked Superman stood in the ring for all to see. He was a closely cropped gray-headed man.

The crowd murmured, and the men around Cal nodded their heads in recognition and talked to one another.

"Who is it?" Cal asked his father and Uncle Orion.

"Lou Nova," his uncle said. "He's been around for awhile. He was a pretty good boxer at one time."

"He was a boxer?" Cal asked.

"Washed up boxers usually end up in the wrestling game, sooner or later."

The crowd filed from the small arena. The mystery of Superman had been solved, and Cal felt left out. He didn't know about Lou Nova, but he wasn't famous, and the Angel was very strange. His head was huge, and his long gangly arms were like a gorilla's.

"He wasn't much of a Superman," Cal said to his father as they walked down the street to the car.

"It's all fake anyway, Cal, it's just supposed to be fun," his father said.

"I haven't heard anything about Lou Nova for fifteen years," Uncle Orion said, "I thought he was dead."

"Can we go again in two weeks?" Cal asked.

"Maybe, if it's boxing. We'll see."

CHAPTER SIXTY-TWO

▼

Cal and Don Grapple sat in a bare room with a peeling ceiling in the University Public Communications building, working on *Kairos* magazine. It was past midnight, and they had been typing master layouts for two hours. A friend of Don's had gotten him access to veritypers once the building was locked at nine o'clock. Don typed on one machine and Cal on another.

"I feel as if I've typed every line five times, not just twice," Cal said.

"Quit making mistakes, dummy. Which one are you doing?"

"Dr. Roth's essay on creativity. He says, 'Spiritually, we must create or die.'"

"I read it, remember?"

"Do you believe it?"

"Sure. What are we doing the magazine for?"

"What does it mean?"

"Read the rest of the essay. He says it straight out."

"He says St. Francis married Lady Poverty because My Lady Wealth turned away the hungry."

"That's just Roth being Roth. He says that at the beginning. You know how sentimental he is. Later he says 'To transform the inner glow into observable color is to create.' That's pretty good. You know it is."

"It's pasty. The best thing we've printed is Longman's article about Camus."

"Dr. Sunday's memoir of Paris is good. Get more from Longman, if you want. What's bothering you, Cal?"

"Everything! Nothing, I guess. How many of us do you think will end up in the Church? Will you? You're not your father. And I won't. Jack may end up directing a big choir in some big church, but he won't end up as a preacher. Can you see Perkins as a preacher? Foster might. He'll be a bishop some day."

"So?"

"Time goes by, that's all."

"I'm going to start my own college."

"With what?"

"My shoestring. How's your girlfriend, what's her name, Clare?"

"You don't want to know. I talked with a guy this afternoon at the ballpark who intrigues me. He's kind of a bum, but he isn't really. I met him once before. Remember when we went down town and preached on the Common three or four times?"

"I was there the day Foster preached."

"The day Jack preached, a guy heckled me and I ended up buying him a meal. He was all beat up, and he was smart as hell."

"He must have been to be a bum."

"He seemed to know all about the Church and the ministry. He quoted Schweitzer and stuff. He just walked away after eating."

"What did you expect?"

"I don't know. Joe and I went looking for him once in the Combat Zone. It was one chance in a million. Joe did it just to mollify me, and we didn't find him. We left a message for him at one of the bars. I actually saw him today at the ballpark and he was different, but he was still intriguing. He actually got the note I left at the bar that day but he obviously had no intention of getting back to me.

"Of course he didn't."

"He was like a guy in a Camus novel. When I got back from the game I read Longman's article again."

"Keep going."

"There isn't anywhere else to go. The guy is just out there somewhere, unattached. He doesn't need anything. He's a complete loner."

"Why was he different?"

"He wasn't looking for trouble. He didn't even want to talk to me. The first time it was like he had the need to go after me, to prove something.

He was angry. Today he just wanted to be left alone and watch the ball game."

"He'd eaten already."

"Yeah, but it was more than that. At least it seemed more."

"And you're here sitting in a safe room typing an artsy magazine, pretending you're going to go into the ministry."

"In *The Fall*, Clamence confesses his complicity, even though he's a judge. Instead of confessing others like a priest, he confesses himself. He's a confesser, not a confessor."

"I don't remember that in Longman's article."

"It's not there, I'm saying it. But Longman pointed it out to me. By confessing that he let the woman drown, Clamence has it both ways. He implicates his listener and transfers his guilt. Longman calls him a Superman who looks down on the human ants, his friends, clients, beggars to 'vehicles of self-aggrandizement.' I memorized the phrase. Longman is fair to Camus even though he doesn't agree with him. He never gets preachy like Konigsbauer does in his article about Eugene O'Neill."

"Camus says, 'No man is a hypocrite in his pleasures.'"

"I didn't understand that until today."

"It's the best line in *The Fall*."

"Joe Stearns has leukemia."

"Whoa! Your plate *is* overloaded. When did this happen?"

"I'm not sure. Joe doesn't know I know. Susan told me. No one else knows."

"I knew that you're close to Joe."

"Since we were kids. I don't know what to do. Ordination's coming up and everything seems to be closing down."

"We don't have to finish this tonight."

"Yeah, we do. We planned to do it and we might as well do it. I only have the poems left in this pile anyhow, and I don't have to justify the margins. How close is your pile?"

"One more to justify. Just Candle's short story, justification by works."

"That's justice?"

"We're slap-happy. What time is it?"

"Three-thirty."

"I can finish by four. Can you?

"Yeah."

"How'd your trip south with Howard go?"

"He kissed me on the forehead coming north."

"No shit."

"It was innocent, but it wasn't pleasant. I just never thought he'd touch me."

"What's 'innocent'"?

"You know Howard. He got enthusiastic about something I said about 'hope.' He jumped out of bed and rushed across the room and kissed me on the forehead, then walked back and jumped into bed again."

"Did you say anything?"

"Yeah. He thinks I misunderstood."

"His feelings are hurt. Are you going to go west this summer with him?"

"It's up in the air."

At five minutes past four, Cal and Don turned off the light switch in the bleak communications room and walked up Memorial Avenue. At the corner of Hiram Street, they parted.

"Say hi to Mary for me," Cal said.

"I will. See you tomorrow."

"When can you print?"

"Tomorrow night."

"See you."

Don headed for Charles River Road and the married student's dorm, and Cal entered the chapel plaza.

CHAPTER SIXTY-THREE

▼

The springtime stars are shining above Boston, and the Back Bay is dead at 4:30 a.m. In a few minutes, the first MTA subway car will roll silently out of the parking yard on the Heights and move towards Brighton and the city, but for now the tracks are empty and the city is silent. The Citco sign over Kenmore Square ripples on and off above the deserted intersection of five converging arteries. An occasional car intensifies the emptiness.

In Copley Square, Trinity Church is locked and silent. The Public Library is dark. The shops along Newbury Street are closed. The Charles River flows blackly and quietly into its basin, the grass banks deserted except for a single walker by the bandstand shell across from the beginning of Arlington Street. The streets of Beacon Hill are abandoned. The Statehouse is dark and empty except for the night watchman who sits on a chair inside the main hall near the staircase, reading yesterday's newspaper.

Goodspeed's bookstore is locked and dark. In Scollay Square, two doorway sleepers darken two entryways, and a man sits on a curb with his chin buried against his chest. In old Haymarket Square, men and women unload vegetables and fruit from trucks into great wooden carts and wheel them over cobblestones to line against the curb. Butchers hang sausages and thighs of animals in front of open displays of meat. On Quincy Wharf, the moorings are empty, the fishermen already miles offshore, and the water in the harbor is calm.

In room 624 at 423 Memorial Avenue in the Back Bay, Cal lies in his bed, listening to his roommate snoring. Cal says "Trav!" and Travis rolls over on his side and the room is quiet. Cal is thinking what it would be like to be in the army.

Cal's father never talked about the war. Sometimes Cal took the Purple Heart from its little box in the dining room chiffonnier and held it between his fingers. One night when he was eleven, Cal heard Aunt Penelope tell his mother that Lem was drunk most of the time he was in France. It was the summer Cal and his mother stayed at Great East Lake in Maine, and Uncle Orion worked for Edmund Rolf on his estate at Mousam Lake. Uncle Orion tended the stables and cultivated a vegetable garden. Cal remembered Uncle Orion feeding sugar to one of the horses, and the horse nibbled some skin on Uncle Orion's hand and it bled.

That night, Cal and his cousin Dick were in bed, and Dick was asleep. Aunt Penelope said, "Lem wasn't in the house five minutes after the war before he headed straight for Effie's, and when he saw her as big as Billy-be-darned, he turned around and walked out without saying a word. He must have gone right over to your house in East Mapleton."

"He did," Cal's mother said, "He just said, 'Come on Sal, let's get married.' We never went out on a date, we just got married."

Aunt Penelope said that the story Cal's father told about riding the donkey behind General Edwards took place when Cal's father was drunk. Lying in bed, Cal liked the official sound of "101st Field Artillery, Battery D." There was a picture in his father's World War I History of the 101st Field Artillery that showed four men loading a cannon during a battle. Cal's father's own cannon blew up, killing one of his crew. His father said that the gun blew up after the picture was taken and Cal did not understand if that was his father's gun or not. When Cal asked him about being gassed, his father said he had gotten only a little bit of it.

Sometimes Cal would get the stepladder from the cellar on rainy days and put it under the attic opening in the hall ceiling outside his mother and father's bedroom. Cal would climb to the top of the ladder and push the wooden cover up and into the attic and then hoist himself in. The attic was cold in the winter and hot in the summer. Usually Cal would go up in the winter wearing a sweater. The attic was pitch black and he needed a flashlight. He had to carefully step on the rafters between the insulation.

Cal put on the German helmet and lifted the rifle in the dark. He put down the rifle and took off the helmet and pulled the gas mask partially over his head, but the mask was tight and he couldn't fit it on without putting the inhaler into his mouth. It was stale and rubbery and he didn't dare to put it in his mouth. He looked at it in the glare of the flashlight and the rubber was cracked. The isinglass in the eyeholes of the gas mask was stained yellow and cloudy. Cal put on the American helmet, but he liked the German helmet better because it was made of heavier dark green metal and it came down over his ears. The attic was dark and cold.

Aunt Penelope said that after Cal's father was gassed at Chateau Thierry, he got pneumonia, and when he got better they made him an aide to General Edwards. "Lem never thought he'd come home alive." Aunt Penelope and Cal's mother talked almost in whispers, and Cal held his breath and heard almost everything they said. He was sure that he would hear something he shouldn't hear, something that would change everything, a hidden secret, something that would crush him.

That same summer, Uncle Orion gave Cal's mother a revolver to keep at the lake where she kept it under her pillow. The Olsen boys had hidden in the dark camp one night when Cal and his mother were visiting Mrs. Olsen up on the hill, and they jumped out and said "Boo!" when Cal's mother re-entered the dark camp. The fright stayed with Cal's mother a long time. She didn't tell Cal how scared she was between weekends when Cal's father wasn't there. Cal found out later that his mother gave him that summer at the lake because she wanted him to have at least one carefree summer at the lake before he grew up.

Lying in his bed in his seminary room, Cal thought of his cousin Everett and tried to imagine what it would be like to be dead. He couldn't imagine being alone forever. He shivered, and his mind shifted. He wanted to go to sleep. When he was a little boy, he was standing in a field in early fall, surrounded by black-eyed Susans and white daisies. He picked several daisies and smelled them. They smelled like urine. He thought, "Everyone else will die, but I won't."

Travis started to snore again as the first light of dawn came into the dormitory room, and Cal studied the white ceiling. It was the ceiling of his childhood home in Maplehurst. He wished he were at the lake.

Waking up at the camp he saw the brown wooden boards overhead. Sometimes at night it would be raining and he would listen to the drops on the roof before he fell asleep. Then it would be morning and everything would be quiet again. One overcast morning after the rain, Cal's father took him fishing in the cove, and there were pond lilies and yellow cow flowers around them in the water, and the newspaper he sat on became damp from the rain on the seat from the night before. It was warm on the water and his father let him take off his sweater. Cal counted four yellow stripes on the side of the first yellow perch he caught.

Cal got out of his dormitory bed and stood at the window. A single rower cut a swath in the daybreak calm of the Charles River. Cal wondered who would die first, Joe or his father.

CHAPTER SIXTY-FOUR

▼

For the next two weeks, Cal went to class, saw Miss Green, helped Don Grapple print and distribute *Kairos* magazine. In his Art of the Religious Tradition class, Konigsbauer acted as if nothing had happened between them. On Sunday nights, Cal went to his Youth Group in Wellesley. Once, Regina was there and afterward they went for an ice cream cone. Regina told Cal that Clare was seeing Vinnie again and working in Wellesley at the hospital. Cal dropped Regina off at home and told her that he would call her.

In the seminary library, Angelica told Cal that *Kairos* was "splendid." She said that her husband Cordell was thinking of writing a short story for it. She said that she especially liked Cal's poem, "Impressions of the Charles," but she didn't understand the image of the "river witches." Cal imagined Cordell sucking Angelica's breasts, and said that he didn't either.

"Ah, a very contemporary poet, this one," she said.

Jim Toffert came by cradling his notebook in his upper arm and said, "Mr. Steinbeck, I presume. I've read your new poem and I commend your imagination. Since this is supposed to be a Christian community, I'll limit my remarks for the sake of sanguinity: you do try one's patience, Newsome, but you are an engaging point of interest."

After Toffert walked away, Angelica said, "I think you caught his attention".

"Is that good or bad," Cal laughed.

"I wonder. Probably good," she said. "Let's believe that, anyway."

James, the British exchange student, came by and said, "Good show with *Kairos*."

"I'm glad you got one, James. I was going to save one for you."

"You Americans are extraordinary—a real literary magazine in the midst of theologians. I'll wager this is the only seminary in America disseminating a literary magazine. It's quite impressive."

"You don't think it's heretical, then?"

"On the contrary. The usual poetry in these sorts of publication is pure drivel, but I'm amazed. And your man Thurman's interview with Gandhi is a valuable historical piece. Really good show."

"I'm glad I heard that," Angelica said. "You should be pleased."

"I am," Cal said. "Thanks. Did you hear him say 'disseminating'?"

"I did. It was clever. Why don't you come over for dinner some night? Cordell needs a bit of creative urging."

"I will. Thank you. I need some creative urging myself."

"I hardly think so. Well, bye now."

Cal found an empty table, read two chapters in Winston's *Pastoral Counseling,* and got an MTA car downtown to see Miss Green.

Later, he called the Newton-Wellesley Hospital and asked for Clare.

"Why on earth are you calling me here?" she said.

"I would like to talk to you, Clare."

"You're talking to me."

"I mean in person."

"I hardly think that's sensible, we don't really have anything to talk about."

"I think we do. We can settle things, and we'll both feel better."

"Things are settled. What makes you think things aren't settled? What you consider talk is just you talking. Every time I listen to you I start becoming somebody I feel guilty about. No, I don't want to talk."

"I heard you were seeing Vinnie again."

"What do you know about Vinnie? That's none of your business."

"Vinnie's dangerous."

"What do you know? How'd you find out where I am? Why are you snooping after me?"

"I'm not snooping, Clare. I care about you. People in the Youth Group know you. They're your friends. I just happened to hear that you were back in the area. Can't we just talk for a little while somewhere? I'm not trying to start anything. I just want to clear the air."

"I know you, Cal. If I don't agree to see you, you'll keep inventing excuses to call me. So I'll tell you what, I'll see you once, and so help me god, if you don't get out of your system whatever it is that itches inside of you, as far as I'm concerned, I'll find a way if I have to move to California, to get away from you once and for all."

"OK. How about Wednesday evening?"

"I work Wednesday evening. It's my only night-shift."

"Thursday?"

"I've got a date."

"When do you get off every day?"

"Four."

"Thursday afternoon at four?"

"Where?"

"I'll pick you up at the hospital."

"No you won't. I'll meet you at Howard Johnson's at ten past four."

"Great. See you there." Clare hung up.

CHAPTER SIXTY-FIVE

▼

Cal drove into Howard Johnson's in Wellesley at four o'clock on Thursday. He brought DeFranco's book to read in case she was late, one of his habits that rarely produced any reading. He looked at the title, *A Theology of the Living Church*. DeFranco made a point in class about it being *a* theology, not *the* theology, not wanting to presume in a liberal rationalist community that he spoke *ex cathedra*, like the Pope. Joe told Cal, when he took the course last year, that DeFranco left room in his theology for angels, so Cal brought the book to read the chapter on angels. Joe said DeFranco wouldn't rule out angels because it would be limiting the power of God. Cal had said to Joe, "Who the hell cares?" Joe had said, "That's a good question."

Cal put down the book and studied the orange tile roof of Howard Johnson's. When he was a boy the orange tile roofs stretched along coastal route 1, people said, all the way to Florida. Twenty-eight flavors of ice cream. Cal remembered the one in Seabrook, New Hampshire where Cal's father would stop on Sunday afternoons on the way back from the lake. Cal's mother always ordered a ten-cent butter crunch sugar cone. Cal's father let him taste his frozen pudding once but Cal didn't like the rum taste. Plus it had raisins.

At four fifteen, Clare hadn't arrived. Cal was agitated. Maybe she wasn't coming. He didn't know what he wanted to say to Clare, he just wanted to see her. Cal wanted to get something settled between them, but he didn't know what it was. He didn't want their relationship to end with her accident, but he didn't know if he wanted the relationship to continue. Cal thought of Regina, and how attracted he was to her. He got out of his car to walk around.

At the end of the parking lot he looked at the deserted miniature golf course. The green carpets were faded and ripped. A pile of dog shit on the second tee was decomposing. The putting cups were full of water from yesterday's rain. Cal started to walk back when a car turned into the parking lot and as he watched it, he saw that a man was behind the wheel. "Good god, it's Vinnie," Cal said out loud. Vinnie caught Cal's eyes and smiled as he pulled in next to Cal's car. Clare was sitting beside Vinnie.

Vinnie rolled down his window and said, "Hey, preach!"

Cal saw Clare put her hand on Vinnie's arm. She got out of the car and walked over to Cal.

"My ride had to work overtime, and Vinnie offered to bring me. He's going to wait for me. I didn't think you'd mind. Let's go inside."

They sat at the counter on the end stools.

"Do you want anything to eat?" Clare asked.

"Eat? You think I can eat? My stomach's all in knots. I come out here in good faith to talk to you about us and you bring that goon with you. Why didn't you invite him inside so he could listen?"

"Is this the way it's going to be, Cal? Tell me now, because if you can't handle Vinnie sitting out there in the car while we talk in here, I'm leaving. It's as simple as that. Which? Tell me what it's going to be."

"You're really playing hard ball with me, Clare. Where's the Clare I knew before?"

"Don't start that, Cal. I knew when you called that you were just going to go through it all again. I'm the same Clare and you're the same Cal, and that's the problem and that's always going to be the problem. We tried. At least I tried. I really tried. I tried everything as a matter of fact, and for a long time I hated myself for it, but now I don't any more."

"I think about that a lot. Sometimes I wish none of it happened and we could just meet for the first time. I know that being a theology student made it difficult for you, but I'm thinking maybe I'm going to do something else. I don't know what, but I've been thinking about a couple of things."

Clare looked at Cal and didn't say anything. She shook her head.

Cal said, "What?"

"You don't know anything about yourself, even now, after everything we went through, and god knows what you and that Joannie you used to talk about went through. You really don't. It's amazing."

"What do you mean?"

"Do you know what kind of a person always wants something only after he has it and turns it down?"

Cal looked away. He knew that Clare understood him better than he did himself. He felt sorry for himself and he let tears well up in his eyes.

"Cal, you're not going to cry. Cal, stop it. If you don't stop it I'm going to go out and get Vinnie. The only reason he's out there is so he won't kick your face in. But it might be a good way to stop your crying."

"OK, OK. I'm not crying, but not because of Vinnie, the hell with Vinnie. I was just thinking of Joe." Cal knew he was lying.

"Joe? What about Joe?"

"He's dying. He's got leukemia."

"Oh my god, I don't know what to say. Is this why you wanted to talk to me? If it is, I'm really sorry about how I've been acting. Joe, my god, that's so awful."

"I haven't even seen him since I found out three weeks ago. He's gone somewhere or he's just staying at his church in Braintree."

"You mean he's going through this all alone? That's even worse. You should go to him, Cal, you're his best friend."

"Joe's got a girlfriend. She's with him. If he wanted to talk to me, he would. I can't do that."

"Oh Cal, you're such a dope. I don't know about you, really. You're so hopelessly full of excuses. I don't know now whether to believe you or not about Joe. You've always pulled me into a million pieces. I know you don't like Vinnie, but I know who he is and I can depend on him."

"You didn't have to tell him about us."

"Of course I didn't have to tell him. I told him because I wanted to. If I didn't tell him I'd be cheating on him, and I'm not doing that any more, with Vinnie or anybody else. I know about the night he came to Youth Group and what they did to Regina. Regina's OK, she can take care of herself."

"I should have called the police."

"Why didn't you?"

"It's a good question. I don't know. But one of these days I'm not going to back down any more. Here comes your bodyguard now."

Vinnie pushed through the door from outside and scooped a fistful of mints as he passed the cash register.

"He's not my bodyguard. Hi Vinnie. Getting hungry?"

"Yeah, sort of. How's lover boy here doing?"

"Lover boy's doing fine, especially without you."

"Oh yeah? Good. Good for you, lover boy. I just came in for an ice cream cone, so don't let me interrupt your *tête à tête*. Pardon my French."

"You could have had the decency to wait," Cal said. "You're just trying to start something."

Clare stepped between them, "Give us ten minutes, Vinnie. I'll be right out."

"You mean I can't get a friendly ice cream cone? Lover boy here is so fragile in the company of three. . ."

Clare quickly said, "Of course, Vin, get an ice cream. I'll get one too in a minute and come out."

Vinnie ordered a large chocolate ice cream on a sugar cone, and Cal and Clare watched the counter girl scrape the dipper several times inside the chocolate bin and load a large ball of ice cream on the sugar cone. She tapped the top twice and wrapped a napkin around the cone and passed it over the counter to Vinnie who took a bite off the side and let it melt in his mouth, then swallowed. "Excellent," he said. "You make good ice cream," he said to the counter girl, who smiled.

"Thanks," she said.

Vinnie walked over to Cal and lifted the cone close to Cal's face, offering him a taste of chocolate ice cream. "Want a lick, lover boy?" he asked Cal.

Cal shook his head, staring at Vinnie.

"I'll be right out, Vin," Clare said.

"OK lover boy," Vinnie said to Cal, lifting the ice cream cone back to his own lips and taking another bite. He savored it, smiling at Cal, and swallowed. He started to take another bite, smiling at Cal.

Cal pushed the chocolate ice cream cone into Vinnie's face. Vinnie stepped back, shocked by both Cal's unexpected violence and the coldness of the ice cream all over his lips and nose. Vinnie's nostrils were clogged with chocolate ice cream.

Vinnie stood there for a few seconds, incredulous. Then he looked at Clare. Clare had shouted "No! Oh god!" simultaneously with Cal's gesture. She expected an instantaneous reaction from Vinnie but he looked more stupefied than angry.

Eyes blazing, Cal dove into Vinnie, dipping his head to one side and putting his shoulder into Vinnie in a perfectly executed football tackle, driving Vinnie first against the wall, then pummeling him again, hard against the wall as he slid onto the floor. Only then did it dawn on Vinnie what Cal had done.

"Call somebody," Clare shouted, "Vinnie will kill him!"

The counter girl disappeared around the cash register, into the dining room.

As Vinnie flailed his arms and swung his fists, Cal got his right hand in Vinnie's face, further mushing the melting ice cream into Vinnie's eyes, and as the struggle escalated, Cal landed punches all over Vinnie's chocolate covered face. Vinnie screamed at Cal, "You fucking little prick, I'll kill you!"

Cal butted Vinnie, opening a gash in Vinnie's forehead. Clare pulled at Cal, trying to pry him away from Vinnie. Cal shook her off and slammed his right fist into Vinnie's nose, breaking it. Blood spurted from his nostrils. Vinnie was dazed, and for a few seconds became lethargic, but then he revived and rolled over, throwing Cal aside for the moment. As Vinnie scrambled to his feet, Cal drilled him again with a shoulder tackle, spreading Vinnie flat on the floor.

In his rage, Cal started to cry, which increased his venom against Vinnie, who swung wildly, trying to land a punch in Cal's face. Some of the blows landed against Cal's shoulders, but most of them missed entirely. Cal hiccoughed and the tears streamed down his face. He bit his lip and drove his right fist into Vinnie's throat, opened his left hand and slapped his palm against Vinnie's ear. Vinnie got his left hand into Cal's face and drew down his fingernails, creating red welts the length of Cal's cheek that soon was crimson with blood. Clare screamed, "Get somebody! Stop this!"

When the police arrived, Cal was sitting on Vinnie's chest, still hiccoughing. He had stopped crying. He kept wiping his nose with his forearm and snuffling back the drainage in his nose, saying "You fool! You fool!" over and over.

CHAPTER SIXTY-SIX

▼

Cal was sitting on the edge of his cell bunk when the fat desk policeman inserted the key in the steel door.

"OK Graziano, you got wings."

"I can go?"

"That's what they tell me. Priest school must be interesting these days."

Cal left the cell and walked down the dark hall. "I'm not a priest," he said, "I'm temporarily attending a Protestant seminary."

The policeman closed the cell door and said loud enough for Cal to hear, "I thought even Prods had priests."

"I'm studying to be a minister. At least I was," Cal said as he walked into the main police station.

He didn't hear the policeman say, "I thought ministers worked for the government."

Joe and Susan were sitting against the wall, whispering to each other. Cal saw them and headed in their direction: "Am I glad to see you!"

A young policeman behind the counter said, "Hey Bud, hold it. Sign this before you go anywhere."

Ten minutes later, riding in Joe's car, Cal said, "I just lost it. I haven't hit anybody since I was in the sixth grade."

"You sure made up for it," Joe said. "The other guy, what's his name, Vincent somebody, is in the hospital."

"You've been hanging out in Braintree, Joe. Can't you tell me what's wrong?"

"Tell him, Joe," Susan said. "You should tell Cal."

"I haven't wanted to butt in, Joe," Cal said, "but it's all I've been thinking about."

"OK, I'll come clean, but we have to deal with this other thing, Cal, there's going to be charges. I talked to Clare, she's pretty upset."

"How'd you find out, anyway? You got here fast enough."

"She called us. I don't know how she got my church number. We're lucky, because Suze and I just got back from Winnepesaukee this morning."

"My car's at Howard Johnson's, Joe, I don't want to leave it there."

Joe nodded.

Cal said, "Joe, are you OK?"

"For now," Joe said. "We ought to go to the hospital and see if the other guy is OK."

"What does 'for now' mean? I don't want to go to any hospital."

"Tell him, Joe," Susan said, "Cal should know."

They were parked next to Cal's car in the Howard Johnson parking lot.

"Let's get the hospital thing straight first, Cal. We don't legally have to go to the hospital, but Clare's involved, and she's upset. She's probably as upset about you as she is about this other guy. He's obviously been hurt. Clare said you did a job on him. He probably deserved it, and it's probably good for you that you finally let someone have it, but now we have to deal with the other side of it."

"I don't want to see Vinnie, and I don't want to see Clare. It's over. Let the hospital take care of Vinnie and let Clare take care of Clare. I don't want to talk about me. The guy in the jail thought I was a student priest. He called me Rocky Graziano. Are you going to die, Joe?"

Joe looked at Susan and she nodded her head. Joe said, "We're all going to die, Cal, it's just a question of when."

"Do you have leukemia, Joe?"

"Joe, there's no point in not telling him," Susan said.

Joe looked at Cal. "Yeah, I've got leukemia. The doctors at Mass General say that I'm going to live a month, maybe six months, maybe six years."

Susan squeezed Joe's hand. They all sat in silence.

"They can't do anything?" Cal said.

"They're doing it, transfusions and stuff. They're still learning."

They sat in silence.

"Suze and I got married last week," Joe said.

"Wow. That's really fine. That's terrific."

"It was my idea," Susan said.

"I still don't think it's fair to her, but we would have eventually, so we did it. And I'm happier about it than I sound.

"Right now, we're just floating on a cloud, like the cliche says," Joe added.

"I sure brought the cloud down to earth, didn't I?"

"Hey buddy, you sure cleaned his clock. What got into you anyway," Joe said.

"I don't know," Cal said, "everything. I can't talk about it."

"You don't have to," Susan said. "Come on, why don't we go to Chinatown for some Sichuan seafood?"

"I'm in for that. Where?" Cal said.

"The Imperial," Susan said. "Remember that time a gang of us walked in on you guys drinking beer there?"

"You were with Lovell and Cripswell," Cal said.

"That was the night I noticed Joe Stearns for the second time."

"That fatal night," Joe said.

Ten minutes later, in his car on the way to meeting Joe and Susan in Chinatown, Cal drove through Chestnut Hill. He was still hitting Vinnie. *His hand mushed into Vinnie's chocolaty face, his fingers in Vinnie's nostrils, then the sound of his flat palm slapping and deafening Vinnie's right ear.* In Allston, Cal took the Cambridge cutoff and turned onto Fielding Drive. The dark river was glazed with lights as he passed Harvard and the Harvard Bridge. Across the Charles, the lighted dome of MIT shone in the darkness. Everywhere universities, Cal thought. Then he was in the tunnel passing Copley Square.

He drove past the Arlington Street exit, a hundred yards from Miss Green's apartment, swung around the half-shell amphitheater, past Massachusetts General Hospital, up the ramp past North Station, onto the Southeast Expressway, past Quincy Market on the right and the Boston Aquarium on the left, past State Street, into Chinatown.

"Miss Green can't help me this time," he thought, as he entered the Imperial Restaurant and walked up the stairs to meet Joe and Susan.

Chapter Sixty-Seven

On the morning of ordination day, Cal was shaving in his room when there was a knock on his door and Phil Whately's voice telling him he had a telephone call.

"It's your mother, Cal."

"Got it, Phil, thanks," Cal called, and continued shaving with his electric razor as he jogged down the hall to the phone. He thought his mother would be asking him for last minute details for their drive to Worcester that afternoon.

"Hi mom, what's up?—dad getting butterflies about parking in Worcester"?

"Cal, this is Bob Briggs, your new neighbor. Your mother asked me to call. I hate like Sam Hill to do this, but I have to tell you, your father just suffered another attack."

"Is he alive?"

"Honestly son, I don't know. I presume he is. They've just gotten him into the ambulance. Your mother's pretty shook up."

"Where are they taking him?"

"Hold on. I'll see if I can find out. I'm going to put down the phone, so don't hang up. Hold on now."

A minute later, Briggs came on the line again. "Lynn. Lynn Hospital. They're taking him to the emergency room of Lynn Hospital."

"Tell my mother I'll be there as soon as I can. I'm leaving right now."

"Yes, I'll do that. They're leaving now. I think I can catch them. I'm sorry about this, son, I'm going to hang up now."

"Please go quickly, Mr. Briggs."

"Yes I will. Bye." The phone clicked.

Cal held the phone in his hand, listening to the dial tone. "Well there it is," Cal thought. *"It's happened. He's gone. I know he's gone."*

Seven hours later, Cal walked up the steps of St. James Cathedral in Worcester and stood at the back of the center aisle. The church was full. Flowers blazed around the altar, and the sun poured through the stained glass windows, lining both sides of the long sanctuary and semi-circling the nave above the altar, casting a bright and warm softness over the dead-still congregation. Up front, sixteen seminary students knelt, all Cal's acquaintances, all candidates for Elder's orders. Cal could not hear what Bishop Lord was saying, but he knew. In the name of Jesus Christ, he was ordaining each in turn an Elder of the Methodist Church, a servant of the Good Shepherd, devoting his life to the Ministry of the Church.

Cal watched the sixteen black robes rise and file back to the front row of pews. Joe and the other candidates for Deacon's Orders would be next. The great organ roared and the music bounded off the walls and through the recesses of the stone church. The congregation was singing "Faith of our Fathers, Holy Faith." Cal did not want to stay, he had had enough, but he remained standing at the back of the church, watching.

An usher noticed Cal and came over and offered to seat him, but Cal signaled with his hand that he didn't want to sit, that he was fine where he was, and the usher returned to his standing position at the side of the sanctuary. Cal could have rushed down the aisle and knelt with them. The bishop would understand. Everyone would understand. He was late because his father died. Cal stood where he was, watched the candidates for Deacon's Orders file to the communion rail. Joe was third in line, slightly taller than the rest. Cal watched the bishop place his hands on each candidate's head and say the words that settle each candidate's life forever. The bishop placed his hand on Joe's head and said the words that Cal couldn't hear. Then Joe lifted his head and the bishop moved to the fourth candidate. Cal left the church.

CHAPTER SIXTY-EIGHT

▼

"GREATER LYNN MEN REGISTER FOR FIRST PEACETIME DRAFT," *Daily Evening Item*, Oct. 16, 1940

In early June, largemouth bass swim slowly around the shore of the lake, and as a boy, whenever he saw them Cal got excited. Later in his life he often dreamed of huge fish in shallow water. Sometimes in his dream he would try to catch one, but the line on his fishing reel would snarl or the dream would change before he got the fish out of the water. Sometimes these fish would be great long creatures with spots on them, but sometimes they were just big fish that he had never seen before. The dreams were not good dreams. There was always something wrong with the lake. The water would be too shallow and there would be large boulders dividing the lake in half. The dirt road leading to the camp was always different. The feeling about the road was a lost feeling.

When Cal was eight years old, his mother and father took him to the lake every weekend in the spring, summer, and fall. This was before the war and there was no gasoline rationing. Every Friday, beginning in early spring, Cal's mother would drive Cal's father back to work after noon dinner so she could pack the car. She and Cal and their dog Pickles would pick up Cal's father at 5:20 outside the gate of the General Electric Company on Western Avenue in Lynn. Cal's mother would have packed the groceries for the weekend in two cardboard boxes in the back seat beside Cal, and they would drive home so Cal's father could change from his chocolate brown double-breasted foreman's suit into his black slacks and a once worn shirt.

As he changed upstairs, she would fry hamburgers and onions for sandwiches to eat in the car. Cal would sit in the kitchen with her. Later, as he grew older, the smell of cooking hamburgers and onions would remind him of the Friday afternoon trips to the lake. His mother and father never fought at the lake, not once in all the years that the family went there together.

After their car reached route 1 in North Mapleton, Cal's mother would unwrap the wax paper from the still warm hamburger sandwiches, and they would eat them. Each had two, and then Cal's mother would pass each of them cookies for dessert. The ride took four hours and they would arrive just after dark if it was spring, and much after dark if it was fall. Cal knew by heart the places on the way, and even when he was a little boy he never asked his father if they were almost there. He knew the big bridges in Newburyport and Portsmouth, and special places like the Old Man of Seabrook on the side of the barn in New Hampshire. Then the wedding-cake house where his grandmother was married in Portsmouth, and the forest of young pine trees in South Berwick which they called "Uncle Nate's pine trees" because Uncle Nate rode in the car with them one time and remarked upon them as they passed. Cal's favorite place was the gladiolus fields in Kittery. He could see the colors far across the long fields as the car passed by.

Sometimes on the way, Cal and his mother played the animal counting game. Whoever saw a cemetery on his side of the road would lose his score and have to start counting over. Cal's dog Pickles slept the whole way above the top of the back seat, against the rear window. Close to the lake, at the turn-in to Red Gate Road, Cal's father would stop the car and let Pickles out so he could run alongside for the remaining three tenths of a mile to the parking space in the bushes on the hill above the camp. When he stopped at Walbitt's spring to fill the water jugs, Pickles would wait at the car and run ahead again when the car moved.

On one Sunday afternoon in late June when the black flies had been gone a week, the water was still high from the melted winter ice and the lake was quiet. Cal's mother and father were sitting in the two wood reclining chairs that Cal's father had built from the leftover tongue and groove second-hand slabs he had used to build the camp. The camp was situated at the lower basin of the lake, and the chairs were positioned on the little slope halfway between the water and the camp itself, so that they could see most of the first lake.

Out of sight up the lake, across from two small islands, a half-mile long narrows separated the first lake from the big lake which was five miles long. The furthest part of the big lake was in New Hampshire. Cal's mother and father were now relaxing after finishing the dishes from the mid-day Sunday dinner. In a couple hours they would sweep out the camp and begin the drive home in time for Sunday evening church. Pickles lay on the ground at their feet, watching the lake with them.

The family rowboat was tied to the pine tree at the water's edge, and the stern had drifted around so that the full length of the boat lay along the built-up rock shore directly in front of Cal's mother and father. Cal was in the boat with his father's fishing pole, a long metal extension rod that could be pushed together into a length of two and a half feet, but was now fully extended to nine because Cal's father had been fly-fishing earlier that day.

Cal liked to play where his mother and father sitting together could see him. When they sat on the front porch steps together at home, he liked to be in the street playing with his balsa wood airplane, looping it over the telephone wires, or riding his tricycle up and down the sidewalk in front of the hedges as they sat together, watching.

Cal asked his father if he could fish with his pole and his father said, "Put a worm on. You might catch one of those big bass that swim by once in a while."

"What about the big pickerel hook that's on now?" Cal said.

"You might catch a big one with it," Cal's father said.

His mother was smiling. She called Cal the "sunshine of her life."

Cal picked up the tin coffee can on the back seat of the boat and pushed his finger into the garden dirt and the night crawlers beneath the moss that kept the dirt moist. With one finger he separated the end of a night crawler from the coiled mass of worms, and pulled it gently. He was careful not to break it apart. He and his father had collected the night crawlers on Thursday night after Cal had earlier watered the lawn after supper. They had gone out with a flashlight as soon as it was dark, careful to walk slowly and quietly on the wet lawn.

"See, they think it rained, so they come up," Cal's father had said. "If they feel the ground shake, they'll go back down. Even if they feel the heat of the flashlight, they'll disappear."

"How can they get down so fast?"

"They don't come all the way out. They leave about an inch of themselves inside their hole. That's why they're so hard to pick up. If you pull too hard, they break in two. When you grab one, just hold it firm and it'll let go after a couple seconds. If we came out in another hour we'd find some all the way out."

Cal baited the pickerel hook by inserting the tip of the barb into the end of the worm and pushing the worm around the curve of the hook as far as it would go. About three inches of the worm wouldn't fit on the hook and writhed in the air. Cal held the heavy pole with two hands and swung the worm out into the water.

"You ought to get a big one now," his father said.

Cal sat down and waited. He rested the pole on the edge of the wooden boat. Cal later remembered this boat long after it rotted and had to be towed over to the cove and sunk with big stones. It was seventeen feet long with three wide seats and a small seat in the bow where Pickles sat when they were trolling for white perch in the evening after supper. It was the only boat in the lower basin that had wooden floorboards. His father put outside signs on both sides of the bow with Cal's mother's nickname, "Sal."

"Here she comes, right on time," Cal's father said. Up the lake they could see a speedboat coming fast, water spraying from both sides. Every Sunday afternoon it appeared about this time.

The boat sped into the lower basin and slowed down, then cruised slowly in a semi-circle a short distance from the shore where they sat. Waves from the speedboat sloshed against the rocks. Cal's boat rocked sideways. Five people in the boat waved and Cal's mother and father waved back.

"You can't beat a Chriscraft," Cal's father said.

"It's beautiful," Cal's mother said.

The mahogany Chriscraft shone in the afternoon sun. Two young women wore identical yellow and red scarves that fluttered in the air as the driver throttled the engine and the bow rose in the air. The boat roared back up the lake.

"It'll wreck the fishing now," Cal said.

"Fish are curious creatures," Cal's father said. "Maybe a big one will come over to see what the ruckus is. You never know."

"I don't think so," Cal said.

The water was calm again, and the lake was quiet. A loon yodeled in the swamp at the lower end of the narrows. Cal wished they could stay at the lake forever.

"Can we stay until after supper today?" he asked.

"We'd miss church," Cal's mother said.

"Why do we have to go to church every Sunday?"

"Because we do, that's why," Cal's mother said.

"Don't start that again," Cal's father said, or we'll go right now."

"I won't," Cal said. "I just like it here, that's all."

"We all like it here," Cal's mother said. "We're very lucky to be able to come every weekend."

"I know," Cal said.

The end of Cal's fishing pole suddenly jerked sideways and scraped across the top of the boat-side where it had rested, and Cal had a fight on his hands. The long metal pole was curved into a half circle.

"It's a big one," Cal shouted, standing up in the boat and fighting against the fish.

"Reel it in," Cal's father said, laughing.

Cal tried to reel, but the fish pulled so hard that it was impossible. The fish was too heavy. Then Cal was able to reel in a little line but again had to hold the pole in both hands. When he lifted the pole it bent more. He began to reel and almost lost control of the pole.

"Try to reel," Cal's mother said.

Cal needed help. His mother and father were enjoying themselves and were not aware that Cal was in a panic. He had never caught a fish this big. He didn't know how big it was but it was big. He couldn't reel and the fish was too far out to reel in.

"I need help," he cried. "Help me."

"You can do it," Cal's mother said. "You'll catch him. Keep trying."

Cal reeled in more line and brought the fish within several feet of the end of the pole. He tried to lift it into the boat but the pole was so bendy that he couldn't manage it. When he got the fish to the surface of the water, it flopped and struggled so that the water splashed in large sprays.

"It's a bass!" Cal shouted. "I can't get him in. Help me!"

"You can do it," Cal's mother said. Cal's mother and father sat and watched Cal's struggle, amused and happy for him.

Cal lifted the fish and the pole bent again, lowering the fish back into the water. He lifted the fish again and it splashed furiously against the surface.

Years later, Cal couldn't remember catching the fish, but he vividly remembered his helplessness at not being able to get the fish into the boat. Later, his mother showed him a small article she had telephoned in to the *Lynn Item* about the incident. He had caught the fish, but when he read the little story in the family vacation column, he wondered again why they hadn't helped him. It was the same feeling, before you could swim, as standing in water up to your neck and losing your balance. The water was above your nose and you couldn't understand why they didn't realize you were going to drown.

CHAPTER SIXTY-NINE

▼

Joe and Cal drove to the lake on a Wednesday night in late June.

"Acton Four Corners! The last three miles are the shortest," Cal said. "It seems like yesterday when this was still a dirt road."

"It was, when I came down with your family the first time," Joe said. "We used kerosene lamps for light."

"The war changed a lot."

"The war changed everything. I remember we used to get water at a little spring just before we got to the camp."

"Old man Walbitt's spring. He was a mean son-of-a-gun. He was always down to our camp complaining that we riled his spring. I never could figure out why my dad was so patient with him. We always held the water jug with the opening just underneath the surface, and when it filled we pulled it out before it sank to the bottom and stirred up the mud. One time my Uncle Orion got me to go to the spring for him and I caught a frog and put it in the jug to get it home. It was one of those brown spotted wood frogs that are really active on a hook. They don't puff up with air and just sit on the top of the water. You can't find them around the shore except once in a while in the deep grass."

"Goat Hill," Joe said.

They were driving up a steep hill beside an apple orchard that they couldn't see, but Cal knew was there.

"Yup, Goat Hill. I don't know where it got its name. It must have been way back. My father used to stop at the bottom and put the '38 Buick into first gear. Then he'd grind the car up to the top. I used to love partridge hunting on the edges of the orchard with my Uncle Orion in the fall."

"What about the frog?"

"Not too much. It just reminded me of my Uncle Orion. He offered me a dime to go to the spring for him and I turned him down because I thought I was being too smart for him. You know how kids are, always making sure they're not tricked into something. But my father was there and started to get mad at me so I went. When I got back Uncle Orion asked me if the tumbler was still at the spring, and I didn't know what he meant. I could only think of a clown tumbling and I thought he was joking with me. I said 'What's a tumbler'? and he said that's what it is, a 'tumbler.' That's the only word he knew for it, so he just said 'tumbler.' He meant a drinking glass, but he grew up on a farm in North Berwick and that's all he ever heard a drinking glass called. When he took the plug-top off the milk can, he jumped when he saw the frog I caught floating with its legs dangling. My father laughed but Uncle Orion wasn't amused. He dumped the water out the side door of his camp and I had to go back for another can-full."

Cal turned off onto Red Gate Road. "This was just a cow pasture road when we first started coming down here. The spring's just in there."

"Let's see if it's still there, just for the heck of it," Joe said.

Cal stopped the car where the path used to be, and got the flashlight out of the glove compartment. The road was still dirt but it was wider and the grass patch down the middle was gone. Cal stepped into the woods and found the path.

"Here's the old path," he said, and Joe followed him to the spring. It was a depression in the ground three by four feet, full of wet leaves, but at the end where a trickle of overflow was running out, the water glistened in the flashlight's beam.

Pointing to the higher side, Cal said, "There's where the stick used to be that held the tumbler. Someone just placed it upside down for anyone to use for a drink."

"Old Man Walbitt?"

"Maybe. I don't think so. Could have been."

"It's not there now. Probably neither is Old Man Walbitt."

"They're all gone. Uncle Orion, even my father."

"Let's come up tomorrow before we go back and clear out the leaves."

"Sure."

Cal found the key to the camp under the coffee can beneath the piazza. Inside, the camp was immaculate, as usual. His mother had come down after his father's funeral to get the rest of his father's clothes. She said she couldn't bear to think of the clothes there without him ever going back to the lake. She had also taken the deer head. That disappointed Cal.

Cal put two beers, a half a loaf of bread, a quart of milk and a half-dozen eggs into the refrigerator and they went out and sat on the screened-in piazza in the dark.

"Still the best time late?" Joe asked.

"Any time after ten if there's no moon."

"You'd think they'd like a moon. They could see the plug better."

"They can see it. Sometimes I think they can smell it."

"It's nice here, Cal, just sitting above the lake, hearing the night sounds."

"Mid-week is the best time. Most people don't come in until Friday night. Not until the July 4th weekend anyway."

"Let's sit here for awhile before we go out in the boat."

"We got all night."

"We've got the rest of our lives."

Cal didn't say anything. They sat in the silence for several minutes.

"I'm going to miss this," Joe said.

Somewhere across the lake a dog started barking. The barking stopped after a while, then started again.

"We had a dog down here when I was a kid," Cal said, "but he didn't bark. I hate a dog that barks down here."

"Pickles."

"Yup, Pickles. He chased chickens. He used to chase Avery Graham's chickens in Mapleville. It's a wonder that Avery didn't shoot him. He'd be gone for a day and I knew that's where he was."

"I always remembered the name, Pickles. What happened to him?"

"He got run over. He must have been chasing cars. Ronnie St. Fleur said he saw him on the side of the road, down on Beechnut Street. I took his collar to bed with me when I found out and prayed for him in dog heaven."

"If I wore a collar I'd leave it for you, old buddy."

After a long silence, Cal said, "Dog heaven, Joe?"

"It's a funny thing isn't it? You try to imagine an afterlife, and it becomes unimaginable. It doesn't have anything to do with faith or hope or anything else. You can say you believe, whatever that means, and you can believe that you believe, but as soon as you try to think in human terms, or human images, it becomes a mystery. You think that there can't be an afterlife, no eternity, no arms of Jesus, no nothing, but you *will* yourself to believe in those things."

"I guess. It doesn't make any sense so you just skip over common sense and decide to believe because you want to."

"Or because you can't bear the idea of nothingness. Maybe it's more, I'm not sure."

"Like what?"

"Like what you believe about the human spirit." Joe didn't say anything else for several minutes. "We're right back in it, Cal."

"In what?"

"The seminary bull session that starts somewhere and ends nowhere. I'm supposed to be dying, and instead of fishing, we're talking again. It's my fault, I started it."

"I know the best places, but we have to row. The motor's on the fritz."

"Let's go."

CHAPTER SEVENTY

▼

Cal rowed quietly across the lower basin of the lake to the opening of a small cove. "This cove is full of pond lilies in August," Cal said.

Joe took a couple practice casts. "How fast should I pull it back in?" Joe asked.

"Slow, just enough to make it wobble. Listen to it."

"It sounds tempting even to me."

"Fred Arbogast was a genius. A jitterbug is the greatest plug ever invented. I can still remember the first time I ever saw one. My Uncle Nate took it out of the package and showed it to my father and my Uncle Orion down by the fish table, and then made a joke out of the printed instruction on the package that said, 'See dope on back.' It struck my Uncle Nate funny to see the word 'dope' used like that."

"I'll bet he wasn't thinking of dope as drugs either."

"He wasn't. He thought dope was a synonym for dumb."

"That was so long ago."

"A century." Then Cal started to whisper. "I'm going to drift from here. I'll tell you when to cast into the opening."

Cal had stopped rowing forty yards from two points of land that formed a narrows into a cove, and the boat's momentum slowly carried them to within twenty yards of the opening. Tall pine trees rose into the sky from both points. "Now," Cal whispered.

Joe aimed his fishing rod between the dark shadows of the pine trees and cast his jitterbug into the darkness. Despite the moon-less night, the outlines of the pines around the lower basin of the lake were still visible against the sky. They heard the plop of the jitterbug landing in the water.

"Nice shot," Cal said. "I think it's right in the middle."

Joe reeled slowly.

"I can't hear it," Cal said, "a little faster. Jerk it a little."

They could hear the bubbling sound as the plug wobbled on the surface of the water toward them.

"Good," Cal whispered, "just like that."

Joe retrieved the plug to the side of the boat. "Nothing," he said.

The boat had drifted to within ten yards of the middle of the channel.

"Let me have the pole," Cal said. "I'm going to try it once down the right shore."

Cal let fly the jitterbug down the shoreline into the darkness. They heard the splash of the plug hitting the water. Cal handed the pole to Joe who slowly retrieved the jitterbug. They listened for the strike but heard only the wobble-wobble of the plug until it clicked against the end of the pole.

"It's early," Cal said. "They'll be here later. I know a couple good places up the lake."

Cal rowed along the shoreline, and Joe trolled with the jitterbug wobbling thirty yards behind the boat. They passed Sam Zwicker's place on the south arm of the cove. Cal had to row out around his moored power boat.

"Congressman Connery from Lynn used to own this camp when we first started coming to the lake in the late thirties," Cal said. "He died of ptomaine poisoning from a can of tuna fish that he let sit too long in his ice box our first summer. Connery's camp was the only place on the lake when my Uncle Orion built his camp in 1936." Cal rowed past Steven's Point and cut in to follow the shore to another little cove across from the first island. "There's a sand beach in there," he said. "One time we were going back to the camp after swimming and Uncle Orion's boat started to sink. I didn't know it until after Uncle Nate dove into the water just as we were rounding Steven's Point. There were too many people in the boat, but it didn't start to sink until Uncle Orion throttled his motor. I don't know what made the boat finally begin to go down, it must have been the speed."

Cal rowed past Hornpout Island and cut across the opening of the first river-cove.

"They're not biting tonight," Joe said.

"They will."

Cal rowed slowly past the opening of a second cove. "I caught a twenty six inch pickerel in here when I was ten," he said. "There's a channel that runs way up into the river. I was fishing with my father's metal extension pole with a dead frog, just flopping it around in the middle of the channel and it disappeared in a little swirl. I knew a small pickerel would have made a big splash so I pulled in some slack line while it chewed the frog, and pushed the pole together so that it was only a couple of feet long, then reeled until the line was almost taut again and yanked hard. I got the pickerel into the boat and I was so excited I jumped on top of it after it flopped once as high as the side of the boat, then knifed it to the floorboards with my fishing knife."

They drifted for a minute or two and Cal said, "One time in the fall Uncle Orion took me way into the cove when the water was down and we picked cranberries."

Cal rowed past the wide opening and the channel leading to the river. "Better reel it in," he said. Joe reeled in the jitterbug.

"Your uncle Orion would say, 'Nary a thing.'"

"That's what he'd say," Cal said. "Up ahead there's a pine tree hanging low out over the water. We should try to cast close to it. You want to do it, or do you want me to try it? If you snag the tree we'll have to mess around and probably spook anything that's hanging around."

"Go ahead," Joe said, "It might change our luck."

Cal took the rod and cast toward the spot, but there was no sound of the jitterbug hitting the water.

"Oh oh," Cal said, "I did it. I must have hung it in the tree."

"Can you tell where it is?"

"I went high so it's at least in the branches hanging over the water."

"Shall we row over?"

"Let me try to get it. Sometimes I get lucky and I can snap it out."

Cal gave the line a jerk and the jitterbug slammed into the side of the boat.

"Nice going," Joe said.

"Your turn," Cal said. He reeled in the slack line and gave the pole to Joe. "Go sidearm, Joe. You might be able to get it under the overhang."

Joe cast the jitterbug and they heard it hit the water. Then they heard the gurgle of the plug wobbling from side to side on top of the water. Joe reeled the jitterbug to the side of the boat. Just as he was about to lift the jitterbug out of the water, there was a tremendous splash at the side of the boat and Joe's pole bent over in a semi-circle.

"It's a good one," Joe said as he battled the fish. Cal reached for the net and picked up the flashlight on the side of the seat, but as he stood up to shine the light in the water, everything was quiet.

"Is he under the boat?" Cal asked.

"He's somewhere," Joe said, "but he's not on my line. He was big, though, very big. I must have screwed up."

"You didn't screw up. He got the jump on us, that's all. Geez, he scared me when he took it. He must have followed it all the way to the boat. They're still in here, that's for sure."

"It sure woke me up," Joe said.

"There's nothing like it," Cal said. "I'd rather be out here on the lake after dark than anywhere else in the world. The silence, the high pine shadows, it's amazing how warm the water is this time of night."

Joe put his hand in the water. "It's warm."

"There's where the North Star would be if we could see it."

"We couldn't get lost if we tried," Joe said.

"I'm going to cross over," Cal said, "You can troll through the islands and we can row down the other side and try the opening to the cove again."

"OK with me," Joe said, and cast the jitterbug behind the boat.

Cal rowed for another hour. The only sound was the oars dipping into the water and the creaking of the oarlocks.

"'Beauty is Truth, Truth Beauty, that is all ye know on earth and all ye need to know,'" Joe said.

"Do you think he was right, Joe?"

"Maybe. He was right about the first part or the second part, but about the whole thing together, I don't know. When that fish hit, something else was in it, whatever it is. I don't pretend to know."

"You've always known things that I haven't, Joe."

"Not really. You've just been working on different entanglements, that's all."

"Fishing is like dreams. Being in touch with things out there and down deep. But in my real dreams, the places I loved the most are distorted and unfamiliar. They're recognizable but they're unknown. I wonder what Keats' dreams were like."

"Like yours and mine probably. He was a boxer, you know."

"His gravestone says that his name was 'writ in water.'"

"I know."

Cal had rowed the whole northern shore back to the end of the lower basin of the lake. Behind the boat, the jitterbug wobbled in the darkness. When they were opposite the opening to the cove again, Cal told Joe that he might as well reel in. Cal angled toward the opening.

"Here we are," Cal whispered. He lifted the oars and gently eased them back into the boat.

"Why are the narrow openings the best?" Joe whispered.

"Mice crossings."

"You're kidding me."

"No. I've found mice inside the stomachs."

Joe cast the jitterbug high into the air between the tall pines on the two points. They heard it hit the water.

"Nice cast," Cal said. "Let it sit there a second."

Mist was coming off the water. Cal put his hand over the side of the boat and felt the temperature. "It's amazing. It's even warmer."

Joe jerked the jitterbug slightly and began to reel. The wobbling sound stopped and Joe's pole was bent toward the opening. "One took it," Joe said, "I didn't even hear it. It's big. I can't even reel."

"Fight him with the tip," Cal said. "Let the pole do it. Get line when you can."

"He's really big."

"Take your time. There are six hooks on that thing. If you don't give him any slack you can fight him all night."

Joe slowly brought the fish toward the boat. Cal had the net and the flashlight in either hand. He shined the flashlight in the water as Joe worked the bass to the boat.

"He seems to be giving up," Joe said.

"He's just taking a breather. Reel faster. Don't give him any slack."

Joe brought the fish closer, two feet below the surface of the water. Cal had it in the light and could see the long form of the fish. "He's huge," Cal said, and pushed the net down into the water. "Bring him into the net."

"He's gone under the boat," Joe said. "I couldn't hold him."

"Push your pole down into the water, Joe. Don't let the line touch the bottom of the boat or it'll cut it."

"Shall I give him some slack?"

"No, let him fight the tip."

"He's coming back."

"Keep the line taut."

Cal held the net down into the water and shined the light on it.

"He's at the tip of the pole," Joe said.

"Keep the tip moving ahead of him. Don't let him shake it."

Cal scooped the net against the bass's head and lifted the whole fish out of the water. The bass shook wildly and sprayed them with warm water as Cal lowered the net with the bass into the boat. The hooks in the bass's jaw were tangled in the net.

"He won't go anywhere now," Cal said. "Nice fish, Joe."

"Thanks," Joe said. "He's wonderful, like an invisible heavenly star pulled up from the deep. To think he was only looking for a mouse."

As Cal rowed back to the wharf in the silence, the bass occasionally flopped inside the net on the bottom of the boat.

Inside the camp, Cal put that day's *Boston Herald* on the round oak table in the middle of the room, and the wet fish glistened under the light from the hanging lamp. The bass was longer than the width of the folded front section of the paper. "He must go six pounds," Cal said, "maybe seven."

Joe forced the jaws open with the fingers of both hands. "Look at the size of his mouth."

"They've been known to take a water snake," Cal said.

Later, after they wrapped the bass in the newspaper and put it in the refrigerator, they sat on the porch and drank a beer. Joe told Cal he wanted to bring the fish back to Susan, and hoped Cal could come over and eat it with them. Cal said he knew a recipe to take out the muddy taste. When Cal went to bed at 2:30 a.m., Joe said he'd sit up for awhile before he turned in.

In the morning, Cal found Joe sitting in the rocking chair, looking out at the lake.

"You're up early," Cal said.

"And I've seen both the early bird and the worm," Joe said, smiling.

CHAPTER SEVENTY-ONE

▼

Cal opened the unlocked door and entered Miss Green's apartment. She was standing across the room, arms hanging down in front of her with one hand holding the other, smiling. "Hello," she said in her quiet way.

"Hello," Cal said, and passed in front of her into her office and sat down. She followed him and sat down in her own chair. The empty couch behind him was still empty, and her Kleenex box with one Kleenex partially pulled out was still available.

"How are you?" she asked.

"I've been dreaming a lot. I wrote some of them down." He handed her the dreams.

"Good," she said, and put the dreams on the top of her desk. "Tell me what you remember."

Cal closed his eyes and images from the dreams came into his mind, *first the giant frog, then the gray deer.* Cal opened his eyes.

"Joe is really dying," he said.

Miss Green nodded and waited for him to continue.

After a brief silence, tears formed in Cal's eyes. He was staring at the wall above Miss Green's desk. "He was a pallbearer at my father's funeral five weeks ago and now he can hardly walk. He can't even drive his car. Last night we were going to go for a little drive down toward the Cape but he got so tired after supper, just walking outside with Susan and I practically holding him up, we didn't go. We sat out in the yard and Tom came over and told stories.

"Kids were playing jump rope in the street. Then they left and we sat in the dark. Tom told a story about growing up in Missouri and his mother taking him on a riverboat trip down the Des Moines River from Athens to Warsaw, then watching the steamboats go by on their way down to St. Louis and New Orleans. He had us laughing. We forgot about Joe, and afterward Susan told me the doctor says it won't be long. I don't know how she does it. He's dying in front of our eyes. I don't know what I'll do when Joe dies. Tom says a person can take as much as he has to." Cal closed his eyes again.

Then the tears came and Cal began to sob. Miss Green let him cry for several minutes, twice handing him a new Kleenex. Then he stopped crying.

"I'm OK," he said.

"Tell me what comes first into your mind," Miss Green said.

Cal closed his eyes again. *"We used to take drives on Sunday afternoon,"* Cal said. *"We'd drive up to Pine Hill and pick up my grandmother and Aunt Bella. My father would either drive to the shore or he'd head out to Marblehead and Beverly Farms. We'd drive for two or three hours and he'd always stop for ice cream cones. One day we came to an ice rink, but it was in the summer time. We got out and walked around. Six or seven years later I played hockey there with the high school team. I knew it looked familiar and then I knew it was where I had been before, when I was a little kid. I wasn't supposed to go with the team but I talked the coach into it when the rest of the team got excused for sixth period. My friend Roger was a better player than I was and he didn't go either. I begged the coach so hard he said I could go, and I asked Roger if I could borrow his shin pads. I remember Roger had study period in Mr. Burl's room and I went back and asked him. He let me borrow the shin pads even though it upset him. When the coach put me in the game, I fell down. I kept asking Kenny Goodwin where I should line up. I felt alone out on the ice. After the game the coach came over to me. I was sitting in the back seat of Mr. Gibb's car for the ride home. He poked his head in the back window and said, 'You told me a wrong story, son.' I felt humiliated and sad. I wanted to be included on the team, but I really wasn't good enough."*

Cal stopped talking and Miss Green waited. Cal had not opened his eyes.

"The deer in the dream had gray hair," Cal said. *He leaped right by my face and it was like musk in my nose. I pulled the trigger but the gun wouldn't*

fire. Then I was on the bridge, climbing toward the dark. The bridge started swaying and I thought about letting go but I was afraid to fall. It was foggy at the half way mark. The girders seemed to melt in the fog and they were swaying. I remembered letting go in a dream once and nothing happened, I didn't even hit the ground. It wasn't really remembering, but I knew it." Cal stopped talking.

Miss Green waited. Cal knew that she would wait for the rest of the hour if he didn't talk. He looked at her and she was looking at him. He closed his eyes again.

"The lake was dry. I had this awful feeling. All the trees were like chalk. I was stepping across big boulders. Across the other shore a great green turtle was crawling away. Then a seashell fell next to me. I wanted to go over to the cove but a giant frog was sitting on its haunches in front of me, looking at me. There were weeds and a green snake dribbling out of his mouth clamped shut. He had gobbled up the whole lake." Cal opened his eyes again and looked at Miss Green. "I feel like I didn't sleep at all. I'm exhausted."

"I can see why."

"That isn't all. I went back to sleep after breakfast this morning. I cut my *New Testament* class. I was so tired I felt like nothing would wake me up. It was like when I came into the camp after deer hunting all Saturday morning in late November after football season and eating the noontime dinner my mother would cook for my father and me. Then I would lie down on the couch in the camp and the need for sleep was like a drug. It felt delicious to fall asleep. My whole body gave in to it and I was totally relaxed, like dying into sleep. I felt like that this morning. I can tell you exactly what I dreamed. It is so vivid in my mind." Cal closed his eyes.

"I was in water in a cave and there was fog on the water. It was a cavern but it wasn't in any place I'd ever been. I wanted to get to the bottom, and I started to swim down. The deeper I dove, the more I wanted to find the bottom. I never thought about breathing. Then there was light beneath me on the sand, and I could see a casket. I was next to it, but I didn't want to open it because I knew my dead mother was inside, like that scene in Gone With the Wind *with the mother's casket in the living room. It wasn't like that visually in the dream but the feeling was like that. The fear was the same fear I felt when I saw the mother dead and rotting in the movie.*

I opened the casket. It became a treasure box and I lifted the cover to see red velvet lining and a large jewel in the middle. I took the jewel and rose to

the surface through the cavern, leaving a swath of bubbles behind me. When I got to the top all the fog had gone. Then I was on the street. I put the jewel in the pocket of my jacket and walked down the street. It was Arlington Street."
Cal opened his eyes.

Miss Green was smiling at him. "Congratulations," she said.

Cal nodded at her and sighed. Miss Green stood up and shook his hand. Cal stood up and they looked at each other.

"This was big, wasn't it?" he said.

"Very."

"How big?"

"You deserve a long rest. You went all the way down and brought yourself all the way back up to the surface."

"I'm the jewel, aren't I?"

"You're the jewel. You're in your own pocket now. You should be proud of yourself."

"It hasn't hit me yet."

"It will. You'll be fine."

"If I ever want to come back, may I."

"You won't want to, but I'll be here."

"I owe you money."

"Pay me when you get it."

"I will."

"I know you will."

Miss Green followed him into the living room and stood outside the door to her office as he crossed the room and opened the door to the stairs.

"Bye," Cal said.

"Good-bye," Miss Green said.

On the way down the stairs, Cal passed a middle-aged man coming up. Cal looked him in the face, wanting to smile at him and tell him it would be all right, but the man passed Cal on the stairway without looking at him. Cal passed through the door and ran down the brick stairs to Arlington Street.

CHAPTER SEVENTY-TWO

▼

Joe died a month after the last class of the spring term. Scores of students from the School of Sacred Thought returned and attended the service at Joe's Braintree Church, including Dean Mueller, Dr. Ruth, Dr. Candle, Dr. Loyalton, and Dr. Jansan from the faculty. Susan asked Dean Mueller to conduct the service, and the *Kairos* Board members were pallbearers. Cal read most of the *23rd Psalm*, but was overwhelmed when he said, "My cup runneth over," and passed the text to Jack Ward who was sitting behind him as organ soloist. Jack finished in a strong voice without looking at the text, and the transition was made so well that the congregation was not aware that it hadn't been planned that way.

After the committal service at Briarwood Cemetery in Braintree, the *Kairos* Board went back to the parsonage where Tom and Regina helped Susan in the kitchen with a tray of tuna fish sandwiches. Travis and the members of the *Kairos* board talked in the living room about their summer ahead. They were all taking assistant pastor jobs except Travis and Ward. Jack had already accepted a permanent job as Choir Director in a large Presbyterian church in Portland, Oregon. Five years later, Jack would resign to become an assistant professor of music at Hunt College.

Of the others, Grapple became one of the assistant pastors for the summer at his father's Methodist church in Minneapolis. Two years later, Grapple became the head clergyman there when his father died, but he left Minneapolis and the Church the following year to become president of a small new college in the foothills of the White Mountains in New Hampshire.

Perkins joined the staff of the Westwood Methodist Church in Los Angeles as Youth Director for the summer. Years later, he became First Pastor of Westwood Church.

Foster became the interim minister for the summer in his home church in San Jose, California. Twelve years later, Foster became a bishop in the Methodist Church.

Travis worked for the summer in his father's construction company in Augusta, Georgia. A year later, as an assistant pastor of the largest Methodist Church in Augusta, Travis became too outspoken on the question of integration in the Methodist Church, and his bishop, Emanuel Moore, denied Travis admission to the Methodist District Health Plan for ministers. Travis left the church and became a labor union organizer. Within ten years he had won re-election to the state House of Representatives twice, but lost a subsequent election to the State Senate by a large majority. Travis later joked that before his father died, he often reminded Travis that if he'd quit talking like a damn Yankee he could have been elected governor of Georgia. Travis took over his father's construction business and almost became a millionaire.

In the late afternoon, Cal and Regina said goodbye to everyone and drove Travis to South Station in Boston for his train to Georgia. Susan drove Perkins, Foster, and Ward to Logan for their flights home. Grapple would stay overnight at Tom's house, and get the train to Minneapolis the next afternoon. The Official Board of Joe's church had asked Susan to fill in for Joe as pastor through the summer, and she was still thinking about it. She later decided to take the job and remained there as the full time pastor for another year while she finished her Director of Religious Education degree. She eventually returned to Akron, Ohio where she became Education Director in her father's church for several years until he died. A year later she married a Brazilian industrialist and moved to Rio de Janeiro.

Cal and Regina said goodbye to Travis at South Station, and Cal headed the car toward Belmont on Memorial Drive. "Well, that's that," he said.

Regina looked at him and waited for him to continue talking, but Cal was silent. He drove to the Cambridge circle beyond Harvard and followed route 2 through Somerville and Arlington.

After a while, Regina said, "They're all fine people."

"I'm going to miss them."

"I'm going to miss you."

Cal looked at Regina, then back at the road. They were in Belmont, still heading west on route 2.

"Would you consider waiting for me, Gina?"

Regina studied Cal for several moments and turned to look at the scenery on her side of the car. They were passing a reservoir that sparkled in the morning sun.

"I love the ponds in late spring," she said.

Cal turned off on the road to Lexington. "I tried to join the army last week."

"What does 'tried' mean?"

"I told the recruiting officer that I had to go to court in a couple weeks over the Vinnie thing, and he told me to come back if I wasn't convicted of assault."

"One of the things I like about you is that I don't know what you're going to do next, and it puts a little risk in everything. Everything becomes a surprise, and I have to tell myself to relax, maybe you'll come through. I know that sounds self-sacrificing, but it also mirrors a part of me, and there's a point where risk becomes adventurism. For instance, where the heck are we going right now? I could ask you and you'd tell me, but if I don't say anything about it, we'll get there just as quickly. Not having a destination is not like not knowing where you're going. Ever since I first met you I've been attracted to that deliberation in you, but I've always thought that it might be temporary, that even though you seem to be floundering, you have an idea of a destination. I think that's important.

"Your going in the army doesn't scare me because in some way that I don't understand, it means that you've decided something big in your life. If you wanted to be a minister, that would have seemed OK to me, but I always knew during this last year when I've watched you from afar, and sometimes a little up close, that you didn't want it. I don't know what made you decide, but I'm glad it's decided." Regina looked out the window again. A farmer was plowing his field, sitting on a high metal seat behind two Percheron horses.

Cal said, "One Sunday when I was a kid, my father drove us to Concord. My grandmother was in the car. It was right after my Aunt Bella died. My grandmother had been taking care of her after her stroke.

She finally had to go in a nursing home but then she died and it was a great relief for everyone because my grandmother was really tired. My Aunt Bella had lived in my grandmother's house all her life. She never married and the only money they had was from my Aunt Bella's piano lessons. My Aunt Penelope and Uncle Orion lived in the house too. They had gotten married when my Aunt Penelope was fifteen, but my Aunt Bella never spoke to them because she originally thought my Uncle Orion was interested in her, not my Aunt Penelope. They all lived together in that house for forty-five years and my Aunt Bella never spoke to them. She would stick out her tongue at my Aunt Penelope if they were alone in a room together.

"Anyway, we went on this ride, which was an unusual one, because my father had always taken his mother and sister on our Sunday drives either to Nahant, by the shore, or Beverly Farms. It's all I remember about it, coming out here on this road between Lexington and Concord, and seeing the vegetable stands in the fall along the side of the road. We stopped and I think we bought some apples. But I remember the feeling of sitting in the car in the back seat next to my grandmother. She was a really nice old lady, and she was happy. She had done her best and my Aunt Bella was better off dead. Nobody said that but everyone thought it. Nobody talked about that kind of stuff in my family. Even after the funeral, when all the cousins and uncles and aunts showed up at the Walnut Hill house, and my other grandmother's adopted daughter Harriet showed up, everybody was nice and said how we all ought to get together more often and not just at funerals.

"My two grandmothers were sisters, and my Uncle Orion and Aunt Penelope were first cousins. My father and mother were also first cousins, but by adoption, because my mother had been an orphan. Harriet, who showed up at Aunt Bella's funeral, was also adopted by my mother's foster mother, so they were sort of sisters by proximity. Harriet left school and worked in a shoe factory in Eliot, Maine, and got herself pregnant. Later she got into trouble with drugs. Nobody talked about it except in private within their own families. My Uncle Art was there at the funeral that day too. He was my grandmother's brother, and he had been a minister until they caught him playing around with young boys.

"Nobody in the room knew much about my other grandmother, my mother's foster mother except me, but that was later. She was a little strange. She and I had the same birthday and she called me her twin. She always kissed me on the mouth and her lips were always wet. I hated it. At their farm in Maine, I had to drink my milk warm, and I still remember that green tinted glass. It wasn't pasteurized milk, but she said it was safe because it came from that cow of hers, Bessie, that gored my father in the leg one Sunday when we were staying there for the weekend.

"My mother told me three years ago that on the night my foster grandmother brought her home from the orphanage, she made my mother play with herself with her hands, in front of my foster grandfather and her. Later, she never let my mother date in high school, but she let Harriet run loose. My mother said 'wild.'"

Cal had turned onto route 2A, between Concord and Lexington, heading toward Concord. "Crazy, huh?"

"That's why we're here. Everything's a little crazy if you take it seriously."

"Yeah, but I didn't know why we were here until I just said it. What I found out in the last couple of years is that everything is behind everything else. Not just something, but everything. My mother lived all her life thinking she was a "nobody," that was her word, because she was an orphan. Two weeks after my father died, she found out from her sister, my aunt Thelma, that they descended directly from seven passengers on the *Mayflower*. So now my mother thinks she's at least somebody, but it doesn't mean anything to her because my father's dead. Aunt Thelma's husband, who was her foster brother, and her son Everett, are both dead. All I know is, I can't accept the 4E deferment from the draft board anymore."

"None of it makes much sense to me, Cal. If you're going to enlist in the army, just don't let your mind wander in Korea."

"I hear you. There's a pond somewhere out here. Maybe we could go there and eat some stuff I brought."

"Walden Pond. Remember, Mr. Sadoski took me fishing there. A Henry somebody with a French name wrote a story about it. I remember it because he went to jail for not paying his taxes or something and somebody named Waldo went to see him and said, 'Henry, what are you doing in here?' And he said, 'The question is, Waldo, what are you doing out *there*?' I thought that was great."

"Thoreau made pencils for a living for awhile. The book is wonderful. He said that he went to live at the pond to see if he could 'improve the nick of time.' Do you remember the pond?"

"Not much. There was a swimming beach below where we parked and we walked through the woods to a cove. I mostly remember how nice Mr. Sadoski was to me, and how he gave me two fish he caught to give to my mother."

"I was there once, on our eighth grade class outing. I remember being embarrassed, walking on the path around the pond with my girlfriend, Barbara Searling. We were on the west shore where they put the railroad sidings to keep the bank from falling into the pond, and I had an erection that wouldn't go down. I don't know if she noticed it, but it was very awkward for me. I thought that if she saw it bulging inside my pants she would think I was a bad person."

"Boys will be boys."

"I'm thinking of driving right now to another pond that Thoreau talks about in his book, White's Pond. I've always wanted to go there. I think I've read *Walden* more than I've read the *Bible*."

They entered the town of Concord, and Cal drove around the monument celebrating the 100th anniversary of the Revolution, passing the Concord Inn. "I think that if we took that road back there we would end up at the Old North Bridge where the Minuteman statue is."

"Let's go to White's Pond. Maybe we can go to the bridge some other time."

"OK." Cal took a right and drove up Main Street toward the Harvard Trust bank where Cal pulled into a parking place in front of Anderson's Market. Inside, they walked to the back of the store where there was wine and big cheesecakes covered with glazed strawberries.

Cal asked Mr. Anderson how to get to White's Pond, and he told him.

In the car, Cal said, "Thoreau says in his chapter on the ponds that he used to sit in a boat on warm evenings and play the flute, and perch came to the boat as the moon traveled over the 'ribbed bottom which was stewed with the wrecks of the forest.' I love that. 'Stewed with the wrecks of the forest.'"

"It is nice. When are you going to show me that magazine with your poems?"

"I'll show it to you. I just haven't thought about it lately."

"The things that mean the most to you, you don't like to talk about, do you, Cal?"

"Open the glove compartment, Gina, there's a book in there."

Regina took out a small leather-bound book. She turned the cover and read out loud the handwritten inscription on the upper corner of the first page:

"To Joe on his fifteenth birthday, from mama and daddy."

"Susan gave it to me yesterday afternoon after the funeral. She said that Joe asked her to."

"It's a special copy."

Susan turned the page and read out loud the title page: "*Walden, or Life in the Woods*: I do not propose to write an ode to dejection, but to brag as lustily as chanticleer in the morning, standing on his roost, if only to wake my neighbors up."

She added, "Let's read some at the pond."

Cal drove to Sudbury and found the road to White's Pond. There was a small vacant beach and they walked along a path that began to circle the edges of the pond, then ended. Across the pond, there were houses, but they were vacant. Cal and Regina walked further until they found a little rise in the shoreline, and a small open space between two pine trees where the sun shone on the fallen pine needles. "Here," said Regina, and they sat down.

Cal took a can opener from the bag of lunch things and opened a small can of Greek olives. He held it to Regina who took one. "I love them," she said. "What else did you get?"

Cal took out a square package and slowly un-wrapped it.

She said, "Feta cheese. How did you know I adore it?"

"I guessed."

"All we need is a bottle of retsina wine," Regina laughed, carefully biting the piece of white cheese. "You have to be careful or it crumbles."

Cal reached again into the bag and lifted out the wine bottle.

"My god," she said. "You must have home made white bread in there too. That's all you need to make it really perfect."

Cal smiled and took out a small uncut loaf of fresh white bread and broke it in half. Regina held it to her nose and breathed in the smell of the fresh bread.

"The last time I saw anyone do that was my father," Cal said. "My mother used to make bread, and she'd put it on the radiator in the living room with a towel over the loaves so they'd rise. When she took the loaves out of the oven, my father would smell them. Once I saw him hold up a warm brown loaf with two hands and kiss it."

"This is *so* nice," Regina said. "Look at the pond, it's ours."

Cal opened the wine and poured it into plastic glasses he picked out of the paper bag. They tasted it together. "It tastes like a pine tree and I love it," Regina said. "It's so perfect with the feta cheese and the fresh bread. She put down her glass of wine and surrounded his shoulders with her arms and kissed him for many seconds. They sat there in the presence of the pond and were quiet, eating green olives and fresh white bread and feta cheese, looking out across the pond, smelling the pine needles in the early summer sun.

Cal said, "May I read a passage from the book?"

"Please do," she said, and lay back in the warm brown needles.

Cal turned the pages of the book until he came to the one he wanted, and read a passage about White's Pond and Walden being crystals of the earth that are so pure that if they were congealed they would be carried off like precious stones for the heads of emperors, but because the ponds are liquid, "we run after the diamond of Kohinoor." Regina listened and Cal read quietly how we could never learn meanness from the ponds, how wild nature only flourishes far from towns. When he came to the end of the passage, Cal realized why he had chosen it, for it said that if you talk of heaven, you disgrace the earth.

They were quiet for a long time, and then Regina said, "We don't have to run after the diamond of Kohinoor, do we Cal?"

"Let's just run after our lives. No more talk about me, no more talk about heaven."

"But not run at first, Cal, let's just start by walking."

"I'm ready," Cal said.

And so they walked back together toward the car.

POSTSCRIPT

▼

Cal pleaded *nolo contendere* at his hearing, throwing himself on the mercy of the court, and the judge let him off with a lecture. Vinnie had two previous misdemeanors on his record, which worked to Cal's advantage, and since Cal was a seminarian, the judge told him that it would be appropriate for Cal to accept his recent violence as the last vestiges of his childhood and henceforth begin to practice the personal ethics of the *New Testament.*

Cal entered the army in August, and after three days at Camp Devens in Ayer, Massachusetts, was sent by train to Fort Dix, New Jersey, for six weeks of basic training. After the first two weeks he wrote short notes to his mother, Tom, Susan, and Travis telling them he was getting good at pushups again and living the healthy life with lots of hiking and fresh air. The notes were ironic and cheerful and identical, for after writing the first one to Tom, he decided to just copy it and send it to the others. He did not write Regina, but he thought about her all the time and composed long letters to her during the forced marches and the combat readiness drills that went from pre-dawn to after dusk. The letters were passionate and full of yearning, but he was never happy with them and he did not write them down.

During Cal's fifth week at Fort Dix, President Truman recalled MacArthur from Korea, and the trainees in Cal's company talked about nothing else for several days. Both Cal's drill sergeant, a tall lean Oklahoman whose mastery of the Anglo-Saxon contribution to the English language was superseded only by his penchant for face to face and very personal oral communication at loudspeaker decibels; and the second lieutenant who delivered an official announcement of the President's action, and made it clear, that they thought it was a pussy act by a pussy president.

The drill sergeant's actual commentary went something like, "OK you assholemouths, today we're goin to bear down real hard to honor a real gen'ral who was no pussy." During drills he said, "get your dongs out of each other asses and move, you look like you're running for a pussy high government office after the war." The second lieutenant read a short statement to the company that said, "Yesterday the Commander-in-Chief of the United States placed Five Star General Douglas MacArthur on inactive duty. General MacArthur, who served our country with valor and loyalty will be welcomed in several days by a ticker tape parade in New York City. That's all, men. Dismissed."

Two days before the six weeks basic training were up, Cal wrote the following letter:

Dear Regina,

I should have written you sooner, but you know me. I guess my short suit is putting things off. I hope that Tom told you I was OK, though you probably would think that, not hearing from me, which I know doesn't make sense. When we filled out our papers before they shipped us to Dix, I put down my mother, then you as my half-sister, so you would get notified in case I got shot from behind crawling under some barbed wire. I have written you parts of long letters in my mind every day. I guess I waited until they sort of came together, not that they were apart but that wine is wine and bourbon is bourbon, or something like that. You know me.

The days here have been long and the nights short, and they have pushed our butts. I'm lucky I played football for seven years. Most days here it's been like fourteen hours of two on one without a breather. The coach here, our drill sergeant, would have been a huge success in the Jurassic age. But I got through it, at least all but the next two days of it, and now they're going to ship me someplace, either another training camp or an embarkation area for Korea. We had to fill out some more papers the other day telling what our specialties in life were, what they called 'previous experience,' and the lieutenant said put down if we play the cello or the piccolo or something like that. I was not about to write that I just escaped from a seminary. I just said I went to college and played football and worked on a school magazine, so I'll probably just end up as a rifleman. Which is what I am probably best suited for anyway. I'm not putting myself down, so don't worry about my frame of mind, it's only still me without the self-pity, taking it as it comes. I asked for it, and here it is, is what I mean.

Please visit Tom. Without Joe it will be very hard on him with only those people in the church he says he hates. He probably doesn't hate them, but he is very impatient with churchy people. He needs you because you are always a little fresh and it will strike him as funny.

I'm getting to what I want to say. Mostly I'm writing this because I trust myself in telling you that I'm not setting you up for something. If you're there when I get back, I will find you. With me there have always been guilt feelings about everything, except with you, even when I didn't write you these five weeks. I know that you know me.

Anyway, last November, actually it was Armistice Day, Joe and I went hunting in Maine, near the lake where my family has a small cottage that my father built in the late thirties and we've always called the camp. I shot a deer and Joe cleaned out the stomach and intestines while I went and bought a license to make it legal. When I got back, we worked like hell to get it out of the woods and home to Massachusetts. My aunt was there with the news that my cousin Everett had been killed in Korea. My father was recovering from his second heart attack and we all sat around downstairs in the living room, and it was one of those family situations where there is nothing to say. Joe and I hung the deer in the garage, and I remember how it was raining and how the smell of the wet deer fur made me feel when we hugged it to lift it and pull the rope around the rafters to raise it off the dirt floor of the garage. It was something I never felt before, like touching an ancient find. My mother and father took the carcass after it hung for three weeks in the garage to a slaughter house and locker plant in Danvers, and made sure that the butcher saved the head for mounting. When the taxidermist finished with it, they took it down the camp where it was going to always be.

Joe told me later, before he got sick, that the deer came to me. We weren't talking about hunting at the time, but about life and stuff. I didn't know what he meant, but he was making a point how life provides openings. He even quoted Shakespeare to me, which he never had done before, something like 'the readiness is all.' Joe always knew that I followed him to seminary, that if he hadn't decided to enter the ministry, I wouldn't have either, but he accepted it, and he never made me feel as if I was tagging along behind him. I can see now as I look back on the last few years that he also could see that I was not cut out, as my father used to say about vocations, for the ministry. But he was my friend, and he stayed with me through all my self pity and he was always positive. There were things about him that I didn't understand, especially why he wanted to enter the church, but I really never questioned him, both because I was afraid that the obvious answer was the true one, that he needed to, and because the one thing he always told me was that I couldn't get answers to questions by asking questions. Clare told me that once also, and even a bum I met on the Boston Common told me, but I didn't get it. I get it now.

The deer I shot came to me in the woods. I was looking down through a grove and heard a noise and all of a sudden this massive buck came walking through the oaks about 90 yards away. For once, the gun fired and I made a good shot. By that I mean that in my dreams whenever I am hunting, my gun won't fire, or if it does, I kill something I didn't intend to. I killed a rabbit once in a dream and it turned out to be a baby. And I pointed a .22 at an airliner and shot it down.

Regina, you came into my life just like the deer, from that other forest. When I went to my mother's house after my dad died, she gave me the deer head and told me that she wanted me to keep it, that she knew it would remind me of Joe and she didn't know whenever any one of us would get down the camp again, now that my dad was dead. I always thought of my time in seminary as my hitch, thinking that it was a play on words because the word is used like that when somebody is talking about the army, but now I can see that underneath that meaning is the real meaning, that my time in seminary was a knot that needed unsnarling. Joe helped me untangle it, and you were there when I did. You didn't spook, as Joe would say, because I was tied up in something else. Because of the MacArthur thing, it looks like the war will wind down sooner than everybody here thought. The idea of actually maybe not getting killed in Korea gave me some of the urge to write this letter. I had to face up to the consequences in my own way, and I am, and now I'm interested more in my next leave than I am in anything else.

Cal